Praise for *Awakening*

"Children of the Solstice is a page-turner of superhero proportions!"

- J. F., Amazon review

"This is a fun and creative addition to the super hero genre."
- J. H. M., Amazon review

"If you like sci-fi and the 'everyday' superhero, this book is for you."

- P. G., Amazon review

"I would find myself out of reading time and then read 'just one more chapter' because I wanted to see what was next, and then 'for real now, just one more chapter.'"

- B. M. M, Amazon review

"Think *Sense8* on Netflix--if you've seen and liked that show, *AWAKENING* will be right up your alley... We all need some heroes in our lives and I'm happy to have spent time with these."

- P. M., Amazon review

By Baltimore Russell and Jennifer Pallanich
Awakening

A novel by

Baltimore Russell

and

Jennifer Pallanich

Art by Alex Sanchez

Published by Pair Tree Ink

An original publication of Pair Tree Ink

ISBN: 978-0-9864104-4-4

.

DEDICATION

To
The woman who helped us dream
The man who helped us soar
And the teachers who showed us how

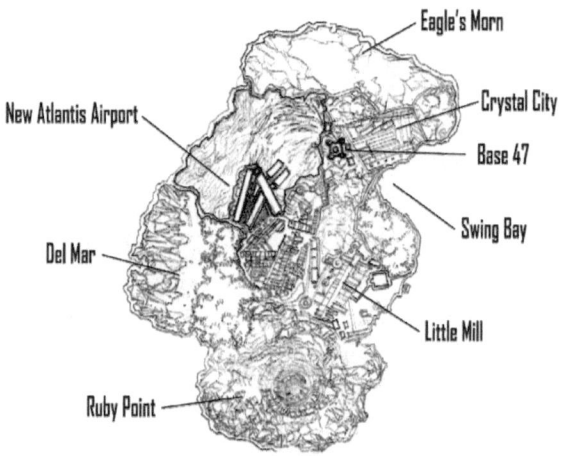

Eagle's Morn

Crystal City

New Atlantis Airport

Base 47

Swing Bay

Del Mar

Little Mill

Ruby Point

New Atlantis

CHARACTERS

SENTINELS
Bayanai Romrico, leader, power booster
Carlos Martin, strong man
Courtney "CoCo" Cooper, illusions
Emilio Diego Santos, probability manipulation
Emma Sheehy, telepathy
Etienne DuBois, intangibility and invisibility
James Chege, speedster
Katrina McGee, psychokinesis
Kirra Wilson, geokinesis
Waleed Gandapur, teleporter

New Atlantis
Arian Nassar, chief of staff to Prime Minister Jaako Aalto, guardian of Emma Sheehy, and former girlfriend of Rami Kazemi
Birgitta Aalto, wife of Prime Minister Jaako Aalto
Ericka Zavatsky, former SENTINEL, police chief of Crystal City, generates green bio-blasts
Jaako Aalto, prime minister of New Atlantis, cryokinesis
Jiya, former SENTINEL, mentor at local ashram, healing
Laura Parks, head of security for Base 47

Marie Gandapur, history teacher on New Atlantis, wife of Waleed Gandapur
Dr. Nicola Patel, scientist at Base 47
Sun Luli, director of public relations for Prime Minister Jaako Aalto
Sun Shining, son of Sun Luli and Sun Yi, force fields
Sun Sying, daughter of Sun Luli and Sun Yi
Sun Yi, husband of Sun Luli
Dr. Yukio Watanabe, scientist at Base 47

The Ascendancy
Anabel Wong, member
Elise Springchild, member
Henry Hastings, member, also founder of The Hastings Foundation
Dr. Julianne Frazier, scientist at The Hastings Foundation
Maksim Wong, member
Dr. Roger Martin, scientist at The Hastings Foundation

The Tribe
Alrick Wagner, mental manipulation
Dafydd Upjohn, self-replication/cloning
Friedrich "Butcher" Metzger, enhanced senses
Jane "Plain Jane" Smith, imperceptible
Jimin "Brute" Pak, converts kinetic energy into strength
Maru Tamatoa, weather manipulation
Quentin Washington, former marine and Base 47 trainer, right hand to Pierce
Taneesha "Flame" Jackson, pyrokinesis
Timothy Ellery, electricity manipulation
Captain Warren G. Pierce, leader of the Tribe, pyrokinesis, density control, strength, teleportation, healing, telekinesis, force fields, remote viewing

Others
Arthur Hastings, Swarm, son of Henry Hastings
George St. John, power of suggestion
Josh "Hollywood" Grant, actor, former SENTINEL, shapeshifter
Juan Pierre del Bosque, chlorokinesis
Luca Florentino, Josh Grant's boyfriend
Maggie Adams, editor and publisher of TheModsBlog
The redheaded man, Swarm
The sand woman, Swarm, sand manipulation
Wally "Focus" Jones, cameraman for TheModsBlog

CHAPTER

1

20 November

Bernard Perry stepped over the body of the Memphis Area Power Plant's chief engineer and entered the central control room. The room was clean and well kept. The machines lining the wall monitored every inch of the power plant. The desk near the window looked over the plant floor.

"Is the system ready?" He wiped his brow.

While Bernard had dispatched all the power plant's employees, Alvin Gavin had hacked the controls to access the plant's system. The partners were complete physical opposites. While Bernard was thin, tall, and fit, Alvin was plump and short and spoke with a wheeze.

Alvin looked at the resolve in Bernard's eyes and wondered how he could have murdered all sixty-three employees of the power plant with no hesitation. The smell of spent cartridges haunted his nose.

"Well?" Bernard prompted.

"Uh, seems to be primed and ready to go." Alvin peered at his encrypted tablet and looked up at the control panel. "Did you insert the cryospore?"

"Of course." Bernard frowned and laid his AK-47 on the

table. "I've also disabled the station fail-safes. Are we ready?"

Alvin looked sharply at Bernard.

"Don't look at me like that. You know that the fail-safes must be disabled so we can test the cryospore integration into the existing grid infrastructure." Bernard dropped his canvas bag next to Alvin, took off his gloves, and slapped them on the table.

"I get that, but it doesn't make me anymore at ease." Alvin navigated the systems on his tablet. "What I don't trust is the scientists' need to test it here. It's already working without being plugged into the system. Why do we have to do this?"

Alvin and Bernard had worked on the cryospore project for about two years. Each had come to The Hastings Foundation as experts in their fields, Alvin in engineering and Bernard in thermodynamics. They had collaborated frequently on energy integration systems.

Alvin knew plant workers would have to die; he just hadn't thought he'd have to work right on top of their bodies. He held back the urge to vomit, calming himself by slowly breathing through his mouth.

The silver desk complemented the silver-and-gray equipment inside the cold box of a control room. Only the safety procedures posters and federal protections notices added any color.

"You going to be okay?"

Alvin scrunched his face tight and gave a quick nod.

"Good, I don't want to babysit you as well."

Alvin tried to push the knowledge and presence of the dead out of his mind and focus on the task at hand. He checked out the tablet, ensuring everything was going according to plan.

"Because the developed world is used to receiving their

power through outlets, this will allow us to provide the energy the cryospore generates and control the entire power grid." Bernard rummaged through the bag and removed an oddly shaped gold artifact.

"What is that? It's not a part of what The Hastings Foundation gave us." Alvin noticed how brightly the gold contrasted with Bernard's dark skin.

"Don't worry about it," Bernard said. "Think of it as a good luck charm."

He set the palm-sized Egyptian artifact on the table. Rubies outlined the eyebrow and curved tail while sapphires circled the pupil. The teardrop was blackened gold.

"But what is it?"

"The Eye of Horus. Been in my family for generations." Bernard braced himself against the window. "Symbol of life and resurrection. They say that looking through the eye will allow you to see with all of your senses."

"Didn't know you were into Egyptology." Alvin was tempted to hold it up to his own eye, but thought better of it.

Bernard caressed the artifact. "Are we ready?"

Bernard snapped his fingers and Alvin finally shifted his attention from the eye-catching artifact to the control panel. "All the indicators are green."

"But?" Bernard asked.

"I'm worried about stability. None of our indicators monitors stability. If the new system proves unstable, this whole plant could—" Here, Alvin was at a loss for words. Instead, he made a hand signal suggesting an explosion and mouthed "boom."

"I'm not worried about that at all," Bernard said, rocking back and forth on his heels. "There's double redundancy with the plant's cooling system. The cryospore will be fine if we maintain the temperature range. Stop worrying so much."

Alvin hesitantly nodded. "Okay."

"Is the system ready to activate?"

Alvin regarded Bernard. He took in the man's angular face and unflinching dark eyes. His lips and eyebrows were drawn into parallel lines. Alvin glanced again at the control panel. "All the indicators are green."

A slow smile stretched across Bernard's face. "History, here we come. Initiate."

"Yes, sir." Alvin punched a command into his tablet, and a handful of the green lights on the control panel flickered, then returned to steady green. When a deep hum sounded from within the machine, Alvin jumped, as though he'd been goosed. He cleared his throat and studied the tablet screen. "The new system is warming up. It'll be a few minutes before it's ready to take the full power load."

"I've been dreaming of this day since I first learned of this technology at The Hastings Foundation," Bernard said as they stared at the contents of the clear cylinder. The item inside gave off a bluish glow. The precious blue orb—about the size of a basketball—would generate all the power this plant could send out to the grid for months. The power generation plant would no longer need to buy and burn coal to make power, although it would still need access to cryospores, upon which The Hastings Foundation would hold a monopoly. Bernard rubbed his hands together in anticipation.

A few minutes later, Alvin said, "Ready to move to the next phase. I'm instructing it to generate ten percent of the power capacity."

"Good."

Alvin punched the command into his screen and peered intently at the control panel. Again, the green lights flickered, but then returned to solid. Around them, the power generation plant began producing ten percent of the plant's potential output by feeding off the blue object in the clear cylinder. The blue ball glowed, and the green lights remained steady.

"It seems all is stable. Shall I bump it up to twenty-five percent?"

"Yes."

Alvin did so, and spotted nothing troubling on the control panel. He looked at Bernard, whose face wore a smile of deep pride. "We're at twenty-five. Shall I jump it up to fifty?"

"Yes."

Again, Alvin did so. The system seemed steady and stable.

"Go ahead and go all in," Bernard instructed.

"Sir, that's a bad idea. We need to ease into this, kind of like easing into a cold pool instead of diving right in."

Bernard drew his eyebrows together. "Seventy-five then."

"Yes, sir." Both men were bathed in azure hues as the cryospore began generating three-quarters of the plant's power potential.

"Now all in." Bernard unbuttoned the top button of his dark burgundy shirt.

Alvin gulped and punched in the command on his tablet. He could have sworn the golden artifact was vibrating. But when the indicators remained steady green, he relaxed a bit.

"We just made history!" Bernard said, offering a high-five.

Alvin was reaching up to meet the high-five when three of the lights blinked yellow, then flashed red. One was the temperature sensor. "Oh shit, the temperature is jumping. I gotta turn this thing off."

"Negative."

"Are you crazy? We'll be in deep shit here if it gets any warmer. I don't want to be here if that happens."

"My source told me that the system, when it first starts, will warm enough to trigger the alarm. I thought I told you that."

"Right, you did, but still." Alvin shuddered, sweat beading down his face, as much from nerves as from the increasing heat. "Think of the possible consequences."

"Leave it a few more moments. See if the temperature self-corrects."

Alvin watched the control panel with single-minded purpose, willing the lights to go green.

A fourth light turned from green to red.

"I'm turning it off," Alvin said.

"No, leave it. It can still self-correct."

A faint crackling sound came from inside the control panel. Inside the clear cylinder, the blue orb seemed to pulse from basketball size to grapefruit size and back again. All of the lights turned red.

Alvin looked from the cylinder to the flashing lights and back at the orb, momentarily mesmerized by its rhythmic pulsing, before saying decisively, "That's it. I'm shutting it down."

Before he could, the new system kicked out an overwhelming surge of hot power. The blue orb wobbled on its pedestal and, even though there was nothing he could do to stop the impending doom, Alvin leapt out of his chair, tripping over a body and falling toward the exit. But it was too late. The cryospore had fallen to the ground. At impact, it exploded, demolishing the power generation plant near Memphis, Tennessee, and killing Alvin and Bernard, who joined the ranks of the dead plant workers.

CHAPTER 2

20 November

From his post by the section D concession stand, Emilio Diego Santos watched for George St. John. He took a swig from a bottle of water, wishing it were beer. Emilio heard the gentle beginning notes of Metallica's "Enter Sandman" and knew the

Emilio Diego Santos

song would soon have the crowd roaring. The Spaniard grinned. The band was pretty good and very loud, but Emilio wouldn't have bought a ticket to attend the tribute concert. Wouldn't be here if it weren't for the threat against George. Where was that man?

During the White Light Wave event five years ago, Emilio had gained the ability to manipulate probability in his favor. While not a flashy power like telekinesis or the ability to fly, it did allow him to count on his luck to turn things his way. Tonight he was counting on it to get George St. John, a short, freckled, sandy brown-haired man, to pass by him at the Cottonwood Pavilion. Two days ago Emilio had gotten inside intel that the SENTINELS' sworn enemies, the Tribe, were after George. To Emilio, anyone of interest to the bad guys was someone his super team—the SENTINELS—would want to protect. That brought him here tonight. He knew George's seat for the concert was in the D section. Sooner rather than later, George would make a beeline circuit of the men's room, the bar, and his seat.

He settled in to wait, admiring the occasional passing hottie but pretending to be absorbed with his cell phone so he could better blend into the concert scene. With his surfer-blond hair, Mediterranean looks, and lean body, he had no problem getting attention. He thought perhaps more than one stared at his blue jeans-clad butt, wondering if he was a boxers man.

"Where's section D?" a big-haired brunette asked, tapping him on the shoulder.

Emilio pointed. "Just through there." Preoccupied with giving directions, he almost missed seeing George walk by, aimed at the men's room. His target was wearing black jeans and a T-shirt from some previous Metallica concert, like at least half of the other men in attendance, so it was George's height and sandy brown hair that caught Emilio's attention. "Excuse me," he said as he sent a pair of prewritten text messages. One was to make sure Waleed was ready to open up a teleportal the instant he saw George.

Man, Emilio thought, this was a lot easier when Emma was around to telepathically coordinate things. Normally, they would use a comms system, but shouted comments to be heard over the throbbing pounding music would have been painful. They had to rely on good old-fashioned text messages.

Up on stage, the tribute band started "For Whom the Bell Tolls," and Emilio waited to see if George would emerge from the bathroom.

"Oh, look what the cat dragged in. Oops, that's Poison, not Metallica," CoCo said, appearing out of nowhere to his right with a tanned bad boy Emilio recognized as Timothy Ellery.

Emilio wasn't a fan of Timothy, who'd long ago had the opportunity to come to Base 47 but chosen to stay with the Tribe. Timothy stood too close to CoCo. Emilio squinted his eyes at Timothy, who could control electricity. They'd had a run-in or three before. Emilio looked at his CoCo, and suddenly he couldn't breathe. Courtney "CoCo" Cooper looked good. Great. Always had. Tanned dancer's body. Confident moves. Wide-set brown eyes and golden brown hair. And she was dressed for concert-going in delicious skinny jeans and a skimpy melon-colored top. She was his love. It felt like all of his luck had taken the last shuttle to the moon.

"What—what—what—"

"No need to stutter." A smirk skirted across her face. "What are you doing here?"

Emilio hadn't been speechless in quite some time. He'd always been glib, sure of himself. But he'd rarely stood so close to CoCo since the very public staged fight they'd had. She'd stormed out and joined up with Pierce and his bad news crew.

It was supposed to have been him.

Now, here she was, and he still loved her, and he wanted to drink her in but couldn't. He had a role to play that he didn't want to play, and it felt like his words were keeping his luck company up on the moon.

"What are you doing?" he finally asked in a voice he didn't recognize as quite his own, hoping against hope their presence here was a coincidence but knowing it wasn't.

"Timothy loves Metallica." She smiled at her companion and Emilio's legs threatened to buckle. "Timothy, hon, you

9

remember my ex, Emilio." She dusted Timothy's cheek with a light kiss, and he slipped a possessive arm over her shoulders.

Emilio thought he felt electricity surge through the air when she kissed Timothy. Emilio glared at Timothy, hating him on sight and on principle. It might be just an act on CoCo's part, but that didn't make it hurt less to see someone else touch his love. His stomach tightened and his chest ached, and he mentally plotted a dozen ways to get Timothy out of her life. Of course, he couldn't act on any of them; that would spoil the plan, his freaking brilliant plan for one of them—him, it was supposed to be him—to go undercover in the Tribe as a mole.

"Yo." Timothy looked like he hadn't shaved in five days. He wore a green T-shirt with an absurdly huge lightning bolt on it. To underscore—or boast, maybe—his Mod power, Emilio thought.

Emilio shoved his emotions into the background and refocused on the present. "Seriously, what are you doing here?"

CoCo didn't answer. She turned and shouted, "There he is," pointing at George, who was banging his head in sync with the last of "For Whom the Bell Tolls" as he headed for the beer line.

Suddenly, Emilio understood that Waleed hadn't been able to get George out. He swore.

Timothy streaked by Emilio, hell-bent on reaching George.

"George!" Emilio shouted.

The short freckled man turned. A grin formed at the corners of his mouth, as though expecting to greet a friend, then fell away when he spotted the man in the green lightning bolt T-shirt running straight at him.

The lights in the concessions area went out. On stage,

the tribute band moved on to the next song in its set: "Seek and Destroy."

Emilio knew he was running out of time. Timothy had sucked the electricity out of the concession area and that would power him up but good.

Emilio was about to run after Timothy when CoCo grabbed his arm. She pulled him toward her and stood on her tiptoes to whisper in his ear. He couldn't hear or understand a word of it and asked her to repeat it. Rolling her eyes, she leaned up and repeated herself. "I love you," she said, and his heart thumped. That's when he realized he couldn't smell her light floral perfume. Dammit. She'd illusioned him, and he'd fallen for it. And she was far better at it now than she had been when she went undercover. He shuddered, knowing she was getting far too much practice casting illusions to keep the bad guys from realizing what she was up to.

He scanned the crowd and spotted the real CoCo and Timothy up ahead.

He hoped Waleed had been following George at a discreet distance and seen CoCo and that loathsome Timothy taking off after George.

He sent a thought upward, as though to the moon, asking that his luck find its way back into his life, and he took off after Timothy and CoCo and George. He pulled out his cell. He ran through the crowd, which seemed to part naturally for him, and called Waleed.

The teleporter answered on the first ring, huffing into the mouthpiece. "I'm right behind him."

"Good."

"Your crazy ex and—"

"Don't say it."

"And that psycho are on my heels."

"Get George, even if you have to teleport in plain sight.

Do not, under any circumstances, let them get him."

"You're the boss," Waleed said.

Emilio heard a weird yet familiar crackling before he could disconnect the call and nodded in satisfaction. Waleed had created a portal on the run and yanked George through it. Emilio imagined the concertgoers gaping at the blatant display of Mod powers and hoped he wouldn't have to defend their actions to any concert security in the area.

Emilio slowed from a run to a purposeful walk and called the recipient of the second text message.

"No sign of him here," Kirra said.

"We had a problem. CoCo was here with Timothy, and they tried to get George."

"Tried, as in failed?"

"Waleed managed to 'port him out right under their noses."

"Nice job."

"Yeah. I'm not far from where it happened. Meet me so we can confront CoCo. They wanted George, and I want to know why."

"Her again? That traitor has it coming. Where are you?"

Emilio bit his lip. It took every ounce of strength to keep this secret. To not defend CoCo every time one of his teammates disparaged her. Shaking the thoughts from his head, Emilio looked around. "Section C."

"Section B. Be there in a jiffy," Kirra said, disconnecting.

He walked slowly through the section's concession area, looking for CoCo or Timothy.

"What do you want with me?" someone screamed over "Seek and Destroy."

Emilio bolted toward the new commotion. What he saw stunned him.

CoCo stood next to Timothy, who was drawing electricity from a wall outlet and pulsing it against a woman

12

convulsing on the dirty floor. At every pulse, she spasmed wildly, crying out.

It took a few seconds too many before Emilio realized this was his teammate, Kirra Wilson. An Australian Mod who was the latest recruit to the SENTINELS, Kirra had the ability to move the earth. He thought she could have been a model if she had wanted that life. A crowd cowered around watching Timothy electrocute her.

Emilio quickly grabbed a plastic black tray from a passing server and flung it like an oversized Frisbee, hitting Timothy square in the back. "You're hurting her!" He pushed two men out of his way toward a pillar and balled his hands into fists. "Stop it."

"No."

The voice was one Emilio hadn't heard in a while but couldn't forget. But the man speaking didn't look much like he had a few years back. Emilio's concerns for the dangerous role CoCo had taken on tripled. The man had been in charge of training him and his fellow Mods back when Base 47 was in Texas. It was the former green beret, Captain Warren Grant Pierce, still wearing the fatigues he favored so much. And he looked scary as hell, like he hadn't slept in a week. A little box stuck up out of the right side of his buzz-cut head, like a little dog house on a gray lawn. A pair of scars ran along either side of his head.

"Why are you here?" Emilio demanded through a mouth that was suddenly cotton dry.

Pierce looked expressionlessly at Emilio and pointed at him. It felt like the old soldier had sucker-punched him, and Emilio lost his balance, falling on the floor near Kirra. How had Pierce knocked him down?

"Pulse Emilio as well," Pierce told Timothy. "For good measure."

A moment later, Emilio knew what it felt like to stick a

wet hand into an electrical outlet and leave it there for an hour. It felt worse than the first time he'd been shocked, if only because it seemed to last much longer.

The concrete floor seemed to ripple, but didn't rise up. Kirra's eyes rolled back in her head. The entire pavilion began to first sway, then violently shake.

"Kirra, no." But it was too late. She had lost control of her powers, and chunks of ceiling fell to the ground. Time slowed as Emilio drew deep inside and willed people out of the way. Even through the agony of being shocked, he pushed his luck powers to the limit. It worked. Every single bystander avoided being hit by falling debris, but it left him drained.

CoCo pushed Timothy out of the way. He narrowly avoided being hit by a falling banner advertising insurance.

"Timothy, stop!" CoCo said, pulling his arm down. "The place is about to go."

Timothy snapped out of his delirium and stopped shocking the SENTINELS long enough for Pierce to notice. As soon as he stopped, the stadium stilled. The musicians went silent. Around Emilio and Kirra, the crowd turned fearful.

The pulses were over but Emilio was panting in pain. Despite that, Emilio clearly heard Pierce berate CoCo and Timothy.

"You're lucky you're not getting the same treatment, falling through on a contract we made with the Swarm," Pierce groused. "We can assume the teleporter took George to safety, probably at Base 47 for now, but that island won't keep him safe forever. Let's go." He snapped his fingers, and a large burgundy door seemed to grow out of the ground in front of him. He pushed the door open and held it, allowing Timothy and CoCo to pass through the freestanding doorframe. He went through, letting the door close behind him with a crack. The door seemed to melt back into the ground. Pierce and his crew were gone.

On the ground, Emilio strove to recover and sort out what had just happened.

"Are you two okay?" a middle-aged guy with a long ponytail asked.

"Those Mods caused this place to fall apart!" another added.

"We're fine, thanks," Emilio said, pushing himself off the ground.

"It was my fault," Kirra said, her brown eyes reddened by Timothy's shocks.

"What?" The middle-aged guy stepped back from Emilio and Kirra, as though he'd just learned they were disease vectors for the plague.

"She means she wanted to stop them, but they overwhelmed her." Emilio gave Kirra a knowing look.

"Sorry, they surprised me," Kirra said.

He studied her. She looked as bad as he felt. Her curly hair was as frizzy as it could be.

She noticed him looking at her hair and reached up to feel it. She frowned. "What I wouldn't give for a hat right about now." Her jeans and slinky tank top were dirty and disheveled. Kirra's face looked dazed yet pained, as though she had spun herself around in circles so many times she would vomit from the dizziness.

In the distance, sirens sounded. "The cops are on their way," Emilio said to the crowd. "We're just going to wait over here."

He helped Kirra up and they walked over some debris to a railing.

"Why did you cover for me? It's my fault."

"They don't need to know that. Besides, it was Timothy's doing. He caused you to lose control." Emilio's words provided cold comfort and he knew it. It wasn't the first time they had been caught off guard.

"Thanks," Kirra said sheepishly.

"They'll be back." Emilio closed his eyes and it felt as though Emma were looking at him with disappointment. He shook his head briskly to clear the feeling, but it lingered. Had he been reckless again? Had he not planned the George grab properly? Was it his fault his teammate was hurting right now? These were all questions he didn't want to consider.

"How did they know to come after George here?" Kirra asked.

He shrugged. "Same way as we did?"

"Which was how?"

"We had intel," he said. "You OK?"

"Yeah, just give me a minute."

Cops were approaching. That wouldn't do at all.

"We've got to get out of here." Emilio grabbed Kirra's elbow and led her away.

CHAPTER 3

21 November

Maybe she should see a shrink.

The idea didn't appeal, but she was about out of options. Or at least almost out of her mind.

Maggie Adams, the editor of The ModsBlog, seeing a shrink? Her investors might like the clicks that would give the site, but she wasn't sure she would.

Maggie Adams

She frowned and looked around her office, but nothing she saw eased her thoughts. In fact, most of it agitated her further. The yellow, green, and white mosaic logo of her blog, which hung over the office door, seemed to taunt her. Her wall of fame—framed images of her with various Mods and well-known people—seemed to mock her. Even the picture of her with the Mod pop star Simone Moyer sang a different tune. The very sunshine streaming in her window seemed to suggest that the whole rest of the world was cheerful.

On the plush office couch across from her desk, a

mountain of a man sat, silently guarding her. Barry's presence comforted her. In the wake of several threats on her life, her longtime cameraman, Wally "Focus" Jones, had suggested she be proactive about her safety. She'd hired two security guards and had to admit they did make her feel better.

Hoping to spot something that might change her frame of mind, she walked to her office window. She twisted her blond hair between her fingers and took in the sun on her face. Her office building was in the Hudson Yards, and her thirty-eighth floor window faced east. She could see the Empire State Building, but even that soaring, iconic New York City building didn't bring a smile to her face.

In the glass reflection she noticed a few more wrinkles around her eyes, a deeper worry line between her brows. If she were a less secure woman, she might have been concerned, but she vowed to age with grace, not to look like her skin was strung tighter than a drum. Still, the last few months had been difficult ones. Shoulders slumped, she trudged back to her desk.

The technician on a ladder working with cables in the drop ceiling in her office offered the merest of distraction. He whistled "Camptown Races" as he maneuvered the cords. She shuddered, watching the sinuous way the cables snaked through the open door, through her office, and up into the ceiling. She closed her eyes and told herself to breathe. There were no snakes here. No snakes. No snakes.

She glanced at the wall clock. Ten a.m. Even time seemed against her. How could she bear to stay at the office for the rest of the day, especially if the technician lingered in her office? How could she possibly accomplish anything? It wasn't even late enough for her to sneak out for lunch. She was stuck, and she most definitely didn't want to work.

"Excuse me, Ms. Adams," said a bubbly brunette in a

fire engine red pantsuit, after knocking on the office door. Maggie waved her in. "I just got something related to the dead Mods story you're working on. This envelope just came for you."

"Thanks, Brenda." Maggie took the large manila envelope. "Good work digging up their background. You've got good instincts—you'll go far."

The young girl's smile reached from ear to ear at the compliment. She blushed and almost skipped out.

The story Maggie was editing about a pair of Mods who had disappeared and recently been discovered dead— apparently killed by a Mod hate group—couldn't keep her attention. Something about the story and the killers plagued her. Something was not right. It should have taken her no more than ten minutes to edit, but the file had been open on her screen for more than an hour, with no progress to speak of. The victims had been brutalized and tortured. Maybe whatever was in the package would help her focus. When she slipped the photographs out of the envelope and looked at them, Maggie sucked in a deep breath. They were among the worst images she'd ever seen; they were so grotesque she wouldn't include them with the article.

She was looking at the last photograph when something long and cylindrical and writhing dropped from the ceiling onto her desk. Maggie screamed. For an instant she was certain the snake would bite her. She shoved away from the sudden threat on her desk, and the casters on her rolling chair squeaked as they sailed her away. Only with distance did she realize it was simply one of the cables the technician had been working with. She panted.

"I'm sorry, miss," the technician said. "Did it hit you?"

Belatedly, she realized Barry was right next to her. The knowledge helped calm her, but for a long moment Maggie couldn't speak. "I'm fine. It just startled me." She didn't dare voice the deep terror that had filled her. Damn that CoCo. Would she fear everything even vaguely snakelike for the rest of her life? She looked up at him and forced a smile. "You know what? Could you just come back a little later and finish that up when I'm not here?"

"Guess so." He reluctantly climbed down the ladder, leaving the cables suspended from above and trailing through her office. As he walked out, Jerry, her other bodyguard, walked in.

Could a shrink actually help with this sort of strange post-traumatic stress disorder? What were the alternatives? She could just go off the ledge. The thought of giving in to the madness, the depression, and leaving behind her responsibilities appealed to her. It would be easier than continuing the fight. Than the constant fear. How long had it been since she'd had a solid night of sleep? One that was free of nightmares? Sometimes the fear froze her for hours, rendering her incapable of even tending to the smallest of human needs. Sometimes it startled her into panicked screaming. Sometimes, she simply curled up in her bed and cried for what felt like days. She had extra-large suitcases under her eyes more suitable for a seventy-year-old than the thirty-nine years she could claim. She was forgetting basic grooming habits. Yesterday, she'd neglected to brush her long blond hair before coming into the office and had only noticed when she'd spotted her reflection in the ladies' room. And forget about eating. She'd lost more than twenty pounds since the terrors had gotten the better of her, and she hadn't really had much extra meat on her bones to begin with.

She was so tired. Her eyes burned from dryness, but she didn't want to close them. She hated what she saw when she did.

Her doctor continued to suggest sleeping pills, but she

refused. She didn't want to become like Uncle Bartie, and she certainly didn't want to risk being haunted by any more unreal visions.

The desk phone rang, and she let it ring twice more before lifting the handset and drawing it to her ear.

"TheModsBlog, Maggie Adams speaking."

"Hey, Mags. You avoiding me?"

Maggie frowned. "Focus? What? Why aren't you calling on my mobile?"

"I did. You weren't answering."

She looked around her office but didn't see her phone. She pawed through her purse, but it wasn't there either. In defeat, she said, "I must have left it at home. What's going on?"

"You tell me. You stood me up."

She jumped guiltily in her chair. "Oh no."

"Oh yes."

"I'm so sorry."

"Did you want to meet with—"

"Yes, of course I do." She didn't. "I'll just get the guys and head on over. We'll be there in twenty."

"The governor's people told me you can't bring your bodyguards into the interview. Jerry and Barry'll have to wait outside."

She sighed. "They won't like that. I don't like that. Are you sure? What if something happens?"

"Mags, I'll watch out for you."

"Thanks, Focus, but neither one of us is exactly equipped to stand up to another Mod who wants to hurt me. Not even friendship could protect me from CoCo."

Focus said nothing. Maggie put her head down on her arms and tried not to close her eyes. When she spoke again, her voice was a bit muffled and she was panting.

"Listen, I'll be on my way in a few." She disconnected.

21

Then she closed her eyes. On the video screen in her mind, CoCo pushed Maggie into a dark and squirming hole. Her eyes flew open, and she yanked her head up off her arms. Her eyes told her she was in her office, but her mind said she was flailing in a pit of writhing vipers. She squelched a scream just as the desk phone rang again. She rocked back and forth in her chair, taking in and expelling lung-bursting breaths, ignoring the shrill ringing. It went on and on and on. She rocked on and on and on and breathed in and out. Finally, the ringing ceased, but not the rocking. The breathing steadied at last, and the rocking stopped.

The phone rang again. This time, she answered.

"TheModsBlog. Maggie Adams."

"Why aren't you on your way yet?"

It was Focus. She didn't answer him.

"You're stalling."

"I'm here." Her voice sounded small, like a scared toddler.

"Mags, come on. Get it together," Focus said. "Listen, I'll try again to get your bodyguards into the interview."

"You think they'll go for it?" She hated the desperation she heard in her own voice.

"Maybe. You have some leverage here. The governor wants to spread his message opposing registration as far and wide as he can, and he knows TheModsBlog has a significant reach. So, maybe. I'll work on them, but shuck your buns. You're going to be late as it is."

"Fine. On my way." She disconnected again and stood. It was time for the mental pep talk. Sometimes it worked. Sometimes not. Today, it had better. She could do this. CoCo wouldn't be anywhere near the governor. There were no snakes and no betrayals. Happy thoughts and deep breaths. She could do this. She just had to keep her eyes open. She could do this. Her shoulders relaxed a fraction, and it felt like the pep talk was working. She gathered her briefcase and purse, which seemed incomplete without her mobile in it, and left her office. "Jerry? Barry? We have an appointment. Let's go."

CHAPTER
4

21 November

The sun hung high in the mid-Atlantic sky as two people walked among the manicured gardens toward a walled enclosure. The man wore a white linen shirt that contrasted against deeply tanned skin. He stood around five-foot-

Base 47

nine inches, all lean muscle combined with the quiet self-assurance of someone much older than his twenty-five years. When Bayanai Romrico, once a shepherd in the Philippine islands, spoke, people listened. This had been true even before the White Light Wave event five years previous had turned him from a mere shepherd into a Mod with the ability to boost other Mod's powers. His dark eyes sparkled with awareness, patience, and intelligence. Now he led the SENTINELS and Base 47, and the burdens of office had added more than few premature wrinkles to his brow and the corners of his eyes.

Bayanai wiped his forehead and looked over at his female companion. She held a tablet and wore the standard Base 47 security outfit: a trim, white, button-down shirt with khaki pants, complete with a Taser. Laura Parks, a middle-aged African-American immigrant to New Atlantis, had been the head of security for Base 47 for the last year. A former US marine, she jogged and did body weight exercises daily, rain or shine.

"Thanks for working with me to update the security protocols." Laura input information into her tablet as they walked.

"I want to ensure Base 47 is secure and that all of New Atlantis is protected," Bayanai said. When they reached the wall, he flipped open a metal keypad and entered a code. The new Base 47 had been built a few years back after the SENTINELS were officially invited to set up on New Atlantis. It happened at a particularly tumultuous period in their history. Their original Base had been destroyed in a siege and the team was in tatters. The move saved them in more ways than one.

"Any news on GRIM?" she asked as a whoosh accompanied a door opening from the wall, and they walked inside the overly air-conditioned building. GRIM, or Global Response Initiative on Mods, was an extremist group that had splintered off of Man First, which was, predictably, an organization dedicated to preserving the human race.

Bayanai paused a moment, waiting for the door to close behind them. "Not really." He studied her a moment and smiled before switching gears. "Is the new and improved MDA functioning as it should?"

"About that, there are some unusual readings."

"What? Why am I just now hearing about this?" Concerned, Bayanai stopped in the middle of the corridor and turned to look at her. "Is the MDA acting up again? I thought we got that cleared up."

The Mod Detection Apparatus was one of the crowning

achievements at Base 47. The MDA was originally based on Emma's Mod-locating powers, but was only able to search for Mods when they used their abilities. Over the years, the MDA had generated an extensive list of Mod activities and locations, all over the globe.

The MDA was only one component of Base 47's security system, but the base and the police force had an information-sharing agreement that gave the police access to MDA data as needed. Similar reciprocity agreements existed with investigative agencies in ally countries. The MDA kept track of whenever a Mod used their powers on the island, although activity by the SENTINELS was recorded but largely ignored in the reporting process.

"It's working. Just some unusual readings, like I said. It doesn't work the same now that Emma is gone."

Bayanai gritted his teeth. "Missing."

"Of course. I didn't mean to imply that—"

"She's not dead." Bayanai's words came out with heat and deliberate enunciation.

"I don't want you to have false hopes."

"There was no body. She is still alive, and we will find her and rescue her." He shook his head to help clear it and switch gears. "What's the problem with the MDA?"

"It's just giving us some false reports. Showing Mod activity when there's none. Some sort of ghost in the machine, maybe. An echo or something. I don't know."

"Are you sure they're false?"

"To the best of my knowledge. I'm doing everything I can to figure it out."

"What are you doing to locate Emma and the Tribe's hideout?"

"Sorry, sir. Wherever she is, it's as if she just vanished. I'm assuming the Tribe's got massive counterdetection measures in place, just like we do. I mean, if the Tribe has her. If she would just use her powers we could ping her with the MDA, but nothing."

Bayanai slowly nodded and resumed walking. To his right framed photos lined the hallway. Each depicted a year in the history of the SENTINELS. He paused and studied the images, considering what had brought them to their current crisis and worries. The series began with a picture of the original Base 47 team in Texas early in their training days, before the events that created New Atlantis, and before they were actually SENTINELS operating under the sanction of the United Nations and the direction of the vice chair of Mod Activity.

Josh, Emilio, Rami, CoCo, Luli, Jiya, Waleed, James, Katrina, Etienne, Emma, and Pierce smiled out at him from the frame. Luli had been pregnant with Shining then, and Rami was still alive. They all looked so innocent. Untested. So … young and shiny.

The remainder of the pictures were all taken on the anniversaries of the White Light Wave event, on the summer solstice.

Pictured at the beginning of their second year were Josh, Emilio, CoCo, Etienne, Katrina, Jiya, James, Waleed, Emma, Ericka, and Pierce. Here, the SENTINELS looked confident, severe even. Happy but oblivious to the turmoil that awaited. If they had only known how precious their time together really was.

The third one saw Bayanai's own smiling face beaming out. His new teammates included Josh, Emilio, CoCo, Etienne, Katrina, Waleed, James, Emma, Ericka, and Pierce.

He'd been thrilled and honored to join the team in Texas, slipping into a life far different than his island life in the Philippines. He remembered when the photo was taken. It was just days after they'd saved the president of the United States from a Mod terrorist attack onboard Air Force

1. He thought she was more upset about the destroyed plane than the attempt on her life.

The fourth one showed a drastically altered lineup, with only Bayanai, Emilio, CoCo, Carlos, Etienne, Waleed, James, Katrina, Emma, and Builder. It followed a schism that had wrenched the team apart. They had learned that their trusted leader, Pierce, had deceived them from the start. The knowledge had almost destroyed the team. With the original Base 47 in Texas demolished before this picture had been taken, the SENTINELS had relocated to New Atlantis. In the aftermath of the Texas base's destruction and worried about the direction of the team, Bayanai had challenged Josh's spot as leader, forced him out, and assumed leadership of the team.

"Have you seen Josh's film, yet?" Laura asked. "It's playing at Grover's Theatre. The whole island is talking about it."

"I keep meaning to catch it. Maybe over the weekend," Bayanai said through gritted teeth.

"Really neat seeing a Mod get celebrity treatment."

"Josh has always been a celebrity. Nothing new there." Bayanai reached the most recent picture showing a scaled-down team. Only Bayanai, Emilio, Emma, Katrina, Etienne, Waleed, James, and Kirra were on the team here. Bayanai thought Kirra a bright—and beautiful—addition to the team during a difficult year.

In the time leading up to the final picture, they had lost Carlos in an explosion and CoCo had betrayed the team by joining the Tribe.

"Sir? Is everything okay?"

"Sorry about that. Lost in thought," Bayanai said. They neared the infirmary, where his teammates Kirra and Emilio were sitting. Bayanai stood in the doorway, Laura behind him, and Emilio looked up.

"What brings you here, *Jefe*?" Emilio asked, a pleased grin stretching across his face.

"Just making the rounds. What are you two doing here?" Bayanai asked. He smiled broadly at Kirra and swung the grin around to include Emilio as well.

"Checkup from yesterday," Kirra said as she stretched her long, toned arms toward the sky. Bayanai took a moment to take her in. She'd managed to tame the frizzy mane from the attack the day before back into her normal thick curly do. The sunlight from the window gave her an extra glow, and it looked like a halo surrounding her.

"All recovered from the electrical surges?" Bayanai asked, looking at Emilio.

"Mostly. I just wish that we had gotten a chance to whack CoCo one," the Australian girl lamented.

Emilio looked down.

"But at least they didn't get George," she added.

"Right. There's a win there." Emilio pursed his lips.

"Come off it, guys. Don't be so hard. We knew that Pierce was going to show up again some time," Bayanai said. "Strangely enough, that's back burner now. One thing at a time. First we have to get over to Tennessee and figure out what happened with the power plant explosion."

"What? Now we investigate explosions?" Emilio asked. "I mean, I heard about it, but isn't that a bit ... mundane for us?"

"This is a case for Nicola. One of her contacts reached out to her and suggested she might be able to provide insight into what happened." Bayanai shrugged. "So I'm sending her in for that."

"Want me to go?"

"No, Emilio. It's okay. I'm sending Etienne. I want you here to help with George. We've got to know why the Tribe was getting him for the Swarm."

"Consider it done," Emilio said. "And Bayanai, I want you to know that I'm sorry about the mistake at the concert. I should've paid more attention. I don't want what happened with Carlos to happen again."

"Stop. Sometimes these things happen in our line of work," Bayanai said. "We'll figure it out." He said it with such confidence that he wasn't sure who he was trying to convince.

"Yeah, okay." Emilio leaned far back and let his head rest momentarily against the wall.

"Looks like you're both good to go," the physician said.

Emilio hopped off the seat and headed to the door before turning back to Kirra. "Wanna grab dinner later on?"

"Sure, sounds great," Kirra said, perhaps a bit too quickly.

Emilio nodded and smiled distractedly at her.

Bayanai looked down to hide his frown before speaking. "All right. Let me know how it goes with George."

"Will do." Emilio slapped the top of the doorframe on his way out.

"How is he really doing? Still blaming himself?" Bayanai asked.

"Of course he is. He's way too hard on himself." Kirra wrapped a turquoise head band around the untamed curls of her hair.

Bayanai and Laura walked out and headed toward the science division.

Bayanai knocked, then pushed through the door into Dr. Nicola Patel's office. "Do you have any leads on the explosion yet?"

"Oh! You startled me. I wasn't expecting anyone until later," the scientist said as she pulled her hands from beside her head. Her lab was meticulous and there was never anything out of place. The only jump of color in the all-white lab were the various ivies draping the tables—a gift from Juan Pierre del Bosque and his solstice-enhanced green thumb. Nicola was medium height and on the skinny side of slender. Her dark hair swung loose and wavy over her shoulders. She had exquisitely expressive eyebrows and a brow free of worry now that she was working for a cause she believed in.

"Sorry about that."

"It's okay. Just a little tense." Nicola glanced at the whiteboard, then back at Bayanai. "Can we take Marie along with us to the site?"

"I don't see why not. The site is secure, and I'm sure Waleed would appreciate having his wife join him."

"He will." Nicola thought a moment.

Bayanai could see the age creep into her eyes. She wore her graying hair at the temples with pride.

"In the meantime, I'll keep preparing for the Tennessee site visit. I'm sure we'll get to the bottom of this."

"I'm sure you will." He smiled a smile he didn't feel and walked out. Suddenly, he found he was ordering himself to get a grip. "You can't lose your confidence now. You'll be useless to the team." He looked around in surprise at hearing his own voice. He really did need to get a grip.

Bayanai reflected on the hard months they'd endured. The losses. The challenges. Was he up for the task of leading the SENTINELS after all?

CHAPTER 5

21 November

"Can you believe what that reviewer said?" Josh slipped into the back of the white Rolls-Royce limo and loosened his tie. His face and voice morphed into a replica of the notorious hates-everything critic. "Josh Grant's performance

Pete Meyers

in *As I Am* is a force of nature. Brutal, honest, damning. A surefire award contender."

Morphing from the critic's likeness back to himself, Josh leaned toward Luca for a kiss.

"Stop doing that!" Luca pushed Josh away. "You left that world a long time ago. If you want to be considered for an award, you can't use your powers."

Josh leaned back and silently nodded. He looked out the window at the night twisting in the smog-filled Los Angeles sky. Luca was right. He had given up superheroics two years ago, and the split hadn't been pretty. After Bayanai had usurped leadership of the SENTINELS, Josh "Hollywood" Grant had left New Atlantis and the team. He distanced himself from the Mods and resumed his acting career. That meant not using his powers in public, a compromise he had mostly been able to maintain. However, there were times when it was just easier to shape-shift into someone else to avoid paparazzi. Or crazed fans.

Be they earned or endowed through the White Light Wave event, abilities want to be used. He missed the variety and fun of using his shape-shifting power. A part of him longed for the rush of fighting the good fight. He had a good life now, to be sure, but the life he'd had before made a difference in the world.

And return he had, landing a revelatory role in a little indie drama that blew up. His star power had grown not only from his exposure as a Mod but also his coming out. He'd given Maggie Adams of TheModsBlog that exclusive. Coming out on a website had been a surprisingly successful move. Shortly after, he'd found Luca Florentino, a rising Italian hotelier who was his match in every way imaginable. Josh had surrendered to love, and they had created a full life together. It was everything Josh had wanted for so long. Everything except a nagging at the base of his skull saying that he wasn't doing all he could. Most nights he could silence that voice by holding Luca closer. Other nights, scotch did the trick.

With all the turmoil of the recent months that he had heard about, part of him was glad he wasn't in charge of the team. All he had to concern himself with was showing up for the latest photo op and where he and Luca were going to holiday.

"*Tesoro*, I love when you play your games, but this is real." Luca's voice started gentle but turned heated. "You promised me when we came together that you would leave your past behind you. I want a long life with you. I don't want to see you hurt. You can't be a Mod anymore. That part of your life is over. You have me. I don't want you to slip into that kind of trouble again." Luca tightened his grip on Josh's hand. "The Mod Authorization Act is gaining steam and you don't want to be on the wrong side."

"I love when you chastise me in your accent. It makes it impossible to be mad at you." Josh kissed Luca. "Hey, Ken, could you raise the privacy window, please?"

The driver slid up the window, and Josh pulled off his tie and loosened his shirt. As Luca rose to open the shirt, there was a loud rumble. The ground beneath the limo seemed to crumble, and the black car tumbled. The moments stretched out and Josh was sure each crunch of metal would be his last. In the chaos, it felt like he and Luca were tennis balls bouncing around inside a dryer. Each hit came harder than the one before. His mind raced for the cause. A drunk driver made them careen off the road? Earthquake? Nothing made sense. For endless moments terror swallowed his ability to think.

When they finally stopped moving, he couldn't tell if they were upside down or right side up.

All Josh could hear was a ringing in his ears. He struggled to pull himself to alertness. Another rumble dislodged the limo and it fell end over end, again tossing them about the inside of the car.

When the car settled and he could finally breathe again, Josh patted himself down and determined that he was okay, mostly. His inventory revealed a dislocated shoulder, lots of cuts and blood. He was sure most of it was his, since he could feel cuts on his cheek and forehead. Add to that a busted lip. "If I'm in pain, then I'm alive," Josh thought as he mentally prepared himself to move. Then he spotted Luca, crumpled in the floor of the limo and bleeding heavily. He crawled over to his boyfriend.

"Luca." Josh coughed and blood dripped from his

busted lip. He wiped his hand over his mouth, then rubbed the blood onto his pants before gently placing two fingers on Luca's neck. For the longest seconds of his life, he couldn't locate a pulse. Then, faintly, he felt something. He recentered his fingers over Luca's neck and felt the pulse, weak as it was. He looked skyward and breathed heavily. "Thank god." Josh heard the driver moan. For the first time since the accident, Josh's attention expanded beyond the miniature universe of himself and Luca. How could he have forgotten about the driver? He was grateful to hear the other man was still alive.

"Ken, are you okay?"

"I'm okay, I think, but stuck. I just don't know what happened," the driver said looking through his rearview mirror. There was no longer a privacy panel between the two sections of the car. Shattered pieces of it glittered like moonlight on the floor of the limo.

"Luca's hurt. I need to get him out of the limo, then I'll help you."

Josh tried to lift Luca up, but his dislocated shoulder screamed at him, and he dropped Luca back on the seat. Luca moaned. Josh frowned and listened for a moment, worried about aftershocks.

"Mr. Grant, you have to get out of here."

"I'm not leaving here without both of you." Josh tried to shift his body.

"I don't know what happened. One moment I was driving along and the next the car just fell off the cliff. I'm so sorry," Ken said.

"It's okay. We're going to be all right," Josh said, hoping he was right. One of the great things about being a shapeshifter was that when he was injured, he could shift into another form and the injuries dissipated. He'd learned that very early in his shape-shifting days. He'd shifted himself into the guise of a cop to play a prank on someone, and when he'd shifted back to himself, the raging hangover that had plagued him all morning was gone. With experimentation, he'd learned that shape-shifting would even heal broken bones. So a dislocated shoulder and all those cuts should be no issue.

But his head wouldn't stop rattling and with his rising panic about Luca's condition, he couldn't focus long enough to make a transition.

"Come on, dammit. Don't wuss out on me now!" Josh slammed his hand against the seat, willing his metamorphic powers to activate.

He looked out the shattered window at the night landscape. He wanted to see police lights. He wanted to see a searchlight. But all he saw was the reflection of the headlights and sparks erupting from the engine. They must have fallen off the road quite a bit if he couldn't see any other car lights. He didn't know the extent of their injuries, but he knew he had to at least get them out of the limo. But how? He was too weak to pull them both out. He reached into his pocket, planning to call for an ambulance, but his cell wasn't there. After a quick search, he spotted it near the dividing wall. He scrambled toward it, stared at it in disbelief, and threw it. He screamed. "No service. Are you kidding me?!"

Josh closed his eyes. "All right, Josh... You've gotten yourself out of bad situations before. This is nothing. Focus and relax. Don't force a change. Breathe. Start small."

He tried again to shift his body. This time, he was able to shift into Luca. He winced in pain as his body started to mend. He had never quite gotten used to the process, but there were techniques to ease the pain. None of which he could remember now. He howled as he grabbed his shoulder. Where did all this blood come from? He couldn't tell. He couldn't remember. Was it just his? Or Luca's? He tried to slow his breathing, to focus, to recall the techniques.

"Mr. Grant, are you okay?"

"Shoulder. Dislocated. But we have to get out of here." Josh gnashed his teeth. Never before had he been in such pain. Waves and waves of pain washed over him until, finally, relief replaced it. The shoulder returned to its rightful place and he heaved a grateful sigh.

"Mr. Grant. It's okay, we've got help." Ken pointed out the front window toward a hooded figure. Josh stared and shifted back into himself. This shift was much easier, now that he was no longer in pain. The various cuts and busted lip were history as well. Blood aside, it looked like he hadn't been in an accident.

Josh peered out. The first feeling, relief, fled when he spotted the figure. Foreboding filled him. "Who is that?" Josh vacillated from feeling saved to a dread that stuck in his throat and back to hope.

"Josh..." Luca muttered as he flailed his head back and forth.

"It's okay," Josh soothed. "Just relax. I'm going to get you home."

Feeling a bit stronger, Josh slammed his now uninjured shoulder against the passenger door, managing to crack the door open. He winced but took a breath and waited for the pain to subside enough for him to speak again.

"Help! We need help. I can't get a signal on my phone. Can you call the ambulance? I think there was some sort of earthquake. We have to get to safety." Josh forced open the limo door and got out. He struggled to pull Luca out of the twisted limo. When Luca's leg got caught on the snarled door, Josh pulled harder. A jagged piece of metal on the door sliced Luca's calf, and the man groaned. Josh, however, didn't notice the additional injury. "I'm all right, but I'm worried about my boyfriend and my driver." Josh slowly laid his boyfriend on the ground before sitting down next to him, out of breath.

"It was no earthquake," the hooded figure replied.

Josh's mouth went dry. He glanced at the driver, stuck in the front seat. "What do you mean, not an earthquake? What else could it be?"

The hooded figure stood there in silence.

"Help us," Josh pleaded.

"Afraid not." He pointed to the limo, where smoke billowed from the engine block. He closed his fist and the ground began to rumble. The figure thrust open his hand and Josh couldn't focus on any fixed object. Everything vibrated. He traced the direction from the kid's hands; they pointed directly toward the front of the limo. Before he could move, the engine exploded. The force threw Josh several yards away. He landed on a rock and felt a rib crack. Through the agony, he saw Luca remained still.

"No!" Josh screamed. It took a moment for his ears to stop ringing. If he didn't do something quick, he feared Luca would be dead.

"Why are you doing this?" Josh beseeched the hooded guy, a lanky figure who thrummed with hostility. "You don't have to do this. I can help you."

"Wrong!"

"What do you mean?"

"I've heard it all before." He pulled back his hoodie. His pale face reflected the moonlight. "From you."

Confused, Josh studied the kid until realization dawned. Five years ago he had saved this kid's life. It was still hard for Josh to focus, but he could never forget the kid who had caused the Devil's Slide sinkhole in Reno. What was his name? It sat stubbornly on the tip of his tongue. This kid had started him on the journey to founding the

SENTINELS. He was there when Josh took a stand and declared himself a Mod for the whole world to see.

"What do you want?"

"You don't even remember who I am?" He scratched what could barely be called a beard. The kid was only around sixteen years old, but his eyes said he'd known nothing but rage and disappointment and self-hatred.

"I do. I do. It's just, my head hurts." Josh looked at Luca lying helpless on the ground and Ken, who was still trapped in the driver's seat.

"My dad was right about you."

"What are you talking about?" Josh screamed as he tried shifting to relieve the agony of his cracked rib, but the searing pain just wouldn't let up.

"You know what I mean." He knelt and placed his hand palm on the ground. A low rumble radiated out, the ground opened beneath the limo, and it started to slip down.

"Stop! You don't have to do this!"

"Yes! Yes, I do!" He walked toward Josh.

"Why?"

"Do you have any idea what the past five years have been like for me?" He clapped his hands together and the ground shook below them. "You told me that everything was going to be okay. You told me that it wasn't my fault."

"It will be okay," Josh said. "And it wasn't your fault."

"You're wrong. It was totally my fault. My powers caused the sinkhole that killed my mom and sister."

Josh instantly regretted not bringing him to Base 47 all those years ago. But the kid had been so young, and he'd truly thought having the kid stay with his family was the best outcome.

"My father said you never cared for me. That you only cared about yourself and your reputation. That you were just a useless, fragile faggot." He pulled his fists up to his face.

"And he was right."

While he was used to hearing all those accusations, the words stung. The kid's words had the hard edge of truth behind it. He had walked away from the SENTINELS over his bruised ego. He had turned his back on so many people. Maybe he deserved this beat-down. The sins of his past had come back to haunt him.

Josh could hear Ken yelling for help. Josh swallowed his hurt and struggled to stand. "I thought you would be better off with your family taking care of you."

"You never checked up on me. Not even once. And when I came to the base in Texas, begging you to help me, you turned me away." Rage filled his words.

"That's not true. I wouldn't do that." Josh hoped that was true.

"You abandoned me!" the kid yelled. The ground below them rippled. "You made me go back to them. Back to that horror."

"I didn't. I didn't know."

"It doesn't matter. I trusted you and you let me down."

Josh was running out of time and options. Ken was screaming in fear and pain as the limo slipped farther down the sinkhole. He hadn't heard anything from Luca in way too long. He hoped it just meant Luca had passed out. But how could he save them both? How would he live with himself if he only saved one of them?

"Look, I know that you blame me for the things that went wrong for you, but nothing's been done that can't be undone. No one is dead. If you want help, if you want to go to Base 47, I can make that happen. You can be a part of the team." Josh neared him. He couldn't tell if the kid was listening or just biding his time.

"Nothing's been done?"

Josh tried to smile.

"Nothing's been done?" He grabbed his head in anger. "How about now?" He pounded his fist into the ground and a boulder slipped from the ledge. It barreled straight for where Luca lay.

"No!" Josh darted toward Luca, barely grabbing him in time and rolling him away from the spot as the boulder careened down the hill. Josh heard a slight pop as they rolled over each other. Josh lay there for a moment as every muscle in his body screamed out.

"What are you doing?"

"Giving you a choice."

"What do you mean?"

"You can save your boyfriend. Or your driver. Or me."

"What?" Josh said as he watched Luca flutter in and out of consciousness. "No. I can't choose."

"You just don't like to make decisions. You run from them." He sneered. "I've seen you run from all the tough stuff. Leave it to others."

"That's not true."

"Really? What happened to Base 47? To the SENTINELS? You gave up on each of them. And for what? A guy? A movie? A career?" Like a predator, he circled Josh. He spat on him and Josh reared back in revulsion. "You can't even begin to imagine how bad my life has been since you left me. My dad hates me for what I did. I hate myself for what I did. I've been watching you. Studying you. Hoping that you'd come back for me. But you never did. You don't care."

"It doesn't have to be like this," Josh pleaded. He tried to muster the strength to do something, anything.

"Tick, tock, Josh." He knelt beside Josh and grabbed Luca by his shirt with one hand and extended the other toward the limo, which shook and rattled.

"Leave him alone!" Josh's voice cracked as he realized

that this could be the end. He froze in panic.

"I've always wondered what would happen if I used my powers on a person instead of the ground."

The kid grinned, and Josh's eyes widened in terror. The horrifying idea of a sinkhole running through Luca's middle, leaving him with a gaping hole rather than internal organs, frightened him badly. "Don't do it!"

"Who are you going to save?"

The ground swayed and Josh couldn't stand up. He had to make a decision. Save Luca? Save Ken? Save the kid who was trying to destroy his life? Even in his prime with the SENTINELS, he had balked at making the tough decisions, relying on Pierce or CoCo or Ericka to make the hard stance. It was the main reason Bayanai had managed to usurp his leadership. There had to be another way. A way for them all to live. But as much as it pained him to the core of his being, he would have to choose, to act, and to act decisively. I've never killed anyone before; but I can't let Luca die, Josh thought as he jumped and grabbed the kid— Pete was his name, now he remembered—by the collar and took him down to the ground. Luca rolled away and heaved. Josh could faintly hear Ken in the distance.

"What are you doing?" The kid and Josh fell backward.

"Saving us all." Josh put his arm around Pete's neck and squeezed. "Shh, Pete," he crooned.

"That won't do anything! I'll never give up!" The ground's trembling intensified.

"I know." Josh fought back tears. He squeezed tighter and tighter until Pete could no longer breathe. Soon the earth stopped moving. Josh let go and Pete rolled over. He was knocked out, at least for a while. Josh panted heavily as he tried to formulate a plan. His body ached like never before but he was now full of adrenaline. Josh got up to check on Luca.

"Luca, are you okay? Say something."

Silence. It was breaking Josh's heart.

"What happened?" Luca faintly asked.

"Oh, thank god." Josh smiled in relief as he kissed Luca gently. "It's going to be okay."

"Who is that?"

"Don't worry about him. Now tell me, where do you hurt?"

"It all hurts." Luca took a deep breath and closed his eyes. Then he stared into Josh's eyes, looking worried. "I can't feel my legs."

"You can't?" Josh looked toward Luca's bloody legs, remembered the pop from moving him earlier, and swallowed hard. "It's, uh, probably shock. You're going to be fine," he said, hoping Luca would believe him. "I'm going to check on Ken. I'll get us some help, and I'll be right back."

"Josh," Luca whispered.

"Shh. Save your strength."

Luca closed his eyes and then opened them again. "Don't leave. I need you here."

Josh sat for a moment, gently stroking Luca's hair, and wishing that the last hour had been a bad dream. Hoping that he'd awake from this dark nightmare and his world would still be revolving. But he knew that would not be the case. Once again he was about to get trapped in the Mods' orbit. He looked up into the sky. There was some sick twisted symmetry to all of this. Five years ago, helping this kid had put him on the path to the SENTINELS. Now, this same kid was pushing him right back in.

"I have to get Ken, but I'll be right back. You're going to be all right, I promise." Josh kissed Luca gently and squeezed their hands together before struggling to stand up. "I'm going to make everything all right."

CHAPTER 6

21 November

"Why'd they want you, George?" Emilio asked.

George St. John and Emilio Santos were in an interrogation room deep in the bowels of Base 47 on New Atlantis. The room held two chairs facing each other

George St. John

and nothing else. But one chair was vacant. While George was seated, his rescuer from the day before paced the room.

"I don't know." George shrank back in his chair from Emilio. "When can I go home? Not that I mind. This place is cool. Does being here make me a SENTINEL? I mean, I am with your team, right?"

Emilio smiled at the rapid-fire questions. "Not just yet. We have to figure some things out first." Emilio continued pacing for a few moments. "You're here for your safety. So. Let's talk about your power."

"Uh, I can, well, one of my friends calls me the Hypnotist because I can get in people's minds and make them do things."

"Like what?"

George hesitated before answering. He wanted Emilio to like him. Was desperate, actually. He was at the headquarters for the SENTINELS. Earlier that day, he'd walked the secured campus. The building, made mostly of an orangey granite, rose out of the ground. The sculpted curves of the base raced toward four peaks, one for each direction, as well as one in the center. These circular turrets were connected via enclosed glass walkways. The central tower contained most of the senior offices. He enjoyed looking out over New Atlantis from Base 47 and feeling like the base was the island's protector.

He was finally at the cool kid's table and he wasn't going to spoil it by being a limp noodle. He had to play this cool. If he could impress Emilio, maybe they'd invite him to join the team. He sat up tall in his seat. As tall as he could. He sucked in his stomach. He wasn't fat, but he certainly wasn't fit.

"Depends. At first, I used to help friends who needed help with managing their emotions. One had lost her father, and I helped with her grief. Another wanted external help to go exercise every day. Things like that."

"Have you ever used your power to conduct robberies?" Emilio asked, recalling an incident involving CoCo's friend Maggie and Maggie's former boss shortly after the Mods first got their powers.

George looked horrified at the idea. "Never. I wouldn't steal or hurt anyone."

Emilio studied him a moment and nodded, believing him, at least for the moment. "You said you used your powers to help people at first. How do you use them now?"

"Pretty much the same way, but I don't use my power very often any more. It kind of creeps me out—other people's minds are as messy as my own is. Maybe messier.

But I don't know my way around their minds like my own. I get lost." He shivered, recalling a particularly unsettling incident. "I try to respect their privacy. People aren't always as nice as they think they are."

"Um hmm. Do they know you're in there?"

"Yeah." George cocked his head and studied Emilio. "Want me to show you? I can make you sit down and feel calm."

Emilio evaluated him a moment. The thought of having someone else directing his emotions made him uneasy, but he had told Bayanai he would figure out why the Tribe wanted George. Reluctantly, he nodded. He felt George jump into his mind, like a kid doing a cannonball into the pool, splashing everywhere.

"Wait. Is it always that obvious? Can you get in there without me knowing?"

George was suddenly out, leaving Emilio feeling curiously lonely. A moment later, he felt George slip back in. This time, it was more like an Olympic diver barely disturbing the water, but Emilio still knew he was there. Then Emilio felt George directing him, like a kindly puppeteer. His pacing halted and he walked purposefully to the plastic black chair facing George and sat. He felt calm, a forced calm that didn't originate with himself.

"OK, get out. That's what I needed to know," he said, and again George left the pool of Emilio's mind. He felt some of the calm wash out of him, but it had taken the edge off.

"That's the quietest entry you can make?"

George nodded.

"Why not dive in so gently the first time?"

George shrugged and reddened. "It's kind of fun to just jump right in. I usually do it that way. Plus, I never want people to think I'm trying to sneak in."

Emilio watched him a moment. "What happens to you when you go into someone's mind?"

"It makes me a little tired, but mostly it weirds me out. Like I said, I can get lost because other people's minds are messy."

"Like being in a foreign country with no map?"

George closed his hazel eyes a few moments before answering. "Yeah."

Emilio thought some, then probed his own mind where George had been.

"Who is CoCo?" George asked suddenly.

"What?" Emilio asked.

"It's just, when I was in your mind I saw her and you. Was she your girlfriend?"

Emilio stood sharply.

"And why do you think they want me so bad?" George asked.

"That's enough," Emilio said.

George jumped at the change in Emilio's voice.

"Did you leave a souvenir in my mind?" Emilio asked.

George shifted in his seat. "That can happen. I didn't do it on purpose."

"You didn't leave a permanent 'be calm' suggestion in my mind?" Emilio glared at George, who slid several inches down in his plastic chair. "How did you do that?"

The man shrugged. "Sometimes, when I try really hard, it leaves an artifact. It usually goes away in a few days, at least according to my ex-girlfriend."

"You played these games with your ex? Is that why she's your ex?"

"That may have been a part of it," George said, and his voice sounded tight.

"But it will go away? Are you sure?"

"Yes, and now that I'm out of your mind, you can ignore

47

it. It won't guide you."

"Okay, then," Emilio said, considering what other questions he should ask. "Can you jump into the mind of someone in the next room, or in another country?"

"No, it doesn't work that way. I have to be close, maybe a few feet away."

"OK, good. That rules out a lot of potentially very bad things."

"What do you mean?"

"That the people who wanted you could use you to hijack someone in another country to assassinate a political leader, or even cause the political leader to commit suicide. And you'd be so far away, there'd be no chance of getting caught. That's one."

George paled, and his freckles popped out in bright relief.

"What kinds of things can you do while you're in someone's mind?"

"Different things. I can make them do things, physically. I can make them have different emotions. I can go in when they're asleep, which I did by accident when I first got my power. I made my ex-girlfriend have—er—have some special dreams." Now he was blushing furiously, and those freckles seemed to pulse like supernovas on his pinkening skin.

He was starting to amuse Emilio, who felt the rest of his foul mood fall away. "Really? You gave your ex sexy dreams and she dumped you? That sounds a wee bit unfair." Emilio swallowed a grin. "Can you plant suggestions in their dreams that they would act on once awake?"

George shook his head. "I have to still be in their heads for them to act. I may accidentally leave an artifact, like you found, but not plant a command or suggestion and still be certain they would act on it once I left."

"Anything else I should know?"

"No, I don't think so. But thank you for rescuing me. I know that whatever they were going to make me do, it couldn't have been good," George said.

"Oh? How do you know that?"

"Well, if it were good, they would have approached me directly, just asked for my help. Right?"

"Pretty much. But then again, we could have kidnapped you and simply be playing the 'good' card."

"But you're not. I know about you. I read about you and Base 47 on TheModsBlog. Plus, I've been in your mind."

"All right, George. Here's the deal. We can't let you go home. It's not safe for you. So you're staying with us until this whole thing blows over."

"Does that make me a SENTINEL?" The words came out too fast for him. But he couldn't take it back. It was too late for that.

Emilio smiled politely. "That's not exactly how it works, amigo."

George looked at the floor.

"You'd have to train first, get strong enough that we could take you on missions," Emilio said.

But all George heard was that he just had to train and he could be on the team. Beaming and purposeful, he jumped up and set off to the training center.

CHAPTER 7

22 November

Dr. Roger Martin stalked down the crowded sidewalks of London, making his way to his office. The last five years had been kinder to him after the WaveMaker disaster than he'd had any right to expect following the disaster on New Atlantis.

Dr. Roger Martin

The Hastings Foundation had gone on a public relations offensive to restore its image and scrub its association with the events on New Atlantis. The PR team had cast the late Dr. Thierry Giraud as the mastermind behind the scheme, a move Roger applauded. Even the efforts of Dr. Nicola Patel, the SENTINELS, and Base 47 could not undo the damage to Thierry's image. Some may have been less trusting of The Hastings Foundation in the aftermath, but the efforts of the PR team had largely paid off.

The Hastings Foundation had reorganized its operations and moved to a high-rise office building in London's Canary Wharf section on the banks of the Thames. The location expanded the group's reach internationally and provided an ideal spot in which to carry out their new plans. When offered the opportunity to head up the cryospore project from the London office, Roger had leapt at the chance. It was not just an opportunity to redeem himself in the eyes of his boss, Henry Hastings, but also a chance to move away from Philadelphia, a city he'd detested. The project he was working on might be the last one he was involved with before he reached retirement age. He wanted to make it count. His mind wandered to thoughts about how he might fill his retirement. The usual—travel—held none of the appeal for him that it did for so many others. Perhaps because he'd already been all those places. Nor did he envision a future in which he shared a career's worth of learnings and love for the art of science with college brats. No, his perfect future involved a country cottage and Ursula. And perhaps the loss of about twenty-five pounds around the midsection.

Roger rounded the corner and stopped at a kiosk to check out the day's newspaper headlines. The first two were "UN Calls for International Registration of Powers" and "MI 5's Special Division in Jeopardy." But when he spotted the last headline, "Josh Grant's Early Oscar Buzz for *As I Am*," Roger turned his nose up. He would never understand why the public idolized that snake of a Mod actor.

He left the newsstand and turned the corner to his office building, a modern high-rise affair with windows that glittered in the afternoon sunlight. Just as he reached the building, his phone rang and he smiled. The ring tone was Ursula's. He leaned against the building and answered the call.

"Roger, you left too early this morning. I wanted to make you a proper breakfast."

He could hear a yawn in her voice. "You looked so

peaceful sleeping I didn't want to disturb you."

"Did you at least get yourself something to eat?"

"I will when I get into my office. Breakfast of champions. Toast and Vegemite. You shouldn't worry." Roger glanced at his watch. He should be entering the building right now. He had a few tasks to do before a scheduled meeting. But he stalled. Her call was too much of a treat for him to want to rush away. "Do you have a busy day planned?"

"Not really. Just a few students coming over to my flat for lessons this afternoon."

"Well, dress warm if you leave your flat today. It's blistering cold out here."

"I will. What about you, love? Busy day?"

Roger smiled when she called him love. "I shouldn't be too late tonight. Are we still on for dinner at Clos Maggiore?"

"Wild horses couldn't keep me away."

"Until tonight then." Roger smiled, hung up, and walked into the building. Even though they had been dating only a few months, he had fallen hard for her. She was the only one who knew he had a softer side. He found himself falling deeper and deeper in love with her. Ursula was easy to talk to and he found himself wanting to tell her about his past and the nature of his job with The Hastings Foundation. But he wouldn't. Such knowledge would not just endanger her; the truth might jeopardize their budding relationship.

He was happier in London than he had ever been in Philadelphia, and his childhood in Melbourne, Australia, hadn't exactly been fun. Remembering the way the morning light shimmered on her short, curly hair as he kissed her forehead goodbye this morning made him grin in contentment.

His mood lightened by Ursula's call, Roger strolled

through the lobby past the guard desk and to a bank of elevators, where he boarded the half-full elevator and hummed as he waited for his floor.

He made his way to his lab and even smiled at the secretary. He flipped the lights on and set his heavy briefcase on the desk. He looked around the lab as he did every morning to ensure everything was in order. As usual, it was. It was sterile. Sleek. Clean. Orderly. No visible papers. No clutter. His lab in Philadelphia had been top-of-the-line, but the London lab blew that one out of the water. Of course, it had newer toys because it was newer, but he'd had input into the actual layout of the lab. As such, the lab was far more efficient than any other he'd worked in.

He removed a paper bag with two pieces of whole grain toast and smeared Vegemite on each. The scent always reminded him of brekkie when he was growing up in Melbourne. As he munched, he reviewed the overnight report from his most recent experiment. A glance at his watch told him it would soon be time to check in with Dr. Frazier in the other lab. He jotted notes and decided to head to the Engine Room so he could get to the other lab.

Frustrations aside, he was enjoying his work on the cryospore project in a way he hadn't his other efforts with the foundation. The problem he was working to solve now would actually help the world, not hurt it. He was making a difference, and he thought that knowing that made a difference in him.

On his way to the Engine Room, he ran into Dr. Evan Spencer, a recent recruit from Oxford, and instinctively stepped back, more out of the need for unscented breathing air than for personal space. Roger eyed Evan, still cursed with acne, and wondered how many days the kid had gone without showering.

"Glad that I ran into you this morning, Dr. Martin."

"Dr. Spencer, you should go home and wash up. Or at least cover up with some cologne."

"Right. Sure. Of course." He pushed a lock of greasy black hair out of his eyes. "I had a thought last night about how to protect the cryospore."

Roger forced himself to count to five before responding. He thought Ursula would be proud of him. "And how would you do that?"

"I dropped my phone into the fountain downstairs and thought I must have ruined it, right?" Evan pulled his phone out and held it up to Roger. "But I didn't! And you know why?"

Roger shrugged.

"Because I had a protective case around it. And then I thought about the cryospores and how we've had problems because they are unstable and thought maybe we could encase them."

"We tried that early on, but we couldn't maintain the protective barrier," Roger said.

"Oh."

To Roger, Evan's look of total chagrin would have been comical had he not had such an urgent need to solve the cryospore instability problem.

As quickly as Evan's face clouded over, it brightened. "But what if we could find a sustainable and regenerating agent that would act as the protective casing, maybe—"

"And how would we do that?" Roger asked. But his mind was already considering the possibilities. Nanoparticles, maybe.

"Um. Maybe we could generate a coating or some material that would engulf the cryospore, allowing it to remain functional, but safe for transport." Evan looked anxiously at Roger.

"That might work," Roger said. "I'll think about this. In

the meantime, why don't you go home, take that shower? Then you can draft a report on this for me, along with a list of potential protective barrier materials and the pros and cons of each."

Without waiting for Evan to acknowledge his new tasks, Roger turned again and walked to the back elevator. He placed his ID badge on the sensor, entered his five-digit PIN, placed his hand on the sensor and looked into the retinal scanner. After a few seconds of processing, the elevator opened. Roger entered it, inserted his key, turned it to the left, and pressed the sub-basement button. Twenty seconds later the door slid silently open.

Roger made his way to the Engine Room. As he walked through the scanning room, he pondered Evan's suggestion for protecting the cryospore. It might work, if they could get their hands on a self-sustaining, regenerating material.

"Morning, Dr. Martin. It'll be just a second."

The greeting pulled Roger out of his reverie, and he mechanically nodded at the engineer and neared the large circular machine, which was whirring to life. The metal frame churned and steam began spilled from the center. Roger donned a heavy, fur-lined coat. The green light flashed on, and the middle of the machine spun in circles, revealing another room peeking through.

"Go ahead, Dr. Martin. Don't get frostbite!"

"Ha. Ha. Ha." Roger walked through the portal.

CHAPTER 8

22 November

"Want to trade first watch, Paul?" Joe, a weathered rent-a-cop, pulled his hat down, tightened his coat around him, and leaned back in his folding chair under a popup tent about a hundred yards from the ruins of the Memphis Area Power Plant.

Waleed Gandapur

"Nope. I'm too cold to sit here for any longer."

"Fine, but you buy the donuts in the morning," Joe said.

Paul adjusted his belt and took out his flashlight. Then he double-checked his gas mask and hung it around his neck. He thought for a moment and added a scarf and gloves to his cold-weather gear. He strode the perimeter of the power plant, on the lookout for intruders and suspicious activities. Two days after the explosion, yellow caution tape still waved in the light breeze. The smell of a huge bonfire lingered. But what worried him most was the story that some sort of unusual chemical had been released during the incident. He didn't really understand it. He thought it was just a basic power generation plant and what use did it have with chemicals? But he guessed it must have since the experts had cautioned him to keep a gas mask within arm's reach at all times at the popup tent and to wear it on rounds.

In the past forty-eight hours, four separate agencies had battled for jurisdiction over the wreckage. ManFirst, an organization dedicated to demonizing all Mods, had even set up a protest near the disaster, blaming it on Mods. But no one knew what had caused the explosion. No one had been allowed inside to even bring out the dead due to worries about radiation poisoning or deadly gases in the air.

As Paul passed his last checkpoint, something snapped. He whipped around toward the sound and waved his flashlight beam around. He saw nothing that could have made the sound.

"God, I hate this job. Should've listened to my wife and not taken it, even if there is overtime." His left hand patted the gas mask, confirming it was still there, but not raising it to his face, feeling certain he was outside the contamination zone. Paul quickened his steps back to the guard tent.

"Thought he'd never leave," Etienne said, maintaining the invisibility power he'd used to cloak his teammates from the roving security personnel. The SENTINELS had used their UN contacts to secure access to discover what had really happened at the power generation plant.

It was a small team. Etienne, a Mod, was there because he could become invisible and phase his body through solid objects, which was a pretty handy power to have on a recon mission. Nearly six feet tall, Etienne DuBois had the kind of dark good looks that got a girl's attention, but the self-centered kind of attitude that just as quickly turned them off. Etienne had left Quebec for Base 47 shortly after Josh Grant had publicly appealed for Mods to join his cause. He'd been seeking a group he could finally fit into. There had been friction at the beginning, to be sure, but over the years he'd learned more than a few things about teamwork. The SENTINELS were his family now, more than his nuclear family ever had been.

Waleed Gandapur, the only other Mod on this team, not only provided the teleportation to and from the investigation site, but he was a history teacher who remembered everything he learned, so he might prove useful to Dr. Nicola Patel's investigation. Pakistani by birth, he'd moved to London in his early thirties, but could find no teaching jobs. He'd wound up driving taxis in London, which is what he was doing when the White Light Wave event turned him into a Mod. He heeded the call to join Base 47 in Texas five years ago. He was forty-one, and he and his wife, Marie, were colonists of New Atlantis. He was once again teaching history when not on SENTINELS duty, and loving life more every day. Marie was also a history teacher. Highly perceptive, she could draw logical—and usually accurate—conclusions about a disparate set of facts faster than anyone else in the room.

"Are you just going to keep us invisible? How will we be able to sneak around?" Waleed asked.

"Relax. I've got the next best thing." Etienne sent a text message. He nodded a few moments later in response to an incoming text. "Okay then. The security cameras have been hacked by Noah in IT, and they'll be on a loop for the next fifteen minutes."

"Cool," Waleed said.

Etienne waited a few more seconds for good measure before dropping his invisibility.

"Let's get moving," Nicola said. She removed pairs of specialized goggles from her pack and passed them around. They already had comms units in place and checked them out now.

Nicola flipped on her dual function spectral goggles and searched for residue traces. "We've got to get in and discover what happened here."

"I'm so glad you brought me along, Waleed. This is so exciting!" Marie twisted her silvering hair back into a bun. She clung close to her husband.

"You should thank Nicola, it was her idea. Besides, you said you wanted to get out of the classroom more." Waleed squeezed her hand and they smiled at each other. Together, they carefully ventured into the plant's remains.

"This is so much more exciting than being at uni." Marie directed her flashlight around the broken columns, over the ash, and straight toward the center of the building, where the reactor once stood.

"Are you sure there's no danger in being here? No radiation or whatever?" Etienne waved his sensor through the air.

"Relax, Etienne. It won't be the radiation or chemicals that will kill you here. It's the unknown that you should watch for," Nicola said.

"Oh, that's comforting." Etienne shot a look at the scientist.

"There haven't been any radiation or chemical leaks. That's just misinformation so we could get a first look at what really caused the explosion." She plodded forward while looking through her goggles. "Besides, that's not what the chemical spectrometer is for."

"Sure. That helps." Etienne frowned as he studied the device.

Waleed looked around. The damage was considerable and absolute. Once-solid concrete walls and support beams were reduced to rubble. Night stars dotted a sky that should have been blocked by a roof.

Nicola surveyed the ruins and walked toward what

would have been the heart of the plant. As she stepped she heard the cracking and clinking of metal. Ash plumed with every step.

"Where are the bodies? Shouldn't we have been seeing their remains?"

"That my dear Etienne, is what we aim to figure out." Nicola cautiously stepped over a steel beam, avoiding several twisted bolts and nails. "We just don't know where the people were or where we should expect to see their remains. If there are any. A fire hot enough would cremate them, but may not have been hot enough to melt metal."

As Waleed and his wife neared the control center of the power plant, avoiding the scattered debris, a sparkle caught Waleed's eye. He tapped his wife on the shoulder and gestured toward it.

"Waleed, what do you think it is?" She knelt beside it. He brushed some of the dust and soot off of the object and they looked at each other in disbelief.

"How did something like this get here?" Waleed held up the palm-sized golden artifact in his gloved hand. He traced over the object, studying it. As he wiped the top of it, he noticed its shape for the first time. The top was about three inches long and curved. Two offshoots stemmed from an almond-shaped center. One pointed straight down and one jutted out and curved farther out.

"Looks kind of like an eye. What's that doing here?" Marie asked.

"Few things in our line of work actually make sense," Waleed said. "But what would it be doing here? And how does it fit into this explosion?" Waleed looked around the destroyed power plant, as though seeking an explanation of the artifact's survival amid the devastation.

Waleed smiled at his wife and flipped the object over. "The only eye artifact I can remember reading about is the

Eye of Horus. I wonder if this is it? See here where the center sort of forms a pupil?"

"Didn't Bayanai say that the Swarm traced its origins back to the Pharaohs?" Marie peered over his shoulder.

"Yeah. And this could have something to do with the Sovereigns of the Swarm. Anything's possible with those jokers, but that's a mystery for another time. Let's bag it." He stowed it for safekeeping.

"What about this?"

"What about what?" The alarm in Marie's voice worried Waleed, and he looked at her. Her face was pale in the moonlight.

She held up an empty shell casing. "Do you think some of the people here were dead before the explosion?"

"Are there any others?"

Marie searched the rubble and leaned down. When she stood up again, she flashed several more casings at Waleed.

"This is bad." Waleed spoke into his comms suit and relayed the finding to Nicola and Etienne. "Bag them."

She did so and slid the evidence into her pack.

"What do you really think happened here, Dr. Patel?" Etienne backed up toward her. Each step gritted and crackled. He tried not to think about what he might be stepping on.

"I don't know but—" Nicola's handheld device beeped, and she looked at it. The readout indicated the cause of the explosion was nearby, and she stopped in her tracks. The culprit was in front of her. She surveyed the area and her eyes lit on a mound of silvery blue dust that glowed almost imperceptibly, as if on the threshold of igniting.

"Don't move." Nicola whipped her head up, down, and sideways.

"Um, Doc, you're scaring me," Etienne said as he stepped back.

"This is bad. Real bad."

"What do you mean? What is it?" Etienne asked as his chemical spectrometer began to blare.

"We have to get out of here."

"You mean, like this could explode bad or what?" Etienne asked.

"Like this is an energy signature unlike any I have ever seen." She peered through her goggles at the mound.

"Then maybe we should just leave it here and go," Etienne said.

"I have to examine this in my lab." Nicola steeled herself, then carefully but quickly scooped a sample of the metallic dust into a containment cylinder.

Etienne frowned as he watched her. Through his communications unit, he told Waleed they needed to meet up and evacuate immediately. Black globules glittered next to Etienne, and Waleed and his wife emerged from the teleportal.

"But we still have five more minutes before the security loop is over," Waleed said.

"That's not the problem. Get us out of here," Nicola said.

But before Waleed could open a portal to Base 47 on New Atlantis, a bright light shone on them.

"Hey! What do you think you're doing? This is a restricted area!"

"Oh man." Waleed looked toward Etienne.

"I knew I heard something earlier," the rent-a-cop said as he held his flashlight in his left hand and brandished a handgun in his right.

"Look, Paul, is it?" Nicola said as she took off her goggles and read his name badge. "You have to get out of here. It's not safe."

"Don't move," Paul said.

The Base 47 team all froze.

"Who are you? No one is supposed to cross the safety barrier," Paul demanded. He reached up to the walkie-talkie at his shoulder. "Don't move. I have to call this in."

"I wish you hadn't said that." Etienne looked at Waleed, who nodded.

A small but deep black portal opened near Paul. Waleed's hand reached out of it, grabbed the walkie, and disappeared with it.

"What the?"

"Listen, I'm a scientist. I don't know what you think you're protecting, but this place isn't safe. You need to get out of here." Nicola inched closer to him. "I need to get this sample to a lab and determine exactly what went wrong here."

"Um, Nicola?" Etienne said urgently as his counter started blaring again. "Something's happening."

Nicola turned and put her goggles back on. She looked back toward the plant and instantly took her goggles off. "Waleed! Get us out of here right now!"

He opened a large portal below all of them and it zipped toward the sky, transporting them far away from the danger. The team, used to teleporting, took the oddness of the location change in stride. Paul, on the other hand, retched up his dinner. Dazed, he asked, "What just happened?"

Marie looked around, surveying the surroundings for something that would tell her where they'd gone. She spotted a huge sign and giggled. "Waleed, maybe we can come back here when Graceland is open?"

"Shame to go to Tennessee and not see Graceland," he said.

"We're all shook up," Etienne joked.

Marie wrinkled her nose at him.

Not a moment later a brilliant blue explosion lit up the

night sky. The team and Paul watched in horror as flames engulfed the property again.

"Was that the plant?" Paul asked in shock.

"Yes, that was probably the power plant," Nicola said.

"Oh my god. What did you people do?" He reached both hands toward Nicola, as though to shake her by the shoulders, but Etienne stepped between them and invited the security guy to step aside and talk about what had happened.

"Nicola, just what exactly is in that thing? Do you have some of what caused that explosion?" Marie pointed toward the containment unit.

"I'm not sure, but I will find out," Nicola said

Waleed opened another portal to return the SENTINELS to New Atlantis.

"I'm not sure who you're working for, Paul, but I'd look for another job," Etienne said as he turned part of his body invisible for effect before walking through the pitch-black portal.

CHAPTER 9

22 November

"Mom, he's touching me." Sying whined, stringing the words out to emphasize purest agony.

Sun Luli

Sun Luli stood facing the kitchen counter, putting the final touches on a lunch dessert of mixed fruit. She glanced over her shoulder at her two offspring and her husband. Shining was indeed clasping his big sister's arm. But it didn't appear to be in the normal pesky little brother way. His eyes were squinched closed and his small face was squeezed tight, and she knew he was in deep concentration. She sighed and was opening her mouth to ask him to quit when he spoke in a voice not his own.

"The mountains will grow."

"What, honey?"

"The dead will walk again." It came out in a deep growl, and the air around him seemed to shimmer with red energy.

"Shining, what are you talking about?"

"The mountains will grow. The dead will walk again."

Again, the same deep growl and red shimmering energy.

"Honey, the dead cannot walk again." She wavered between rushing in to fix everything and letting her children settle their conflict on their own. After all, she and Yi wouldn't be around forever.

"Mom, make him stop," Sying broke in. She used her right hand to try to force Shining's grip off of her left arm, but his force field kicked in. The bubble sent her right arm flying up. She wailed in frustration. "Mom!"

The noise seemed to make it through his concentration, and the shimmering red energy snapped out of existence. The boy opened his eyes and smiled.

"Shining, what just happened?" Luli knelt next to her son.

He looked at her with questions in his eyes. "What do you mean?"

"You said the mountains will grow and the dead will walk again. And in a strange voice."

Shining dropped his eyes to the table in front of him.

"Shining." The name came out sharp, edged with worry.

Her son wouldn't make eye contact. He muttered. "Not me. Amir."

"What have I told you about blaming your imaginary friend?"

"But Mom, not me. It was Amir," Shining protested.

Luli sighed. "Why were you touching your sister?"

The question startled him. He looked at his sister. She was rubbing her arm.

"Shining, what just happened?"

"I don't know."

Yi silently watched the whole incident, though Luli detected the beginnings of a worry frown on his forehead. She wished he would say something, anything, but Yi had never been good at articulating his feelings about Shining's powers. She'd have to talk to him before they went back to work.

Luli's cell phone rang, but she ignored it. Lunch and dinner every day with her family were nonnegotiable. She'd read the studies and knew that kids who sat down at home to eat most of their meals with their parents were better adjusted, less likely to get in trouble, and generally more aware than their counterparts. She and Yi were going to do everything they could to make sure both children had the best possible foundation for life.

"Shining, son, can you repeat the things you said a few minutes ago?"

He looked confused.

Luli exchanged glances with Yi, who shrugged, although she thought that worry frown seemed to grow fractionally. She decided to drop it for now. She turned back to the counter and scooped the chopped mango, pineapple, and passion fruit onto four dessert plates.

While they waited, Yi and their children talked about plans for the holidays. Like most children, they were eager for Christmas to come.

Sying, now nine, was a studious but independent child. Her brows were often drawn together, as though she were perpetually in deep thought. She was a slender girl who preferred to wear her long hair back in braids or a ponytail to keep it out of her face. She hoped for books and a bike. Shining, born on New Atlantis mere weeks after the island itself emerged from the depths of the Atlantic Ocean, was now five and wanted any number of toys. He was a short, round-faced boy who smiled easily. That smile currently displayed a pair of missing front teeth. Shining was still at the age where he found delight and wonder in simple things, like a spinning pinwheel. But more than that, they were beyond excitement with the idea that they were going to travel first to San Francisco, then to China for the holidays, so they could learn about their family history.

Luli carried the dessert to the table, placing plates in front of each of them. She ruffled Shining's short dark hair before sitting. She gave her son a wink and looked lovingly at Yi, who was engaged with Sying. She had a spoonful of fruit salad halfway to her mouth when the phone rang again. She shook her head, ignoring it. Another ten minutes, and she'd see who had needed her so urgently. At that point, Yi would walk both kids back to school, and she'd head off to the capitol. But no one interrupted meals at the Sun house.

"What's San Francisco like anyway, Mom?" Shining asked as she forked a piece of mango.

"Well, honey, it's a lot different than here. It's a lot cooler, even during the summer. And there are many more people. Lots of hills."

"And what about China?" Sying asked.

"Many, many more people," Luli said. "All speaking another language."

Sying frowned. "Not English?"

"Mostly not," Luli said.

"Then how will we get around?"

"Bié dānxīn wǒ de bǎobèi, wǒmen huì hǎo de. Don't worry, my precious children, we'll be fine," Luli said. "And while we're in San Francisco, I'll be sure to take you on the trolley. Remember seeing the trolley on TV?"

"Cool," Shining and Sying said at the same time.

Sying sang loudly, "Clang clang went the trolley."

Shining giggled.

"Sying, finish your dessert, my sweet," Yi said.

Agreeably, she dipped her fork down to snag a piece of mango, but she couldn't get to it. Her fork hovered in midair, an inch above it. "Shining, stop it!"

"I'm not doing anything," he protested.

"Are too. Let me have my mango."

Shining chortled, watching his frustrated sister. "Say please."

She shot a frosty glare at him but said nothing.

Sighing, he relented. "Fine." He released the force field he'd formed over her dessert plate, and she scooped up the last of her fruit.

Holiday chatter resumed until Luli spoke up. "Kids, go get your backpacks ready."

As soon as they were out of earshot, Yi said, "Have you seen him do that before?"

"A few times. Yesterday, I caught him making a force field around his sister to keep her from the TV remote control," she said.

"Really?" Yi considered this. "His powers are growing fast. Did it ever occur to you to try to put your force field around other stuff when you had that power?"

She shook her head. "But you know kids. They experiment endlessly."

Yi thought about that. Finally, he voiced his growing concern. "I'm not sure this Amir is just an imaginary friend."

"Yi, of course it is. Haven't you read the research? Lots of kids have imaginary friends. He's smart and precocious. I'm not worried about it."

"But this Amir isn't saying your typical imaginary friend stuff. It sounds like—" Yi looked down and swallowed hard before looking up at her and continuing, his deep brown eyes pools of worry. "It sounds like prophecy. Like from before."

Luli narrowed her eyes at him and shook her head fiercely.

"Yes, Luli, it does. Remember those bits of prophecy you told me Emma and Rami used to say? This sounds a hell of a lot like that, and it scares me. Not to mention that red aura that surrounds him from time to time."

"Stop being impossible. There is no way Shining is reciting prophecy. You're overreacting."

"I don't think I am, and I don't think I'm wrong about this," he said in a steady but quiet voice. "We'll be better off if we confront the possibility of this than if we bury our heads in the sand like stupid ostriches. Forewarned is forearmed."

She stepped back from him, shaking her head.

"Think about this. Being an ostrich exposes our family, puts us in danger. If we try to figure out this prophecy, we might have a chance."

Luli shook her head again.

"Don't you think Rami spent all his time thinking about that prophecy? Where is he now?" Luli's panic and anger filled her to the shaking point. "This Amir, he's not talking prophecy. He's an imaginary friend."

Yi sighed. "We'd be protecting Shining by looking into this." He studied her for a moment. "Have you heard anything about new prophecies? From the SENTINELS?"

Those last questions came out so quietly she almost didn't hear them. Once she parsed the meaning, though, she felt cold inside. "No."

He only raised his eyebrows at her. "No?"

"No."

"Luli, listen, we only have one job here, and that is to protect our children. Everything else is secondary. If you know anything, I need to know it. Bayanai needs to know it."

"There's nothing." She turned from him. "I've got to get back to the office."

Yi sighed and leaned forward to hug her, but she didn't turn back to him. In a strained voice, she said, "Time to go back to work," and moved to gather her things.

Yi walked the kids back to school while Luli headed back to work. As she walked the few blocks through Crystal City back to the capitol building, she sniffed the ocean air and tried to put all thoughts of prophecy and Amir out of her head. Instead, she thought about how much her life had changed in the last five years. She and Yi had expected to spend the rest of their lives in San Francisco, but the White Light Wave event had changed that. She had gained the ability to project a force field over her body, preventing any injury to her. Over Yi's objections, she had gone to Texas and joined the other Mods. Even then, she'd felt a duty to show her family that doing the right thing is worth the risk. When she went into premature labor on the newly risen island, she was stunned to learn her ability to create force fields had only been temporary. It wasn't her power, but her unborn son's. When the opportunity to be one of the first colonist families for New Atlantis landed in her lap, she couldn't turn down the chance to help form a new nation. A true multicultural experiment on a brand-new island.

The island didn't look brand new any more. Buildings had sprung up quickly once the UN sanctioned the development of New Atlantis. Roads, bike paths, and sidewalks cut throughout the heart of Crystal City, which was on the eastern part of the island. Mass transit in the form of buses and light rail carried people all over the city. An airport on the outskirts of the capitol city gave visitors easy access to the island. At the western edge of the island was the volcano responsible for the rise of New Atlantis from the Mid-Atlantic Ridge.

New Atlantis was habitable largely because Mods with a variety of powers helped out. A gentle Colombian named Juan Pierre del Bosque gave plant life a jump-start on the former swath of lava. Now, the island was green and lush, thanks to his chlorokinesis power. Many of the fruit trees he had started already bore fruit.

Kirra Wilson, an Australian who had joined the Base 47 team, had helped, too, using her geokinesis powers to access underground aquifers that would ultimately provide the nascent island with plenty of fresh water. She also reshaped the island to better accommodate the infrastructure that made modern lives possible.

Unable to fully shake off Shining's latest Amir episode because of Yi's insistence they address it, Luli walked back to the capitol building on autopilot. The Amir appearances were becoming more frequent, more troubling, and Yi's belief that it wasn't a simple imaginary friend terrified her. It had started off innocently enough, with Shining blaming Amir for mischievous actions, but in her book Shining reciting prophecy fed to him by someone named Amir amounted to the worst-possible-case scenario. She hoped against hope that this wasn't the case.

"Ouch!" Luli said in surprise. A short man in khakis and a sports jacket was obviously in a much bigger hurry than she to get into the capitol building and nearly knocked her to the ground as he jogged past. It was times like this that she missed her protective shield and being an integral part of the Base 47 team. Then again, as a mother she was pleased that at least Shining had that protection. Though she would never admit it, that connection with Shining was so strong that she felt guilty she didn't feel the same with her daughter. But Yi seemed to pick up the slack and their father-daughter bond reassured her. Without that shield and position on the team, sometimes she felt like she wasn't making as big a difference in the world as she could and should.

While patiently waiting to go through security to enter the capitol building, only two people behind the hurrying man who had run into her, she checked her mobile for voice mail. She listened to a long-winded message from the prime minister's chief of staff, Arian, who sounded near-panic about the winter festival. Luli wondered what she had to do with this. She was just responsible for public relations. The second message was also from Arian, but this time the anxiety revolved around powers registration. Now that, Luli thought, she could do something about. Smoothing her pale gray knee-length skirt and adjusting her ruby red blouse, she entered the New Atlantis capitol building and headed toward the office of Arian Nassar, a striking Iranian with dark brown hair and darker eyes. Luli had once told Yi that she thought Arian was the kind of woman who could only love one man, no matter the circumstances. Rami had been her heart's one true soul mate, Luli had said, and with him dead Arian would keep all other comers at arm's length. Yi, once he finally met Arian, had sensed her melancholy and agreed.

Arian was typing away on her laptop. Luli knocked lightly on her doorframe and walked in at Arian's nodded invitation.

"Sorry about the lunch calls," Arian said. "Needed to call while I was thinking about it. First, it looks like we're going to have a blogger from the US filming the Christmas party. Maggie Adams."

"Oh, she was here when—" She stopped. She'd meant to say, "when Rami died," but saying that to Arian, a woman she both liked and respected, seemed cruel. Instead, she asked a question of her own. "Why is she coming to the holiday party?"

"It's the prime minister's idea. He thinks that we need to go heavy on a PR offensive, pushing all the reasons that requiring powers registration is a bad idea. So you need to prepare press releases and talking points opposing powers registration. Also, he wants Maggie and her cameraman to film the party, to see life on New Atlantis and how the hub of powers is a peaceful and harmonious place."

"OK," Luli said. "I'll get these things to you. Anything else?"

Arian closed her eyes and drew a deep breath before responding. "The prime minister had an idea about footage while Maggie's here filming. He wants to do an interview early that day near the memorial to Rami." Five years later, and her voice still hitched every time she said his name. "Then he wanted to let her have free rein around Crystal City—with you in tow, of course—until about an hour before the party. At the party, the prime minister wants either you or me to be with Maggie at all times."

Luli struggled to keep her disappointment from showing on her face. She had been looking forward to enjoying the party with her family, not working.

"Don't worry, Luli. It will mostly be me, but in case he needs me for something, you're next in line."

"Am I supposed to trot out Shining? Because that's not going to happen."

Arian offered a half-smile. "Down, mama bear. The prime minister will probably make ice for her, but you're under no obligation to let her film Shining's power."

Luli shrugged and smiled apologetically. "Just had to check. I'll get to work on the talking points." She paused before asking the question she really wanted to ask. "Any word on Emma?"

Arian sagged but immediately brightened. "Emilio's looking into something new that he thinks will help the team find her. I don't want to talk about it too much, or I'll get my hopes up."

CHAPTER
10

22 November

For a moment, Roger struggled to keep his breakfast of champions in his belly. The Vegemite gurgled, and he had to place a hand against the wall to steady himself. The wall was reassuringly cold to the touch, so he pressed

Dr. Julianne Frazier

his forehead against it and breathed deeply to smooth his stomach.

The instantaneous teleportation from one of the world's most crowded cities to the research base on the world's least populated continent was possible due to Isaac "Builder" Bowmester, an exiled SENTINEL. He'd seen how to harness the power of the cryospore as the unit's energy source and envisioned the machine itself, which featured two doors that acted as folds in space, allowing teleportation between the lab and the office. The teleportation had improved over the years, but it still made Roger feel like he might throw up every time. His stomach finally settled as he waited for a scan to proclaim the teleportation had been incident-free. He dreaded what could happen if things went wrong. He thought it might be like that "splinching" that occurred in the Harry Potter books when disapparating went wrong.

Cleared by the scan, Roger met Dr. Julianne Frazier in the hallway. It was long and featureless and led from the teleportal to the labs and research zone of the base.

"London seems to be treating you well."

"No more so than usual."

"You should keep her around." Julianne's soft smile warmed her face.

It was an expression Roger had rarely seen on her, and he looked at her with a cocked eyebrow. He shrugged and smiled back at her. He'd tried diligently to keep all his professional relationships at arm's length, but Juliane had the uncanny ability to look at him and know his inner thoughts. It annoyed him, but in the four years they'd worked together she had never broken his trust.

She was a little older than he but looked more than a decade his senior. As far as Roger knew, she had no interests outside the laboratory. He'd never heard her mention dating men or women. She shunned makeup except penciled-in eyebrows, and probably had never dyed her hair. It was silvery, parted just to the right of center, and she wore it efficiently short. She wore the same diamond stud earrings and simple gold chain necklace every day. When she was angry, her already thin mouth nearly disappeared, and a vertical line appeared between her eyes.

"I'd like you to look at the samples we took yesterday." She handed him a manila file folder, but he didn't open it.

"Any progress in the extraction process?"

"No. We can barely extract enough to supply the teleportation and the Tribe's carrier and still have some left over for experiments. It's not so much a matter of drilling, but of finding, collecting, and storing."

"You know how vital this project is."

"I do. That is why I urge caution. We can't have another explosion like in Tennessee."

Roger nodded. Stabilizing the cryospore was as essential to the long-range plans of Henry Hastings and his secretive group as retrofitting the power plants to handle the cryospore. He was feeling comfortably warm and appreciated the fact that he was safe and comfortable inside the complex instead of outside facing the bitter cold of the Antarctic. He still marveled that the Ascendancy had managed to set up the base, undetected, in direct opposition of the Antarctic Treaty, which forbade development of the icy continent. Money, capability, and determination were a potent combination.

About five years before, Ascendancy-funded scientists had discovered an elemental energy source buried deep in ice. The Ascendancy planned to mine the material and control it completely, and they had built an innovative base in Marie Byrd Land in West Antarctica near the Ross Ice Shelf. While the base had only one level above ground, three more levels extended below. The surface-level portion of the operations were outfitted with holographic devices to disguise the base from satellite surveillance. Random holographics made the base essentially invisible. Other cutting-edge technology created by Builder kept the base operational.

The mining annex stood about a quarter of a mile from the base for safety reasons. It was accessed by snowmobile.

Roger looked out the porthole at the mining annex. The Ascendancy had funded all of this in a bid to mine the spores. The plan was to bring truly clean energy to the world—and eliminate fossil fuels—by harnessing the energy of the cryospore. And, of course, to gain the power and money of holding a true monopoly.

They entered the lab that held the spore samples. It was a small room but looked like most basic laboratories. Large and bulky equipment stood resident on some of the counters. Chemicals and test tubes were arrayed neatly in cabinets. Safety signs hung through the lab.

Roger looked at a clump of glowing cryospores inside a plastic display case. That containment box kept the cryospores at a specific temperature and pressure and was all that stood between life and the obliteration of the whole base. The ball of cryospores was the size of a basketball, and its blueish light pulsed with energy. That thing could power London for a month.

But there were two fundamental problems, and they had plagued him since he started working on this project, shortly after the WaveMaker debacle on New Atlantis.

The first problem was how to extract the spores without damaging the shelf.

The second was how to keep the cryospores stable.

He couldn't help with problem one, but, thanks to Dr. Evans' clumsiness, he thought he could help with problem two.

"I've got an idea about how to stabilize the cryospores," Roger said. "I want to revisit the idea of containing the cryospores within a protective barrier."

"But that was a dead end. We couldn't find a way to make it work."

"I think if we can encase the cryospore in a protective sphere, bond it to that sphere, it would neutralize the instability."

Julianne considered his idea. "That might do it." After another moment of thinking, she squealed as only a woman in her fifties who should not be squealing does. "I think that will do it!"

"Good."

"I'll get on that immediately."

"It still doesn't resolve the problem of the extraction." Roger grinned inwardly as he popped her bubble. "We need to get the cryospores out of the earth, keep them frozen and stable without damaging the ice shelf."

"One problem at a time."

CHAPTER
11

22 November

Somewhere in the Southern Indian Ocean, the crew of a deep-sea fishing trawler passed the evening swapping stories. Though sipping tea instead of alcohol, they still traded more than a few tall tales about conquests back home. Ivan, however, was

Courtney Cooper
"CoCo"

solemnly extolling the virtues of a loving marriage when one of his compatriots interrupted.

"What is that?" The crewman pointed toward an approaching vessel.

"I'll be damned! It looks like a cruise liner without their lights on." The captain put down his thermos and capped it.

"No, it's not. It's a ghost ship! And it's headed right toward us!" another crewman shouted.

The crew sprang into action to veer out of the vessel's path. It also altered course and passed within yards of the trawler after many tense moments.

"Reckless sons-a-bitches," the captain said. Anger and

adrenaline from the close call pounded in his head. He shivered as they bobbed in the wake of the large ship. "Was it just me or did you hear laughing when it passed?"

The vessel the trawler crew couldn't describe was actually a former Soviet aircraft carrier decked out with the latest and greatest anti-surveillance technology.

If you were to look at the ship for too long, you wouldn't be able to properly describe it. The shape, colors, and size of the ship constantly shifted, defying identification and description, and leaving witnesses unsure what they saw.

That next-generation military upgrade, developed by a Mod, was financed by the Ascendancy. The group on the carrier could do whatever jobs they wanted, as long as they also carried out the orders of the Ascendancy and kept secret the connection.

Over the past four years, the Tribe, mostly led by Taneesha before Pierce took over, had been behind heists, breakouts of powered people, and one violent uprising against a Mexican drug cartel. More than once, they'd infiltrated a sovereign nation to eliminate a leader. And it seemed like they skirmished with the SENTINELS monthly. One of the more epic battles had resulted in the complete destruction of Base 47 in Texas two years ago.

CoCo spent a lot of time on the deck of the carrier. She enjoyed the solitude she found on deck. Noise in the distance caught her attention, and she spotted a boat, maybe a trawler, in their path. She frowned. She knew the vessel's captain, a hooligan nicknamed Bones, liked to play chicken with small vessels he happened to spot out and about. She was powerless to help the trawler's crew, who likely thought the large craft was going to ram them. She could hear their panic as they worked to move the trawler out of danger.

She knew the vessel wouldn't run into the trawler. But the close call Bones was going to pull upset her. She watched it happen, and her anger mounted. Gone was her tranquil evening.

She'd come up to the deck simply to drop her guard for a while. Undercover work was exhausting. She'd been working with the Tribe for nearly a year, and it seemed like she was still learning the ins and outs of the carrier. Life with Timothy and the Tribe, run with Captain Pierce's iron will, was worlds away from life with Emilio and the SENTINELS.

Timothy. They'd had some grand adventures together since she had gone undercover with the Tribe. Once, he'd shorted out the lights in Paris, so he could woo her with a romantic dinner atop the Eiffel Tower. Another time, they "accidentally" got lost from the team and had a weekend away on a secluded island in Thailand. Sometimes, when particularly excited, his hands crackled with electricity around her, sending short pulses through her. Unfortunately for him, their whole relationship was an illusion, part of her cover.

CoCo leaned over the railing and felt the hairs on her neck stiffen. Timothy was close. She created an illusion of herself turning toward him. He sent a short series of sparks through her as she reached out her hands. CoCo watched her illusory self kiss him.

"That was... nice," Timothy said as he pulled away, brushing her hair back down.

"Nice?"

"Let's try that again, see if we can't do better."

CoCo's illusion leaned into him, and they kissed again, deeper this time. Sparks crackled and danced around them. "Better?"

His grin said it all.

"What do you think Pierce wanted with George?"

He shrugged. "Who knows." Timothy slid his hand into

hers.

"You've been with the Tribe for a long time. Do you ever wonder who Pierce gets his orders from?"

Timothy turned away from her toward the ocean and said nothing for a long time. "There are questions you just don't ask here."

CoCo changed gears. "Don't you ever want to leave the Tribe?"

"Sometimes. But how? I don't have any options." Timothy looked at the unending sea. "That night in Miami... Those deaths... It's my fault." He squeezed CoCo's hand. He paused, and CoCo thought he was remembering all the harm he'd done when he was learning how his powers worked. "I'm not a bad guy, not like the rest of these guys. But look at you. You were kicked out of the SENTINELS and your so-called friend wrote those terrible things about you over at TheModsBlog. If we hadn't saved you from that crowd in Johannesburg, you might have ended up in one of those Mod prisons."

"I don't want to talk about that." Now CoCo's illusion turned back to the ocean. After a few minutes, she stroked his arm. "Where do you think he gets his information?"

Timothy grabbed her arm, pulled her close, and whispered in her ear, "Be careful. This entire ship is bugged and monitored, and you know it. We aren't free to speak. I don't want anything to happen to you."

CoCo reluctantly nodded. Months of careful digging, and she had little to show for her time with the Tribe. She had to suck it up and get what she could.

"Let's go grab a snack," Timothy said.

"Sure." She merged into her illusion and they moved toward the stairs.

"Well, if it isn't the lovers."

The Germans—Alrick and Butcher—approached them.

"I thought I smelled lavender and weakness." It was Alrick Wagner, wearing another of his cheap suits.

His slow cadence reminded CoCo of a serial killer from a movie she'd seen once during a sleepover with her friends back in high school. CoCo looked at him through slitted eyes. He wore a chin curtain. His cold, piercing blue eyes seemed to examine every part of her body. She instinctively stepped back from him because he had the ability to make people do whatever he wanted. He could scratch his way into the back of his victims' brains and influence their behavior to such a point that the victims wouldn't know whose desires—their own, or the manipulator's—were directing their actions. In her book, that made him creepier and more dangerous than anything she'd ever known.

CoCo thought the other German, Friedrich "Butcher" Metzger, looked like what would survive if a child were abandoned in the woods. Vicious and gnarled, he sharpened his teeth regularly. He seemed to grow more sadistic every day and obeyed only primitive commands. CoCo had rarely seen Butcher by himself and knew Alrick kept him on a short leash because, otherwise, the feral man could not be trusted to not to maim or kill anyone he happened to meet. She hated working missions with them, particularly because Friedrich's tracking skills and enhanced senses had helped them find their targets. CoCo had heard that in his former life he was a butcher in a small east German town, but she thought his nickname more likely stemmed more from his cruel nature than his former profession. She wondered if Friedrich was like this before the solstice five years before, or if the White Light Wave had fundamentally changed his personality.

"What do you think, Butcher? Aren't these two just too sweet? Almost makes you sick, doesn't it?" Alrick took out a comb to pat down the few gray hairs that flew out of place in the breeze.

Friedrich snarled and licked his lips. He spoke no English.

CoCo suddenly regretted concentrating so strongly on her conversation with Timothy. If she'd kept some of her senses alert, she would have noticed the Germans coming and created an illusion to avoid interaction.

"Oh Alrick, you're just jealous that someone on this ship is getting action and you aren't." CoCo laughed and grabbed Timothy. Together, they walked straight past the Germans and to the commissary on the main level.

Although CoCo had been with the group for almost a year, Timothy was the only one she trusted, and that relationship was based on lies and illusions. She hadn't made any true friendships within the group, not that she had expected to. She had not realized how lonely undercover work could be.

As Timothy and CoCo passed the workshop, they saw Isaac "Builder" Bowmester hard at work on another project. He was dressed in his usual overalls, which strained across his growing stomach. He was balding, which he tried to cover with a varied hat collection. He was happiest when inventing something, or tinkering with and repairing machines. He kept the carrier afloat. He devised a system that used seawater to propel the ship. He'd invented the ghosting process the ship used to deflect surveillance and keep hidden from view. CoCo knew Builder from Base 47. He was once a SENTINEL and had designed all the safety and security systems there, but he didn't have a scrupulous bone in his body. He was kicked out of Base 47 for selling the base's security plans to the highest bidder.

Timothy and CoCo walked hand in hand through the commissary and chose the table closest to the wall.

"Oy! Timmy!"

CoCo knew Timothy hated when anyone called him anything but Timothy—all variations, but especially Timmy. CoCo knew from the voice exactly who it was. Dafydd sat a table playing cards. Dafydd was rarely alone. He generated duplicates of himself at will. He was playing poker against himself and, by the looks of it, losing. His longish brown hair was disheveled and greasy. She had a difficult time understanding his heavy Welsh accent, but in the interests of establishing rapport with her targets, she usually tried to make nice. Today, though, she wasn't in the mood to spend time with him.

"Sit down and play a round with us," Dafydd invited. He blinked, and another duplicate appeared.

CoCo masked their presence and projected an image of Timothy sitting down to play cards with Dafydd.

"Oh. You just did your thing," Timothy whispered as he saw himself sit down with Dafydd and his duplicates. "Nice."

"I just didn't want to stay down here any longer. Let's go back to your cabin."

"Oh, yeah." Timothy grabbed her hand.

"I'll just have to keep the illusion going for a little while after we're gone."

As they left, CoCo looked around the commissary and noticed a shimmer on the far side. Did the shimmer suggest a secret entrance? She wondered how she'd never noticed it before. Perhaps it led to an off-limits area she had heard about. She filed it away as a mystery to investigate another time.

CHAPTER
12

23 November

Henry shuffled through his grand foyer. A storm raged outside his secluded Philadelphia mansion. A lot had changed for the Ascendancy in the past five years. After the disaster at New Atlantis, Henry had fought his way back into their collective good graces.

Anabel Wong

It had been an arduous task, as he had simultaneously rebuilt The Hastings Foundation and worked to repair his own financial situation, which had taken a beating in the aftermath of the failed Reckoning and WaveMaker debacle.

The exertions had taken a toll on Henry, now sixty. Just five years ago, his hair had been salt-and-pepper. Now it was almost all salt. At least he still had a full head of hair. His shoulders slumped a bit more than they had, and the wrinkles creasing his forehead and crinkling the corners of his eyes had deepened. A full night of sleep? Forget about it. Hadn't happened in more years than he cared to admit.

Henry had long shielded his son from the inner workings

of the Ascendancy, but Arthur had grown increasingly eager to learn all he could about the Ascendancy and its purpose. At first, Henry delighted in finally having someone close to him to share the secrets and power with, but Arthur's obsession with forcing a new reckoning worried him.

Henry entered his secret room. This room, at least, remained a secret from his son. Partly because Arthur wasn't a full member of the Ascendancy, and there were plenty of Ascendancy secrets in his room, but also to preserve the room as his refuge and throne of power. He simply wasn't ready to share that yet, not even with Arthur.

He zigzagged through the stacks of newspapers and magazines cluttering his room. Gone were the days where he took pride in maintaining a clean work space. Empty glasses and bottles lined tables and shelves like dead soldiers. No food, though. He couldn't abide the thought of sharing his sanctuary with the cockroaches and rodents that food remnants would surely draw. He'd begun retreating into this room more and more often over the last five years. Recently, he had taken to sleeping on the couch a few nights a week, not that his wife even noticed. It was also a symptom of how hard he'd worked to try to restore his foundation and finances to their former glory.

The Hastings Foundation had been rebuilt, and he had kept Dr. Roger Martin under his control. With the potential of the cryospore, Henry felt he could come out on top.

As Henry prepared to discuss his latest progress with the other Ascendancy members, he ruminated on the struggle they faced as New Atlantis developed. Since their original plan for domination had failed, the Ascendancy had needed to help make up for that loss. They had chosen to pursue the cryospore, which could provide the world with the clean energy it needed. Not to mention that it would make the Ascendancy a fortune. Henry was in charge of mining the cryospores, the twins would handle shipping the cryospores to market, and Elise was overseeing the end user market, which entailed getting power plants onboard with the new energy source and adapting electrical appliances to operate off cryospores.

The Ascendancy was busy. They also had worked to devise new ways to bring about the Reckoning since the Sentinel had been killed on New Atlantis. Elise Springchild, the head of the European branch of the Ascendancy, spearheaded the purchase of the Soviet-era aircraft carrier that was the new mobile base of operations for their strike division. She stayed in close contact with Captain Pierce. Anabel and Maksim Wong, the twins who killed their father for membership into the Ascendancy, were making strides in solidifying their shipping monopoly in Asia.

Henry himself was as focused as ever on lost art and scrolls dealing with the topic of the Reckoning. With the first effort failing so spectacularly, he was determined to redeem himself. Such a vast collection of art he'd collected, and all of it secure in his secret room. His latest acquisition was a set of scrolls located recently in the Parisian catacombs. He'd devoted hours to their study. He was close to learning their true secrets. He leaned over his desk, where the most important of the scrolls was spread. As he often did when he just stopped to admire it, he spotted a word that triggered his mind. He slid into his desk chair and lost himself in the scroll. Before long, a beep alerted him to a text message. It was from Elise.

"Where are you? It's time for our meeting."

He sighed.

Henry checked himself quickly in the mirror and turned on the video monitor. Everyone was waiting for him.

"About time," Maksim snapped as he put his champagne down.

"Sorry. I had to get some items in order. Let's go ahead with the status updates," Henry said politely, grateful they couldn't see the mess and squalor that had swallowed up his personal sanctum.

"I'll start," Elise said. In the years since the disaster on New Atlantis she had spread her influence far and wide to second- and third-world nations, reaching Brazil, Tanzania, and Laos, to name a few, under the guise of her charitable organization, which trained teens in different skills and trades. Now she was ready to take advantage of that influence. "I've redirected funding toward our interests in Africa, propping up local leadership through our charitable organizations. Our mole at New Atlantis is providing actionable intelligence. The reserve funds have still not been touched, and they are proceeding with the infiltration process."

"Thank you, Elise," Henry said.

"What have you got, Anabel?" Elise asked.

"Because we control two-thirds of the shipping lanes, we are able to move our products without governmental interference," Anabel said.

"That just leaves me, I suppose," Henry said. "I am almost finished with the lost scrolls found in the Parisian catacombs. It is really quite fascinating—"

"Enough with the history lessons, they bore me."

"Maks!" Anabel snapped. "Apologies, Henry, it seems my brother is still without tact." She glared at her twin. "Please continue."

"Of course." Henry paused to order his thoughts and conceal his loathing of Maks. "As I was saying, the scrolls reveal much and I believe that within the next few days, we will have a detailed description on how to proceed without the Sentinel."

"That is great news," Elise said. "Anything else?"

"As you know, my son has become more and more involved in the day-to-day monitoring of the activities of The Hastings Foundation, while I have been focusing on the cryospore situation."

"And what exactly is the 'cryospore situation'?" Maks asked.

Henry ignored his tone and simply answered the question. "We believe we are mere days from being able to extract large volumes of cryospores from Antarctica." He beamed. "My scientists have developed a method that will allow us to retrieve the cryospore from its icy holding. They are solving the problem of storing it safely so it can be turned into actual, usable renewable energy."

"Any update on the Tennessee explosion?" Elise asked. "According to my network, the investigators are chalking it up to PM—pure magic. In other words, they have no clue."

"Pure magic. Good, that's real good. Once we've got all the kinks worked it, it will work pure magic on our bank accounts, that's for sure," Henry said. "Anyway, to answer your question, it was a minor setback. It shows us we are not quite there yet on the integration side. But soon we'll be ready to roll out the public phase of the cryospore."

"But for now?" Elise prodded

"We can't functionally extract the cryospores at the rate we need to turn a profit, but I believe we'll be there within the month." Henry shifted in his seat.

"We're running out of time," Elise reminded him.

"Don't you think I know?" Henry drew a deep breath. "I'm well aware of the deadline."

"Failure to have the cryospore available as a viable alternate energy source before all the major countries sign the Stockholm accords could mean a loss of billions," Elise said. She was referencing the Stockholm Accords to Minimize Climate Impact.

"I know. I'm working on it."

"Not to stress you further," Maks said, smirking, "but what of the missing cryospores that you've already mined? Or did you think we hadn't noticed?"

"Those missing cryospores aren't actually missing," Elise said. "They are powering the Tribe's ship. Not to mention the teleportation device connecting the London office of The Hastings Foundation to the Antarctic Base."

"Thanks for letting us know about it," Maks snapped.

"I briefed you on this a few weeks ago," Henry said.

Maks rolled his eyes.

"And what of the extraction?" Anabel asked.

"I don't foresee any issues," Henry said.

"Just like you didn't see any issues coming up with the Sentinel?" Maksim asked.

"If you have something you'd like to say, kid, just come out and say it."

"I'm just saying that you were so sure five years ago that we'd be unstoppable with Rami Kazemi and the device. Look how well that turned out for us."

"We all agreed to the plan, and it didn't work out," he snapped at Maks. "Now we're working a new plan." Henry stared at each member in turn.

They were all silent for a moment before Elise spoke up. "Henry, we have complete faith in your abilities. We just don't want any surprises."

"Not to put your hand over the fire any more, but we have heard some disturbing rumblings about the Swarm being active again," Anabel said.

"I've heard the same rumors and can assure you that they are just that. Rumors. The Swarm are far too scattered and disorganized to function." Henry poured a double shot of bourbon. As he tilted his head back to savor the drink, he saw Elise wrinkle her nose and Maks roll his eyes. Screw them, he thought. Maks could drink champagne on the call, but he couldn't savor a bourbon, himself? Bolstered by the alcohol freshly coursing through his system, he added, "And besides, they have no real infrastructure like we do to operate."

"Let's make sure that they don't," Elise said. "It could be ruinous if they did."

"I understand. I won't let the Ascendancy down," Henry said, signing off from the conversation. He took a deep breath and drank down the rest of his bourbon.

CHAPTER

13

23 November

"Are the holiday party arrangements all on track?"

Arian looked up at her boss, her glass of water halfway to her mouth. She hadn't heard the prime minster come in. At six foot three inches, he towered over

Arian Nassar

her. He'd been lean when she took up her role as his chief of staff, but even the daily gym visits couldn't combat all the fat cat dining he'd indulged in over the years. He was starting to pudge in the middle. That said, she thought the fifty-year-old politician still managed to look quite dapper in his expensively tailored suits. She felt chilled by his proximity. He looked anxious, but she didn't think it had anything to do with the planned festivities. She set her water down. "Of course. Contractors are confirmed and guests have been invited."

"Good, good." He blinked his icy blue eyes a few times, as if in thought, then nodded and turned away. "We have to make sure all the world can see that New Atlantis is a success, and the winter festival will show that."

She nodded, grasped her water and held it out toward him. "Mind?"

Jaako Aalto, who had once been a member of the Finnish parliament, held his hand to the glass, and four ice cubes formed in it.

Arian watched in fascination at the display of his power despite the fact that this was a near-daily ritual. "Thanks, Mr. Prime Minister."

"No problem. I'll be in my office. No disturbances."

"I'll be leaving for lunch in about fifteen minutes, so I'll set everything to roll into voice mail in my absence, as usual." She looked at him. "Do you want me to bring you anything?"

"No, no, just back from lunch with Bayanai."

"What? That wasn't on your schedule. How can I keep track of things for you if you keep me out of the loop?"

"Relax. We ran into each other, and I had a hankering for kebobs, so I suggested we visit over lunch at the grill. It's been a while since I've gotten an update on things at Base 47. And it's good to hear from my constituents with powers."

"How is he?"

"Still worried about Emma. They've reached a new point in their investigation, though."

Arian perked up. "Really? That's great. What did he say?" No one on the island was more worried about Emma than she was. Arian had become guardian to Emma after the child's parents died in a car wreck. Arian's own life had improved immeasurably when Emma had come to live with her, fulfilling her in ways she'd never imagined. In the months after Emma went missing, Arian had done all that she could think of to try to find Emma. She refused to fall into despair. She kept herself strong for Emma. For Rami.

"I knew you'd ask, but he didn't divulge any details."

"I'll have to stop by and ask him later. Maybe bribe him with something sweet from the bakery."

The prime minister shrugged. "Might work. He said his team is very busy, what with patrolling against malicious Mods activity, searching for Emma and chasing down what they believe is a whole new Ascendancy plot."

The last words hit Arian like a gut punch, rendering her short of breath and slightly dizzy. She clasped the desk to steady herself. The Ascendancy? Couldn't they just leave well enough alone? They'd stolen her love, and now who knew what they were up to. She struggled to bring herself under control as she assessed her boss. Were those waves of stress emanating off him because of something specific Bayanai had told him? Probably. Unless he'd had some communication from a fellow global leader while he was away from the office. "Okay, then. I'll just head out. Back in about an hour."

She gathered her purse and phone and left the prime minister standing in her office. She hadn't been hungry, merely in need of a break from being indoors. But her boss's mention of kebobs had caused a stomach rumble. She hadn't eaten since lunch the day before. She'd been too preoccupied with her guilt and grief to consider eating. But her growling belly told her even grief and guilt need to eat. Maybe a fish kebob was in order. She could get it to go, and still have time to enjoy the fresh air. She called and placed a carry-out order from Smokin' Kebobs, her current favorite quick-food eatery near the office.

Ten minutes later, she left Smokin' Kebobs with her lunch and considered her transportation options. Since the island's infrastructure design had the benefit of being planned before buildings were erected, the transportation systems were logical and geared toward mass transit. She could take a bus, if she chose, or the Crystal City Light Rail. Both would get her where she wanted to go. But the day was lovely and she was in the mood for minimal contact with strangers. She waved down one of the local open-air taxis, which was a glorified golf cart, and hopped in. When the golf cart glided to a stop, she paid the driver and slid out, looking around.

She was alone and grateful that was the case. This place might belong to everyone on New Atlantis, but she wanted it to herself today, especially after hearing that the Ascendancy might be up to its nasty tricks again. Sometimes being around the memorial made her optimistic for the world's future. Sometimes it broke her heart. She thought today would be one of the latter days.

Her heels clicked along the concrete path as she circled the memorial. It was clean and clearly well cared for. Though she visited the memorial almost daily, and at varying times of the day, she had never seen anyone tending to the memorial. She wasn't sure who was responsible for the upkeep, but she remembered with a quick smile the day she'd seen Carlos hoist the statue up on its base. Tio Carlos, as Emma called him, was the strongest Mod she'd ever seen, but the strength was his outside story. Carlos' inside story was as gentle as could be, and he treated Emma like his own niece. She shook her head to clear it. She only wanted to think about her one true love at this moment.

"Rami, my sweet," she whispered as she drew up in front of the memorial. "I miss you."

Of course the statue didn't whisper back. She simply couldn't stop her heart from wishing Rami were still alive. She had moved to New Atlantis to escape the memories of Iran, and she felt a connection to the island that she could not explain. The likeness of Rami was marble, and larger-than-life. It wasn't him, but it would do. How she pined for him, even five years later. Wasn't heartache supposed to ease with time?

One morning over breakfast, she had asked Emma that very question. Emma had gently suggested she quit visiting the memorial every day if she wanted to "get over" Rami, or else start dating someone else. She did not plan to act on Emma's recommendations.

Emma. Emma was part of the problem.

She was missing Emma and the child's quick smile and intelligence. She had lightened the mood in Arian's house tremendously. Arian also ached for the son, stillborn, that Rami didn't even know he had given her. How different would her life be if they both had lived? There was a gaping hole in her heart. She missed them all. The sadness washed over her, as it often did when she stood near the memorial to Rami, but she only felt guilt over Emma. How could they get her back? And what was whoever had her doing to her?

She nibbled at her kebob while pondering what she could do to help get Emma back. Being able to get Emma back might help her, in some weird way, to feel like she'd partly avenged Rami's death. The beginnings of an idea started to form. She knew most people looking to save Emma were operating on the assumption that whoever had taken her wanted access to her telepathic powers. Suddenly, Arian wasn't so sure. Everyone had overlooked Emma's other ability—the power to locate other Mods. She wondered if Emilio, who was heading up the search for Emma, had considered this. If they could figure out who would want to track down Mods, maybe they could figure out who had Emma. She pulled out her mobile phone and selected Emilio's number.

CHAPTER
14

24 November

Jane Smith walked through the revolving doors of the First National Bank in downtown Chicago. She walked past the security guard, who couldn't say for certain that Jane had actually entered the establishment. That

Jane Smith
"Plain Jane"

was Jane's Mod gift. It was also her curse. She was so unremarkable that no one paid any attention to her. But because she couldn't affect electronics, she still had to be careful about videographic evidence. However, video surveillance of her was so unremarkable that officers rarely remembered her long enough to investigate her.

As a shy and retiring librarian, she barely made an impression on her customers or colleagues. She was a fifty-two-year-old woman of average looks. She was neither fat nor thin. She had short mousy brown hair and brown eyes with a light fringe of eyelashes. She was neither tall nor short. She had a penchant for khakis and pastel polos during the summers and pastel sweaters during the winter. When the White Light Wave changed everyone, she became even less noticeable. As long as someone looked at her, they could remember her, but as soon as they were distracted or turned away from Jane, she immediately faded from their short-term memory, as if she had never been there. She was Plain Jane, the woman who wasn't there. She'd gone to Base 47 seeking help from the other Mods, but no one could remember her after she left the room, except Pierce. His promise to find a way to help her kept her going for many long years. He'd yet to deliver, but Jane chose to give Pierce the benefit of the doubt because he was that rare person who never forgot her. But, she wondered, did he remember the adoration with which she looked at him? Did he know that she craved his attention as a lover?

When the schism split the SENTINELS, she happily left with Pierce and helped keep the operation afloat with cash grabs around the world. Her great ability gave her bittersweet satisfaction, and part of her hoped that soon she would be relieved of these powers, if only so she could fully be with Pierce.

Jane located and entered the First National Bank's vault, took a stack of bills, and quietly exited through the lobby, nodding politely to the security guard.

She only took small amounts at a time, so it was often days or weeks until the banks realized a theft had occurred. This was her greatest skill, but also her greatest fear. If no one could remember her, did she even exist at all?

Outside she walked through the plaza and sat on a bench. While she was waiting, she people watched, a pastime that fascinated her. It was lunchtime and the plaza was humming with the energy of office workers enjoying an unseasonably warm fall day.

Soon a young African-American woman with flame patches sewn into her leather jacket and a physically imposing Korean woman consulting her tablet walked up beside Jane.

"It might be time for you to take some cover," Taneesha "Flame" Jackson told the former librarian. Under her leather jacket she was dressed in city camo fatigues. Her hair was tightly braided to her head. She glanced down at her own tablet, which helped her keep track of Jane.

"Have fun robbing the bank?" Taneesha asked.

"Always," Jane said primly. "Ready to have fun of your own?"

Taneesha's grin widened to display her molars. "Starting a riot is my second favorite way to spend my lunch time."

"How long until the SENTINELS appear?" Jane asked.

Jimin "Brute" Pak answered the question. "I estimate a response of between two and five minutes." Jimin checked her watch. "Let's not waste time." She removed a light jacket, revealing her chiseled physique. The South Korean had used the enhanced strength given to her during the White Light Wave to give her an advantage in weightlifting competitions. She had won her third Ms. World title and a gold medal at the Olympics before the sports governing bodies discovered her Mod status and stripped her of the titles and medal.

Jane marveled at the woman's gorgeous face and beautiful long hair. She would definitely not want to cross Jimin in a dark alleyway. Shortly after Jimin joined the Tribe, she had usurped leadership from Taneesha, who wanted so desperately to restore her status that sometimes Jane thought she could hear her blood boiling when Jimin issued commands.

"Let's get to it, Flame," Jimin said.

Jane scooted away from Brute. Jimin needed to be hit in order to gain her vaunted strength.

"You asked for it, Brute!" Taneesha smiled as she rolled

up her sleeves. They had called her Brute for a while and Jimin seemed not to mind. Taneesha wailed her fists against her teammate's arms and shoulders before sneaking in a jab to Brute's nose.

"Enough!" Jimin shouted and waved Taneesha away. She stumbled over to a hundred-year-old oak, ripped it from the ground, and tossed it like a Major League ballplayer might toss a baseball bat. The tree sailed through the floor-to-ceiling window of the bank. Twigs and dirt littered the sidewalk outside the bank. The tree's massive root structure occupied a spot on the sidewalk the size of a van.

Security guards rushed out of the bank to confront Brute. Taneesha rubbed her hands together and ignited the oxygen molecules in front of her, causing a flame to emerge. She rolled the flame in her hand into a ball and threw it at the guards.

One guard yelped and fell back after the fireball hit him in the chest. He rolled over on the ground to extinguish the flames.

"Come on, rent-a-pig! You want a piece of me?" Taneesha created a three-foot-high wall of fire around her and Brute.

"Didn't your mother teach you not to play with fire?"

Taneesha turned around to see three members of the SENTINELS emerging from a deep black portal. Etienne, Bayanai, and James each wore the standard black-and-purple armored uniforms, but added their own flair. James Chege, a Mod from Kenya, was a speedster. He was almost twice as old as Etienne but had the readiest smile of any of the SENTINELS.

"Oh come on, you know she just likes the heat!" Etienne joked as James got all the pedestrians out of harm's way.

"Thank you so much, young man," an older lady said to James before he took off again. She watched the

SENTINELS in action and knew they'd never remember her.

"About time you showed up." Taneesha formed a fireball between her hands. It glowed and flickered in the midday sun.

"Just glad that CoCo isn't with them," Etienne said as his body faded from view.

"I should have known they would send boys to do a man's job," Brute said. She charged them. James sprinted out of the way as Etienne grabbed Bayanai, phasing them from the rampaging Korean.

"How did you get here so fast?" Taneesha threw her hands up and a fiery dragon leapt high in the air.

Bayanai ignored her question, instead looking at James and pointing at Taneesha. James sped in circles around her, slowly extinguishing her flame.

"Burn in hell, speedy," she yelled as her dragon blew fire balls around the plaza.

"I'll take care of the civilians. Etienne, you take on Brute." Bayanai set about taking a group of young kids to safety.

"You know you'll never be able to touch me, Brute, so why even try?"

Jimin punched at him incessantly, missing his phasing body every time. "You've got to become solid sometime. And I don't get tired."

Nearby, James circled around Taneesha. Frustrated and alarmed by the diminishing oxygen in the air, she shouted at him. It didn't help. She began to drift in and out of consciousness. As she fell to the ground, her flames died down. Brute noticed the waning flames, picked up a large ornamental rock, and threw it toward a gathering group of onlookers.

"James! Get the rock!" Etienne shouted.

James stopped and rotated his arms, creating a funnel of wind that slowed the rock's descent.

"Oh come on! Too easy, Brute!" James laughed as the rock slowly dropped to the ground.

Etienne was tiring, so he jumped on Brute's back and made her as intangible as he was. "Wish that Carlos were still here. He could take you on punch for punch."

"Too bad your strong man didn't survive that explosion," Brute said. "He was fun to fight. You? You're just so-so."

Hostility and anger and loyalty flared in Etienne. "You shouldn't have said that." Etienne phased her through the ground, but knew that wouldn't really stop her. He pulled a pair of escrima sticks from his leg holsters. The foot-long sticks had several improvements over the commercially available weapons traditionally used in Filipino martial arts. Instead of light flexible rattan, they were metal. Etienne's souped-up pair came with a charger that gave the sticks an electrical kick. They could deliver a shock that would incapacitate the opponent. He jabbed the sticks into her shoulders, delivering a full measure of the shock into her. "This should hold you for a while."

Brute, whose body increased in strength in response to kinetic energy, could not stand the assault. Stuck in the ground, she screamed and blacked out.

"Bayanai, let's wrap this up," Etienne said as he put his escrima sticks away.

But Brute came to moments later. "Wrong move, rat!" Enraged, she smashed her arms on the ground in a bid to free herself from her earthen prison. She sent rock fragments flying like an exploding firecracker. Finally free, she spotted Maru in the sky. Maru Tamatoa, a deeply tanned Samoan, was capable of manipulating weather. He'd teamed up with Flame from the beginning.

"Time for an exit," Brute called out to Flame, who was stirring on the ground.

"Great timing, Maru." Flame stood as Maru created powerful winds to carry them up. The three were soon just a narrowing spot in the sky.

"We could pursue them," Etienne suggested.

"No good. They turned tail quick enough. We'll see what the authorities say about the damage," Bayanai said as James skidded to a stop beside him.

"So they just get to escape?" James kicked some rocks. He wanted to put the Tribe away. They had been going back and forth with these jokers for years. Each time they put them away, they somehow escaped. It was more annoying than any reality show ever.

"They'll be back. That you can count on," Bayanai said.

"So we should be going too, then. We can only operate on US territory as long as there is clear and present danger. We don't want to overstay our welcome, and they look like they want us to get out of here." Etienne gestured at a couple of cops frowning at the SENTINELS.

Several bystanders approached the SENTINELS. One reached out a hand to shake. "You saved our lives, mister. Thank you so much," Jane said as she walked toward the heroes.

"You're welcome ma'am." He walked away and failed to notice her walking alongside him.

"Right here, guys," Waleed said as he opened the portal back to Base 47.

"All right. Let's get out of here. Lunch won't eat itself." James chuckled as he raced through the portal.

Etienne followed Bayanai through the portal as Waleed waited for everyone to clear the portal. He walked through but didn't realize that he wasn't alone. Jane Smith had grabbed his hand and walked through the portal back to

Base 47 along with him.

"And that is why it pays to be The Woman Who Wasn't There." Jane grinned. Her mission was just getting started.

CHAPTER

15

25 November

"How is this even possible?" Dr. Watanabe stared at the containment tube. Her dark hair was back in a ponytail, and her brow wrinkled so deeply it drew her eyebrows together. She slipped her right hand into her lab

Dr. Yukio Watanabe

coat pocket and drew out a small notebook. She jotted a few notes.

"It's a mystery for me too, Yukio," Nicola said. She rounded the table and flipped through the chart.

"I know this isn't really my field of expertise, but I just can't get over this." Yukio turned the tube upside down and watched the contents filter down. Dr. Watanabe had joined Base 47 when it relocated to New Atlantis. An expert in experimental cybernetics, she had created training drones and enhanced the advanced security systems on the island because they couldn't trust the system put in place by Builder, who later got booted from the SENTINELS for selling the designs for Base 47's security system to the highest bidder. Builder had then joined the Tribe, and Dr. Watanabe oversaw a completely new security project to rework the existing protections.

"You said this residue was all over the place at the plant?"

"Pretty much." Nicola studied the image from her electron microscope.

"And what about the artifact Waleed found at the site?" Yukio asked.

"Another mystery."

"But maybe not for much longer," Bayanai said as he entered the lab with Emilio.

"What do you mean?"

"We've long suspected that the Swarm was still active."

"No matter how hard the Ascendancy tried to destroy them," Emilio added.

"I believe this artifact is tied to the Swarm. This suggests to me that the Swarm is somehow involved in the power plant explosion." Bayanai walked to the counter.

"But what is the connection? Why would the Swarm leave this behind?" Dr. Watanabe lifted the jeweled artifact and studied it.

"I'm thinking it wasn't intentional. Whoever took it to the site was vaporized." Bayanai leaned over to look at the artifact as well.

"It's an eye. Have you tried looking through it?" James zoomed into the lab, picked the artifact out of Dr. Watanabe's hands and peered through the eye. "Hmph. Nothing." He dropped it back into the scientist's hands.

"Careful, James. We don't know anything about it," Dr. Watanabe said.

"Is the Swarm making a comeback?" Nicola pumped out some sanitizer and rubbed her hands dry.

"I certainly hope not. We barely defeated them last time.

I don't look forward to fighting them again." Emilio held his hands out and Nicola pumped some sanitizer out for him.

James spun around on the stool until Bayanai stopped him.

"Thanks," Emilio said.

"Bayanai, do you think whatever caused the power plant explosion, this material we found, the eye and all that could be tied to Emma's disappearance?" Nicola asked, desperate for an answer.

James looked again at Dr. Watanabe and the eye. He rushed over and took it from her hands. Doing so, he accidentally cut his hand on one of the jewels.

Noticing his blood trickle down the artifact, Dr. Watanabe said, "James, you're bleeding."

He tentatively pulled it to his eye.

Dr. Watanabe saw things happen in slow motion. There were almost imperceptible changes in James as the Eye of Horus awakened something in him, possibly his consciousness. His eyes rapidly shifted left to right and his body vibrated. It became so significant that Emilio held him down. Finally, James collapsed back onto the stool.

"What happened?" Emilio asked as James regained composure.

"I could see. I could see everything. It's the Swarm. They're back." His voice deepened with concern. "We have to go to Cairo."

"What did you see?" Bayanai asked.

"I saw everything so clearly. Flashes from the past. Way past." James could barely catch his breath. "But it was all in reds and browns."

"How is that possible? None of us saw anything. Why did it work for James?" Dr. Watanabe sounded partly concerned and partly annoyed.

Bayanai only shrugged. "Only time will tell."

"Bayanai, we need to get to Cairo. That's where the eye showed me," James said.

"All right. You and Katrina take the next plane to Cairo. Take the eye with you. We need answers." Bayanai motioned for James to get started, and James zipped away, taking the eye with him.

"But we aren't finished studying the eye yet," Nicola said. "I mean I've been with the SENTINELS since the beginning and you've only been here a while, Bayanai, but in my experience this sort of mystery usually involves the bloody Ascendancy in some way."

Bayanai closed his eyes and thought. He frowned and looked at the group, then stood to leave.

"And where are you going?" Emilio asked.

"If things really are as bad as this seems, we're going to need help, and I know just who to reach out to." Bayanai grabbed his gray jacket, the one he often wore when leading meetings. "But first, let's go check on George's progress."

"Sure, *Jefe*." Emilio followed Bayanai out.

Their departures left the two scientists alone in the lab again.

"Oh, sweet silence returns." Nicola laughed as she turned back toward the monitor and double-checked the calculations in front of her.

"Now we can actually think and work," Yukio said, grinning. In the silence, she focused on the scanner. After a few long moments, she pointed at one of the numbers on the scanner readout. "Nicola, come look at this."

Nicola studied the readout.

"We could adjust the scanner to search for the new element using these values, right?" Yukio asked.

A slow smile grew on Nicola's face. All she had to do was set the right parameters so the scanner could find the element in question.

"That's brilliant. And I can calibrate our dedicated satellite to search for it as well. Maybe we don't have to send anyone to a dangerous place."

"That would be great," Yukio said. "How long before you can initiate the search?"

"The programming will take some time, say half an hour to code, and then I can start the search."

CHAPTER 16

26 November

Bayanai perched on his favorite bench in Dini Square and noshed on cubed papaya from a nearby fruit stand. He was so absorbed by his thoughts that he didn't even notice beautiful bright orange-red petals of the royal poinciana tree swaying in the

Ericka Zavatsky

ocean breeze. A faint grape-like fragrance hung in the air. The so-called "flame trees" usually reminded him of home. None of those cacti in West Texas made him feel welcome the way these vibrant trees did. The island would be a much different place if Juan Pierre, a Mod from Colombia, had not used his power over vegetation to amp up the growth of flora.

He mulled the problems the team faced. There must be a connection he just wasn't seeing. Did something aside from the artifact tie the power plant explosion to the Sovereign of the Swarm?

The idea of a secret society operating to influence the

world was a difficult concept for him. His good-hearted nature found it difficult for him to understand those of more vindictive persuasions. Back in his simpler times on his family farm in the Philippines, he had dreamed of a life filled with adventure and excitement. Since he'd become a Mod and found his way to Base 47, he'd begun to regret those youthful desires. On his second mission as a SENTINEL, he had faced the full wrath of the Swarm. During the fight, he didn't think he'd survive, but he had.

A police siren pierced the silence, and Bayanai's mind snapped back to reality. Curiously, he turned toward the sirens.

Three police cars skidded to a stop just outside the square. Six cops jumped out and some of them ran inside the square. One called for the crowd to disperse and seek shelter as two worked to cordon off the square. Bayanai observed from a distance.

A spry older man wearing a backpack leapt through the square. Suddenly, Bayanai understood. This was a small-time crook named Leonard Levit, who had the ability to jump great heights. The SENTINELS knew he was on the island and that he might attempt to pull off a jewelry heist. Levit, also known as Leaping Leonard, was part of the Scarlet Syndicate, an up-and-coming crime gang that the SENTINELS were watching.

Bayanai assumed the man's backpack contained diamonds and other precious jewels. He looked to be in his late sixties, and something about his facial expression made Bayanai think of Don Knotts, although the man was actually balding. The man bounced through the square, leaping above the heads of people who had, until then, been enjoying their lunches.

"Watch out!" The man kicked over the very fruit stand that had sold Bayanai his snack. Papayas, guavas, and mangoes went flying and its proprietor stumbled to the ground.

"That's definitely Leaping Leonard. Once he gets really going, he can jump upwards of fifty feet high. Approach with caution. Stun guns only. If things get crazy, use the power-dampening weapon." The orders came from a woman whose dark brown hair was pulled back in a bun. She turned to the criminal. "Leaping Leonard! That's quite enough."

"Leaping Leonard." He snarled back at her. "I hate that name." He jumped toward the officers. "I was going to leave you alone and just bounce, but you've upset me." He skipped toward the officers. "I know you won't shoot me. It's against the law."

On New Atlantis guns were illegal. The citizenry was not allowed to have firearms. Even the police force had only stun guns or batons.

"We may not have guns, but we've got plenty to stop you with," a tall officer said as he stepped toward the Mod.

Leonard smiled and leapt on top of the officer, dropping him to the ground. With a speed that defied his age, he jumped again as an officer fired a stun shot at him.

"I don't think so." Leonard squinted his eyes and jumped toward the officer. Out of nowhere, two officers tackled the Mod and pinned him to the ground.

"That's about enough. You aren't going anywhere," one said as he held Leonard on the ground.

"No!" Leonard used his feet to launch the two officers fifteen feet in the air. They landed hard, and both groaned. Leonard rose, and he was confronted by the last officer standing. It was the woman with brown hair pulled tight in a bun.

"Look, honey, I make it my policy to not hurt pretty ladies." Leonard neared the officer, who held her ground.

"I'm flattered."

He cocked his head and jumped on top of her, knocking her stun gun away from her. She was compact and strong, but still she gasped at the force of his impact. She nearly lost her balance at the surprise of his weight. He wasn't quite on her piggyback style, but close.

"That's what you get for underestimating me, honey."

Even from afar, Bayanai could see the officers' concern for their chief. Leonard could cause some serious damage to her from that position, should he have a mind to. They began to approach.

"Stay away."

The officers backed two steps away. In the distance, Bayanai stepped closer.

"Hmm, let's see. These stripes mean you're important, don't they?" Leonard asked her.

"You could say that." Her eyes glowed green against her clear pale skin, but Leonard was behind her and couldn't see that. Without warning, green energy burst from her eyes, hitting him on the left forearm as she whipped her head around in that direction. He yelped and released his left arm from around her neck. She aimed an energy burst at his other arm. Another yelp, and she was free. She turned around and let him have one more big blast. He reeled and crashed back toward the white marble fountain in the geographic center of the square. With a radius of fifteen feet, it was the focal point of the square.

Leonard shook his head hard and slapped his hands over the backpack straps to make sure his stolen goods were still with him. He stood in the knee-high sparkling blue water with a fierce scowl on his face.

"I wondered where you've been." He jumped out of the fountain and landed next to her. "The girl with green energy blasts. Although shooting them out of your eyes is something new. What else can you do?"

"Gotta keep you off balance, Leaping Leonard." She felt an unexpected boost in energy. Like she was suddenly amped up to eleven. It was familiar, but unexpected. She went with it.

"Stop calling me that!" He grabbed her by the safety vest, leapt high into the air and landed across the plaza on the arch, which served as another key feature in the square. "If you value your island, don't do that again."

"You made the wrong choice." She grabbed his arm and flipped him off of the arch as she snatched his backpack from him. She watched him fall toward the ground.

With cat-like reflexes, he righted himself and landed on his feet. She jumped off the arch, using her green energy blasts to slow her descent.

As she landed next to Leonard, she removed a power dampener from her belt pouch and slapped the bracelets on his wrists.

"This will hold you for now." She activated the dampener, and Leonard was visibly drained. She expelled a long breath as adrenaline continued to course through her body.

The crowd in Dini Square erupted in cheers and applause. Her officers approached with congratulations.

Bayanai also approached her. He smiled and said, "Great work."

"What are you doing here?" Crystal City Police Chief Ericka Zavatsky grabbed him by the arm and steered him away from the crowd. "Are you checking up on me?"

"No. Nothing like that," he said. "I was here having some fruit and thinking. But I do have something I want to talk to you about."

"I'm not interested."

"You don't even know what I was going to say."

"Listen, maybe what we're doing isn't as glamorous as the SENTINELS, but it's equally important."

"I didn't say anything."

"Someone has to keep the island safe. Your crew is busy all over the world. We—" She turned and pointed to her officers and then herself before continuing. "We're busy here. We take care of Crystal City and New Atlantis. That is our mission. Says something like that on the car door."

"Ericka, I don't want to argue or fight with you. I am proud of you. You are an amazing police chief in a tough job. You set a high standard."

She struggled to keep her emotions in check.

"I didn't need the power boost, you know," she said as she wiped her hands.

"I know, but it doesn't mean it didn't help." Bayanai smiled.

She sighed. "What do you want, Bayanai? I've got my hands full here, plus I'm short-staffed since I have officers on loan to help deal with illegal shipments in Swing Bay, the refugee crisis in Eagle's Morn Settlement, and designer drugs in Little Mill. This island may be your Base 47 now, but it's my home and I aim to keep it safe." She wiped her brow.

Before Bayanai could say anything, she sighed and spoke again.

"If I hear anything about Emma, or any suspicious Mod activity on the island, I'll pass that along."

"We've worked well together in the past, departmentally speaking. I just want that to continue." Bayanai touched her shoulder.

"The SENTINELS constantly overstep their boundaries. That's part of why the public has trouble trusting Mods, Bayanai."

"I hear what you are saying. But we only go where we're

welcome." Bayanai could see Ericka's attention wane. "Look, all I'm saying is there is something coming. Something that will take all of us to thwart. I just want to know if push comes to shove, where will you stand?"

"I wish I could help you, Bayanai, I really do. But I've different responsibilities now. These officers, this position, this force are my purpose. I won't abandon them."

"And I'm not asking you to. I just need you to keep a lookout for anything suspicious. There's the winter festival with the prime minister coming up."

"I know. Arian has been begging me to come—and not as security detail."

"Come. We'd all like to see you there."

"Will Josh be there?"

Bayanai grimaced. "We haven't heard from him in a while," he said. "But he's officially been invited."

"Well, I'm sure with all the hype for his new movie, he and his huge ego couldn't fit on one island." Ericka laughed sourly as a fellow officer approached. "Listen, I'll do what I can. Just remember that my life with the SENTINELS is over. I'm glad for that time, but I'm done with that phase of my life."

Bayanai nodded and turned to leave. He hadn't expected her to jump at the request to help, but he'd hoped she would at least hear him out and consider the request. He hoped that with time she would change her mind.

Ericka put her hand on his shoulder and whispered into his ear. "Between us, I would keep a close eye on your support team. There's been a breach in my files about Base 47. I wouldn't put it past the Tribe to exploit it to get back at us. At you." She turned and walked toward her latest detainee. "All right, big guy, we're going to get you into a special cell, right away." She watched her officers carry the Mod to one of the cop cars.

Bayanai mulled this new information as he walked toward one of the secret entrances to Base 47. If Ericka was right, he had another problem to deal with. He looked around to make sure no one was watching him. Seeing no one, he opened a meter reader box and input his identification code. A door slid open in front of him and he quickly walked through.

CHAPTER 17

26 November

James Chege

"Too bad Waleed didn't join us. He would've loved to tell us all about this part of town," James said as he and Katrina walked through the crowded streets of Old Cairo.

"He does love his history lessons," she agreed. "I kind of missed the teleporting. Flights are so—"

"Don't say it!"

"Fine. I won't." She paused a beat. "I bet he's having a blast celebrating Thanksgiving with Marie's family."

"I hope he brings leftovers."

"Always you and the food," Katrina teased.

They walked companionably through the busy streets. James soaked up the vibrant reds, splendid yellows, bright blues, verdant greens, and deep blacks all mixed together in fabrics, ornamental designs, and clothing against a backdrop of sun-drenched beige buildings. Vendors sold fragrant perfumes, spices of all varieties, and brightly colored clothing. Each person they passed on the street sounded as if they were trying to speak louder than the next person. It made him nostalgic. It was home, Africa, but not Kenya.

Katrina McGee, a twenty-two-year-old Canadian who had joined the SENTINELS at the beginning, back in the days when she wore goth black, couldn't get enough of the travel that she got to do. She had one of the showier powers on the team: she could move things with her mind. The twist was that she was psychokinetic, not telekinetic. What that meant, basically, was that she harnessed the energy in the area to move things with her mind. The more energy— positive or negative—the more she could accomplish. That power was quite something to heap onto an angsty goth teen prone to being bullied. Most of her SENTINELS training had focused on emotional balance.

They passed a large, ornately domed Coptic church next to a mosque.

"Why do I feel like there should be a snake charmer on the next corner?" Katrina asked.

"You've been watching too many old romance movies."

She neared a kiosk and pulled her violet head scarf a bit tighter. The owner greeted them, showing off his silver and gold baubles. Katrina liked a pair of silver earrings and matching bracelet.

"There will be plenty of time for shopping after."

Katrina sighed and handed the jewelry back to the vendor. "Next time."

James weaved through the throng of Egyptians. He'd brought them to the area he sought, and it was time to get to business. "The first Sovereign of the Swarm is buried around here."

"How do you know?"

James shrugged. "Back on Base 47, when I looked in the Eye of Horus. I saw it. I saw... everything. It feels like it's around here."

"Feels?" Katrina asked.

James' jaw jutted out.

This time, Katrina shrugged. "Why don't you take a spin—"

Moments later, James skidded into one of his famous stop-slides right in front of Katrina. "Nothin'. I found nothin'."

"Well, before you took off, I was going to recommend using this." Katrina held out the Eye of Horus.

James' eyes lit up in happy surprise. "That's a great idea." He held the eye to his own for a long time before lowering it and sighing. "Nothing. I can't find anything."

"What do you think you'll find, just holding that old thing up to your eye and looking around?"

He shrugged. "Who knows."

"Maybe we just need some perspective?" Katrina looked around, but there were people everywhere. She spotted an empty side alley and pulled James into it before levitating them to the roof. "We can get a better view from here. Now, what you can see?"

James put the eye to his own, but there was nothing to experience. He frowned again. "It's not working."

"Calm down. Let's think this through. How did it work when we were at Base 47? Step by step, what did you do?"

James closed his eyes and recalled the incident in the lab. He looked down at his palm, where a scar should have been. "I think I know what to do." Holding the Eye of Horus in his right hand, he gouged his left palm over a rough sapphire and grimaced as blood trickled out and onto the golden artifact.

Katrina gasped but James ignored her. He held the eye to his own and suddenly a whole new world revealed itself to him. "Whoa."

"What is it?"

"The colors, it's like sepia tones with bright spots leading toward..." James paused, pulled the artifact away from his face, and pointed left toward a distant conical structure. Without warning, James grabbed Katrina and sped them down the building, zigzagging through the crowd and across the Nile to the tip of Rhoda Island. The island in the Nile featured a central road and connected to western and eastern Cairo via a pair of bridges. A hotel and hospital dominated the northern area of the island. James' destination was on the southern tip of Rhoda Island.

"A little warning next time would be lovely," Katrina said as she regained her balance.

"Sorry, I think time's of the essence."

"What is this?"

"The Nilometer. It used to measure the height of Nile during the annual floods. If it was too low, there would be famine. Too high and devastation followed," James said.

"How did you know that?"

"The plaque here." James pointed to the description.

"Cute."

"Super speed reading and all." James glanced over his shoulder.

"Wait..."

But it was too late, James had already raced them through security and deep inside the Nilometer. He avoided the caretaker. They descended into the interior well used to measure the actual floodwaters.

"Is this safe?"

"They don't use it anymore. It's like a museum now." James skidded to a stop.

"What now?" Katrina looked around the well.

"Let me see." James winked as he put the Eye of Horus up to his eye and did a slow turn around. Putting to the back of his mind why it took his blood to activate the powers of the eye, James lost himself in the immersive sensory experience that the eye provided. Sight and hearing, as well as physical and historical perception, were all enhanced. He could see Cairo, past, present, and future. It might have driven a lesser man crazy.

"What is it?"

But James was in a different world. A slight shift in James' breathing told her the eye was showing him something. He slowly turned around in the room and nodded. To Katrina, he seemed lost in the glyphs etched in the Nilometer's walls. She wondered if the eye was providing him with an understanding far deeper than just knowledge.

"The Swarm is trying to protect a lineage. Something about bringing back something long lost." James struggled to explain the glyphs he was seeing. "The Ancient One will Rise; The Four will Protect Him; A New World Ruled by Suns—no, Sons." James pulled the eye away from his own eye. The sensations were overwhelming.

"What does that even mean? And how did they hide a message in something that's been open to the public for more than a thousand years?"

"I wasn't reading the wall. It wasn't in these glyphs," he said, flicking a hand toward glyphs that covered one of the walls.

"Then how?"

"I have no idea," James said.

The sky darkened above them. Something ground against the floor. "James?"

"Wait. I think I've got it figured out."

"James." Urgency filled her voice.

"What?"

"Sandstorms aren't normal for this area, are they?"

James brought the eye down. "No, why?" He turned around. But it was too late. A deluge of sand swallowed them up.

CHAPTER 18

26 November

Luca Florentino

Josh quietly slipped back into the hospital room. He sipped coffee and sat next to Luca. It had been five days since the accident. While an ambulance had taken both Luca and Ken to the hospital as quickly as possible, the damage had been done. Ken had come out of his coma and was on the road to recovery, but Luca...

Josh replayed over and over in his head the events of that night. All he could see was the crash and him trying to pull Luca from the wreckage and that one moment. That one moment, that popping sound, that stung him to the core. The doctor told him that Luca's paralysis came not from the wreck itself, but from being moved while injured. He was certain that pop marked the moment. It was his fault, his responsibility to fix. And Luca wasn't going to like the only alternative Josh could come up with.

The hard thing about waiting for someone you love to wake up in a hospital is being locked up in your mind.

There's too much time to fret, worry, and anguish over how things will be in the future. To try to feel your way through what this altered life will mean for you, your relationship, and your loved one. To think about different ways of delivering terrible news and how to suggest an alternative. To wonder if you'll be strong enough or found lacking.

Josh feared he was lacking.

Ever since that blasted White Light Wave event, his life had been thrown upside down. Luca was the only real thing in his life, and now even that was threatened. In his mind all he could hear was the last thing Emma said to him when he left the SENTINELS: "You may be leaving us, but you can't walk away from who you really are." Those words had haunted him many times, and never more than in the last few days.

Josh gently held Luca's hand and cursed himself. Everything that had happened was his fault. He was responsible for Pete, which in turn made him responsible for Ken's injuries and Luca's situation. If he had just taken a bit of time to make sure that the kid was okay, to actually listen to him. Things were far from okay now.

Still reeling from the terrible aftermath of the accident, Josh had pulled some strings. Instead of turning Pete over to the Feds, Josh had contacted GRIM, who had arranged Pete's imprisonment in a remote facility designed to contain Mods. At the time he hadn't cared about the consequences of dealing with GRIM, he'd just wanted to punish Pete while having the certainty that the boy was locked down and could harm no one else.

Josh looked at Luca and closed his eyes. He hoped to see his love's piercing green eyes light up the room again. Josh put his tanned hand against Luca's olive-hued skin. It was still warm to the touch. Some things never changed. Luca always burned hot. He remembered them scandalously walking hand and hand down the red carpet at the premiere. No one could keep their eyes off of them. Luca was the perfect companion for him. Together they were the personification of tall, dark, and handsome, doubled.

"*Tesoro*?" Luca whispered. It came out dry and quiet, without vivacity. Josh snapped out of his daze and placed his best "everything's going to be okay" smile on his face.

"I'm here," Josh said. He stood, grabbed some ice from the bucket, and leaned over. Josh let the ice drip on Luca's lips and the moisture parted them.

"How was the surgery?" Luca's voice was hopeful.

"How are you feeling?"

"How was the surgery?"

Josh could hear true fear in Luca's voice. He brushed Luca's thick black hair back.

"That bad?"

"We don't have to talk about it right now."

"Then when?"

Josh looked down, unable to look into Luca's worried eyes.

"Tell me." Hardness crept into Luca's demand.

"If you'd just let me take you to New Atlantis—"

"Why?" Worry edged into his voice.

Josh said nothing.

"Just tell me. Why are you delaying this? It's not going to change the news."

Still, Josh couldn't speak.

"Get it over with."

"Look, the surgeon says you're never going to walk again! Don't you understand? He couldn't repair your spinal cord. There's nothing more the doctors here can do for you." The dismayed sorrow on Luca's face made Josh instantly regret his harsh tone and blunt words, but he was tired and scared and angry and just wanted to make things better. Gently, he added, "Jiya can heal you."

"That's enough," Luca said.

"You aren't making sense. You—"

"Don't tell me what I'm thinking. Isn't that part of our whole problem? You somehow still think you're in charge of it all, don't you?" Luca struggled to sit up, but couldn't. His arms were too weak, his body was too heavy, and his legs and spine refused to move. "This isn't going away. I'm going to live like this for the rest of my life." His voice faltered.

"You don't have to. Let me help you." Josh couldn't understand how the whole conversation had gone completely off the rails. He knew why Luca wouldn't leap at the chance for healing, but that didn't change Josh's mind about it.

"I'm not some broken watch or car that you can just mend. I won't take the easy way."

"Why do you have to be so stubborn?"

"Mod powers aren't natural. You aren't supposed to have these abilities."

Josh had hoped that Luca, faced with the full reality of paralysis, would allow Jiya to heal him. That, he realized now, was a fundamental impossibility. In panic, he lashed out. "I can't have this argument again."

"*Tesoro*, I don't know why you were given this—this curse, but God doesn't want this. This is not natural."

"What are you talking about, Luca? This is who I am. Who I've always been. You think that the White Light Wave just gave me abilities, but I say that it awakened me to who I was meant to be. Before that I was just a self-centered actor who didn't care about anyone else. When I changed, when I became a Mod, I got clarity. A purpose. A family."

"I thought I was your family," Luca said coldly.

"You are. And so was my team." Josh swallowed hard.

129

He'd abandoned the team. He wouldn't abandon Luca.

"Is it true?" Luca asked.

"What?"

"The night of the accident, through all the pain I could hear him yelling. Did he come to you for help?" Luca looked straight into Josh's eyes.

"No," Josh quickly said. "Maybe. I don't know." And finally, softly, "yes, I think so."

"That's your answer. All this," Luca tapped his legs, "is your fault. Your inaction and arrogance have led to this."

Josh tried several times to speak, but nothing he could say would make the situation any better.

Luca sank into his pillow. His next words to Josh were cold and distant. "I can't have this conversation with you anymore. You're going to do what you're going to do. I won't let you drag me into that world."

Josh's heart dove into his belly. How could he fix this? "What do you want from me? I thought the point of us being together is to make sure that we are taking care of each other, but you won't let me."

"It's a cheat."

"You won't walk again."

"Maybe. Maybe not. But that's my choice."

Josh threw the plastic ice bucket against the wall. The flimsy container landed with a clatter and splattered ice chips and meltwater all over the floor next to the bathroom, and Josh stared at it in surprise. When was the last time he'd thrown something in frustration and anger? "You infuriate me," Josh said.

"And you, me." Luca dropped his head to the side and looked away from Josh.

"I'm going to make it right." Purpose replaced the despair in Josh.

"Don't do it," Luca said softly.

"I can't see you like this. I won't. Not when I can fix it," Josh said. He kissed Luca. "I love you."

"Don't go. There's still a chance for us if you don't go."

"I will be back. And you will walk again." Josh turned, squared his shoulders, and summoned the courage to walk out.

"You walk out that door, don't bother coming back."

Josh paused for what felt like minutes. He had to make things right for Luca, help him to walk again, even if it meant it was over between them. No one deserved to live a life of paralysis when there was a means to repair it. Especially Luca, who was the other half of his heart. He grabbed the handle, pushed, and hoped for the best.

CHAPTER 19

26 November

"James!" Katrina raised her right arm above her head, using her powers to shield them and prevent them from drowning in the piling sand.

The sand woman

"This is weird."

"You think?"

The sand continued piling on them inside the tiny sitting well at the bottom of the Nilometer.

"We have to get out of here. I don't like this." Katrina's voice shook. The weight of the sand above strained her and sweat beaded on her forehead. The thought of being buried in a confined space overwhelmed her. She was certain the walls were swaying.

"Kat, calm down. I'll get us out of here." James tried to run, but sand on the floor kept him from getting any traction. A raspy voice boomed and the sand retreated.

"You should not be here. That does not belong to you."

"What? What are you talking about?" James looked

around, unable to locate the source of the raspy voice. That they couldn't determine who was there made them more anxious.

"I am the Swarm's protector. I will not spare you."

"The Swarm?" James grabbed Katrina's hand.

"Who's there?" Katrina squeaked. She watched through the thinnest of eye slits as the sand formed into a humanoid shape in front of them.

The sand creation was at least three feet taller than Katrina and proportionally larger, lacking definition. Katrina couldn't tell if the shape was male or female. The merest suggestion of features shaped the face.

"We have to get out of here," Katrina said.

The sand person had required much of the sand in the room to form, leaving less sand on ground. James was finally able to gain traction and raced around the walls in circles, climbing toward the sand creature. James speed-punched, but his fists punched uselessly through the sand. The sand formed hands, picked him up, and held him upside down.

"You cannot find the one. The one is sacred and is ours to take."

"What?"

But instead of clarifying, the sand creature threw him against the wall. James clattered onto the steps, landing in a sandy, gritty heap.

"James! You okay?"

He patted himself down, checking for injuries. "Think so."

Psychokinetic energy bubbled off Katrina, and she levitated herself off the ground. "You're gonna regret that."

"No, I don't think I will," the creature rasped.

A sand avalanche poured mercilessly over Katrina, who created a psychokinetic wall to push the sand back, but it was a fight. The sand moved like a living thing.

James spotted the eye lying on the ground and snatched it up. He placed the eye in front of his face and gasped. "There's a real person!"

"What?" Katrina sent out bolts at the sand creature. "How do you know that?"

"The eye. The sand is being controlled by a woman. I can see her!" James pointed over to the edge of the structure.

Without a word, Katrina manifested a psychokinetic hand that grabbed the sand controller. At once the sand dropped to the floor. She brought the woman closer. The woman was so gritty with sand that at first Katrina couldn't make out her features. Her opponent was not much older than Katrina and had an athletic build.

"Who are you? Why does the Swarm want this eye so much?" James sped around the walls, climbing higher with each revolution.

Katrina glared at the woman and a wave of hatred and intense anger swept over her. It had been quite some time since she had felt such strong emotions. It was far and above beyond what she should have felt, and she wondered if the sand person was manipulating her emotions. She almost lost herself but, helped by the thought that the sand person might be causing it, used the emotions to strengthen herself.

"I will never tell you." The words reverberated in the well like a haunting whisper.

"I'm done playing nice." Katrina's eyes darkened and glittered, and her grip on the woman tightened.

"You caught me by surprise. That won't happen again." The woman twisted her wrist and commanded the sand to form spears that shot across the room directly at Katrina, who erected her psychokinetic shield. The sand spears crashed into the shield and the sand splattered to the ground, landing in muffled clumps. "Pity you can't protect him too."

The sand swallowed James up. As fast as he was, he just couldn't keep his head above the crushing sand.

Katrina saw the fear in James' eyes and reached out to him, but the sand toppled over him. She struggled to levitate him under the onslaught of covering sand but couldn't. Her powers were stretched too thin.

"You can save him or you can take me down. But not both."

She looked back at the woman and cursed her. As she let her go, Katrina blasted the sand away from James and pulled him up. He was safe. The sand pooled on the floor, stripped of its essence, the woman gone.

"What were you thinking? James coughed. "You let her get away."

"I had to save you."

"You could have done both."

"It's not like she got away with everything. We still have the eye, right?"

James slumped and shook his head. Katrina psychokinetically punched the wall in her frustration.

"But I did see everything before. And I think I know what—or who—she was talking about."

"We have to get back to New Atlantis," Katrina said, levitating her teammate.

"Oh no." James leaned against the wall.

"What is it?"

"It's just that. A moment ago I was sure who she was talking about and now…"

"Now what?"

James looked at her in despair. "It's like a dream. The details are slipping away."

"Damn it! Our first real lead into all this and now nothing!" Katrina yelled.

The walls began to shake.

"Kat! Stop. That's not going to help us." James sped to her side. "Let's just get back to the base and sort this out."

CHAPTER
2 0

27 November

"Love what you've done with the place." Josh smiled as he walked into the lush garden of Jiya's ashram. Situated near a park on the western coast of New Atlantis in Ruby Point, Jiya's ashram was dedicated to healing and peace. She had created the sanctuary in

Jiya

her second year on the island as a way to give back to the citizens.

Her students studied and lived a frugal life so they could be a force for peace and understanding. Some of those students were practicing yoga at one end of the garden.

"It's good to see you, *beta*," Jiya said.

She seemed more energetic than when he'd last seen her, and more at peace than ever. She wore a sunshine yellow sari and matching sandals. He came in for a hug and she held tight and long, giving him a surprise healing boost.

"Jiya, you didn't have to do that."

"I know. But it's been too long." She held his hand.

"Come with me."

They walked along a stone path through ornamental trees toward a small bungalow. Jiya sat on a bench swing on the porch and patted the seat next to her. Josh sat uncomfortably next to her.

"Katrina told me that you might get an award for that movie you did."

"That's what they say." Josh wrung his hands and waited silently.

"What's troubling you, *beta*?"

"I need your help." Josh looked down at the porch. "There was an accident. Luca's been hurt. He's paralyzed."

Jiya scooted closer to him and wrapped her arm around his shoulders. "We've no time to lose."

Josh looked at her through red eyes and wanted to immediately leap up and leave, but knew that he couldn't. "It's not that easy." Josh sat wordlessly on the bench swing next to her. Bird chirps and wind chimes tinkling in the light breeze filled the silence.

"How so?"

"Luca doesn't want to be healed by a Mod."

"Then I cannot help you." Jiya took a deep breath.

"Please."

"You ask me to violate Luca's wishes."

"I know that. I know why he doesn't want this help. I just don't understand it, and I certainly can't accept it." Unable to meet her eye, Josh looked at the people tending the garden in front of him. The yellows, reds, and greens all seemed to be brighter after the little healing boost.

"People have to follow their own path and at their pace. Forcing this onto him... Josh, it's not right." She went silent for a long moment. "For instance, healing my leg would have been wrong, although it's entirely within my power to do so."

"Does it pain you?"

"Not much." They sat companionably, listening to the birds and thinking their own thoughts. She clasped his hand.

He was surprised by how soft her strong hands were, despite the wrinkles and obvious yard work.

"You do know that even actions carried out with the best intentions can have unintended consequences?"

He nodded. "But I am supposed to take care of him. It's my fault he's in this condition in the first place."

"You want me to take away his choice."

He could barely look at her. He knew she was right, but he couldn't stop the sharp twist in his heart.

"Go to him. Talk to him again. If he agrees, I will heal him."

CHAPTER 21

29 November

Pierce lay face down on the table, hooked up to monitors. The lab technicians had strapped his legs and arms down. If he reacted as before, those restraints would be necessary.

Warren Grant Pierce

One of the techs popped open the metallic wrestling-style belt to reveal a port and a small crystalized spore that glowed a dim blue. The spore gave Pierce the energy needed to harness his stolen powers.

Surgeon and Builder had figured out how to transfer Mod powers to Pierce via transplants and cybernetic surgeries. Surgeon handled the actual medical work but the transplants alone hadn't been effective. Pierce had needed an external power source to be able to operate the grafted powers, so Builder had developed a belt and port system that Pierce could use as an energy source. The cryospore provided the energy.

Pierce had scoured the earth looking for Mods to supply

his power set, although he had recently found an easier way to locate his next donors.

Surgeon had replaced Pierce's right hand with that of a Russian telekinetic. It had taken Pierce two weeks to recover and accept the new grafted hand, and another two weeks to awaken the power. By the next month, he was levitating jets off the carrier with his stolen power.

Pierce's left arm showed the tanned skin of a certain strong-armed Argentine. His chest bore faint scars from a heart transplant procedure that had granted him self-healing powers. Mixed into the captain's short, gray hair were scars running along each side of his head. One was for his ability to control density and one for his ability to control fire. On the left side of his head was a two-inch cube cybernetic relay mount that controlled his access to teleportation powers.

Today's surgery would give Pierce a personal force field. The unwilling donor was a young Portuguese girl Quentin Washington had captured while she was napping in a library.

Surgeon was a tall, thin Moldavian. Balding, his brown curly hair grayed at the temples. He wore a monocle, and he rarely left the infirmary. If he was trying to look like the stereotypical James Bond villain, he was succeeding.

"The surgery should take no more than two hours to complete. You will be at the ready for the implantation?" Surgeon asked Builder.

"Of course."

Surgeon made his way over to the young girl, who was strapped down in the room's other bed and wearing a power-damping device. He checked her eyes and saw she was conscious.

"Girl, can you hear me?" he asked.

She blinked rapidly and nodded, tears streaming down her face.

"I am going to remove part of your brain stem and attach

it cybernetically to Pierce. It's the only way, since your powers come from your nervous system."

"No!" she wailed.

"You won't feel any pain during the surgery, but you can expect to be paralyzed from the neck down afterward."

The girl began to cry.

"There, there, *crianca*, it will all be over soon."

"I'm ready when you are, Doc." Builder worked on the belt and port system to enable it to fuel yet another power.

"The patients are prepared," one of the lab technicians said.

Another started playing Surgeon's favorite operation music over the room's sound system. The bold intro of Verdi's *Dies Irae* swelled through the room.

The Portuguese girl, who happened to be familiar with the composition and aware that it dealt with Latin funeral rites, screamed.

Surgeon made the initial cut on the girl and blood dripped from his knife onto the floor.

CHAPTER

22

30 November

The pro-registration camp drummed up a sizable turnout for the latest protest in Dini Square. Royal poinciana trees lined the square leading up to the fifty-foot-high arch. Their fiery petals acted like a buffer from the city.

Jaako Aalto

On opposite sides of the arch, thousands thronged shoulder to shoulder in Dini Square waving signs and chanting.

"Register all Mods!"

"Beware the Mod Agenda!"

"Police the powered!"

"The only good Mod is a dead Mod!"

"Mods not welcome!"

Jaako and Arian watched the scene from an open third-floor window of the restaurant Caldera just off the square. They were there for his weekly lunch date with his wife, Birgitta, one of his ways of keeping up public appearances.

Through the window they could hear the chanting, but not quite make out the words. Each side made their points but kept their distance from each other. The Crystal City Police Force stood at the ready in case either side got too rowdy.

"Mods make the world go 'round!"

"Give peace a chance!"

"Mods are people too!"

"Some people are Mods. Get over it!"

"I'm surprised to see this much support here, of all places, for registration. Do you think GRIM or Man First helped get any of these protesters out here?" Arian wasn't alone in feeling like GRIM was stoking the fires between the two sides. With GRIM's affinity for Orwellian doublespeak, she feared they might win the conversation. On the pro-registration side, GRIM had set up tents and volunteers were passing out water and pamphlets.

"Most likely both of them," Jaako said.

Arian was grateful to live in a place where protesting didn't land people in jail, in contrast to her home country of Iran, which had imprisoned Rami for political dissent.

"It's like they don't even realize what a rat's nest of problems registration opens up," he said.

"Right, and if it's like this here, how much support is there globally for registration? A lot of countries aren't as progressive as New Atlantis," Arian said.

The prime minister shrugged. "We always knew the anti-registration stance was going to be an uphill battle. After all, how many people are Mods? And how many people are scared of the Mods?"

The doors of Caldera swung open and Birgitta strolled through, her designer heels clicking on the marbled floor and bringing her height up to a full six feet. Her wavy blond hair fell loose below her shoulders. While she wore the barest hint of makeup, she was devastatingly beautiful, even for a woman of a certain age. While there were rumors she'd had some work done, it wasn't true. She simply took her gym and spa day commitments very seriously.

"Hold that thought." He walked over to greet his wife. They turned their faces to opposite sides and gave a quick kiss. Jaako held up his finger to his wife and crossed back to Arian, who stood a respectful distance away.

Arian turned to him, a frown creasing her brow. "You're not reconsidering your position on this, are you? Is that why you wanted to check out the protest?"

"Of course not. I just wanted to see what we're up against. Who we're up against."

CHAPTER 23

1 December

"Stop!"

"Hold still. It'll be over soon."
The redheaded man's gloved
hands tightened its squeeze
around the other man's neck.

The redheaded man

"Why? I didn't do anything, I
don't even know you." The man
choked out his words as he tried
to pull his attacker's hands away from his windpipe.

For a long moment, the redheaded man said nothing. He
only looked at the writhing, scared man and continued
squeezing. His tanned skin. His blond hair. His lean build.
"You look like him."

"What?" Confusion and disbelief momentarily halted his
struggle.

"Look at this," the redheaded man snarled. He took his
left hand off his victim and pulled his shirt down, revealing
a crusty rash that ran diagonally across his chest.

His victim took advantage of the lessened pressure
around his throat to renew his life-and-death battle.

"Stop that." The redheaded man moved his left hand to the man's head and tilted it so his wide eyes could see the scabs, which pulsed in the street's amber lights.

"Stop, you don't have to do this," the man managed to say.

The redheaded man moved his gloved hand back to the man's throat and squeezed as though he could pop the man's head off if only he exerted enough pressure. The man's eyes bulged and he gurgled. His hands fought the redheaded man's unrelenting grasp, to no avail. At long last, the redheaded man released his victim, who crumpled to the ground, his lifeless eyes glazed in the street's amber lights.

The redheaded man knelt next to the victim and caressed the pustules, which now oozed a blue liquid. He lifted some of the blue oozing liquid and smeared it across the man's forehead. For a moment, peace mingled with relief in him.

A rush and a surge of power coursed through him. His chest vibrated. The blue liquid beaded up on his skin in cathartic release. He panted as the pain subsided. He buttoned his shirt back and leaned against a brick wall.

He had been chasing relief for five years. The more they reminded him of the one who'd nearly killed him, the better it felt at the end. This had been one of the better ones. If only he could get his revenge on Emilio. But those he worked for had prohibited that course of action, citing Emilio's potential importance in certain long-range plans.

A streetlight bathed him in amber and he looked down at the man lying on the ground with a mixture of contempt and gratitude.

"Believe me, buddy. You're better off gone," the redheaded man said. He felt the phone in his pocket vibrate. He pulled out his cell along with a cigarette.

"Henry! It's been a while." He lit the cigarette and inhaled deeply. "No, not interrupting me at all, just cleaning up. What can I do for you?"

"I need you to go to New Atlantis and kidnap Shining and the prime minister during the winter festival."

"The prime minister? You mean Jaako Aalto? That sounds pretty high-level. And a kid?"

"I'll triple your fee."

He considered this for a minute. It had been a while since Henry had contacted him. He knew the Ascendancy was working on a scheme that involved a new energy source. "All right. But I need something else from you." The redheaded man took a slow drag off the cigarette, watching the cherry glow bright.

"Make your request."

"Write this down. Locker 2816 in the Kansas City Union Station. Put that fancy watch of yours, the Excalibur Quatuor, in a bag and leave it with the money. I'll pick it up in two days." He hung up, sucked a long drag off the cigarette and exhaled, considering his next move. Smiling, he drafted and sent a text: "Henry contacted me about the job. Things are going according to plan."

CHAPTER
24

1 December

Nicola breathed in hot and humid air as she took in her new surroundings. New Atlantis was surprisingly lush for a five-year-old island, thanks largely to Juan Pierre and his power of chlorokinesis, but it was no

Juan Pierre Del Bosque

comparison to the Amazon. Rubber trees. Bromeliads. Dozens of varieties of ferns. Liana vines. Toucans. Tree frogs. The Amazon had it all.

"Wow, it's been so long since I've been out in the field, I'd almost forgotten how fun it can be," Bayanai said.

"The instant this trip goes south, I'm going to remind you that you said that," Emilio shot back.

"The instant this trip goes south, I'll take everyone back to Base 47," Waleed promised.

"It is beautiful, though," said Nicola, who rarely went on SENTINELS missions. "I can see why this place is home to so many medicinal compounds."

"What you see here can help you, or it can kill you." The

voice came from behind them, and the team turned to see who had spoken.

"Juan Pierre!" Emilio bounded over to hug the newcomer. "How's the reforestation project going?"

"Pretty good," he said, smiling. He greeted the rest of the team and turned serious. "I'm glad you could get here so quickly. Like I said when I called Bayanai, I'm a bit worried about what I found at that village near here."

"Why don't you explain it?" Bayanai invited.

Juan Pierre del Bosque nodded and paused to gather his thoughts. Juan Pierre, a Colombian, stood about five-foot-six inches and looked every bit a naturalist in the prime of his life. He wore the uniform, at any rate. Green cargo pants with bulging pockets. A khaki vest with more full pockets. A Panama hat that kept his flowing brown hair out of his face. A backpack full of supplies, along with a canteen or two. He was a serious man, slow to crack a smile, but once it came out, more were sure to follow. He walked much lighter now than he did five years before. In those years, he'd dropped nearly fifty pounds. He was a trim man who looked like he might run marathons in his spare time, possibly without needing to train. The White Light Wave event had granted him the power of chlorokinesis, or the ability to stimulate plant life. Wherever he wandered, he left signs of his green thumb, though sometimes the plants weren't evident until a later season. Juan Pierre had spent a month or two on New Atlantis jumpstarting the plant life on the island. He had returned to the island periodically to visit his pals at Base 47, always leaving new plants and trees in his wake. Sometimes, little sprouts and flowers trailed a few steps behind him like a congregation following its minister.

"This whole region is sparsely populated. The people who are here have primitive lives. Huts. No running water. No electricity. At least that's the way it was when I was through here a few years ago. But when I got here yesterday, I saw that had changed. I visited the village chief, and he had a refrigerator. Lights. A television, which seems to always be playing some American sitcom. Still no running water, but definitely some sort of power source."

"What do you mean 'some sort of power source'?" Emilio asked.

"It's weird. That's why I called Bayanai. First, not a single appliance is plugged into any sort of power grid, but they all function. According to the chief, they've had these things for several months. The fridge even has an ice maker, but since there's no running water that part doesn't work." He shook his head. "I walked all the way around the village, looking for the source of power. There were no electrical lines, no easement. Nothing. I looked at the appliances, but I don't understand how they're being powered."

Bayanai looked over at Emilio and sighed.

"But if anyone would have a way to figure out what's going on, it'd be you guys." Juan Pierre reached inside his backpack to pull out a few nuts. "The whole thing could just be plain weird, but I suspect whatever is happening isn't on the up and up." He popped the nuts into his mouth and chewed silently while he waited for the SENTINELS to respond.

"I might have an idea on that," Nicola said.

All eyes turned to the scientist, and she blushed.

"Not too long ago, there was an explosion at a coal-fired power generation plant in the United States. It left a strange residue behind. Investigators called for the help of the scientific community in figuring out what it is. Our team went to the site and collected samples. Hypotheses are all over the place. My own is that the residue came from a new and strong power source that is inherently unstable. Perhaps your strange power source could be like the one from that power gen plant in the US."

"An explosion? Then it's dangerous?" Juan Pierre asked.

Nicola quickly summarized what she knew about the explosion, then added: "If it is what I think it is, it can be. Anything with that much potential to help can have at least that much potential to damage."

"But the Tennessee plant was connected to the grid. This, apparently, isn't connected to anything," Emilio objected.

Nicola thought for a moment. "That could be a variable that the people behind this are testing."

"Can we meet the village chief?" Bayanai asked.

"He probably already knows you're here. He knows everything that goes on in the area. But yes, you must meet him." Juan Pierre motioned them to follow him. They fell in behind him. "Remember what I said. The Amazon is a dangerous place. Try not to touch anything. And watch where you put your feet."

"Still having fun?" Emilio asked Bayanai.

"It's good to be out of the office," he said stolidly.

Emilio shook his head and grinned. His luck kept him from tripping over a thick and woody liana vine snaking across their pathway. Nicola, right behind him, wasn't so lucky. She shrieked as she went down. She put her hands forward to cushion her fall and squealed again as a beetle squished under the weight of her hands. The team instantly gathered around Nicola to help her back to her feet.

"You okay?" Juan Pierre asked.

"Fine, fine. I'd like to wash my hands, though," she said, looking around as though wishing a sink with hot running water and soap would materialize. "Emilio, could you get my sanitizer out and squirt it on my hands?"

As Emilio obliged, Juan Pierre looked at her hands. "You got lucky," he told her.

"Lucky?" She almost shrieked.

"Yes, you could have smushed something much worse. All you got is disgusting. You missed out on dangerous. I'd call it Dr. Patel 1, Amazon 0." He grinned at her. "Now, once again. This time, watch your feet."

After a fifteen-minute walk through the Amazon, they spotted a dozen huts. One was much larger than the rest and stood a distance away from the smaller huts. Juan Pierre approached the door of the chief's hut. "Davi!"

A serious-looking man opened the door and stepped out into the humid air. His thick black hair was cut short. He wore a feather on a cord around his neck and a pair of denim jean shorts.

He nodded at Juan Pierre and looked at the three men and woman behind him.

Juan Pierre and Davi spoke quietly for a few minutes and then Davi backed into his hut. Juan Pierre beckoned the others and followed Davi into his home.

The inside was a study in contrasts. A sleek flat-screen television sat atop a chunk of wood. A woven hammock hung opposite the TV. A refrigerator hummed away. A light shone overhead. The floor was dirt, covered with a woven mat. On a tiny altar sat a clear tube containing a tiny blue glowing orb.

"Wow," Nicola said. "Juan Pierre, could you ask him if I could look at the TV or fridge?"

Davi seemed to understand the words TV and fridge. He stepped toward the TV and beckoned her. He punched the power button on the remote and the television launched its warm-up sequence. Nicola stepped to the side and studied the TV. It had a cord, but it was not plugged into any outlet. There was, however, a lightly humming blue box, about six inches wide, six inches tall and three inches deep, attached to the back of the set. It had a red light indicator, now bright, that read "receiving."

Suddenly, *Seinfeld* interrupted nature's soundtrack, and she jumped.

"Never thought I'd see New York City in the Amazon," Waleed joked. "I like this episode."

Impossible as it seemed, the way the shiny blue orb glowed made it clear it was wirelessly powering the TV and fridge.

Bayanai found the remote and gestured to Davi. "May I?"

Davi cocked his head and nodded.

Bayanai muted Jerry Seinfeld.

Nicola motioned picking up the television and Davi nodded at her. She inspected the unit more closely, paying close attention to the after-market blue box. It felt about as heavy as a flat-screen TV should be. She set it down and wandered over to the fridge. It, too, had an unused electrical plug and its own blue box. Experimentally, she opened the freezer door and peered inside. She spotted a half dozen neatly stacked full ice trays nestled to one side, next to the nonworking automatic ice maker.

"Ice? You made ice?" she asked Davi.

"Is good. Cold." He grinned, his wide teeth gleaming in the reflection of the TV.

"Juan Pierre, ask him when he got all this stuff. How he got it," Bayanai said.

Juan Pierre and the chief conversed. The longer the discussion went, the more Juan Pierre frowned.

"Some white people, one with bright red hair, came to the village a few months ago and brought all the toys. They didn't have a translator, so Davi doesn't know much, although he learned their words for light, TV, fridge, and ice. It was more like show than tell. They showed him the fridge and how it works. They showed him the TV and how to change channels. They gave him the blue orb on that altar and gave him the impression it must remain in his hut. But he doesn't know who the people are. They haven't been back. He is starting to learn Portuguese, Spanish, and English, though, from the programs," Juan Pierre finally reported.

Emilio had frowned the moment he heard "bright red hair" and now spoke up. "Why am I not surprised to find out that Code Red is involved in this?"

"He's not the only redheaded man in the world, but I must admit that is a distinct possibility," Bayanai said. "Juan Pierre, is he the only one with toys or do the other huts have new things as well?"

Another brief discussion—this one much more animated. "Everyone got goodies, and everyone got a blue orb. But Davi says the goodies have divided the village. Some want to embrace the new way of life, and some hold onto the old ways. There have been fights."

Nicola pulled the customized goggles she'd used when investigating the Tennessee explosion from her bag and donned them. She slowly surveyed the room. Viewed through the goggles, the blue orb took on an oily sheen. She took them off and moved toward the altar. In one silent and fluid motion, Davi stood between her and his prized blue orb. His chest bowed out. "No touch."

"Ask him if I can look at it," Nicola said to Juan Pierre.

After a brief discussion, Nicola was allowed to study, but not touch, the blue orb, as Davi hovered protectively next to her.

"Fascinating," she said. "This thing has got to be somehow powering the TV and fridge, using those blue boxes. Maybe this is like wireless charging, only it's wireless power. If so, this is pretty cool stuff. To really figure it out, I'd have to dismantle it, and I don't have any tools with me."

She looked at Davi. "And I suspect he'll protect his new toys as much as he can." She moved back to the TV and Davi relaxed fractionally. "Ask him if I can take pictures of everything, to study it for later."

Juan Pierre and Davi discussed Nicola's request, and Juan Pierre nodded. Nicola pulled out her cell phone and documented the hut, the TV, the fridge, the light, the boxes behind the devices, the unplugged nature of the electronics. When she moved to the blue orb to snap pictures of that, Davi was right by her side.

"No touch," he repeated.

"No touch," she agreed. "Just pictures."

Holding up her phone a few inches away from the clear container encasing the blue orb, she clicked the snap button on her phone. Almost instantaneously, a series of booms sounded. For a few confused moments, Nicola thought taking a picture of the blue orb had caused those explosions.

A lot of things happened at once. People shouted. Following behavior learned from years of training, Bayanai, Emilio, and Waleed all dove to the ground, shielding their heads from anticipated flying debris. Nicola, however, stood still, dumbfounded until Emilio yanked her to the ground. She looked at her camera, then at the blue orb. It was still intact. The room around them was undamaged. Understanding set in and wiped out her confusion.

"That must have been another one of the orbs," she said. "We have to go see."

Davi flew out of his hut but stopped short as he took in the chaos. He sank to his knees. Where there should have been eleven other huts, none remained intact. Only Davi's hut, set apart from the rest of the huts, had been spared from the daisy-chain of explosions.

"Oh my god," Nicola said.

Behind her, Waleed, Bayanai, Emilio, and Juan Pierre

exited the hut.

"You three, go look for survivors in the rubble. Split up. Juan Pierre, tend to Davi," Bayanai ordered.

As one, the team moved. Juan Pierre put his hand on the chief's shoulder, and he jumped at the touch.

The search was a brief one. Waleed, guided by wailing, found two kids near one hut. One had a broken arm, and the other was bleeding copiously from a cut on his head. He pulled them to Davi, who seemed to still be in shock.

The rest of the huts appeared to have been empty. The majority of the village's residents had been away, fishing or gathering plants, and so were spared. The residents streamed back to the village, drawn by the sound of the blasts. Most milled around looking at the destruction and talking in hushed and angry tones, but one administered first aid to the two crying children.

Nicola told Bayanai she wanted to collect evidence from the explosions so she could study it in her labs, and he gave her the go-ahead. Again, she documented the scene with the camera on her phone. She selected one hut and concentrated on it. She located part of a blue box from a small, relatively undamaged flat-screen TV and collected it for further study. Wearing her goggles, she also found plenty of residue similar to what had been found at the Tennessee power gen explosion. She collected that, too. She searched unfruitfully for actual pieces of one of the orbs or one of the containers.

"Bayanai, I have all I think I'm going to get. I'd like to take Davi's blue orb, but I don't want to risk bringing it into my lab. I don't know enough about how to keep it stable, and we don't know what caused the other orbs to explode," Nicola said.

"I don't like leaving that thing here, but you're right, I don't want it at the base either. I wish Waleed could teleport it somewhere, but I'm afraid even that could be a bad idea," he said.

Further discussion was cut off as several of the surviving residents started shouting at Bayanai and his team.

Juan Pierre, the only one who understood the local language, paled. "We have to go, right now. They think we caused the explosion."

Some of the villagers waved knives as they slowly advanced on Bayanai and his team.

"Waleed, now!" Bayanai said.

Waleed looked up, took in the situation, and nodded. He opened a teleportal back to Bayanai's office at Base 47. The shimmering black portal appearing out of nowhere alarmed the villagers, who screamed and ran toward the group.

The team and Juan Pierre hurried through.

Something whizzed past the team and thunked into a wall as the portal closed.

"What was that?" Bayanai asked. A knife that had been fashioned in the Amazon quivered to stillness in a sheetrock wall in the War Room. "That was a close one!"

"Remember how fun fieldwork can be?" Emilio teased.

Nicola stared wide-eyed at the knife and shivered. "I'm just glad they didn't send the orb through."

CHAPTER
2 5

8 December

Pierce was getting used to the feeling of turning his new force field on and off. Each time, he felt a trio of twinges he tried to ignore. One was at the suture site, one in his heart, and one where the cryospore belt's port made contact with his body. Together,

Quentin Washington

they hurt but assured him the transplant was taking.

He spent most of the afternoon bumping around his quarters. Each time he knocked a cup off a table or a book off the shelves, he better understood how to deploy it and what its range was. He learned to extend and retract the length of his field.

This new power was, perhaps, the most important of them all. He would now have protection from energy blasts, bullets, gas and, he hoped, telepaths. God, he hated telepaths. Worst of the powers. No one else should ever be in his head.

He tried a force field again and the twinges trebled in

intensity. He frowned. This shouldn't be happening already. He'd only deployed a dozen—or maybe two dozen—practice force fields. Or had it been more? He'd been having so much fun, he'd lost track.

Something clattered to the floor behind him, and he spun around, instinctively activating his force field. He doubled over. His heart pounded. His sutures pulsed, and a trickle of blood oozed from them. The energy flowing from the port flared and dried up. He fell to the floor and curled up. From that vantage point, he could see what had fallen. It was the sword he had taken off of Quentin Washington the first time he'd practiced with telekinesis. The fixture that was holding it was halfway out of the wall. For a moment, he was lost in the pride of that success, recalling how he had telekinetically tormented Washington with the sword for several long minutes before taking mercy on the man. Then the pain brought him back to reality.

It was too soon for this to be happening. He rolled onto his back and pressed a switch on his belt. The metal buckle popped open and he propped himself up against the wall.

He had depleted his supply of cryospore energy.

"You got this." He pushed his feet to the ground and grunted with the exertion needed to slide up the wall to standing. He needed to switch out the cryospores. And quickly. He only had a brief amount of time to make the replacement; otherwise, he might not be able to control any of the powers.

Builder had worked alongside Surgeon to perfect a method that allowed Pierce to operate the stolen superpowers by drawing on the energy generated by the cryospore. However, each additional power sucked up energy reserves at a faster rate. The more powers Pierce acquired, the more quickly his cryospore drained. Builder had told him part of the reason for the quicker cycles is that the powers were at constant war with Pierce since he had acquired them in an unorthodox fashion.

Surgeon and Builder had both cautioned him against running out of cryospore energy. Each had described consequences ranging from upsetting to terrifying. The powers might atrophy and never fully replenish if left unpowered too long. Even worse, the powers might turn on him and eat away at him like a cancer. Sweat beaded on his forehead as he fumbled the combination into his pressurized, refrigerated safe.

"Come on."

The lock opened and he flung open the door. An icy mist engulfed the room. Inside was a new cryospore clump to insert into the port in his belt. His hands shook as he placed the spent clump into the containment unit and carefully grasped the new one. Need and fear clouded his vision. He took a deep breath and with dexterity belying his age, popped the cryospore into the port in his buckle. A click and whirr signified the process was complete.

Pierce clamped the buckle and sighed. Relief surged through his body as the cryospore glowed blue. Color seeped back into Pierce's face.

Pierce studied the calendar and his cryospore inventory and calculated. At the rate he was using them up, he'd have none left by New Year's Day. He needed an endless supply. No more simply accepting some from the Ascendancy and acquiring the rest he needed by skimming off of the supply chain. His life now depended on securing unlimited cryospores. And if the Ascendancy thought they were going to keep him begging for scraps like some whacked-out junkie, they had another think coming.

His eyes flashed.

He headed to the Training Room, where a mock battle was in progress. He stopped to watch.

"You can't keep avoiding the fight, Washington!" Jimin, an overly muscled Mod, shouted as she charged him. "Being Pierce's right-hand man won't save you." She threw a metal bench at the tall African-American soldier. "And I don't give a rat's ass that you and Flame are together. She can't save you if she isn't here."

"You don't scare me, Brute." Washington sidestepped her punch. His years in the Marines had taught him well. He knew when to fight and when to play it safe. While he was built like a brick house, he had the energy of full health and youth. Understanding that being bald was a choice but balding was not, he had recently shaved his head. "I'm not gonna help you increase your strength."

"Butcher!" Jimin urged the vicious German toward Washington. "Sic him!"

Butcher snarled and rushed at Washington. Butcher was already foaming at the mouth, a sure sign of his further descent into mindless savagery.

Washington danced away to avoid Butcher's advances. He snagged a bo staff from the weapons shelf and twirled it.

The snarling and foaming German launched himself at Washington.

Washington slammed the bo staff down on Butcher, bringing him to the ground.

Butcher rolled over as Washington slammed the staff toward him a second time. Butcher chomped it into two separate pieces.

Washington paused briefly as he took this in before breathing, "Oh shit," and backing toward the ropes.

"Poor little human, no match for a Mod." Jimin closed in on him.

Butcher was up again. He bared his sharpened nails and leapt at Washington. Washington tried to slip out of the way.

"Not so fast, Washington!" Pierce telekinetically lifted Washington off the ground. "Get back over there and fight like a man."

"What? Not all of us have powers."

Pierce telekinetically floated Washington into the boxing ring in front of Butcher's clawing hands. "Fight."

Pierce thought he would see terror flash in Washington's eyes, but instead the man was steadfast. That resolve pleased him.

"Do you think you could handle this?" Pierce said as he brought Washington closer to Butcher, who was clawing to maim him.

Washington said nothing. He focused only on Butcher.

"Get him!" Jimin shouted. She toyed with the ring's ropes in her meaty hands. But she wasn't paying attention. Pierce telekinetically picked Butcher up and slammed his claws into her. Jimin screamed.

"Get up," Pierce said. "You can take a simple blunt force."

"Not so simple." Jimin held her bleeding side. Even the increased strength and resilience she got from her powers wouldn't counteract the loss of blood.

"Now, Washington. You have her in your sights."

Washington took the broken bo staff pieces in his hands and charged the bleeding Korean, intending to deliver a knockout blow. As soon as he ran toward them, Pierce levitated Butcher into his path. There was a fantastic crash as flesh shredded and bones cracked.

"Never take your eye off of any of your enemies. You must be aware of all your adversaries at all times." Pierce telekinetically dropped Washington to the ground. "You know this. After all these years by my side, you know this."

Pierce turned to Jimin, grasped her with his tanned grafted arm, and lifted her up so they were eye to eye.

"You want to be my second-in-command over Flame. You need every advantage you can get. Viciousness, callousness, and cunning will only take you so far." Pierce telekinetically threw Butcher against the wall, knocking him out, then pointed at him. "Both of you get down to the infirmary and have Surgeon take care of you. You'll be fine. I just hope you learned a lesson here."

CHAPTER
2 6

10 December

Roger looked up in surprise as his door swung open, instantly on alert. No one barged into his office. Everyone knocked and waited for admission.

Henry Hastings

Everyone, that is, except for the man in his doorway.

"Henry! What are you doing here?"

"These are my offices, are they not?" Henry stepped into Roger's tidy office and let the door shut behind him.

"I wasn't expecting you for another week—"

"Things are progressing at a pace that requires I visit."

"How was your flight?"

"A bit turbulent." Henry made himself comfortable on the couch.

"Scotch then?" When Henry nodded, Roger pulled a bottle of Macallan 18 out of his lower right desk drawer, along with a tumbler. He poured and handed Henry the drink. Anything to take the edge off. "What do—"

"Stop wasting my time." Henry sniffed the Macallan and frowned. "No ice?"

Roger called an assistant and asked for a glass of ice to be delivered to his office immediately. Roger and Henry passed an uncomfortable two minutes in utter silence. Once a single cube of ice had joined the scotch in his tumbler, Henry sighed and drank deeply. At last, he spoke. "The cryospore. You said we need a safer transport containment system and to figure out a way to extract it while maintaining the integrity of the Antarctic Ice Shelf."

"Of course. I want to make sure the shelf doesn't calve because of the drilling and extraction processes, but the only way so far that we can get the cryospores out of the ice is quite detrimental." Roger smiled at his boss. "After all, we aren't in the world destruction business anymore, right?"

"We've grown beyond that. And I've just the solution for our little problem." Henry removed a magazine from his coat and tossed it to Roger.

Roger glanced at the cover. "I don't get it."

"You're a scientist, Roger, you should." Henry sipped and closed his eyes in pleasure as the scotch coursed through his system.

Roger looked at the cover. It touted the prime minister of New Atlantis as a revolutionary world leader. "He's a Mod. One who can control and create ice."

Henry smiled. "That solves one problem. Then there's Shining and his force field. Between the two of them, Shining's force field can contain things and Jaako can keep it cool, so to speak."

Roger tried to keep his face neutral. "You want us to use these Mods in the extraction process?"

"They'd be effective."

"That's not a sustainable answer, Henry."

"We have a timeline, and you haven't come up with a

better one yet. This buys us both time."

Roger held in a sigh. "Your suggestion would probably work."

"I'm having one of my agents take care of the abductions. Just make sure the Antarctic base is ready for them."

"Of course." Roger stood to walk Henry out.

"Tread easy with Pierce. I fear his powers are affecting his frame of mind more than we anticipated."

"And if that's the case?"

"Then we do what we've done with other problems. Take care of it in the Dark Past room." Henry opened the door.

"And Arthur?"

A flicker of surprise crossed Henry's face. He closed the door and turned to Roger.

"I don't mean to pry, but he's been in and out of the office lately. I've heard he's been taking some extended trips to—"

"Let me take care of my son," Henry said in a voice that left no room for argument.

CHAPTER
27

11 December

"Again," Bayanai said as he flipped George onto his back. George landed on the mat with a thud. He slowly rolled over and sighed. Bayanai offered his hand and George took it.

Bayanai Romrico

"I'm never going to make it, am I?" George wiped sweat from his forehead. He had been on Base 47 for about three weeks. Every day he had been training in some fashion. Personal trainers guided his weight-training exercises. Emilio helped him hone his powers and increase his ability to stay in someone's mind. He pushed George to expand his creativity.

"Don't think that way. You've only been here a little while," Bayanai said.

"Yeah, and I'm sore in places I never thought I had." A chagrinned smile swept across George's face.

"Then it's working. Remember, this is a process. We all start off at zero." Bayanai charged George, who completely unprepared. Bayanai body slammed him to the ground. He jumped back up and took a few steps back.

"What was that for?" George asked.

"You have to prepared for anything. That's the best we can do here. Whether you're a SENTINEL or just living your life. Be aware of your surroundings and keep alert."

George slowly got up. "Okay, but maybe don't take me down so hard."

"No can do. Your enemies will never allow you that kindness." Bayanai threw a roundhouse kick, which George barely dodged.

"You can't always rely on your powers. If they have power dampeners, then what? You have to be strong. That's why we're working you so hard." Bayanai closed his eyes and recalled his own tough training under a much harder mentor, Captain Pierce.

George lunged at Bayanai, who ducked and swept George's feet to the ground. It was the last straw.

"Stop!" George yelled, but not just out loud. He had jumped into Bayanai's brain and was now in charge of the team leader. Bayanai's body stiffened as he struggled against George's control. George walked Bayanai over to face the mirror. He could feel Bayanai fighting with every fiber of his being, but he wasn't going to let go. Not that easy. He forced Bayanai to stop breathing and to watch himself as his face turned blue. Panic filled Bayanai's eyes and still the breathing wouldn't come. George refused to relinquish control until moments before Bayanai was on the verge of passing out. Before he hopped out, he left a souvenir in Bayanai's mind. It was an almost imperceptible image that was the sum total of George's dream.

Bayanai gasped as air rushed into his lungs. Once he'd caught his breath, he grinned at George. "There you go, George. I was waiting for the fighter to show up."

"That's what all this was for?" George asked.

Bayanai nodded. "It's the only way you're going to get better. And what exactly did you leave in my mind? I can feel it, but every time I come close to remembering it, it just disappears." Bayanai threw the towel into the hamper.

George looked down. "I left a souvenir. A framed photo. Like the ones in the hallway. But I'm on the team too."

Bayanai nodded at him. "Good work today, George. You just might have what it takes."

George beamed.

"You're coming to the festival tomorrow right?"

George's eyes lit up. He had heard the entire base buzzing about the winter festival, but he had not gotten a formal invitation. Finally, he'd be at the party, instead of just hearing how amazing it was. He had trouble keeping his smile from bursting from his face.

CHAPTER
28

12 December

"Looks a lot different than it did the last few times we came here, hmm?" Focus asked.

Maggie glanced around and nodded. "It's hard to believe how quickly Crystal City has grown up. From nothing but a rocky island to this. Almost a million people in less than five years."

They passed through Dini Square on their way to the Museum of Happiness, a contemporary art museum on the southern edge of the plaza. An absurdist sculpture that reminded Maggie of an upside down, deconstructed armadillo greeted them at the door. Inside, the walls of the museum were covered in large-scale paintings. Some were just splatters of paint, and others used found pieces to tell a cheerful story.

They walked by Bayanai, who nodded at them. He was with two other SENTINELS she recognized, but also a wide-eyed guy who had a bounce in his step and a grin that he couldn't wipe off. She had expected them to be helping with security but they were headed out of the event. She wondered what would call them away from a party like this.

It was already dark on the island, and Crystal City was lit

up for the festivities. A thirty-foot-high evergreen tree was decked with what appeared to be rose quartz crystal ornaments, hung alongside white lights and silver garland. Focus had gotten some footage of the tree in the daytime and now trained his camera on it for a night shot. After, he turned to Maggie and saw Luli hurrying their way in a sleeveless dress.

"Hi, Maggie. The prime minister will be along soon, and you can ask some of the lighter questions you didn't cover during your interview earlier today. But you only get five minutes. That's about all I can manage to keep others away for," Luli said.

"OK, thanks. Remind me, about how many people are on hand for the party tonight?"

"Close to two thousand. Some residents of the island will be here, as well as dignitaries from other countries. Ah, here's one of the scientists, Dr. Yukio Watanabe." Luli gestured at a woman wearing a bright yellow party dress.

Focus trained his camera on the scientist.

"Dr. Watanabe, good evening. I'm Maggie Adams. How is everything at the lab?" Maggie asked.

"It's good. Lots of interesting research into how everyone's powers work, and why they work. We're making good progress, and it's a great research environment. In fact, Dr. Patel's finishing up some work on this at the lab and will be late to the party."

"What can you tell me about the applications of your research?"

"The holy grail of this type of research is to figure out if there are latent powers in people, and if so, how to activate them. There are a lot of unknowns," Yukio said.

"Good luck with your research," Maggie said. "Focus, why don't you see about getting footage inside?"

Focus peered into the magnificent assembly hall. Guests

circulated and waiters passed trays of appetizers. On stage a string quartet played holiday music. He looked at Maggie, flashed three fingers, and was off with his camera.

Smiling, Maggie turned back to Luli. "Has Sying had any problems adjusting to the schooling system here?"

"Not at all, actually. She's excelling and recently started taking violin lessons. She surprises me every day. I love seeing her experience and learn," Luli said with a beam of parental pride that Maggie had never felt.

"Are you willing to talk off the record about your family?"

"Depends."

"Are they coming tonight?"

"The children are inside with Yi. I'll join them when Arian gets here to help you."

"Babysit me," Maggie teased.

"Maybe a little of that," Luli acknowledged.

"So, again, the force field, that belongs to your son?"

"Yes. It was quite a shock to find out I'd lost it. But I'm grateful to know he'll be as safe as possible with it. And the island's very safe."

"But is it?" Maggie asked. "Someone managed to kidnap Emma, didn't they?"

"Where did you hear that?"

"Luli, I'm a reporter. Any leads?"

"You did need a babysitter, it seems," Luli muttered. "We've been searching for her."

"I hope you find her. I liked her from the first time I met her, back at the beginning of all this." Maggie gestured at the island in general. "Spunky kid."

Just then, the prime minister arrived with his wife, Birgitta, and his chief of staff, Arian.

"Hello, Ms. Adams. I seem to have caught you without your cameraman," Jaako said. He was dressed in a classic black tux, and his wife wore a champagne-colored floor-length satin gown.

"Perhaps I'll catch you inside, then, Prime Minister?" Maggie asked.

He nodded, but before he could head into the party, Emilio appeared at the prime minister's side, apparently neither noticing nor recognizing Maggie without Focus by her side. He tapped Jaako on the shoulder.

"Sir, Laura just alerted us to some unexpected Mod activity across town. The team has gone to check it out."

CHAPTER
2 9

12 December

"Wake up, kid, it's time to work."
The voice belonged to Captain
Pierce. The overhead lights flared
on.

Emma Sheehy

The child groaned and pulled
her pillow over her face.

"No," she said, her words
punctuated with preteen angst. "Sleep."

"Work first, and then more sleep. Or breakfast, if you
like."

To this, she simply squeezed the pillow down harder into
her face. Her left leg hung off the twin size cot, toes inches
from the floor.

"If you find me what I want, I'll see to it that the kitchen
makes you waffles and bacon for breakfast," Pierce said.

"Not hungry. Need sleep."

"Up, Emma. It's time to work."

"What do you want?" Resigned.

"Same as always. Just go see who's out there," he said.
"And if you don't do this quickly, it's going to be even

longer before you get to go back home."

She couldn't read his mind to see the falsity of his statement, but she didn't need to. She knew him. No, he wouldn't send her back home. Escape from this boat was unlikely, but she hoped her teammates would finally rescue her. She worried, actually, that they hadn't come yet, and she worried that anger, followed by despair, loomed around the corner. Just how long had she been there? And what sea were they in, anyway?

Emma slowly sat up, looked down at her purple pajamas, and frowned. They smelled like thousands of haunted dreams. She rubbed her eyes trying to find some semblance of normalcy in this nightmare. She finger-combed her thin blond hair, which hung in tangles. Whatever they were giving her clouded her brain, making coherent thought almost impossible. This fog she had been living in was an easy escape. If only she could pretend she were somewhere else. Someplace fun. But the horrors kept dragging her back.

"Emma." Pierce's voice was cold and commanding.

Startled, she looked at Pierce and, behind him, Alrick. Her stomach spasmed. Pierce had become gruesome in the time since his split from the Base 47 team. He didn't look like a regular military man anymore. He had changed more than her, and she was twelve now. He looked cobbled together. She fought down revulsion. He wore camo, but with a wide black belt. Its centerpiece was a massive belt buckle showcasing a ping pong ball-sized glowing blue orb, and she wondered again at its purpose. He wouldn't worry about the way accessories looked, so this belt must be functional. But to do what? Could she somehow exploit that? She studied him, waiting for him to direct her search. He looked repulsive but also tired, and she wondered why, grateful she'd never been able to read his mind.

Alrick sneered at her from behind Pierce. If Pierce

frightened Emma, her feelings for Alrick were closer to pure, unadulterated terror. He was old and balding. Vivid but small blue eyes glared out from under nearly invisible eyebrows. His white-and-gray chin curtain emphasized a humorless mouth. As she looked at Alrick, she felt the tickling in her mind that was his prelude to taking control. She closed her eyes and resisted him. Sweat beaded on her forehead, and she retained autonomy for ten precious seconds. Ten seconds of alone. Ten seconds where she wasn't Emma, the captured Mod. Ten seconds where she wasn't Emma, the Mod Hunter. Just plain, regular Emma. And it was glorious. Better than last time. No tears this time; she didn't let them see her weak.

Without choosing to, she opened her eyes.

"I'm ready," she said, speaking as Alrick directed.

Pierce propped the door so it stood slightly ajar, just enough to deactivate the room's ability to dampen her powers. A red light flashed on the panel next to the door, indicating the power-dampening circuit had been broken. When Pierce closed the door once again, the completed circuit would once again dampen the telepath's powers. It wouldn't affect his own or Alrick's powers because Builder had tuned the system specifically to block Emma's powers. Opening the door, of course, broke the circuit and allowed her to use her powers, but under Alrick's guidance.

"Go find a Mod you haven't found yet," Pierce said.

With Alrick the puppet master directing her, she had no choice. She could think her own thoughts and she didn't think he was privy to those, but she couldn't act her own actions. He directed those with a heavy hand. Alrick forced her to cast her mind out, seeking the powers that had originated with the summer solstice five years previous.

Pierce stood by her bed, watching her with greedy impatience. The sooner she found someone, the sooner he would go away. But what would he go and do? Dare she ask?

"Come on, child, you should have found someone by now," Pierce interrupted.

"She's searching," Alrick said.

For some reason, Tio Carlos felt very close to Emma, even though she knew he was dead. Alrick was directing her movements, but she tested the boundaries like any child or unwilling participant. She tried to send her mind out to the SENTINELS while simultaneously continuing the search for other Mods. She gasped when Alrick tightened his grasp on her actions. Had he understood her intent?

She missed her friends, and she missed the family life she'd had back in Ireland before Base 47 happened and before the car wreck that had robbed her of her parents. She had been so cut off from other humans since she'd been on the boat that she even wished she could hear prophecy in her head again. The voice hadn't spoken to her in years. She had never felt so far removed from everyone, and it made her sad and angry. Why hadn't her friends rescued her yet?

She yawned and rubbed her eyes again. Tired. So tired of trying to rescue herself.

She kept thinking, trying to find a way out of this problem. She needed to offer up someone who would be satisfactory. But what would happen to the person she found? Who could she show him?

Emma sought powers, still directed by Alrick the puppet master.

"She has someone in Alaska who can speak with cats and dogs and other animals," he said.

"Tag him," Pierce said.

Emma created a connection between the two of them that would allow her to find the animal-talker when needed, and let him out of her mind.

"He's tagged," Alrick said.

"Again," Pierce demanded.

Emma slumped in her bed and, directed by a shove from Alrick, sent her mind back out for the new search.

"Enhanced smelling ability, in Paris?" she asked.

"Tag him," Pierce ordered.

"He's tagged," Alrick said.

"Again," Pierce said.

Thinking about Tio Carlos, Emma sent her mind back out, specifically seeing strength, but she only found Pierce, which confused her. She tried seeing teleportation, hoping to find Waleed, but all she locked in on was Pierce. Another confusing result. She finally found a teleporter in Belarus, and said so.

"Tag him," Pierce said.

"He's tagged," Alrick reported.

Emma's heart sank. What did he want?

A few minutes later, still under Alrick's direction, she located an old man with remote vision. She sent a mental apology to him while Alrick told Pierce what she'd found.

"Good, where is he?" Pierce grinned a horrible grin and rubbed his hands together.

"In Paraguay. He's reading his grandson a story," she said.

Suddenly, Alrick was gone from her mind. Despite her relief at his abrupt departure, she felt wrung out and dirty. Violated. Never before had she wanted a shower so desperately. When these cretins left, she'd have her shower and mull over why she'd fixed on Pierce during her searches for strength and teleportation.

Where were her friends?

CHAPTER 30

12 December

Jaako frowned at Emilio. "That doesn't work for me. Leave some of the SENTINELS here."

Emilio glared at him in disbelief. "What?"

"I need the whole world to see that the Mods are no threat. I need some SENTINELS here at the party to show that. How else am I going to have any success with the anti-registration act?"

Emilio grabbed Jaako's arm. Three feet away, Jaako's security detail bristled. Emilio might be a SENTINEL and cleared for interaction with the prime minister, but this was clearly unwanted, potentially aggressive contact.

Jaako looked at Emilio's hand and then at his face. "Let. Go."

Emilio did, and the security detail relaxed fractionally. "We don't know what kind of Mods we'll be up against, so we need access to all our powers. We'll be back when we can." He strode off before Jaako could say anything else.

Arian approached and smiled at the prime minister. "It's time for your speech. Come with me."

Trying to conceal a frown, he followed his chief of staff

to the outside podium and glanced around. He knew monitors inside the hall would show his speech. He spotted Maggie and her cameraman, as well as the official Crystal City staff cameraman. Ever the politician, he smiled for the cameras.

"I am so pleased to have all of you here for our winter festival. You know, growing up in Finland, we never had a shortage of snow. In fact, it was one of the best things about winter, the snowy landscape. It was the wonderland of my childhood.

"But here on New Atlantis, we don't have the pleasure of a winter like that. We have wonderful weather here, and life here is beautiful. We are so grateful for the privileged life that we all live here. Our tiny island is only five years old, and our nation even younger, but we have accomplished so much already. It is a grand experiment, a truly multicultural nation. We pride ourselves on our commitment to the values of equality, freedom and liberty. I welcome the world to visit our nation. See our black sand beaches, the Pele Rain Forest. Take in an opera. Admire the contemporary art here in the Museum of Happiness. See just how much we have accomplished in such a short amount of time. New Atlantis is the green and pleasant land you've always dreamed of." Jaako raised his arms in the air in a sign of victory.

"Although I absolutely love the weather here in Crystal City, I still long for the snow of my childhood during this festive time of the year." Jaako raised his hands again. Focus sharpened his camera on the prime minister. Tiny snowflakes appeared, lightly dusting the area.

"Snow!" Shining shouted.

Jaako smiled as he watched Luli's children try to catch the snow in their hands. Luli and Yi grinned at their delight.

"Happy holidays to all!" Jaako proclaimed as the snow fell gently from the sky. He bathed in the happiness and wonder of his audience.

Five years ago, he never would have dreamed of showing his power to another person, let alone showcasing it during a speech. After he was exposed as a Mod, he thought his political aspirations were destroyed. According to polls, however, his ice powers somehow humanized him. He and Birgitta had not struggled much with the decision to leave Finland to become New Atlantis colonists, as they thought he had a high chance of winning the island's first election for prime minister. He'd been a popular leader, running a tight and efficient government and refusing to push through bloated budgets that would sink the island's nascent economy. Like any planner, he was always thinking about his next steps. In this case, it was the philanthropic foundation he would start when he finally left office. He already had a good start on the funds for that.

As Jaako looked out from the balcony, he saw children run to investigate the white fluff. Some had never seen snow in real life.

Arian smiled as she walked up to him. "Looking very good, PM," she said. "Let's go back to the hall. I've got plenty of people you must be photographed with."

"How do you think this will play?"

Arian cocked her head and considered. "This plays right into your Families First campaign as well as shoring up your base with the right. Contrasting this with your stance against powers registration, you are in a very good place."

"That's what I thought, too. It's never too early to think about the next election, even if it's years away," he said as they entered the hall. He noticed a redheaded man making a beeline right to them. "Arian."

She rushed to intercept the man.

"I'm sorry, but the prime minister is not meeting with anyone at this moment," she said. "You look familiar, but

I'm sure we haven't met." She extended her hand. "I'm Arian Nassar, Prime Minister Aalto's chief of staff."

The redheaded man maneuvered around her and approached Jaako directly. "Prime Minister Aalto. Nice to see you." The redheaded man extended his hand to shake.

Reflexively, Jaako shook his hand and smiled his politician's smile at both Arian and the newcomer. "Arian, go get Maggie and her cameraman so I can do the interview I promised her," Jaako watched her walk away, then turned back to the newcomer. "How can I help you?"

"I'm glad you asked. Come with me."

"Where? Why?" Jaako asked.

Instead of answering these questions, the man pulled out his phone. He punched the screen a few times and held it out for Jaako to see.

Jaako absorbed the information on the tiny screen, and the color drained from his face, leaving him almost as white as the snow he'd created outside. "How did you find out about my foundation's seed money?" His voice rasped, hoarse with concern about the career-ending documents in the stranger's possession.

"Doesn't matter. Fact is, I know, and I'm not the only one. Looks like kickbacks to me. That's grounds for impeachment, isn't it?" The man circled around Jaako as if he were chum in the water. "As I said, I need you to come with me."

"Why? Who are you?"

"Who I am is inconsequential. Who I represent is important. And, of course, what I want."

Jaako stood his ground. "What do you want?"

"You may have heard we have a real global energy crisis at hand. My employers have located the next clean energy."

"What does that have to do with me?" Jaako asked.

"Well, it's in quite a precarious place. A little difficult to retrieve at the moment. That's where you come in. My employers require your special abilities to securely extricate the cryospore."

"Special abilities?"

"Your ice."

"You need me to give you some ice?"

He grinned a grin with too many teeth. "It's much more complicated than that."

Jaako leaned toward the man and the temperature dropped significantly. The man's chin quivered. Across the room he noticed his security detail detect the chill. He shook his head and they relaxed.

"Then explain it to me before I freeze you any further. What is a cryospore?"

"I wouldn't do that if I were you," he said through chattering teeth. "Be a shame if I have to reveal this." With great effort the man took out a device and showed a few images to Jaako. Immediately, Jaako let the heat return. What he had seen was enough to warrant further discussions.

"And I need more than just you."

"I don't understand."

"I need him." The redheaded man pointed at Luli's son.

"Shining?" Jaako asked. "Why?"

"Simple. We need your ice, his force field."

"Why not just approach Luli and see if she'll help?"

"She'd never agree."

Jaako's eyes narrowed at the newcomer. "This is a kidnapping?"

"Kidnapping." The redheaded man smiled and his face tilted to the left. "Just a matter of perspective."

"No. If you want me, fine. But I will not help you take Shining." Jaako stared at the redheaded man with all the authority he had.

"You misunderstand me. It's going to happen. You are going to help. And you are going to come along with me." He placed his arm around the prime minister like they were frat brothers.

"You can't expect me to—"

"Oh, but you will. All you have to do is distract the parents in five minutes, then come to the back exit of the museum without your security detail. And it will all be over. Just to make sure that you comply, I will be entertaining your lovely wife."

Jaako frowned, worried what kind of damage this might do to his reputation and future, along with his marriage and the nation if he did not follow his orders.

"As long as I let you take the boy—"

"We need you, too."

"Right. What kind of assurances do I have that we won't be killed?"

"Assurances are for pussies, Jaako. This is serious. You're scared. But if you come through as requested, I'll make sure you are both returned home safely."

"You'll never make it out of New Atlantis without the SENTINELS knowing."

"You're kidding me, right?" He laughed. "You should really take a closer look at your security protocols. Not as tight as you would think." The redheaded man backed away from the head of New Atlantis and pointed at the Excalibur Quatuor on his wrist. "Tick tock, prime minister."

CHAPTER

31

12 December

About an hour after telling Captain Pierce exactly where to find the Paraguayan with night vision, Emma received breakfast, carried by a cafeteria worker. It was as promised. Waffles and bacon along with a glass of milk

Surgeon

and another of orange juice. It smelled terrific, and she realized she was famished.

She had long ago given up the pretense of civility. She pulled the tray up to her knees while she was still in bed.

As was her custom, she said grace over her meal. It was more a way to keep her parents near her than a religious act, as she had lost much of her faith since being captured by the Tribe. She lifted a slice of bacon and began to eat. As she chewed, she realized something marvelous. For some reason, the power dampener in her room was off. The unmuted voices of another's thoughts crashed into her mind; the cafeteria worker was at once scared of and scared for Pierce, which intrigued her.

She saw fragments of the worker's memories: Pierce creating a teleportal, Pierce exerting super strength, Pierce telekinetically flying objects through the air. Pierce had a number of new powers, each associated with a different body part. Guilt crushed over her. However he got those powers, she might have helped him steal some of them.

"Hurry up," he said. "I need to get back to the caf."

She said nothing. She munched slowly on her waffles and drew out her meal as long as she could. This was a golden opportunity not to be wasted.

Then she cursed her stupidity. The power dampener was broken. Why was she wasting her time and power on this nothing cafeteria worker? She tried knocking in the minds of everyone she knew. She tried Waleed most often because of his ability to teleport. No one else could directly rescue her.

No one answered. What was wrong with her?

Too soon, her plate was clean and she reluctantly handed it to him. She was once again left alone. She was so lonely. She even missed being in school.

Her inability to reach her friends demoralized her. She sank back into her bed and tried not to think about what might be happening to the man with night vision. She felt sorry for him and didn't know what to do. Sooner or later, Pierce would be back, wanting more. What would she do? Who would she give him?

With any luck, she would have managed to get off the boat before he came back asking for another person with special powers. But if not, she needed a plan. As her pa had liked to say, the best defense is a good offense. Escape would be the best offense, but now she needed another plan. As she lay there, she thought about ways to get her location to the people on Base 47, since she couldn't telepathically reach anyone.

Carefully, she lay still in bed while she thought and tried to reach out for rescue. She wondered how long it had been and when she might have dinner. The waffles and bacon hadn't stuck around very long, and she was hungry again.

The door to her room burst open, and she knew immediately there was trouble. It wasn't the cafeteria boy. It was Pierce, and he strode purposefully to her bed, trailed by Surgeon.

"Get up." Pierce barked at her.

Emma played at being rousted from a satisfying nap, but she could see on his face he didn't buy it. He looked angry. There was something frighteningly familiar in his eyes, an anger she'd seen many, many times back in Base 47 in Texas. And even though she was once so confident and self-assured, something about Pierce made her feel defenseless.

"We've had a technical difficulty. It seems the power dampener here for your room is acting up. We have to make alternative arrangements." He pointed at Surgeon, who held up a syringe full of blue liquid and crept menacingly toward her.

"No, don't!" Emma pleaded. As he neared she gasped. She couldn't breathe. Her throat tightened. Her pulse raced. Her vision blurred.

Surgeon advanced and Emma shrank back in her bed. He loomed over her, holding the syringe in front of him. She fought, and she screamed, but in the end, Surgeon planted the needle in her arm and delivered the foul power-dampening formula.

Emma felt all the hope she'd ever had leave her. She crumpled back into the bed and wept. She could see what Surgeon, still standing behind Pierce, was thinking. It terrified her.

As Emma drifted into oblivion, she had one last thought: that she was grateful she didn't have to see what was in

Surgeon's head anymore. She slid into a dream of her old dance studio.

CHAPTER
3 2

12 December

CoCo closed her eyes again and willed herself back to sleep. But the whirr of the engines and howl of the wind did not comfort her tonight. She rolled over again in her bed. The clock said 1:00 a.m., but she could have sworn it was later. She had not slept well for weeks. It was these moments at night, alone in her cabin, that she struggled most with the burden of her undercover mission.

She missed sleeping easy next to Emilio in their bed on New Atlantis. Would this nightmare never end? Would she be able to help the SENTINELS stop Pierce before he went overboard? These thoughts plagued her, but they were not top of her mind. Top of her mind was trying to make sense of something she thought must be a dream. She didn't remember dreaming it, but her recollections of it had that hazy quality of all dreams relived upon waking. She replayed it on the video screen in her mind as she lay in her bed.

It all started in a dance studio. When she made her way to the barre and looked at the dark mirror reflection of herself, she recognized it. She was in Emma's dance studio, a place she hadn't been since she'd gone undercover. Surely it wasn't a coincidence. With trepidation, she stuck her hand out toward the mirror. An old, wrinkled hand appeared in the mirror. Was that supposed to be her as an old woman? She made contact with the hand.

"Why did you leave him? He fell apart without you," a voice bellowed from the darkness. Her own voice. But who was she talking about? Emilio? She recalled that the mirrors in Emma's dance studio reflected potential futures, not a set future, but the dream vision frightened her badly.

"Who's out there? What do you want of me?"

Just as quickly as the hand appeared, it vanished. CoCo looked down the barre and spotted a little girl sitting with her back toward her. Was it her as a kid? She approached and put her hand gently on the girl's shoulder. The girl turned around, but only a skull looked back at her.

"You never found me. I died because you failed."

CoCo jumped back and her lips quivered, formed the named Emma, but didn't say it. Maybe there was something she could do about this potential future.

Another image appeared in the mirror. She stepped closer and saw herself.

"Why am I here? Because of Emma?" For a moment, the ludicrousness of trying to talk to herself in a dream vision almost snapped her out of it.

The reflection did not answer.

"What can I do to find Emma? Where is she?"

The figure turned and walked away. CoCo was about to yell when she glimpsed a hallway in the mirror. It was a hallway in this ship. She watched herself walk through the area she had just found in the forbidden zone of the ship.

"There? You want me to go there?" But there was no response. The images went dark and the hazy dreamlike video replay in her head ended.

"Holy mudbugs," CoCo said. "This is a sign. You knew

something was wrong on this ship. Now you know where to look."

She wondered about trusting this seeming recollection. After all, she cast illusions all the time, and people couldn't always believe what they saw around her. She knew others could cause hallucinations and do things like force someone to act in certain ways.

But there was something about it that sparkled with innocence and desperation. It felt like Emma. And, after all, it was Emma's dance studio. She wondered why she might be in Emma's dance studio when, as far as Emma was concerned, CoCo no longer played for the angels. Pragmatic as ever, though, she just decided to go with it.

What could she do? What should she do? When she had infiltrated the Tribe, it was with the intention of taking them down from the inside. To stop the incessant back-and-forth battles they had been locked in. She stormed out of Base 47, and then carried out a series of attention-drawing actions, including breaking a few Mods out of prison, publicly hurting Maggie in a way that would establish her to the world at large as unredeemable, and "hooking up" with Timothy Ellory.

Pierce creeped her out, and she worried about his continuing deterioration toward madness. Timothy seemed uneasy with the way Pierce ran the show but felt he had nowhere else to go. Posing as Timothy's girlfriend helped her avoid the unsavory characters onboard.

She regretted having to manipulate Timothy because she sensed his feelings for her were true. Every single interaction and moment between them was an illusion. When this nightmare was finally over, she would be back with her love, Emilio. She hoped to convince Timothy to leave the Tribe for good as well, although she would be unable to offer even her illusory self to Timothy if he did leave.

After discovering that Pierce had stolen Mods' powers for himself and the strange dance room dream, she hoped the hidden room would give her enough ammunition to take him down.

She'd explicitly avoided the off-limits area of the ship until now because she didn't want to twig Pierce's antenna against her. But maybe it was time, especially if it could yield information that would help the SENTINELS.

CoCo put on a blue pair of yoga pants and hot pink camisole and took a deep breath before opening the door. She tried to push the disturbing dream images from her mind.

CoCo cast a simple misdirection illusion around her, allowing her to make it past most of the guards. Making it all the way through to the labs would be challenging since her misdirection had its limits, but she was stronger than ever thanks to Pierce's unorthodox training methods.

She made it to the first checkpoint and waited for a technician to come by so she could enter with him. She wished her powers could work on technology so she could just bypass all the sensors and doors in order to see what exactly Pierce was up to.

It wasn't too long before a lowly tech on the overnight shift walked past her. She projected her image on the other side of the hall speaking to him. The real CoCo then snuck up to him and took his security badge and gained access to the second lab. She would keep the badge so she could get into the medical center.

She carefully made her way through the ex-Soviet aircraft carrier to the off-limits area. On one side of the hall was a room labeled Hazardous Materials and the other one said Project Isolation. CoCo cleared her mind and tried to sense any energy coming from behind that door. There was absolutely nothing coming from the Project X room, but she detected faint energy behind the Hazardous Materials door.

CoCo pressed the security badge to the sensor. The door clicked open and the intense smell of bleach filled her nose. It was a fair-sized room. Three empty large clear tubes and three draped with white sheets filled the room. The empty ones stood against the room's left wall while those covered with sheets lined the right wall. She glanced at the ceiling and walls for surveillance cameras and spotted none. She crept to the first covered tube and pulled down the white sheet.

As soon as she did, CoCo wished she had just stayed in her cabin. She covered her mouth with her hands, willing herself not to scream. The old man's face was badly mutilated. One of his eyes had been gouged out, and the wound looked caked over, the scab uncared for. The eyeless socket gaped at her. The other eye was closed as though in sleep. He wore a hospital johnny. Aside from the eye, he seemed unharmed. A steady yellow indicator light above the clear tube caught her attention. Three words over a trio of lights. It reminded her of a stoplight.

Dead.

Stasis.

Animated.

Under dead was a red light. Under animated, it was green. Stasis was yellow.

Stasis? Animated? Dead?

What was going on here?

And what had been done to this poor man with the missing eye? She pulled the sheet back over his face and whispered a quiet sorry.

The silence of the room unnerved her. Shouldn't machines be beeping, she wondered?

CoCo quieted her mind again and let her mind reach out.

She didn't know how she got in the dance room, but it seemed possible that, despite everything, Emma was reaching out to her. She looked across the room and felt drawn to the tube on the end. She slowly pulled down the sheet. What she saw felt like a punch in the gut.

It was Carlos Martin. Her friend and teammate from the SENTINELS. His left arm was missing. Amputated. The stasis status light glowed yellow, as with the eyeless man. The sight shocked her so greatly that for a moment she let go of her illusion. And one second was all it took to for the technicians to discover something was off and to ring the alarm.

The blaring klaxon broke CoCo out of her horrified paralysis. She threw the sheet over her lost friend and ran back to the door. She carefully opened the door. Techs on the overnight shift were running around trying to figure out what was happening. You got this, girl, CoCo thought as she planned her next move. She crafted an illusion that she was just another tech amid the chaos.

"Do you know what happened?" CoCo, the fake tech, asked.

"I have no idea, but let's get to the reporting deck. I'm sure Pierce will question us all." He urged her to follow him.

"Right behind you," she said as she got through the restricted area with relative ease. She looked down the corridor and saw no one there. She dropped her illusion and walked around the corner only to run right into a very real Timothy.

"Where have you been?" Timothy asked as he grabbed CoCo by the arms.

"Timothy." She searched for something else to say, but nothing would come out.

"What are you doing? What if those German pervs saw you dressed like this?" They scooted to the side of the hallway, allowing the guards to pass them.

"Sorry. I suddenly got this strange feeling. I had to figure out what was going on here."

For the first time, she was letting Timothy touch the real her. She panicked.

"You know this area is off-limits to us. We could be killed if we were found there."

"Timothy, there is something seriously wrong here. You have to listen to me—"

But before she could tell him, Flame and Washington raced down the hall.

"You know what Brute had the nerve to say?" Flame said to her beau.

"What?"

"That I'm redundant because Pierce has pyrokinetic powers." She spat. "He can't even make flame animals."

CoCo watched, fascinated at this insight into Flame.

"Don't listen to her. She's just trying to get into your head," Washington said. "But I am worried. Every power makes Pierce less stable."

"You noticed it too? Let's talk about that later."

They stopped and kissed before heading down the hall.

"Come on. CoCo, we should go." Timothy held CoCo's arm and tugged her forward. She didn't dare say anything now. Who knew who might be close by listening in.

CoCo tried not to think about her friend lying in that clear stasis tube in the lab. Everyone thought he'd died when the mountain came down. She'd gone to his funeral, although there had been no body, no casket. How had Pierce found him? How could Pierce do this? She'd seen that tanned, strong arm on Pierce every day since she'd been here, but it had never occurred to her that he'd stolen Carlos's Mod powers. This thought made her stomach retch a little, but she pushed down her fury.

And then there was Timothy. If he knew about Pierce's secret actions, it might be what it took to convince him to break away from the Tribe.

As they made their way to the commissary, CoCo saw Pierce walking toward them. She wanted to use her power against him, but thought better of it. Maybe he had grafted a power capable of deflecting her skills. They had barely passed him when he called out.

"Ellery!"

They both stopped, turned around, and walked back to him.

"What is it, Captain Pierce?" Timothy asked.

"It looks like we had a power shortage. I need you to take a look at it with Builder."

"Of course," Timothy said. "I'll meet you back in your cabin, honey."

CoCo watched him leave and turned to head back to her cabin.

"CoCo. A question." Pierce said. It sounded like a command.

CoCo swallowed her rising rage. "Yes?"

"It seems some of our techs got confused earlier. Some say that they saw you in the lab areas. I told them they must be mistaken because you know you aren't allowed down there." Pierce searched her face.

"While I do enjoy a good mystery, I can assure you that Timothy and I were in my cabin until we heard the alarms go off," CoCo said. "We went to check it out but found nothing very interesting. We were just heading back to bed." If she could sell the story to Pierce, her misdirection power could account for filling in any gaps he had. "If I were looking for someone questionable, I'd take a long hard look at Jimin. She and Flame are constantly at each other's throats."

He scrutinized her for so long she thought she wouldn't be able to stand it. At long last, he seemed to reach a decision. He turned and stalked away without a further word. As he rounded the corner, CoCo exhaled her tension in one long breath.

CoCo hustled back to her cabin, hoping she had allayed Pierce's suspicions, and closed the door. Finally, she was alone. The only thing she wanted to do was to run into Emilio's arms. She curled up in the chair next to her bed and wondered how things could have gotten so bad. From Carlos to Emma to Pierce's powers. And she had walked right into the lion's den.

"All right girl, pity party is over with. You have your mission. Save your team."

But how?

CHAPTER
33

12 December

Inviting the blogger and the international press corps to Crystal City had seemed like such a good idea at the time. Now, Jaako cursed it. Things were going to be tricky enough to manage in the next little while without

Sun Shining

having to worry about what Maggie Adams and her cameraman or any of the other press in attendance might capture on video.

Jaako was no longer in a festive mood. Not even the sight of the virgin snow outside could improve his disposition.

How the devil had he gotten in this fix? How had that odious redheaded man acquired the documentation about his foundation's seed money? More importantly, what was Jaako himself going to do about this? He ran his hand through his short blond hair as he considered.

He took Dale Carnegie's advice on the matter of trouble seriously. Carnegie promoted that one should figure out the worst that can happen, accept it, and do what one can to improve on it. In this case, he wasn't really sure what the worst was. Would the worst be abetting the strange redhead or would it be the fallout if certain information came to light? Either way, he could be impeached. Utterly unacceptable. The prime minister just didn't have enough information, and he couldn't possibly ruminate properly on the topic with all these happy people partying around him. Yet he dared not leave the festival. He could see the redheaded man charming Birgitta.

What was he going to do? He was running out of time in which to decide before the redheaded man's deadline. His political career would most assuredly be over if he did this, and maybe his life, too. But his political career would also be over if he didn't. The island's constitution stipulated that any sort of bribery or business collusion was unacceptable and anyone found guilty of participating in such activity would be immediately impeached from office. While what he'd done wasn't technically bribery or collusion, it would be awfully hard to explain away. The images of his banking records that the redheaded man had shown him made that clear. Coldness grew inside his chest.

He asked his security detail to give him some room. It was a normal enough request and they relocated across the museum floor. He knew they would still be watching him, but hoped that they would be distracted enough for him to carry out his task.

He groaned, and a passing waiter offered him a champagne flute. He shook his head. Definitely not in a celebrating mood. But vodka would do nicely, he thought. He beckoned Arian, who waited nearby.

Jaako asked her to bring a strong drink from the bar. Arian raised an eyebrow at him but left to fetch the requested beverage. In her absence, he watched Luli and Yi and thought hard.

"Here," Arian said when she returned, handing him a drink that had to have included four shots of vodka, one shot of tonic, and a twist of lime. "Want to talk about it?"

Jaako looked at her without really seeing her, took a deep drink of the vodka tonic, and made his choice. He turned and strode to Luli and her husband.

"Luli, Yi, come with me a moment," he said.

"Mind your sister," Yi told Shining.

The couple followed him outside, and Jaako realized he had nothing to say, nothing of enough consequence to justify taking them away from their kids or the party. He grasped around for ideas. "I just want to make sure you two are happy here at New Atlantis. Luli, are you still loving your job?"

"Yes, sir," she said slowly. Her eyebrows drew together.

"You've been very effective and I just wanted to tell you that I am going to approve a raise for you for the work you've done this year. I wanted you to know so you would understand why your next check is bigger than normal."

"Oh, thank you, sir. That is a nice gesture," Luli said, shaking hands with him. Next, Yi shook hands, and they visited for a few minutes.

Back inside the party, the redheaded man passed by, without noticing, a woman with mousy brown hair. He walked toward two children standing by the dessert table. The redhead leaned down to speak to Shining and his sister, Sying. They grinned and pointed at the cookie tray.

"This one?" the redheaded man asked. "That's the cookie you want?"

"Yes, please," Sying said.

"The other one for me, please," Shining said.

"Here you go," the redheaded man said, passing one cookie to each child.

"Thank you, sir," they said in unison.

"You both have such great manners. Sying, you must go tell your mother that I have said so. I believe she is outside. I will watch Shining while you go tell her," he said.

"Thank you," Sying said, smiling shyly. She turned toward the front door but looked back at the redheaded man uncertainly. "What's your name, mister?"

"Guess."

She studied him a moment. "Joey."

"You're a great guesser." He lifted a half-smile at her. "I'm an old friend of your mom's."

"Oh." She slowly walked off to find her mother, munching on her macaroon.

"Shining, what are you doing for Christmas?"

"We're going to San Francisco."

"Oh really?"

"I'm going to ride the trolley."

"That sounds like fun. Are you having fun tonight?"

"Yes."

"What did you think about the snow?"

Shining's face lit up, then clouded over. "It was excellent. I wanted to go out and play in it but my mom said no."

"Why is that?"

"No coat," he said, glum.

"Ah, well, let's sneak out the back door and you can play in the snow. I won't tell if you won't," the redheaded man said conspiratorially.

Shining lit up. "Okay. But promise I won't get in trouble."

"No trouble, no way. I might even teach you how to make a snow angel. Have you ever heard of those?" The man steered the child toward the back of the museum. Once they were outside, the man looked around. "Jane?"

"Here."

The area was empty. The ground was coated in a pristine white snow blanket that glistened in the moonlight.

The redheaded man told Shining how to make snow angels. While the boy enthusiastically flapped his appendages in the snow making angels, they waited for Jaako. "Where's Pierce?"

"Right here," Pierce said, appearing from the shadows, and Jane looked at him longingly.

"Okay, good. We'll leave the moment Jaako gets here. Or do you want to send Shining through the door now while we wait on Jaako?"

The point became moot, as Jaako appeared just then, exiting the museum's back door. He drew his eyebrows together as he recognized Pierce. "You're involved in this?" He took in the old soldier's physique. "My god, man, what happened to you?"

"The less you say, politician, the better."

Pierce snapped his fingers, and a large burgundy door seemed to grow out of the ground in front of him. He opened the door and pushed Jaako through.

Luli, just stepping out the museum's back door on the hunt for her son, saw Jaako disappear. Then she spotted Pierce and her son. "Shining! Come here. Now!" Hysteria ringed the edges of her voice.

The boy was turning toward his mother when Pierce shoved him through his teleportal.

Luli screamed. "No, Shining, no! Come back!" She rushed toward the door, determined to barrel through the portal after her son.

Shining was gone. The redheaded man stepped through, followed by Pierce. He let the door crack closed behind him an instant before Luli reached the door. She slammed into it and fell back onto the snowy muck that had accumulated in front of the door. She watched as the door seemed to melt back into the ground. Pierce and his crew were gone. She wailed and beat her fists into the ground. They had taken a part of her world with them.

CHAPTER 34

13 December

The Engine Room in the Antarctic Research Station roared to life and energy filled the air. The door connecting London and the polar station opened and Dr. Roger Martin walked out and shivered. A tech greeted him and handed him a coat.

Antarctic Research Base

"I make this trip maybe twice a week, but it always surprises me that even inside it's cold." Roger complained as he accepted the coat. He strode past a thermometer that indicated it was fifty-eight degrees Fahrenheit inside the facility and paused long enough for the post-teleport scan. Once complete, he stalked to the security doors, keyed in an entry code, and came face to face with Dr. Julianne Frazier. She was drumming her fingers on her thigh more nervously than normal.

"I know it's cold, but we're still focused on minimizing any chance of destabilizing the cryospores we've managed to extract. And so, it stays cold inside." Julianne smiled at

Roger. "Maybe once we figure out how to keep them stable we can start warming the facility to comfort."

"Where have we gotten with the Finnish icicle and wonder boy?"

"We have yet to run any substantial tests since we just got them. It's all very theoretical at the moment," Julianne said.

"Damn theoretical. We need to start immediately."

"We just got them last night. It's going to take time to figure out how to utilize their abilities to extract the cryospore." Julianne led Roger toward the holding cells.

"Get them to do as we demand. Sooner rather than later. I don't care what it takes." Roger peered at the monitors in the hallway. The monitors showed the captive Mods in separate cells, which Roger knew were equipped with power dampeners. "Why do they look so comfortable? They should be in the annex ready for testing!"

As Roger watched the New Atlantean prime minister, he felt like Jaako could tell he was being watched. Jaako stood to pace his room.

"Look at the boy and his chart," Julianne said, leading him to the other cell. The child was playing with a bunch of blocks. The child spoke and then acted as though he were listening to someone in active conversation. Probably just a coping mechanism, Roger thought as he picked up the chart and flipped through the pages.

"The information looks promising. How soon can we get him into the machine?" Roger asked.

"I think we can try soon. I understand time is of the utmost importance, but isn't it better that we take all precautions to ensure everything works as required?" Julianne drummed her fingers along her thigh.

Roger handed her back the file with a huff. He knew she was correct, which infuriated him further. "I need results in two days. I don't know how long we can detain them without anyone from New Atlantis and Base 47 looking at The Hastings Foundation for this. That's the last thing we need."

"There haven't been reports about Jaako's disappearance. They must be hiding it from the world. I wonder why," Julianne said.

"They're probably too embarrassed to admit they've managed to misplace their prime minister and are furiously searching for him." Roger paused and thought. "But I understand they'll be distracted from the search to some extent. Let me know when you can get the boy working. I've got to get back to London." Roger turned to head back to the teleportal and Julianne followed.

"Leaving so soon? I thought perhaps you could stay and run through—"

"I just came and see for myself how things are running now that you have the, uh, the extra elements to work with."

"I'll keep you posted on everything." Julianne watched the techs fire up the teleportation machine to take Roger back to London. Roger tossed the jacket back on the hook, turned, and stepped through the doorway between Antarctica and London.

Julianne waited a moment after he left, gritted her teeth, and turned to her technicians. "We must speed up the drill procedure. I want drilling trials in six hours with Shining and Jaako both helping. Make it happen."

CHAPTER
3 5

13 December

Black globules bubbled and expanded in Josh's large living room, and he groaned and rolled over on the couch. Empty pizza boxes and scotch bottles littered the room. Blackout curtains hid the midmorning sun, leaving Josh to sleep the day away yet again as

Josh Grant
"Hollywood"

he had for most of the last two weeks. The globules merged and formed a portal.

"Woah," Waleed said as he stepped over a broken vase. "This place is a mess."

"You're telling me." James looked around. The once-immaculate Hollywood Hills home of Josh now looked more like the day after a frat kegger. Empty plates and bowls were strewn about. James drew his eyebrows together in consternation when he spotted broken picture frames and a shattered chair.

"And the smell," Waleed said as he recoiled. "What is that?"

"That would be me." Josh sighed and pulled back the blue-and-yellow patchwork quilt, a gift from his paternal grandmother. He looked a mess: eyes shut tight against the dim light, hair that would send any Hollywood stylist into shock, and a beard nearing hippie gone wrong. "And you are both much too loud." His head throbbed. He sat up anyway. "What the hell are you doing here?"

"Are you drunk? It's eleven a.m." James zoomed over to the couch. The liquor on Josh's breath was so pungent that James leaned back.

Josh scoffed. "It's almost impossible to get drunk when you're a shapeshifter."

"Doesn't keep you from trying, I gather." Waleed picked up a frame containing a photo of Josh and Luca at the beach.

"Giving it the old college try." Josh collapsed back into the couch.

"Well, time to sober up. We need you."

"No can do."

"We know you came to New Atlantis a few weeks back. Jiya told us," Waleed said.

"Why didn't you tell us about Luca?" James asked.

"What's there to say? I broke him. He hates me. I can't do anything." Josh choked on the words.

"Well, you can't just stay here wallowing in filth and self-pity." Waleed leaned over the couch.

"Just watch." Josh collapsed back onto the couch and rolled over.

"We need your help."

"You have Bayanai. And all the SENTINELS. You don't need me."

"Yes, we do," Waleed said quietly.

James looked at Waleed and nodded.

"Sorry," Waleed said.

"Wha—" But before Josh could complete his question,

a teleportal opened below him. Josh slipped through and resurfaced a few feet above the couch. He plopped on the cushions and immediately sat up. He leaned over the side and heaved. Not wanting to deal with the mess, James fled the scene. He returned with towels and a glass of water. He dumped the towels on the vomit and handed the water to Josh.

"That was uncalled for." Josh wiped his mouth with the quilt. "You killed my buzz, man. You know how long it took me to get and stay that drunk?"

"Good, we need you sober. Drastic times." Waleed wobbled his head as he finished the rest of the phrase. A faint smile curled on his lips.

Josh slowly faced his former teammates. Miraculously, his headache was gone. He was beginning to think clearly again.

"A little upset you didn't come see me." James sat down next to Josh. "We're supposed to be friends."

Josh avoided eye contact. He wanted to curl up and disappear. Ever since he'd gotten Luca's diagnosis and realized the dilemma he faced, he'd been frozen. He'd spent the last two weeks bingeing and drinking and avoiding. Friends, his agent, family. He'd even refused Clarita entry into the house to clean anything. He was paying the maid to stay away. Anyone who could have pulled him through this he had pushed away.

"You don't understand. This has never happened to me before. I've always gotten things to go my way. Even when it was hard, it really wasn't. But now Luca won't even see me. He refuses my calls. It just hurts too much." Josh fought back the emotions he'd driven underground in the weeks of drinking.

"So that's it? You just give up?" James asked with a harshness wholly uncharacteristic of him.

Josh stood and looked at his friend. "Who do you think you are?"

James stared right back at him. "We're friends. And friends don't give up on one another."

Josh lunged to tackle him but James easily dodged. He didn't even need his super speed to evade Josh's lumbering attempt. Josh fell flat on the ground and groaned. Waleed echoed Josh's groan in sympathy, but the humor of the situation got the better of him and he started laughing.

"You think my pain is funny?"

"You know we don't. But you aren't acting like the man we know you to be," Waleed said.

"You don't know what it's like to lose something like this. And I am the cause. Luca would be just fine—"

But James wasn't having it. "Don't finish that. Luca's alive. You saved him. The rest, it's going to be hard. But you aren't doing yourself any favors by doing—this." James gestured to the empty liquor bottles. He sat next to Josh. "I know you feel like you can't handle this, but weren't you the one who convinced me that walking away from something just doesn't work?"

Josh looked at his ruinous home, then up to Waleed and back to James.

"We need you. Quit falling apart," James said.

"You can't just keep running away when things get hard," Waleed added.

Josh let his head fall back toward the couch and lay there. Was he falling back into—or even seeking out—old, destructive patterns? He didn't have to look around his living room to know the answer. But was going back to the SENTINELS the right decision? After all that had happened? Ericka. Bayanai. Could he really just walk back in? Did he even want to? But he knew he wasn't going to save Luca by being loaded.

"What did I do to deserve friends like you?" Josh shakily stood. "What is this big emergency? What is so important that Bayanai would actually need me?" Josh picked up a shirt from the chair, sniffed it, made a face, and threw it back.

"It's Jaako. He's been kidnapped," Waleed said.

"What?"

"Yeah. But there's more," Waleed said. "We'll fill you in when we get back to Base 47."

"But before we do any of that, let alone take you back to New Atlantis, you need a shower. You stink something awful." James wrinkled his nose and waved his hand in front of it for emphasis.

Waleed and James laughed and their laughter spread to Josh.

"You always could find a way to make me smile," Josh said.

"Of course, Hollywood, now get cleaned up. We've got important work to do," James said.

CHAPTER
36

13 December

"Why didn't you just get him while you were there the other day?" CoCo wanted to know. "They certainly were preoccupied."

Dafydd Upjohn

Pierce narrowed his eyes and CoCo backed away, realizing they no longer matched one another. She thought of the eyeless man she'd found in the Hazardous Materials room and fought down rising gorge.

"I was more concerned with getting Jaako and Shining. But we still need George. So you and Dafydd, here, are going into the lion's den to collect him for me. No more errors," Pierce said.

"Timothy could be helpful on a mission like this."

Pierce frowned at her. "You two together screwed it up the first time. This time, you and Dafydd. I'll open the door and be on standby for your return."

"What about the MDA? It'll go off the second we teleport onto the island," CoCo said.

"I've got that covered. My person on the inside has it down for maintenance."

CoCo looked at Dafydd. "Do we have a plan?"

He grinned. "You divert. I'll provide all the extra bodies we need."

CoCo shook her head. "For finding George."

"Word is he's got a bunk at Base 47. I'll get you onto the island, as close as possible to the base. You'll have to find him from there," Pierce said.

"What about surveillance? My powers don't work against cameras, and if we're going into Base 47, there will be a record of it," CoCo said.

"If you're fast enough, it won't matter. But assuming you have trouble finding him, I'll have someone take care of any footage they capture," Pierce said.

She nodded. "Let's go."

Pierce opened a door onto New Atlantis, and Dafydd and CoCo stepped through. The burgundy teleportal door clapped shut behind them, and CoCo looked around for a landmark. She spotted the orangey granite turrets of Base 47 in the distance. "It's going to be about a fifteen-minute walk. Let's go."

CoCo set out an illusion that made the sidewalk appear empty. It had been almost a year since she had been on New Atlantis. She had told herself she would only step foot back on the island once she had helped take down Pierce for good. Her heart skipped a beat as she passed by Grove Street. Just two blocks over was the house she shared with Emilio. She forced herself to not look over. They passed few people, but she saw no one she recognized as they made their way to the base.

"How are we going to get in?"

She sighed. "We'll just have to wait until someone comes or goes and follow them in. But for now, we need an illusion, or no one will let us in." She reused her empty sidewalk illusion. "Simple is best."

A few minutes later a janitor left the building. CoCo reached out and held the door open behind him. She gave the janitor the illusion that the door had clicked shut. Dafydd entered the building, followed by CoCo.

"Dorm rooms are down a few levels. George may be there," CoCo said, taking the lead.

They reached the elevator, and CoCo punched the down button, still casting her trusty illusion of an empty hallway.

The elevator doors opened, and CoCo felt a pang when she saw Emilio and Katrina already in the car. They looked out and appeared to see no one.

CoCo held up her hands in a "what do we do now" gesture and Dafydd pointed to the elevator car. CoCo held back a groan. She reworked her illusion so Katrina and Emilio neither felt nor saw them enter the elevator.

Unlike three weeks ago, when she had been near Emilio, she couldn't steal a moment for the two of them. She couldn't afford for Dafydd to sense any weakness or hesitation. But for a moment she let herself go. For a moment, she closed her eyes and breathed in Emilio. She could tell he had just showered from a workout and she longed to slip her hand into his and never let go. She wanted to tell Emilio about finding Carlos on Pierce's boat. She couldn't leave her friend to rot there, not if she could do something about it. CoCo cursed herself for failing to master running two illusions at once; her goose would be cooked if Dafydd thought she was passing information to her former boyfriend or teammates.

Nonetheless, CoCo formulated the basics of a plan that would help her to give her friends a fighting chance. It relied on her being out of sight of Dafydd for a minute or two so she could scrawl a note for someone to find. And if the gods were good, they'd somehow find the Tribe's shielded ship. She could provide information about the ship's location along with its coordinates from the day before. If the SENTINELS could crack that, they could rescue Carlos from stasis.

They reached the fourth-level underground, and Katrina got off the elevator. Emilio, however, lingered a moment. Frowning, he pressed the door open button and looked around at the seemingly empty elevator cab. CoCo caught her breath. They'd be sunk if he somehow saw through her illusion.

"Emilio? You coming?" Katrina hollered.

He shrugged and stepped out of the elevator.

When the doors slid closed, CoCo punched the three button, and they rode up one floor to exit at the dorm level. Leading the way with her empty hallway illusion in place, CoCo walked toward the dorm rooms.

"The visitor rooms are at the end," CoCo whispered.

"Why are you whispering?" Dafydd wanted to know. "Aren't you countering out sound with your illusion?"

"Of course I am," CoCo said.

Just then, the fire alarm went off. CoCo whirled and saw that while one Dafydd stood beside her, another stood at the fire alarm, looking self-satisfied.

"More efficient than knocking on door after door," Dafydd number two said.

Hastily, she cast an illusion over Dafydd number two before any of the residents could come out of their rooms. "Not helping," she said.

One after another, doors on level three flew open, as their residents, a mix of technicians, trainers, and scientists, headed to the surface.

Not a single one was George.

The alarm was still blaring, so CoCo looked at the two

Dafydds with her hands held up in a "what now?" gesture.

Dafydd duplicated himself into more selves and at once opened all the doors that hadn't opened in response to the alarm. Still no George.

From the north stairwell came Emilio and Katrina. Per Base 47 procedures, they sought the source of the alarm and would double-check each room to ensure no one was left on the floor.

Again, CoCo looked at Dafydd and raised her hands in the eternal "what now?" gesture.

Dafydd grinned, but CoCo could barely contain her frustration.

"Here's just the one you wanted. Make an illusion that Emilio is keeping up with her. I'll take him in here and grill him on the whereabouts of George." Dafydd pushed Emilio into one of the dorm rooms.

She incorporated this into her illusion. "Done." This was the best opportunity she'd have to pass along the Carlos information. She had to manage it just right, though. First, she had to get Katrina to leave the area, giving her time to duck into a dorm room and scribble a note for Emilio.

CoCo walked behind the illusory Emilio accompanying Katrina. She made the fake Emilio act like he was sending Katrina on and that he wanted to double back to check something. Katrina nodded and headed up the south stairwell. As Katrina started up the steps, CoCo released the illusion. Blessedly, the fire alarm shut off, leaving a deafening silence in its absence.

CoCo found an empty dorm room and raced to the desk. She hastily scrawled a note: "E—Can't trust normal communication. Pierce has Carlos. Alive on boat. I saw him. Love, C."

She folded the note and tucked it in her pocket before making her way back the dorm room where Dafydd held the true Emilio. When she saw how the Dafydds were interrogating Emilio, she almost shouted at them to stop hurting him, but that would blow her cover. Two Dafydds held Emilio's arms while a third punched and asked questions. Emilio was a bloody mess.

He spotted her. "You. I should have known you'd be in on this," Emilio snarled at her.

"Well?" she asked, turning to Dafydd, fighting to continue playing her role without betraying her emotions.

"Nothing."

"You'll never get him to talk like that," she said. She saw an opportunity to get close and pass the note. "Let me try."

Dafydd shook his head. "No. We're going to have to search every floor."

"Good luck with that," Emilio said.

"What? Why?" Dafydd asked.

CoCo answered. "Any time an alarm is pulled manually, it sounds only on that floor until a team member verifies it's an emergency."

Emilio picked up the explanation. "I haven't called up to security to confirm, so they cancelled the alarm. Right about now, they smell something fishy and will be checking out the footage from the security cameras to see who yanked the alarm."

Dafydd cursed. CoCo's powers of illusion only worked on humans, not equipment.

"Then we don't have much time," Dafydd said. "What's downstairs?"

"The gym," CoCo said.

"Sounds promising. Let's start there."

CoCo cast an illusion of her leading the way to the stairwell, with the two Dafydds marching Emilio along behind her. In truth, she was behind Emilio and able to slip the note into his back pocket and whisper a gentle apology.

She prayed he found it soon.

The group headed down a flight of stairs to the gym. People were streaming back into it after the aborted alarm.

About a hundred feet down the hall, the dark-green walls changed to glass. All the latest toys for gym rats, and quite a few were in use. The group surveyed the gym-goers for George.

"There he is," one of the Dafydds said, pointing at a man climbing onto a rowing machine.

"CoCo, give an illusion of Emilio here going in and telling George that he's needed immediately for something. Doesn't matter what. Just get him out here in the hallway. Then I'll grab him," the original Dafydd said.

CoCo nodded and yanked open the gym door. When she spotted him, she realized he'd become fit since his arrival at Base 47.

"Yo, George, man, we need you upstairs," the false Emilio called.

"What? What's wrong?" George asked, not slowing his rowing pace at all.

"We think your family might be in danger," the false Emilio said.

He let go of the rowing handles. "What? How?" The machine stopped, and George stood on shaking legs.

The false Emilio pointed out the door and George went. Just as he was about to turn left and see the true Emilio, CoCo swapped illusions. To the other gym-goers, she was still Emilio but now George couldn't see he was about to walk into a trap.

As soon as they all cleared the glass and the regular wall provided some semblance of privacy, CoCo dropped the illusion.

Shocked to find two strangers in front of him holding Emilio captive instead of Emilio walking behind him as he thought had been the case, George stopped short.

"Keep going, George," CoCo said.

"Who are you?" he asked.

"Shut up. We'll release Emilio if you'll come in peace," Dafydd said.

George stepped forward, as though to offer himself up, but Emilio's bloody and fierce head-shaking pulled him up short and made the step look more like an ambulatory stutter.

"Sorry, Emilio, you don't get a vote here," Dafydd said. "George wants to come with us. CoCo, grab him."

CoCo had just put her hand around George's wrist when one of Pierce's doors opened up right next to her. George was confused by its sudden appearance, and CoCo, despite every fiber of her being telling her not to, took advantage of his momentary bewilderment to push the man through the doorway.

As she followed him, she heard Emilio yell, "We'll come for you, George. Don't let them use you." Her heart lurched as she heard Dafydd punch Emilio, in the stomach, it sounded like, based on the grunt and coughing that followed. And then she was far enough from the door that she couldn't hear New Atlantis any more. Moments later, the Dafydds joined her, leaving Emilio doubled over in the corridor near the gym.

"George," Pierce said as a grin spread across his face. "I have plans for you."

CHAPTER
37

13 December

Jaako had no idea where he could be, although something
about it reminded him of his native Finland. Maybe it was
the crispness of the air, even inside, that brought him home.
Only a day ago he was leading his island nation in a winter
celebration and now he was bitterly on his own.

He was in a small room filled with all-white furniture. He
assumed Shining's room next door was similar.

He'd tried several times to create a little ice, or snow
even, but couldn't. His room was probably equipped with
some sort of power dampener.

Jaako turned his attention back to his current situation.
As long as he and the kid were useful, they would live, and
as long as they lived, hope for rescue or escape lived as well.
He hoped the SENTINELS would rescue them soon, but
he wouldn't just rely on them. He would be proactive.
Before he could consider his options, the door opened. In
walked a woman in a white lab coat.

"Who are you?" Jaako demanded.

"I'm afraid, prime minister, you do not get to demand
answers here."

"What do I call you?"

"Dr. Frazier."

Jaako nodded but said nothing. The scientist's eyes studied him for a moment before she spoke again. He wondered what she was thinking about him.

"Aren't you going to ask about the boy?"

"You need him, too, so I'm sure he's fine. Look, I was assured that we would be returned to New Atlantis after I did whatever you needed me to do."

"And that is still the idea," Julianne said.

"What do you need?"

"We need you to convince young Shining to help us. All you need to do is get him into a machine and we can take it from there." She folded her arms across her body.

"And what about me?"

"We need you to keep the temperature stable and replenish any ice that is lost in the extraction process." Julianne drummed her fingers against her arms.

"Where are we?"

"Bottom of the world." Julianne reached down and clicked a button on her key ring and a wall shimmered to reveal a window looking out onto a barren snowy landscape.

"Antarctica? Are you kidding?"

"Believe you me, this is no joke." She clicked again and the window shimmered back to solid.

"How does all this figure into the new energy source?" Jaako asked. "Is it safe? What is Shining supposed to do?"

"Are you saying you actually care what happens to the boy?" Julianne asked.

"His mother works for me." He wondered if she knew that already, but the mention of an energy source got him thinking about the American power plant explosion that the SENTINELS had investigated. He wondered how dangerous this new power source might actually be.

"The energy is the first around that won't emit any carcinogens or pollutants into the atmosphere. The only problem we have is that it is stuck in the frozen Antarctic. Well, that and a minor instability problem," Julianne said. "We have developed a machine that will, in layman's terms, unstick the cryospores and allow us to extract them. We need you to maintain the ice shelf and make sure that the process does not damage the region. We are scientists after all, not a soulless corporation."

"Why do you need a kid who can make a force field?" Jaako asked.

"His force fields will coat the individual cryospores so we can safely and easily transport them."

Jaako frowned.

"If you don't help, there could be dire consequences for anyone or anything north of us," Julianne said.

Jaako sensed she was telling the truth. And if these cryospores were as volatile as she suggested, then he had to cooperate for the time being. But he didn't want to be stuck here forever, forced to slave away with his ice power only to enrich The Hastings Foundation. Once they got a taste of free-flowing cryospores, he thought, they wouldn't be willing to let him or the kid go. They had to be rescued, or escape.

"Now, come."

Uneasy, he followed Dr. Frazier out of his cell and into the next one, which held Shining. Jaako the person wasn't a big fan of kids, although Jaako the politician was.

"Hello, Shining," Jaako said as the door opened. The small child threw down his blocks and ran to him, hugging his legs tight.

"Where are my parents? Why am I here?" Shining asked through tears.

"You'll be fine and we'll get you back to your parents as

soon as possible," Jaako said.

"Really? You'll take me back to Mommy?" Shining asked in relief as he looked up at the tall blond man.

"Of course. I just need you to help me with something. Can you do that? Can you be a brave boy?" Jaako knelt closer to the boy.

Shining wiped his tears away and nodded. "That's what my friend wants me to do."

"What friend?"

Shining hung his head.

"You can tell me."

"My friend told me that I should help them out. That the world is hurting but I can make it better," Shining said.

"Who is your friend?" Jaako wondered if Shining had cracked up from the trauma of the kidnapping.

"He is looking. Always looking. I have to help so that he can find—"

"Find what?" Jaako asked.

Shining slowly shook his head.

"What's your friend's name?"

"Amir."

"I'll do what I can to help Amir. Will you help me now?" Jaako asked, playing the hand he had to great effect.

Shining nodded.

"Good boy. Okay. We'll do this together," Jaako said. They turned around and faced Dr. Frazier.

"Follow me," Julianne said. They all walked out of the cell and toward the entrance of the lab.

CHAPTER
38

13 December

"Henry, it's been ten days—"

"Maks, you know these things take time. Rushing puts us in a position to fail." Henry tried to hide his complete hatred of Maks and his exasperation for the thirty-year-old's total lack of patience.

Elise Springchild

"You mean for you to fail. You have shown time and again that you can't succeed." Maks's scornful face filled the screen in Henry's secret room.

"We reached a breakthrough yesterday and we are on the brink of success. The scientists are working overtime on a new approach they feel certain will work. Have a little patience." Henry leaned forward in his chair.

"Every day we don't have the cryospore is money and world domination down the drain," Anabel said. "Look, Henry, we know all that you have done for our organization. But despite all your efforts, you have let us down again. Maybe it's time for a new perspective."

Elise spoke up. "After the New Atlantis debacle, a lot of our revenue sources were strained. But we still had to cover the research for our other operations." She frowned, but her forehead didn't move. Henry recognized the signs of Botox injections. She paused, as though to gather her thoughts. When at last she spoke, her voice came out gently. "Henry, let me be honest with you."

Henry bristled at the phrase, knowing nothing good ever followed.

"You've made incredible sacrifices for the Ascendancy and we would never discount those. You pulled the missing pieces of the prophecy together so we could move forward with our goals," Elise said. "You've made significant progress on the cryospore development, but—"

Henry's mouth went dry. "I have given my entire life to our cause. Everything. Everything I have done was for—"

"We know that. And don't think that for one instant this is a reflection of our opinion of your contributions over the years," Elise said.

"Then what?"

"What she's trying to say is you're out." Maks cut him off with a sadistic grin.

"What? You can't kick me out." In his shock and mounting anger, the words burst out of Henry's mouth.

"Henry, this decision wasn't easy. We debated and discussed this for some time," Anabel said.

"Our three families created the Ascendancy. You can't just force me out. It's my birthright."

Three stony faces glared back at him from the video monitors, and Henry's heart sank. He couldn't lose his spot on the Ascendancy.

He pleaded. "It doesn't have to be like this. Give me one last chance. Let me give you the cryospore. I can deliver it to you in a week."

"It's too late. We're taking over," Elise said with a finality Henry had not expected to hear from her.

"Basically, Pops, it's over. You're done."

Henry whirled around, his back now to the video monitors. His son was just a few feet away from him.

Arthur stood erect, eyes glinting in the soft light of Henry's secret room. Arthur looked past Henry into the video monitors, where he saw surprise on Elise, Anabel, and Maks' faces.

"Arthur? What are you doing here?"

"I told you I had an interest in the family business, Pops." Arthur unzipped his biker jacket and brandished his Ruger Mark III pistol. Arthur aimed the gun and squeezed the trigger. Henry fell to the floor, shrieking. Arthur walked up to the wall of monitors showing the other Ascendancy members.

"Arthur! What have you done?" Elise moaned.

"What none of you had the balls to do." Arthur holstered his gun. "You wanted dear old Dad out of the Ascendancy. I just made it permanent."

Elise and the twins looked back at him in stunned silence.

"From now on, I'll be your point man in the Americas." Arthur slammed his fist on the recording device, disconnecting him from the meeting. He sat down in his father's chair, spun it around, and smiled.

CHAPTER
3 9

13 December

George opened his eyes and tried to focus, but the pain was excruciating. His head was pounding. He tried rubbing it, but found himself handcuffed.

He tried reaching out with his powers, but he couldn't, and not just because there was no one else in the room. He couldn't even make the jump out of his mind, when normally he could do that at will. Slowly, George realized there must be some sort of power-dampening technology in use. He'd known it existed, but had never felt its effects. Maybe that was what was causing his pounding headache, his sudden confinement to his own head.

He had no idea where he was. The room itself was nondescript. White, white, white everywhere. He was sprawled out on a white couch. White walls. White floor. He heard the hum of machinery but couldn't place the sounds. The air, though, smelled of salt.

He thought back to the all too brief training from Base 47 and wished he'd paid more attention when Emilio explained basic escape techniques. He'd been more interested in lifting weights instead of practical skills like how to survive or escape bad Mods. He knew he couldn't rescue himself just now. He wished bitterly for another intervention from the SENTINELS. They knew he was missing. That was at least something.

He assessed his situation. Bad Mods had him, and they were probably going to make him use his power of hypnosis to do something wrong. Maybe try to make him do one of the things Emilio had questioned him about. If there was a silver lining, George thought, it was that his Mod power couldn't be used at a distance. At least they couldn't make him cause someone far away to commit homicide or suicide. But that still left many other things possible. He swallowed down rising gorge.

Nearly a month ago his life had been normal. He only used his gifts to help others with their problems. Now he was locked up and in the hands of the bad guys.

The room's only door opened, and two men entered. George stared at the first man in mingled fascination and revulsion. He stood with ramrod posture but seemed almost cobbled together, as though he'd been assembled in a spare body parts warehouse. The second man was older, with a chin curtain. He looked as though he enjoyed pulling the whiskers off kittens and the wings off butterflies in his spare time.

"I'm Pierce."

George merely nodded acknowledgment at the introduction.

Pierce telekinetically levitated George, who panicked and flailed in the air. His eyes darted around the room.

"Eyes on me, kid." Pierce snapped his fingers.

George didn't want to look at Pierce. He looked everywhere but at the man who had suspended him in midair, afraid anything he said might set him off.

"Don't make me repeat myself," Pierce said.

As Pierce spoke, George felt pressure all over his body, but particularly in his chest. Was he having a heart attack? In his panic, he actually looked into Pierce's glittering eyes.

Pierce turned him upside down and brought him closer.

George looked at Pierce with horror. His head pounded. All the blood in his body felt like it was pooling in his head. The pressure on his chest felt like it might crush him.

"Frightened? Good." Pierce chuckled.

George wanted to deliver a snappy comeback, but he couldn't think clearly. He was scared, and being upside down discombobulated his thoughts. Again, he wished for the SENTINELS to step in and save him.

"Don't think about trying to escape. You won't be here very long," Pierce said. "Someone thinks you have some value."

Pierce finally turned George right side up but kept him suspended in the air.

George's stomach clenched. His deepest fear had been confirmed. He shook his head in denial.

"Why me? I'm not even very good at hypnotizing people."

"Believe me, you weren't their first choice. They tried Alrick first, but his powers require the other person to be awake." Pierce gestured at the other man, who drooped at the mention of this shortcoming. "Yours don't."

"You want me to hypnotize someone asleep?"

Pierce didn't answer George, but dropped him unceremoniously on the ground. George rose on shaky legs.

"I'll take it from here," another voice said, entering the room. George turned and saw a well put together redheaded man who somehow frightened him more than Pierce had. His stomach tightened and he fought to keep control over his bowels.

"He's all yours. Take him away," Pierce said. A burgundy

teleportal door appeared next to him. "This is where you leave me."

The redheaded man took George's elbow and walked him through the teleportal.

CHAPTER
40

14 December

"Okay, let's start at the beginning.
Fill me in on what went down,
and I'll see how I can help you."
Ericka leaned forward in her
chair. It had been a long time
since she had been in the War
Room at Base 47. She had settled

Katrina McGee

into her new role as police chief for Crystal City and thought
she'd put superheroics behind her. Even so, being back in
the War Room tugged at her. She was present as not just as
a cop but also a reluctant SENTINEL.

"Pierce and his crew kidnapped the prime minister and
Shining from the winter festival, then came back the next
day and took George as well," Bayanai said.

"Why doesn't the world know about that yet?" Etienne
asked.

"We're keeping his disappearance a secret for right
now," Bayanai replied.

"Why?" Etienne asked.

"We're hoping to get him back before anyone figures out

he's missing. Until then, cover up." Bayanai looked at his team sitting in the War Room at Base 47. All he saw were various shades of despair. They needed a win.

"Security on this island is in serious need of an upgrade." Ericka looked at Bayanai.

"Isn't that something a police chief is in charge of?" Etienne said.

"Etienne, that's enough," Katrina said, lightly bopping the back of his head.

"Question stands," he said.

"There are some glaring breaches here, but we have to get on top of this," Bayanai said. "I spoke with Laura just before this meeting, and she's running diagnostics, trying to figure out why the MDA failed to warn us that we had been infiltrated, as well as how CoCo was able to access Base 47 in the first place."

"Yeah, it's getting a little old that the Tribe can just get in and out of our secured base whenever they want and we can't even locate theirs," James said through a mouthful of candy bar.

"There's that, but I'm more concerned about Carlos," Emilio said. He rubbed an eye that had been blackened during the interrogation with the Dafydds and subsequently healed by Jiya. "Now that we know Carlos is still alive, we have to rescue him."

"And how do we know that?" Ericka asked.

"I told you, I overheard one of the Dafydds talking about it when he was here to capture George."

"And we're supposed to just trust that duplicating freak?" Etienne raised his hands to emphasize the question.

"Could be a trap," Ericka added.

Emilio tilted his head at them and nodded. "It could be. But it might not be. For the first time, there's hope, a chance that Carlos is still alive. And that means we need to redouble our efforts to find Pierce's base of operations."

"As much as we'd like to believe he survived—" James said.

"We never found a body," Katrina said.

"What are we going to do?" Kirra asked.

"We're going to get them all back. We don't leave anyone behind. We just have to be smart about this so we don't walk into a trap." Bayanai's eyes lingered just a few moments too long on Kirra.

"Why do they want George so bad that they'd come here to get him?" Ericka asked.

"We believe they need his power to jump into people's heads," Emilio said.

"But they have Alrick," Ericka countered.

"Maybe that German creep wasn't strong enough. Maybe George's powers work just a little differently," Katrina speculated.

The room grew silent.

"I know everyone is upset. That's why I asked Ericka to come in. I hope she has some insight that will help us piece this together," Bayanai said.

"What I know right now, without more information, is that we're woefully unprepared for whatever their scheme is." Ericka pressed a button and the screen behind her lit up a world map. She clicked a button and Cairo popped up on the screen. "An artifact found at the Memphis site led to the Nilometer in Cairo where James and Katrina had a run-in with an empowered minion of the Swarm."

"Yeah, and we lost the artifact," Katrina said.

"Can you remember what you saw with the eye?" Ericka asked.

"I can't. Maybe if Emma were here, she could help me recover those memories," James said, glum. "I can't believe I lost the eye." He ripped up the candy bar wrapper in frustration.

"We have to figure out how the Swarm is connected to all of this," Etienne said.

"We need to figure out if the Swarm and Tribe are working together, and if so, to what end," Ericka said. "Or are they simply trading favors? Knowing this will help us figure out what we're up against."

"We know the Ascendancy and the Swarm are enemies, and that the Tribe does some work for the Ascendancy," Bayanai added. "That's another wrinkle. Is the Tribe playing the two against each other? Or helping them both as mercenaries? Either way, the Tribe has definitely been involved in three kidnappings from Base 47."

Ericka pressed a button and the world map changed. She stood and pointed to Memphis, Tennessee. "Let's piece this puzzle together. Here we have the first explosive appearance of a new element or energy source." She pointed at Brazil. "Then here in the Amazon Basin. I think we can all agree that The Hastings Foundation has discovered a new fuel source and is experimenting with it."

"Aren't they behind everything?" James shook his head.

"Not to mention that the latest target of the Tribe was a guy who has mental abilities of indeterminate strength. But they sought him out for a reason." Ericka leaned against her chair.

"Maybe they wanted him to work with CoCo's illusion powers?" Etienne offered.

Emilio gave him a look.

"What? Not my problem that your ex-girlfriend dropped us for Pierce's team."

"Not helpful, Etienne," Katrina said.

Once again the room was quiet. Ericka could sense their concern and despair. "We need to focus on what we can actually do. Back on topic. We know that Pierce has powers, that he has Carlos, and is keeping him captive on his boat. I have a hunch that he also has Emma. And Pierce also grabbed Jaako and Shining. Just one of these by itself would be a bad thing, but all of them together and we've got a nefarious plot. Whatever Pierce... The Ascendancy... The Swarm is planning, it has to be huge," Ericka said.

"Again, we've got to figure out what they're after, and who's actually working with whom, if we have any hope of defeating them," Bayanai said.

Katrina sighed as she ran her fingers through her brown hair streaked with blue.

"Sorry to interrupt your meeting," a voice said from the back of the War Room. The team looked back as two figures emerged from a teleportal.

"Josh?" Emilio smiled and went to hug his old friend.

"What are you doing here?" Stunned to see him, Ericka struggled to keep her face neutral.

"This is an all hands on deck kind of situation, isn't it?" Josh asked.

Ericka glared at Bayanai.

"I can't wait for your movie! It's gonna show at Grover's Theatre downtown! Will you come for a premiere here?" Katrina asked as she crowded in on the hug.

"Perhaps if you had been at the winter festival like you should have been, this might never had happened," Ericka snapped.

"I had other things going on," Josh said tightly as he pulled away from James.

"Yeah, movie things, press and such," Ericka said.

"Actually—"

"Save it. I already know about the wreck," Ericka said.

A few of the SENTINELS looked on in confusion.

"There was an accident. Luca is in the hospital," Josh said, then reluctantly added, "We had a run-in with a Mod."

"Why didn't you say anything? We could have helped you," Emilio said.

"What's important is that we find out how this is all connected." Josh walked with his former teammates to the table.

"What's wrong with Luca?" Luli asked.

"Something I can't fix," Josh said.

"Not that I'm not glad to see you, but should you be here? Shouldn't you be by Luca's side?" Luli frowned.

"It's ... complicated."

Bayanai spoke up. "I'm sending Etienne and Kirra to Sydney. Laura uncovered details about a Swarm outpost that we believe might provide some information about what they're up to." Bayanai handed a briefing packet to the pair. He wished he could have taken the mission with her, but he was needed here. Maybe when she got back, he'd finally ask her out.

"And what about the rest of us?" Katrina asked.

"We've got our hands full here. Nicola and Yukio are helping us on the element tracking, and Josh can minimize the Jaako situation. He'll be the public face of New Atlantis while we search for Emma, Carlos, Shining, and Jaako."

"And why, again, are we keeping the kidnappings a secret?" Etienne asked.

"This isn't just the kind of news you share," Luli said.

"I'm surprised at you," he said. "I'd expect you, of all people, to be on board with making this public. After all, the more people looking for them, the better the odds that they'll be found."

Heat bloomed in Luli's cheeks. "This isn't some Amber Alert scenario where the kidnappers are likely to take the kid into a store where he'll be spotted by some eagle-eyed citizen. The Tribe has them. Pierce has them. And we know Pierce. Pierce is not going to make a stupid mistake. They're locked up tight, wherever they are. So our best bet is to work the Tribe and Swarm leads and keep the whole thing quiet." Luli's voice was shaking. "As hard as that is for me. My baby has been ripped away from me."

Bayanai smiled at her. "We'll find them, Luli."

Her eyes went flinty. "You bet you will. I won't let anyone rest until my boy is safe here at home."

Ericka waited a beat. "Pierce. The Swarm. This energy element. Emma's disappearance. Pierce's stolen powers. George's kidnapping. The eye, which led us to Cairo. Shining and Jaako's abductions. And now this new lead down in Australia. Not only that, but the SENTINELS have been fighting the Ascendancy and the Swarm since the day we lost Rami. We are locked in a tug-of-war."

"If we don't win decisively, this could still be going for the next five years. Who else will we lose?" Luli's knuckles were white from holding them so tight.

"Luli, it's going to be okay." Emilio rose toward her.

"Don't tell me that. You don't know that. We don't know anything. My baby—"

"We'll get Shining back. I promise you," Bayanai said. He so fully believed it that an enhancing aura spread across the War Room. The more confident he was, the better and stronger everyone felt. He had supercharged everyone's abilities. "Let's start by getting Etienne and Kirra out to Sydney. We'll figure the rest out after."

Etienne and Kirra walked with Bayanai out of the War Room, followed by most of the others. Josh, Ericka, and Emilio remained behind.

"Look, Ericka. I know we've got some—"

"Not now, Josh. I really don't have the time to deal with this." She brushed past him.

"Hmmm. Still on her bad side, eh?" Emilio teased.

"That's putting it mildly."

CHAPTER
41

14 December

In a darkened and twisty corridor lit only with candles, a barefoot man draped in a scarlet hooded robe scurried, his fingers grazing the rough stone wall. He rushed past several doors before stopping, placing his hands on his knees and panting. As soon as he regained his composure, he rapped three times and waited for the wooden door to open.

The lock slipped and the door swung into the chamber. The man in scarlet crept in. The chamber was extravagantly decorated. Masterpiece paintings covered the walls. Gold figurines glittered in the torchlight. At the center of the chamber was a solitary intricately carved ivory chair

"I have news about the Scion," the man in scarlet said. He knelt before a cloaked figure sitting in the ivory chair.

For a long moment it was quiet in the chamber. Winter chilled the air, but he never once felt cold even as he knelt on the stone floor.

"And what say he?" The voice was a baritone, deep and rich.

"He has heard from the Sentinel."

"Get on with it."

The man in scarlet genuflected and swallowed as he opened a handwritten note. He read it to the sitting figure.

"The time is near, the earth will crumble.

"The center is nigh, old gods will tumble.

"Children must be punished.

"Axes will revolt.

"The four forces rise anew."

The cloaked figure rose from the carved chair and strode to the single window in the chamber. "You know what we must do. Prepare for the New Reckoning. We must go to the cave."

"Yes." The man in scarlet backed away from the cloaked figure, never looking up, and left the chamber, quietly closing the door behind him.

The time is close, he thought, smiling, as he scuttled down the twisted stone corridor.

CHAPTER
4 2

14 December

"Thought I might find you here," Josh said, walking into Blue Ribbon Grill near Dini Square.

A glass of whiskey sat untouched on the gleaming wood bar in front of Ericka. Josh looked around the empty bar. Sunlight poured through the windows and lit the dark oak walls.

"We don't have to do this." Josh motioned between the two of them.

"It seems like we do." Ericka stared at the liquor bottles on the shelf.

"I am really sorry for—"

"How's Luca?"

"Pretty mad at me actually."

"He deserves better."

"Ouch."

"In your heart, you know it. It's only a matter of time before you just walk away from it all." Ericka drummed her fingers on the bar.

"We should talk."

She stared down at the bar, refusing to meet his eyes.

"You want to talk now? A little late for that. Years too late. You should have been there. You were my best friend. We were supposed to do this together. You betrayed my wishes, and then you left. That's hard to forgive and impossible to forget." She looked up at him, her eyes welling with tears that refused to fall.

Josh lowered his head. "I didn't know what to do. I was scared too. I was weak."

"You sound like you think it's over." Ericka looked sideways at him. "I'm not over it. You stole my one good opportunity to have a child."

Josh sighed. "Ericka, I'm sorry. You know I never wanted to hurt you."

They sat there in silence for a few moments.

"Whatever is happening is bigger than us." Ericka wiped the tears from her eyes. "We're going to need to work together."

Josh was about to say something but Ericka's phone rang and interrupted the moment.

"What is it, Bayanai?" She listened, then added, "Actually, he's right next to me."

She pressed the speaker button, and placed the cell phone on the bar. They leaned in to listen.

"I just came into some information about the Swarm. I need you to check it out. I'm sending you the files right now," Bayanai said.

Ericka squinted her eyes but said nothing.

"I need you to check with your sources, Ericka. We need to be on top of all of this," Bayanai said. "Let me know as soon as you know anything. And, Josh, this means your timetable has moved up too."

"OK." She hung up.

"Sounds like he's got things in order, right?"

Ericka shot him a cold look. "He'll be fine. He's got a

good team behind him."

Josh cut his eyes down to the drink in front of Ericka.

"I'll read the files and check with my sources. You go play prime minister and keep this country together."

"Maybe after all this is over, we can actually—"

"You think you can put your self-interests aside to do what the team, what this nation, needs you to do?"

"I'll do it," Josh said.

Ericka eyed him intently. When she was satisfied with his answer, she slid off her bar stool and walked to the door.

"What about your drink?"

Ericka turned around and studied him for a brief moment. "It was never for me."

Josh watched her leave, then turned back to the bar. He pulled the file toward him, opening it as he sipped the whiskey Ericka left behind.

CHAPTER
43

14 December

"You can't be serious." The words came out harsher than she expected, but she didn't apologize.

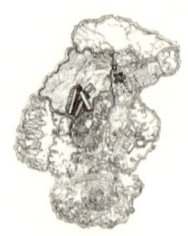

New Atlantis

"What choice do we have, Arian?" Bayanai asked as they stopped in the elevated glass walkway that connected the peaks of Base 47.

"You of all people should know how fragile democracy is. If this ever got out—"

"It won't." He looked around to make sure no one could hear their conversation.

"We both know what it's like when a few people take control of a government."

"This isn't like that."

"Isn't it?" Arian stared down the leader of the SENTINELS. She was so angry she could hardly contain herself.

"We won't let it be like that." Bayanai countered and

turned to face her.

"Iran and the Philippines have both had our share of dictators." Arian's brow furrowed. "The right things, for the wrong reasons—"

"I understand what you're saying, but this is our best option."

"This isn't right." Arian tried to not let her past bubble to the surface, but it was too late. "Rami was imprisoned by the government for speaking out. They came and took him away from me." Her voice began to shake. "I lost him to fascists and extremists. We can't be like them."

"I know that. But we can't let the world know that our prime minister was kidnapped. Not now with all the added spotlight of Mod registration. This could quite literally seal our fate. Not only as a nation but as a people."

"There's a process for this. That's why we have the deputy PM."

"You and I both know he's incapable of making the tough choices. Besides, we're in a legislative break. The only thing Josh will have to do is show his face as Jaako. Just public appearances, no actual government work."

She looked deep at Bayanai, wondering just how they had slid down this particular rabbit hole. "I can't support this."

"Arian, you must. We won't be able to pull this off without you. You're Jaako's right hand." Bayanai stepped closer to her.

"This is a slippery slope. We can't be seen as subverting our own government."

"I know. We both lived through some harsh times before we came to New Atlantis, but I believe we can still be a shining example to the world—"

"Bayanai, stop. I won't do this."

She turned and looked out of the floor-to-ceiling

windows of the walkway that connected the base's four peaks. In the distance she could see the memorial to Rami. The promise she'd made in Rami's memory to protect this island and its people weighed heavily on her. She wanted to do the right thing.

"We can't do this without you."

"I know." She felt his hand on her shoulder. Every part of her body wanted to stop the plan to have Josh masquerade as Jaako. "What if we don't rescue him in time? Or ever?"

"We will."

"What if he's dead?"

"He's not."

The surety with which Bayanai replied appeased her, and she turned reluctantly toward him. "All right. I'll help. But the world can never know about this."

CHAPTER
44

14 December

"You ever come out here as a kid?" Etienne gestured at one of Sydney's most famous beaches.

Etienne DuBois

Hundreds of swimsuit-clad people lay on beach towels soaking up the sun. Tanned men and women played volleyball as kids ran with their boogie boards. The turquoise water lapped ashore the golden sandy beach known as Manly Beach, but there was little breeze to break up the sweltering summer day.

"I grew up in Arnhem Land," Kirra said dryly. She hated the rest of the world's perception that anyone from Australia was from Sydney. Then again, she had thought for far too long that all Americans were gun-toting super-size zealots. It was a view she had only partially revised. When he drew his eyebrows together in a question, she added, "but I've been here bunches." She wiped sweat from her brow. Her curly hair was pulled back in a French braid, but some of the tendrils had come loose and framed her face. "Wish that you making us invisible would prevent us from sweating."

"If only," Etienne laughed. They hopped up on the rocks. "So is this the spot?"

"Yeah, just through there is the Wormhole." Kirra pointed at what looked like the opening to a cave partly up the rock wall.

"That name just gets me." Etienne laughed. "You sure we won't end up in China?"

"Are your jokes always that lame?"

"People usually like my jokes. They find them endearing."

They entered the tunnel. The floor was uneven and the tunnel itself was not very wide. The sudden shade cooled them both.

"Lucky no one else is here."

"You had to say that, didn't you?" Etienne said as a group of kids carrying pails, umbrellas, and shovels walked in from the other side. The heroes pressed up against the wall to let them pass.

"They seriously can't walk a straight line?" Kirra whispered as the kids fanned out in the four-foot wide tunnel.

"I got it, just hold your breath." Etienne grabbed Kirra's hand and phased them inside the rock. Like always, the feeling reminded her of the time her older brothers had pushed her into a squishy mud puddle after a huge storm.

Staying unmoving inside the rock was not as scary as Kirra thought it might be. Though she had officially been with the team less than a year, she had known them for a while and had helped terraform New Atlantis along with Juan Pierre at the very beginning of the colonization effort.

The kids blissfully walked past them and out the other side.

"That was close," Etienne said as they emerged from the

rock. With no one else around, he made them visible again.

Kirra touched the rocky walls of the earthen tunnel, seeking entry into the Swarm's abandoned outpost, which was said to be accessible from the Wormhole. Bayanai had said he thought it might offer insight into whether the Swarm was connected to the new energy source. She felt Etienne looking at her as she communed with the walls and blushed. "I'm trying to feel for anything unnatural."

"What?"

"I can't really describe it but I can feel when there's something different about the rocks." She walked along the wall, hands spread wide and barely touching the walls. She stopped abruptly and waved him over. "Like here."

"When we get back to New Atlantis I'm going to take you out to dinner," Etienne said, gazing at her and smiling.

"Don't look at me like that," she said.

"Right," he said. "Right, because that would be ridiculous."

"Exactly." She directed him to the spot on the wall. "Now watch."

There was a slight rumble and chunks of plaster fell from the wall, revealing a steel door.

"I think they covered up the door with plaster to hide it when they left this little hideout, tried to make it look like real rock," Kirra said.

"Guess we should take a look-see."

"Yep," Kirra said.

He grabbed her hand and phased them through the steel door. Behind them, the sand on the bottom of the tunnel moved toward the crack Kirra revealed.

"This is unreal!" Etienne said as they emerged from the rocks into a large but ink-dark chamber that was part rock, part reinforced steel.

"Got a flashlight?" Kirra asked.

"Sure. Hang on." Etienne fumbled in his pocket, removed the flashlight, and flicked it on. The beam revealed a bank of obsolete monitors and computers and lots of cobwebs.

"Much better," Kirra said. "What do you think they used this place for?" How long had the Swarm been gone from this bunker in Australia? The state of the cobwebs—she tried not to think of the spiders they implied—suggested years, as did the ancient computer hardware. She wandered around the room and spotted some papers. One caught her attention. It had four figures drawn inside a circle, and above it two words.

"What is the Dark Splinter?" She traced the letters with her finger. Pulling her finger back, she examined it and wrinkled her nose at the dust she'd stirred up. She wiped the tip of her finger on her pants.

"The more important question is why they left this place behind." Etienne waved the flashlight around to see the rest of the bunker.

"Who knows. Let's just look for any clues as to what they could have wanted here in Sydney. Maybe something will help us defeat them."

Etienne tried to open a file cabinet but couldn't.

"Hmph. Locked, but not for long." He phased his hand through the lock and pulled the drawer open. Searching through the files, he came across a file labeled Four. Right behind that, he saw one labeled the Reckoning, and he whistled. He put all the files into his pack and turned around. "Kirra," he said, low, pointing behind her. "I don't think we're alone."

"What do you mean?" She turned around. There was a mounting pile of sand growing behind her.

CHAPTER
45

14 December

"You sure you want to do this?" Bayanai sat next to Josh in Jaako's office.

"There's not much choice, is there? Either we let the world know the prime minister was kidnapped by Mods or we play it close to the vest and try to solve this on our own."

"What we're doing is quite sensitive, not to mention highly illegal," Bayanai said.

"Well, there's that, but we both know this is the only reason you had me come back." Josh had pretended that it was the SENTINELS who needed him, and they did, but the truth was that he needed them too.

"Besides, it's the safest way to cover his disappearance up," Josh said. "You say Arian and Luli have handled the staff and made convincing excuses to Birgitta. Now, it's up to me. Don't worry, I've done this before." Josh laughed and his body began to change shape. His face morphed with his nose thinning out, his eyes turning ice blue, and his hair copying the missing prime minister's hairstyle. "After all, it's what I'm good at." With that statement, Josh was lost and there was only the reflection of Jaako.

"Wow."

"What?"

"I just forgot how good you were at this."

"We don't have to do this now," Josh said as he sat down.

"No, we do. I regret the way it all went down in Durbin. I didn't want you to leave." Bayanai crossed his arms.

"We're both adults. And the better man won. And truth be told, it was the best thing. For the team, for me, and for you," Josh said. "I mean, I went back to Hollywood and now I've got this film coming out and there's serious award talk about it. I'm doing fine." A moment after speaking, Josh wondered whether he was trying to convince Bayanai or himself.

Back in Durbin, South Africa, the long-simmering tensions between leader and would-be leader had come to a head, rising to a level that affected the team's effectiveness. It had come to blows. When Bayanai won, Josh decided to leave and return to Hollywood, rather than linger as a hostile second-in-command.

"You don't blame me for it? For any of it?"

"Maybe then, but not anymore." Josh morphed back into himself. "Bayanai, you have to get past this. I have. I made a great comeback. I found someone... I'm happy."

"Really?"

"Absolutely." Josh looked out the window. The sun was setting through the palm trees. Brilliant pinks, blues, and purples hung in the sky like swirls of paint. "Some view, huh?"

"Josh, Luca will be okay."

Josh's shoulders slumped. "He's never going to walk again. And he won't let me do anything about it." He could barely keep his composure. "Luca is the love of my life, and I can't look him in the eye. He's in that bed because of me.

Because I failed that kid. Because I turned my back on my kind. I didn't come back for Carlos' funeral. I never asked about Emma. And Ericka. That was unforgivable. I let myself get wrapped up in the artificiality of LA. Let that easy life seduce me, where I never had to make a real decision. It was so easy."

"Maybe Dr. Watanabe could help. She's making great strides in advanced cybernetics, or Jiya could—"

"He forbade me to do any of that." Josh's face sunk into his hands.

"Why?"

"He has his reasons." Josh slammed his fist onto the table, knocking his phone onto the floor.

Bayanai stood and touched Josh's shoulder. "Want to talk about it?"

For a long moment, Josh didn't respond. He searched Bayanai's eyes and came to a decision. "Luca is, um, no fan of Mods."

"But you two got together anyway," Bayanai said.

Josh shrugged. "It's complicated."

The two sat in silence for moments before Josh spoke up again. "It's my fault. All of it. I knew the Mod who attacked us. He came to Base 47 back in Texas and I ignored him. I was too wrapped up in my own—whatever—to pay him any attention. And it came back to bite me hard. I caused my own problems." He hadn't meant to say all this, certainly not to Bayanai, but it felt good to say it.

"I don't know how, but I think things will work out for you. Thanks for trusting me enough to talk about it with me," Bayanai said. "We'll figure this out."

"And you?"

"What do you mean?"

"When are you going to ask Kirra out?" Josh could tell the question caught him off guard. "Come on, Bayanai.

We've all seen how you look at her."

"I don't know. It's complicated."

"Then uncomplicate it. What's the worst that could happen?" Josh said.

Bayanai considered it for a moment. Maybe he would take a chance for himself.

Josh smiled and for the first time since the accident, felt like he knew what he had to do. "Well, enough of this," Josh said. "I've got a country to fool." He shifted himself into the prime minister. "And you've got a team to lead."

Bayanai walked back and fidgeted with his papers. "None of it makes sense. Just what is the Swarm after? How is The Hastings Foundation tied into it? What is the cryospore?" Bayanai held his head in his hands for a few moments. "I want my team back together."

"We'll get them back. And we'll kick Pierce's ass but good," Josh said.

Bayanai gave a slight nod and smile. "All right. Let's go over this again. You just need to go through his daily routines. There's no actual work you have to do. And Arian will help you out if you get stuck. Here's the schedule." Bayanai handed the faux prime minister the official schedule.

"Don't worry. I've got this." Josh knew that pretending to be the leader of New Atlantis would be a cakewalk, but he had some concerns about the implications of impersonating a world leader. "Just get them back." He started to walk out, then turned back. "I know this may not be my place since I am in and out of here, but you shouldn't blame yourself for anything that happened."

"It happened on my watch. I was supposed to protect us all. If it wasn't for me, Emma would still be here. Carlos would be here. CoCo wouldn't have done all she did, and Luli wouldn't have lost her son—"

"And if it wasn't for you, we would have lost too many times to count. You can't blame yourself for what CoCo did. That's on her." Josh took Bayanai by the shoulders and looked him square in the eyes. "Don't doubt yourself. You are tied to every good thing we've ever done. You are invaluable."

Bayanai sighed and the tension drained from his body. "Get out of here."

Just as Josh-as-Jaako was turning away from Bayanai, Arian walked in and stopped dead in her tracks. She stared at the faux prime minister. "I don't think I'll ever get used to your metamorphic abilities."

"I aim to please." Josh turned toward the door.

CHAPTER 46

14 December

"Oh man," Etienne said just as the sand rose up and morphed into a woman.

Kirra Wilson

"You shouldn't be here. You don't belong!" The sand woman stretched out her hands. Sand flew out, blasting the heroes against the wall.

"What a—" Etienne started to say before sand filled his mouth.

"Watch your mouth," the sand woman said primly.

"Etienne!" Kirra created a rock fist and threw it against her opponent. To her disappointment, the sand parted, making a hole that the rock fist passed right through. Etienne was choking on sand. "Phase!" she yelled and he struggled. "Get away from him!" Kirra peeled several layers of rock from the wall, fashioned them into spears and launched them at the sand woman.

Each of the rock spears passed through her sandy body and crashed against the wall.

"Who are you?" Kirra asked.

"I'm the Protector of the Swarm. I am the keeper of the Dark Splinter," the sand woman said.

"What does that even mean?" Etienne's voice was raspy but at least he was no longer choking on the sand.

"You won't be alive long enough to find out, Etienne. I've already reclaimed the eye. You are just a nuisance."

"What do you mean I won't be alive long enough?" Etienne made his body intangible. The sand passed right through him and he coughed.

But the sand woman gave no response.

"We need answers," Kirra said.

"Leave now. Heed my warning, Kirra. Your future is marked."

Kirra opted not to worry about the future, instead focusing on the present and their mission. She drew in a deep breath and stood as tall as her five-foot, seven-inch frame would let her. "We need answers," Kirra repeated as Etienne spit out more sand. "And we aren't leaving without them."

"I'm afraid that won't be possible. I already fought your little friends back in Egypt, and the two of you are no threat." She shaped the sand into a mace and swung wildly at Kirra.

Kirra blocked the swings by calling up rock pillars, which broke up the mace attacks. Every time she went on the offensive, the woman just shrugged off the attacks or, worse, let them zip right through her.

"Etienne! A little help!"

"Right-o." Etienne pulled his souped-up escrima sticks from their holsters and flicked a switch near the base to charge them. "Let's see how you handle this!"

Etienne slammed the amped-up sticks into the moist sand. The sand woman lost her cohesion and disintegrated.

Sand spattered to the floor of the Swarm's old outpost.

"Kirra! Let's get out of here." Etienne smiled as he turned around to his teammate.

"Not yet, mate. She's still kicking." Kirra pointed behind him. Etienne grimaced and slowly turned. While their adversary struggled to reform, the sand swirled, rising up toward the ceiling.

"You just made me madder." The sand woman, whole again, threw her hands out, blasting them with the sand.

"Oh great," Etienne muttered. He rushed the sand woman and made contact with the charged escrima sticks several times. The brunt of the attacks was dispersed by the sand.

"I can go on forever. As long as there's sand, I'm up." She swung a sand mallet, which would have clobbered Etienne if he hadn't phased.

"Can't you control her? Sand is of the earth."

"I've been trying. But I can't get a grip on her," Kirra said.

The bunker filled up with sand.

"Etienne! The more sand she has the stronger she is!" Kirra said. Their opponent kept adding it to her mass to increase her strength.

Kirra called up the rocks from the ground and tossed them haphazardly, hoping to distract her opponent.

"You really think some stones are going to do anything to me?" She laughed.

"No, but I was hoping that it would distract you long enough."

"Long enough for what?"

"For this." Etienne threw his overcharged escrima sticks deep into the sand woman. The electrical charge flash fried the sand woman, who completely lost her form. The damp sand sizzled and scattered all over the floor.

"Etienne! That was amazing!" Kirra climbed up the rising sand mountain toward him.

"I impressed myself actually." He shrugged and laughed.

But the laughter was short-lived.

"I don't think that stopped her," Kirra said.

"Aw, come on!" Etienne cursed. Everywhere they turned, sand was rising. They would drown in the stuff if they couldn't get out of the bunker.

Kirra took a breath and reached her hands in front of her. The rock walls began to shake. As she pulled her arms down, she ripped a hole in the rock to the outside. She grabbed Etienne and they ran through the newly made exit. The explosion of rocks hadn't hit any of the beachgoers, who were still hundreds of yards away, but some had turned to see what the source of the noise was.

"What now?" Etienne said as they trudged through the sand.

"We've got to get these people out of here." Kirra brushed sand off her body.

Etienne looked around. They were definitely drawing attention. Men in speedos and bikini-clad women turned and stared.

"Run! Get out of here!" Etienne shouted as he ran toward them, waving his arms above his head.

Kirra ran behind him until she heard a sound that drew her attention back toward the Wormhole. The sand was gathering together and growing. The sand woman was now the size of a house.

"Etienne. We have to stop her."

"How? I'm out of charges." He pointed to his escrima sticks, tucked back into their carrying case.

"We can't let her hurt all these people."

They stood there for a moment surveying the beach. Most had deserted but there were still a few stragglers who seemed to be recording the incident on their phones.

"Let's fight sand with sand," Etienne said.

Kirra looked at him blank-faced.

"You control rocks. Sand is rocks. If you can't control her, maybe you can create something to fight her!"

Of course. Why hadn't she thought of that? She closed her fingers into a tight fist and created a golem composed of sand and rock that was twice as large as the sand woman.

"Whoa," Etienne breathed out. He turned and ran toward the remaining people on the beach.

"Get out of here!" He was able to get most of them to move away to safety. But he could still hear them. They talked about Mods. About how this was the exact reason why the Global Mod Registration Act should be passed. About how they should call GRIM on them. He tried to tell himself that they were just scared and that cooler heads would prevail once the drama was over. Satisfied that the bystanders were safe, he ran back toward Kirra. He watched in awe as Kirra's sand golem took on the sand woman blow for blow.

The sand golem punched and the sand woman fell down to the ground. But Kirra wasn't done. She picked up broken rocks from their escape and slammed them down on the sand woman.

"There," Kirra said with a satisfied smile of a hard battle won.

"That was incredible. You are incredible!" Etienne said as they embraced. They slowly pulled their heads back. Just far enough for their lips to almost touch. Any other occasion, he would have kissed her. Sunset on a beach. A perfect first date spot by any standards. He closed his eyes as she leaned toward him. But before they could meet, an awful screech came from deep within the sand and the sand golem dispersed. They looked toward the sound. She was reforming. Bigger.

They let go of each other and faced their attacker.

"I've got an idea," Etienne said.

"I'm all up for it."

"But it's risky. Might not work," Etienne said.

"How about this? If it works you get that date." Kirra winked and Etienne smiled.

"Launch this rock toward the center of her body." Etienne pointed to a rock the size of baby carriage.

"What? She'll just let it pass though her."

"Exactly. But when it's just inside of her, break it up."

"But why?"

"Because then she'll absorb it."

The light clicked on for her.

"Then I can control her."

"Exactly," Etienne said as Kirra used her power to launch the rock at the sand woman. As expected, she created a hole for the rock to pass through, only this time when it was hurtling through, Kirra exploded the rock with a thought. The rocks joined into the sand woman and became part of her.

Etienne looked over at Kirra. Her smile was enchanting.

The sand creature glided over the sand toward them, but the next moment lost all control of her body. Kirra was in the driver's seat.

"All right, Kirra. She's somehow able to control the sand. Pull it all away. All of it," Etienne said. Thousands of pounds of sand shot in all directions as Kirra used her complete mastery of the earth to neuter their enemy. But it was a fight. The sand woman screamed and tried to stop her, but it was no use.

Etienne watched as Kirra pulled layer after layer off to finally reveal a dark-haired girl, no more than twenty, sobbing in the middle of the beach.

"You did it!" He grinned at her.

"It's not over yet."

He ran toward the girl. Before she could react he phased his hand inside her head.

"I see one grain of sand move and I will solidify my hand into your head and you will die," Etienne said with complete seriousness. He looked down at her. She was shivering in anger. A series of hexagonal tattoos lined the inside of her right forearm. The honeycomb structure cemented, in his mind, her association with the Swarm.

"You lie."

He narrowed his eyes and made his hand incrementally solid. The pain was excruciating and the girl wailed. Kirra grabbed Etienne.

"You think she'll stop on her own?"

"It doesn't matter. We aren't like her!" Kirra said as she motioned with her eyes to the growing crowd. Etienne took a deep breath and released his hold on her. Immediately, the woman dissolved into sand and was gone. They had to get back to Base 47, and they didn't need to give the public any more reason to fear them.

CHAPTER
47

15 December

Laura Parks

"How'd we find this place, anyway?" Katrina trailed her SENTINELS teammates out of Waleed's teleportal and into a decommissioned train depot in southern Poland.

"Every time I searched for the Tribe's base using the MDA, the location bounced around the globe," Ericka said.

Laura picked up the thread. "All our information pointed to dark spots. Places where there should be something, but something was blocking our scanners. So I created an algorithm to monitor that and find the source. And here we are."

Waleed studied the depot. It was dusty and cobwebby but otherwise tidy. "I'm not sure about this place. I mean, if the Tribe was here, it must have been a while ago. Don't they use that warship? What's this train depot thing all about?"

"I think this is an old hideout of theirs," Laura said.

"If that's the case, maybe they've left something behind that will help us find them. Or maybe even George." Ericka scanned the room.

Waleed pushed a cobweb out of the way and moved toward one end of the depot.

"Don't move!" Emilio put his arm out to block his teammate.

"What? Why?" Waleed looked from side to side.

"It was about to be your last step." Emilio pointed to a brick on the ground that was far darker the others. He stepped on it and leapt to the side. Poisoned darts shot through the corridor and slammed into the wall.

"That was lucky," Waleed said.

"Was that trap set for us or just anybody who wound up here and didn't belong?" Ericka asked as they inched forward through the depot.

"Knowing Pierce, probably the latter," Emilio said.

"Uh oh." Katrina pointed to a burgundy door that had just materialized in front of her.

"Get back!" Emilio shouted. His teammates were doing just that when the door opened and Pierce walked through.

"Well, look who we've got here. I wondered who was stupid enough to come crawling through one of my old bases." Pierce telekinetically levitated his body and ignited a flame around him. "This is going to be fun."

Ericka's hands glowed green as she powered up. She nodded at Katrina, who psychokinetically lifted an empty train car and threw it at Pierce. He merely waved his hand and blocked the attack before lowering himself back to the floor.

Laura pulled her handgun—something she carried while on missions with the SENTINELS but was not permitted to use on New Atlantis—out of her holster and fired shots at Pierce, whose force field deflected the bullets. Out of bullets, frowning and dejected, she stood off to the side watching the battle.

Emilio ran at Pierce. Using Mod strength, Pierce grabbed the train car with his left hand and lifted it above his head. A broken handrail fell off the train car. Emilio slid between Pierce's legs, snagged it, and swung wildly at Pierce's back. But the handrail bounced off the force field. Emilio's hands clanged from the vibrations. Eyes wide at the surprise impact, Emilio dropped it and shook his hands out.

Ericka took advantage of distraction and sent her green blasts full force at Pierce, but his force field repelled the damage and sprayed the blasts back against the wall.

Waleed opened a teleportal and moved the train car Pierce was holding through it. "Can't use it against us if he doesn't have it," he muttered.

"Keep the pressure on!" Ericka shouted as she charged Pierce.

Katrina aimed her fists at Pierce and let loose the totality of her psychokinetic powers. Combined with Ericka's green blasts it seemed like they were tiring him down.

Sensing that Pierce was wearing out, Emilio grabbed the handrail and struck at Pierce's back again. This time he connected, and Pierce howled.

"Lucky shot, eh?" Emilio grinned as Pierce hit the floor.

Katrina and Ericka stopped their blasts and watched a smoldering Pierce with his hands on the ground.

"You really shouldn't have done that," Pierce said. He reached out his hand, clenched his fist, and suddenly they all dropped to the ground as an unseen force pressed on them from above.

"No!" Ericka shouted.

"Now, this is more like it." Pierce stood.

Out of the corner of her eye, Ericka noticed his large belt buckle and the blue light streaming from the center. She motioned to Emilio and Katrina and pointed at it.

"I admit my fires aren't as interesting as Flame's, but they can still burn you." Pierce reignited his flame and shot a fireball at an errant railroad car. It blew up and flames spread. "Feeling the heat yet?" He levitated toward them. He telekinetically picked up metal shards and whipped them around the room, as though in a whirlwind. The flying shards cut some of the SENTINELS as they lay on the ground, still unable to move.

Suddenly, Pierce dropped to the ground with a cry of anguish and denial. His flame flickered.

The SENTINELS could breathe again, could move again.

Emilio wiped blood off his brow as he looked at Pierce, whose face soured.

"Not now. Not like this," Pierce said, covering his belt buckle. The blue light from inside it flashed and seemed to lessen in intensity.

The flashing caught Emilio's attention, and he signaled to Waleed. "Look familiar?"

Waleed squinted at it for a moment and then lit up with recognition. "Amazon?"

Emilio nodded.

"Katrina!" Ericka pointed a bloody hand at Pierce.

"On it." Katrina psychokinetically ripped up train tracks and launched them at Pierce, who barely waved them off.

Pierce looked at his opponents and telekinetically grabbed Laura, who despite standing off to the side of the battle was closest to him, and brought her near him. He pulled out a blade and held it to her throat.

"You better stop, if you know what's good for you," Pierce told the SENTINELS.

"Pierce, stop. You don't have to do this," Laura whispered.

Wild-eyed, Pierce grunted and flung her to the ground. He leaned down and said, "You're lucky my force field deflected your bullets." He lowered the blade to her left leg and sliced. She screamed and held her leg.

In what seemed like a Hail Mary move, Pierce scrunched down and splayed back his body, releasing a wave of telekinetic energy that pushed them all back. He called up a burgundy door and escaped.

For a few moments no one moved. Then Emilio roused himself from the ground, crawled over, and checked on his teammates.

"What happened?" Ericka ran the fingers of her uninjured hand through her mousy brown hair.

"Your guess is as good as mine. He is totally unhinged, though," Emilio said.

"Why do you think he let us go?" Katrina struggled to catch her breath.

"Something's not right with him." Waleed knelt over Laura, inspecting the gash in her leg. "You saw how his powers seemed to dry up a little, or maybe lessen in intensity?"

"What if it's his powers? What if his powers are making him mad?" Emilio armed blood off his forehead.

"You mean madder than usual?" Katrina put her hand against the wall for support.

"We have to get back to Base 47. Laura needs medical attention." Ericka looked down at her own bloody hand. "She's not the only one."

"Yeah, it's just going to take me a moment," Waleed said. "I need to regain my strength." He pulled out a bag of trail mix and chewed.

"There was something familiar about how he flattened us like that, it's like it was—" Katrina leaned back against the wall in thought.

"Like that African warlord we faced a while back?" Emilio offered.

"Just like that." Katrina snapped her fingers in agreement. "You think Pierce stole his powers?"

"Entirely possible," Ericka said as she wrapped her bloody hand with a bandanna. She didn't want to think of the implications.

"And that belt?" Katrina asked.

"Yeah, I think it's connected to his powers. Maybe we can exploit that," Emilio said. "It looks like something Waleed and I saw in the Amazon with Nicola."

"We barely survived that. If he's as strong and unstable as that, maybe we don't have a chance," Katrina said.

"We can't think like that," Ericka said. "Besides, we now know that Pierce isn't as omnipotent as he thinks he is."

"Are you kidding me? We just took a thorough stomping from that monster." Katrina curled her fists for emphasis.

"We need to get out of here. Pronto." Emilio pointed to the corridor they entered through. A fire, triggered as an intruder deterrent, raced toward them.

"Waleed?" Ericka looked at him.

"On it." He opened a portal back to Base 47. They ran through. He barely managed to close it before the entire depot went up in flames.

CHAPTER
48

15 December

Later, the seismologists would claim the 7.3 earthquake that devastated East Falkland only lasted thirty seconds. Later, Ian Abbott would disagree, saying the scientists could only say that because they weren't there. To Ian, who had been contentedly sweating out his daily run before the world moved, it felt more like the longest, most frightening hour of his life.

Earthquakes weren't common in the Falkland Islands, and at first he hadn't understood what was going on. One moment, he was running, left right left, stuck in the relaxed empty state that comes with good exercise, and the next moment he was off his feet, rolling in the grass. Vertigo set in and he felt like he was falling even though he was already on the ground. He hadn't known what to do other than watch in disbelief as the ground bucked and heaved around him and hope for the best. The forty-five-year-old history teacher was sure he survived by nothing but pure dumb luck, with nothing but a few bruises caused by his unexpected fall to show. Not that he wouldn't take that— survival was, after all, survival.

But what about his family, back at the house? Panic wrapped around his heart. He'd left them asleep, left them to enjoy the chance to sleep late, while he enjoyed an early-morning run.

When Ian was sure the ground was still beneath him, that the only pounding left was his frantic pulse, he shakily stood, though still fearing aftershocks.

He surveyed the damage. He lived quite outside Stanley, the country's capital, and he enjoyed running in the rural area. Looking east toward town, he could only see billows of dirt blowing around.

Conscious of his heavy breathing, he lifted the neck of his sweaty T-shirt over his nose. Wouldn't do to breathe in all that dirt. He looked west, toward his house, and what he saw took him to his knees. The once familiar Mount Kent, Wickham Heights, and Mount Usborne seemed much taller than he remembered.

He ran, hell-bent for home.

His cottage lay in shambles, the stone walls no longer intact, the roof caved into the guts of the house. Panicked, he began calling, "Maddy! Paul! James! Where is everyone?"

But they never answered.

Couldn't.

Ian wished bitterly for the hope he'd felt on the run home, the hope he'd felt before he found his wife and two sons crushed beneath the weight of the roof and falling walls. He hoped they had slept through the earthquake. That they had not had the chance to feel fear or pain. That the last things they had known were good-night kisses before sleeping. He felt his own heartbreak and feared the vast wasteland of a life that stretched out ahead of him. He screamed and cried as he held the broken and crushed bodies of his loved ones.

CHAPTER
49

16 December

James slid to a stop in front of Maggie and Focus. "I've got one. Over there at the bank two blocks away. First floor, left corner. Katrina is on her way there, so if you get there fast you can video the rescue." He pointed and, without waiting for their response, was off again on his search for other earthquake survivors who could use the SENTINELS' help.

Maggie looked at the rubble near the building in question, and they hustled to it.

"Look, the window's out of the office James mentioned," Maggie said as they drew near the bank.

Focus lifted his camera and shot video as they approached. Careful to avoid stepping on broken window glass, he picked his way toward the opening and sucked in his breath as he looked through. "I see someone's feet," Focus said quietly.

Maggie peered through the window. Feet in sensible low black heels stuck out from under a table. She looked along the legs and spotted a downed pillar trapping, but not crushing, the woman. "Oh god."

"Did James send you?" Katrina levitated herself over to

them.

Maggie nodded her head toward the glassless window. "There's a pillar on a woman, just in there." She moved out of Katrina's way.

Katrina assessed the situation. She stared at the pillar, and it levitated off the woman. The woman groaned but did not move. Katrina pursed her lips and stared at the woman, gently levitating her off the floor.

Maggie watched in mute awe as Katrina mentally held both the deadly heavy pillar and the woman suspended in midair. For a moment, the pillar seemed to tremble, as though threatening to harm the woman a second time. Maggie sucked in her breath and watched as the woman floated to the side a few feet. Katrina let the pillar drop. It landed with a bone-rattling boom, and the force sent glass shards flying through the window. Maggie and Focus jumped to the side, but Maggie didn't move fast enough. A piece of glass nicked her left arm, and she clasped her right hand over the cut.

"You okay, Focus?" she asked.

"Yeah. You?"

Maggie lifted her bloody hand off the cut and peered at it. She lifted it to her mouth as though to suck it clean, but seemed to think better of it. "Small cut. Not too bad. I just need a bandage for it."

"You think they asked us here to counteract what GRIM is saying about Mod incident in Sydney?" Focus handed her a bandage from his photo bag, which held a few first aid supplies just in case.

"It's entirely possible. But the fact remains, they are helping here. And they have an advantage that other aid organizations don't." Maggie stuck the bandage over her cut.

"The almighty Mod will save us all!" Focus chuckled,

thinking about the latest GRIM pro-registration ad campaign, which heavily featured raw footage of the SENTINELS fighting another Mod on a Sydney beach.

"Hey! I need your help." Katrina levitated the injured woman right through the window, but saw no good landing zone for her on the glass-strewn sidewalk. She frowned, and the shards flew up and back through the bank's open window. Finally, she lowered the wounded woman onto the cleared sidewalk.

"Check her vitals," Katrina said.

Surprised into action, Maggie did just that. She knelt beside the injured woman and grasped her hand. "Are you okay?" There was no response, so Maggie slid her fingers up to the woman's wrist and sought a pulse. She frowned and moved her fingers to the woman's neck. At last, she found a pulse, faint and slow.

Maggie shook her head. "I don't know. She has a pulse, so she's alive. But..."

Katrina spoke into a comms piece. "Waleed, I need a teleportal over here next to the bank."

Black globules crackled into existence, and Waleed stepped through the glittering portal. Like James, he wore a backpack. Maggie knew Waleed's contained cookies that he could eat when his energy depleted from making so many teleportals during the rescue effort, while James' contained candy bars to help fuel his super speed. Waleed looked around and spotted the victim. "Hospital or Jiya?"

"Hospital, I think," Katrina said.

"Got it." He opened the portal, and Katrina once again levitated the woman. This time, she entered Waleed's portal to deliver the woman to an emergency room in Rio Grande, Argentina, where the SENTINELS were sending those whose injuries were not life-threatening, since the local hospital in the Falklands was a shambles. When the woman was safely on a bed, Katrina returned through the teleportal and Waleed let it close.

As Katrina came through, she tilted her head, listening to her comms unit. "Okay, I'll tell them." She raised her eyebrows at Maggie and Focus. "James said you should go to the local library. It's that way." She pointed down the block.

"Sure," Maggie said. "We'll go now." But she was talking to the air. Katrina and Waleed had vanished through another of Waleed's teleportals.

As Maggie and Focus hurried in the direction Katrina had indicated, she thought about some of the early reports she'd read on the internet posted by the earthquake's survivors. One man claimed a serious amount of mountain building had transpired during the thirty-second quake. The mountains were there, sure enough, but she had no idea if they were taller than they had been. Despite years as a travel journalist, she had never before been to the Falkland Islands. Maybe some building had happened, but the bulk of the equation was firmly on the side of destruction.

According to news reports, part of Stanley had sunk into the ocean in one fast landslide, as was the case for most of the island's coastline, although scientists couldn't agree on the mechanics of just how or why that had happened. One after another, scientists posited hypotheses, each more absurd than the last. The one Maggie found most unsettling was that this earthquake signaled the onset of a new set of weird disasters, such as those that led up to the White Light Wave event five years ago.

Maggie was grateful the islands weren't home to many. Around three thousand people lived in the entire archipelago, although an estimated two-thirds of them were Stanley residents. Early accounts indicated at least half of the city's residents had been injured or died in the earthquake. She worried about what they would find at the library. She imagined row after row of book shelves, toppled like so many dominoes.

Her thoughts kept coming back to the latest GRIM ad fanning the flames with anti-Mod rhetoric. How long would it be before there was actual bloodshed against anyone who supported Mods?

Ahead, Maggie spotted people milling around someone lying on the ground outside what she thought must be the library.

As they neared, Maggie saw her initial impression was wrong. The group stood around five people stretched out on the ground, not one. Four people lay on the grass, unmoving. Victims. Jiya, the SENTINELS' healer, knelt by the fifth victim and held her orange-glowing hands over a gash in a young man's head.

Focus filmed and Maggie watched in awe as the bleeding slowed to a trickle and the wound began to stitch itself up.

"Thank you," the young man said through gritted teeth. He had slicked-back brown hair and a determined expression on his face.

"You can't keep putting yourself in danger, Ian," the healer said sternly yet lovingly.

Maggie saw that the man could not look Jiya in the eye.

"Can't stop now, have to keep up the rescue effort. There's got to be more survivors out there." He pushed himself off the ground and used his sleeve to wipe blood off his head. He waved over several men, who grabbed first aid kits and flashlights and headed off inside the damaged library.

Maggie watched the healer knee-walk to the next victim and study him. She brought her hands close to his neck, and orange glowed on his face despite the daylight. His eyes fluttered open and he took in his surroundings.

"How? Why?" He patted his head.

"Shh, shh, *beta*, you're okay. You've been in an earthquake, but you're alive and okay. Rest now while I tend the other wounded." Jiya knee-walked to the next victim and studied her. The healer placed her hands over the woman's chest, and the orange glow appeared again.

Focus continued filming.

James blurred to a stop in front of Focus' camera. He looked at his teammate, intent on her patient, and then at Maggie and Focus.

"We're shifting from rescue to recovery work. We're starting with that building. It will mainly be Kirra and Katrina who carry out the heavy lifting, so to speak, and Waleed will 'port them directly to a field on the outskirts of town. I'll be scouting each location for the deceased. Let's go." James turned and took off.

Maggie and Focus looked at each other. "Recovery. Damn," she said. "I was hoping a lot more people had survived."

Focus seemed glum. "Me too. Let's go."

Maggie looked at him. "I know this was nothing like what happened back with Kili, but I just can't shake the feeling that we might be on the same path as we were back then."

CHAPTER
50

17 December

Emma struggled up from the depths of her drug-induced stupor. Every morning had been like this since Surgeon started giving her the power-dampening shots. Every lunchtime was like this. Every evening was like this.

Alrick Wagner

She could not take it any longer. The days passed like weeks for her. She could never concentrate long enough to make sense of it all. Despair had sunk its hooks into her. In her heart of hearts, she still held out hope the SENTINELS would rescue her, but expectations of her rescue had diminished greatly.

Someone bearing a tray woke her. He waited patiently while she groggily used the toilet and washed her hands before returning to the bed. How she hated the bed. She felt like she had been in it for years, not mere months. When had she last run barefoot through the soft grass in Crystal City? How she missed island life and its fresh, fragrant air. Her friends. Her freedom. She missed her parents, too, but she'd have to go to heaven to see them.

Once she was sitting up in the bed, the cafeteria worker placed the tray table over her lap. He slumped in the chair while she ate. This morning's breakfast was a cold ham and cheese omelet, orange juice, and milk. Sighing, she tucked in. She took her time. The longer she could stretch it out, the more time she had to think. As soon as she was done eating, nothing pleasant remained on the schedule. She worried next would be a visit from Pierce, telling her to fish for more people with powers. That would also postpone Surgeon, who frightened her beyond measure. Surgeon typically arrived after breakfast and dinner and to administer that vile blue shot.

A sleeping shot.

A shot that stole her powers.

Mostly.

It combined with some kind of dampening device that kept her from being able to send her mind beyond the walls of her room. Her cell. Her prison.

While she could, she ate, thoroughly chewing each tiny bite. She sent her mind out looking for someone who could help her. A couple of days ago, Emma thought she had sensed someone familiar, someone she might trust, someone with good energy. She felt as if she had seen this person in the dance studio of her mind. But whoever it was, the shot and the dampener dulled her senses.

Rescue, if it was going to happen, would require much more of a helping hand from herself. She systematically sent her mind out, looking for cracks in the dampening device.

"Come on, kid, I need to take the dishes back to the cafeteria. Hurry up," the boy said, finally losing patience with her slow eating. He fidgeted with the key chain on his belt, and she tuned out the jingling and clanging keys.

Without answer, she continued cutting off small bits of

omelet to eat.

There had to be a weakness somewhere.

The door opened, and Emma saw the weakness all at once. Hurriedly, she sent a blast out to any and all who might hear. "Help, it's Emma. Captain Pierce has me on his boat. Come get me before he hurts anyone else." She repeated the message until the door fully closed behind Pierce, completing the circuit of the room's power-dampening technology. Behind Pierce was Alrick.

Cheerfully, Pierce greeted Emma.

That's new, she thought. He's never in a good mood. She shrank back from him, and her fork clattered onto the plate. The more she saw him, the more she hated him. She certainly had lost her appetite.

"Don't look so scared. We're just here for a little information," Pierce said.

Emma did not respond. She avoided looking at Alrick.

"I have a little project that I've been working on. We're about to move out of the planning and preparation stage and into the execution phase. But I have a few problems. I need more powers. This time, child, you will find the specific powers I seek."

Whatever color might have been left on her face after months of captivity fled. Resigned, she asked what power he wanted her to find.

"Metal manipulation," Pierce said.

"Okay," she said. She settled into her bed and felt Alrick slip into her head. The creepy German descended further and further into her mindscape. A shiver shot down her spine and she shuddered. Compelled to do so, she sent her mind out but got nowhere. She looked at him and said so.

"Right, forgot to turn the dampener off," Pierce said, propping open the door to break the circuit of the room's power-dampening technology. "No funny games."

This time, when Emma sent her mind out, she was able to search. But with Alrick the puppet master guiding her, she could only look for the power of metal manipulation. Eventually, she found it and said so.

"Good, where is he?"

"It's a she, not a he," Emma said with an eye roll. "But you already know about her."

"What do you mean?" Pierce cocked his head at her.

"Margaux. She's in Zurich." She hadn't thought about the Vietnamese Mod since she'd left the Tribe years ago.

"Margaux, eh?" Pierce looked at her through slitted eyes. "What else did you do, girl?"

"Nothing," she said. "It just took a long time to find her. It's those shots. They slow me down."

For a long moment, Pierce said nothing. He just looked at her. "Find me some invisibility."

Emma silently stifled a scream. She hated being forced to help Pierce. It was bad enough being prisoner here, wherever that was, but worse to have to do his bidding. She fought tears and glared at Pierce.

"Yes, sir," Emma said, and began the new search, directed by Alrick.

"There's a man in Mozambique who can be invisible. What now?"

"That's all," Pierce said satisfied with the find. "Come on, Alrick, there's still work to do."

Emma had a sinking realization that she had just signed their death warrants. Unable to actually connect to them because of the room's power barrier, she wished the two Mods would be strong enough to resist Pierce.

CHAPTER
51

17 December

Maggie had never heard an explosion until now, and only sheer luck—her taxi had been in a fender bender on the way back to the office—had kept this explosion from being the last sound she'd ever hear. Maggie and Focus, along with Jerry and Barry, were at the entrance to the building TheModsBlog called home. They had just walked past a glut of GRIM protesters, and as usual had ignored them. The automatic door slid open, and they were about to enter the building when something boomed and the building shook. It sounded like an explosion on one of the upper floors.

"Oh god," Maggie said just as Focus grabbed her arm.

"We have to get out of here," Maggie heard one of the security guys say, but her ears were ringing and she wasn't sure if it was Jerry or Barry.

As a group, they stepped back onto the sidewalk and looked up. About where her windows should be were jagged holes instead. Maggie swore.

Near her, bystanders and GRIM protesters alike were pointing and gawking at what Maggie was becoming sure was her office.

"We have to get up there," Focus said.

The pair ran into the building, and Jerry and Barry chased after them. Focus looked at the elevator and shook his head. "We'd better take the stairs."

"Are you kidding? We're on the thirty-eighth floor."

He looked grim. "It's going to be a fight to get up there, too, because they will evacuate the building."

Maggie nodded and pulled out her mobile phone. As the four ran to the stairwell, she punched the receptionist's name on her phone. Upstairs Janine's cell phone rang and rang and rang before rolling over into voice mail. Maggie swore. Janine always answered the phone.

Maggie felt like a salmon swimming upstream as they raced upstairs while everyone else in a blind panic shoved downstairs. If she hadn't been so focused on her employees and company she might have commented on this. Maggie spent the entire climb imagining the worst. She was so upset and worried she didn't even notice the burning in her legs until they reached the thirty-eighth floor and she stopped climbing. Jerry and Barry took the lead in exiting the stairwell.

When Maggie saw no immediate damage, she cautiously began to hope. As they neared the office doors, however, the sound coming from inside quashed her hopes. She followed Jerry and Barry through the office door and stopped so suddenly that Focus bumped into her.

It was chaos in the reception area of TheModsBlog. The reporters were the ones who were in action—talking on their phones or helping others—while most of the remaining support staff reeled from the trauma. Some walked around in circles, muttering, their eyes vacant. Others sagged in red leather couches. It appeared that many of the employees had evacuated. Part of the wall dividing the reception area from the corridor behind was splattered on the floor. From the looks of it, the chunks of the wall narrowly missed hitting the receptionist's desk. Janine was nowhere to be seen.

"Janine?" Maggie called out. "Are you okay?"

The receptionist didn't answer, but a reporter named Ashley broke off from a phone call for a second to answer. "She's fine. I think she's still on the phone with 911. But some people are hurt and the blast killed Brenda, Kevin, and Carrie."

"Oh god," Maggie said again. A wave of guilt swallowed her and she sagged against Focus. Brenda was just out of college and reminded her so much of herself at that age— fearless, ready for adventure, looking for trouble. And now she was gone. Just like that. It took every ounce of self-control in her not to burst into tears right then.

Jerry set about securing the office while Barry stayed glued to Maggie's side.

Maggie heard sirens. It sounded like they were right outside the building. She tugged at Focus. "Let's go see."

What she saw made her stomach sour. Most of the wall of her office was gone. TheModsBlog mosaic lay shattered in the hallway. Pieces of it were next to Kevin's bloody body. Holding back dry heaves, she peered into her office. Her office as well as the neighboring office to the south had been destroyed. That office, however, hadn't been empty at the time. Both Brenda and Carrie sprawled lifeless on the floor.

"Damnit!" Maggie screamed. Behind her, Focus kept a steadying arm on her shoulder.

"We should go back to the lobby," Barry said. "It's not safe here."

Mute, Maggie shook her head and pressed on.

She could hear the sirens through the shattered window, and wind whistled into her office. Her desk was a pile of rubble. The wall separating her office from the meeting room just north of her had also been heavily damaged. Fortunately for the people in that room, the brunt of the blast had gone toward the south. All four had been injured, but the damage didn't appear to be life-threatening.

The bomb had clearly been in her office. Dumb luck. A traffic accident had kept her from being in the wrong place when it mattered.

"Who do you think did this?" Focus asked her.

"Take your pick," Maggie said. Her voice came out bitter and sad. "Let's see. I've been called a mouthpiece of the SENTINELS, so maybe it was someone who hates them. Or it could be just about anyone who hates the Mods. It could have been the GRIM protesters outside. Or somebody who maybe personally hates me."

"You don't think CoCo—"

"No, she's done some bad things, she's in with a bad crowd, but I just don't see her doing ... this," Maggie said, gesturing around at the damage. "Focus, I just don't think I can keep doing this." Her voice was small and petulant, even to her own ears. The fear came and went, and she felt spent from the grief.

"You're going to just quit TheModsBlog? Over this?" Focus waved his hand at the mess that had been a bustling newsroom earlier that day.

"They attacked us. Brenda, Kevin, and Carrie are dead, Focus, and four people are going to the ER. We're lucky to be alive, and I won't endanger anyone else by keeping the blog going."

"This blog is important. No one else is so unbiased in their coverage of the Mods and the calls for powers registration," he argued.

"I'm not unbiased. Remember, I'm the 'mouthpiece of the SENTINELS'?"

"You know you're not."

"I've written more good stuff about them than the other Mods. We were just in the Falkland Islands documenting their heroics. And when the other Mods get my attention, it's usually a bunch of bad actors who got up to no good. So maybe they have a point." She shrugged unenthusiastically, a few tears trickling down her cheeks.

"We're doing something worthwhile here, even if you feel a bit lost from time to time. You can't bow down to the fear tactics. You have to stay strong." Focus studied her a moment. "This is awful, I won't say it isn't. But you can let whoever did this win, or you can fight back. The Maggie I know would never let them win. If you fight, I've got your back."

"How, Focus? Hmm? How did they do this? I had security, but they managed to get the office, would have gotten us if our taxi hadn't had that fender bender." She closed her eyes and shuddered at the close call. She sagged against him, leaned her head back, and covered her eyes with the crook of her elbow. A few more tears slipped down her face. "I just don't know if it's a fight worth fighting anymore."

CHAPTER

5 2

18 December

Chaos reigned in downtown Brussels near the Europa building. When Ericka and her pals from Base 47 teleported to the European Union Council building, she saw a quartet of Mods from the Tribe attacking

**Jimin Pak
"Brute"**

protesters. The air was crisp and cold. Maru was using his weather manipulation powers to create a localized hailstorm that pelted the registration supporters. She recognized Dafydd immediately. He was hitting one of the protesters with his own sign. It read, "Register all Mods!"

She realized belatedly that there were two throngs of protesters. On the east side of the building, scared protesters held signs opposing the powers registration effort, although most of these posters hung limply by their sides. They seemed to have forgotten the legends on their signs—one read "The rights of the minority should never be subject to the whim of the majority." They watched in fascinated horror as Mods bullied protesters calling for the EU to set registration of Mods as its policy.

Ericka's eyes glowed green as she took in the situation. Jimin, Butcher, Maru, and multiple Dafydds were physically assaulting members of the pro-registration camp.

Experience from her time as police chief for Crystal City helped her quickly size up the situation and give orders. The self-replicating Dafydd tipped the scales against them. She wished she'd been able to bring several more Mods, but no one else had been available when they'd gotten the panicked call from a source at the EU. Waleed had teleported them in but was still spending most of his time helping in the final stages of the Falkland Islands crisis.

"James, get those gawking protesters to safety first, then start helping the ones under attack. Etienne and Kirra, you take on Dafydd and Butcher. I'll handle Maru and Jimin. James, once you're done moving the protesters to safety, come help me."

"On it!" James buzzed back and forth, ferrying the protesters to a safer place a couple of blocks away. Many, oblivious to the danger, objected to being removed from the scene of such excitement.

From the corner of her eye, Ericka saw Etienne and Kirra make a move for Dafydd and Butcher. Most of the powers registration protesters and supporters were no longer in evidence, and she saw James blur by carrying another to safety. Ericka focused on Jimin and Maru. She went on the offense, shooting green energy from her hands at Maru and Jimin.

Maru fell in a groaning heap on the sidewalk. Without his full concentration, his hailstorm halted fully, leaving the ground littered with grape-sized pieces of hail. Jimin, however, absorbed the green energy and converted it into strength. "Thanks for the power-up!" She flipped into the air, over and above Ericka.

Ericka was spinning to face her when Jimin kicked her side and sent her sprawling. Ericka's right ribs exploded in agony and she struggled to breathe. She was grateful to be wearing the SENTINEL armor, which provided impact absorption, instead of her regular police uniform. How could she fight Jimin if everything she did to her increased Brute's strength? She took a few shallow breaths—deep breathing felt out of the question given her aching ribs—and struggled to her knees. In relief, she saw James had finished moving all the bystanders. He raced up and ran circles around Jimin, keeping her from moving.

"Thanks, James. Keep it up!" Ericka said.

"No problem. Just glad to have you back on the team," James said.

"It's temporary," she said, her voice tight. She surveyed the scene. Kirra seemed to be holding her own while fighting the two Dafydds, calling up the cobblestones from the street to toss at her targets. In much the same way Katrina could control objects, anything from the earth was hers to do with as she pleased. Her ability to twist, rotate, and launch the cobblestones allowed her to pelt only the intended opponents.

Etienne struggled against the vicious Butcher. Ericka, still reeling from the pain in her ribs, sent two green blasts at Butcher, but missed. Butcher whirled and seemed to forget about Etienne, who faded invisible while Butcher's back was turned. Butcher charged at Ericka. Again, she aimed green blasts at him, but they only seemed to slow him down, not knock him out.

Butcher leapt at Ericka, who dodged. She sent a green blast right at his chest, which he narrowly avoided. He jabbed at her but missed. Again, she sent her green blasts at him, and this time, he went down, snarling. She blasted him again, for good measure, and wondered where Alrick was, since where one was the other often was. She was grateful, at least, they didn't have to worry about Alrick. Perhaps Jimin was minding Butcher for the time being, Ericka thought.

She turned from Butcher to see Kirra fighting with four Dafydds. Apparently, an invisible Etienne was helping her out because one of the Dafydds crumpled to his knees even though Kirra hadn't touched him.

Holding her side, Ericka ran toward Kirra to help her out.

"Ericka, behind you!" James called out. He halted his speeding cyclone around Jimin and raced off to help Ericka. He slipped on a hail pellet from Maru's storm and collided into a column. James screamed in pain and buckled limply to the ground.

She was turning to see the threat and the reason for the scream when she smelled Butcher's breath. She reflexively held her hands up in front of her face, sending a double dose of green blasts right into Butcher's face. He stumbled back, then seemed to regain his footing. She sent a steady stream of green blasts at him.

Why wouldn't he just go down, already? Ericka hadn't encountered someone who seemed to be able to power through her blasts like Butcher, other than Jimin, who could absorb them and use them to increase her own powers.

She heard Etienne whisper in her comms piece and she nodded. She couldn't see him, but she felt a breeze as he sprang past her at Butcher. Suddenly, Butcher convulsed, and Ericka knew Etienne had used his charged escrima sticks on him. Butcher seemed to sense where Etienne was, because he savagely clawed at him.

Etienne grunted. Blood started dripping in midair, then Etienne's ripped and bloody uniform appeared. Finally, Etienne himself materialized, clutching at his chest. A gash spanned his chest from right shoulder to left hip. Etienne seemed to be trying to hold the gaping wound together. He sagged and fell to the ground.

Ericka resumed shooting green blasts at Butcher. They were in trouble. She called for Waleed on her comms device. A few people had again congregated around them and were watching the scene. Kirra seemed to finally have come out on top of the Dafydd fight by entombing him and his replicas in the ground.

Waleed teleported in from Base 47 and took stock of the situation.

"Waleed! Get James and Etienne back to the base! They're both hurt," Ericka said.

Waleed opened portals back to Base 47 for the injured Mods. Then he turned his attention to the others. He opened a teleportal beneath Butcher's feet, and he fell through and disappeared, but that particular kind of teleportal cost Waleed. He'd need to rest, Ericka knew.

"Bring him back right now!" Jimin demanded. When Waleed refused, she advanced on a trio of passersby who'd just turned the corner. She grabbed a woman dressed in a pants suit and held the cowering woman up. She pulled her limbs in opposite directions, as the woman screamed. Her two pals shrank back in fear. "You get him back here right now and maybe I won't split her in half."

"Stop! We'll do it! Just leave her alone," Ericka shouted.

Grudgingly, Waleed opened a portal three feet above the ground. Butcher fell out of it and landed with a grunt.

Jimin dropped the woman flat on the ground.

Butcher snarled as he wiped blood from his face.

The effects of Ericka's energy blasts had finally worn off, and Maru rose to his feet. He whipped up the winds around them and flew himself and the rest of Pierce's Mods away, leaving Waleed, Kirra, and Ericka to face an angry crowd.

The group descended upon them, shouting, "Mods, go home!"

"I think it's best we take off. We've already created an international incident. Don't want to give the fearmongers any more ammunition," Ericka said as she signaled to Waleed.

Waleed opened a portal back to Base 47. "Kirra, Ericka, after you." He pushed them both through and followed. Kirra and Ericka stumbled into the War Room.

***

"There you go," Jiya said to the newly healed Etienne. He took off the bloodstained uniform. Jiya turned to the Kenyan speedster. She held onto the twisted leg and closed her eyes. A warm healing glow emanated from her hands. James held his breath while she worked her healing magic, and Ericka and Kirra watched.

"What happened out there?" Bayanai strode into the War Room.

"We were outpowered. We couldn't get an upper hand," Ericka said.

"You're lucky Jiya was here to heal you. And lucky Waleed was around to teleport you out. I don't want to yell, but this is exactly the kind of danger we need to avoid. You're all too important to lose." Bayanai studied the group. "Maybe we are too close to truly see the machinations at work here."

The team listened to him, fuming at constantly being one step behind the bad guys.

"We're not looking at the whole picture," Bayanai said. "We're not seeing the connection. After what we found out in Sydney, we have to plan this carefully. He's already thrashed us once." He looked at his team. "We can't go in half-cocked. We have to be better than this. We have to save them. We have something that could work in our favor. We know Pierce's powers are causing no small amount of physical and mental distress—"

"I'll say," Emilio interjected. "He's falling apart. He's unstable."

Bayanai nodded. "Right, it could be in our favor, or it could work against us. But we need to be aware of it. He's powerful, but there's a great cost associated with it." He paused and considered his next words. "It's time to get out from behind the eight ball."

CHAPTER
53

18 December

Arthur barged into Anabel's penthouse. In a blink, he took in the scene. Ten guests around a formal dining table went from laughing and chatting to silent. The remnants of a huge meal filled the table. Everyone was in

Arthur Hastings

evening wear. Maks and Anabel, natural entertainers and hosts, were also in formal wear.

"What? No invitation for me?"

"Excuse me," Anabel said to her guests, rising from her spot at the head of the table. "How'd you get past my guards?"

He shrugged and grinned. "I'm kind of a badass."

Anabel passed her champagne glass to a waiter and rushed over to Arthur. "What are you doing here?"

"I was in the neighborhood and thought I'd just check in on my partners. I mean, after all, I did kill my father too," Arthur said, raising his voice enough to ensure all the guests could hear him.

In hushed tones, the guests speculated about the accusation.

"How dare you." Anabel hissed so coldly at him it should have covered the windows in frost.

"We're a little busy right now, why don't you come back tomorrow?" Maks sipped his martini and advanced toward Arthur.

"Ah-ah! I don't think so." Arthur slid his jacket back just enough for Maksim and Anabel to glimpse the firearm they'd most recently seen used to shoot Henry. Anabel blanched.

"You should have called first, Arthur," Maksim said.

"Yeah, I don't see it that way, partner." He snickered. "Besides, it's much more fun to drop in unexpected."

Anabel turned back to her guests. "I'm sorry, my friends. My brother and I have some business that needs our immediate attention. We'll just be in the other room for a few minutes. We'll be right back, and then we'll have dessert." She led her brother and Arthur into the drawing room and closed the door firmly behind them.

Arthur sauntered over to the bar and spotted a bottle of fifty-year-old scotch. "That's more like it." He opened it and filled three tumblers. Rather than handing them to the twins, he left theirs on the bar and strolled to the middle of the room.

"What do you want?" Anabel asked.

"You make it sound so ominous, Ana. Don't be such a wet blanket. I'm here to visit with my new best friends." Arthur sipped his drink and smiled appreciatively.

Anabel frowned and looked at her brother, who shrugged.

"Not sure what you think that we owe you." Maks walked over to the bar and took his drink.

"Let's be honest here, we only came to power by killing

our dads. The only one who stands in our way is sweet, old Elise. If we can pick her off, we can consolidate the operation for ourselves." Arthur removed his pinstripe suit jacket and tossed it over the couch.

"What are you suggesting?" Anabel folded her arms across her chest and stared at him.

"A little game." Arthur smiled.

Maks looked over to his sister and raised his eyebrows.

"What's your plan?" Anabel asked.

"You're on board?" Arthur whipped his brown hair out of his face.

"Let's say that we are. I'm sure Elise is taking precautions after what you did to your father." She walked over to the bar, grasped the final tumbler of scotch, and took a sip.

"We can still take her out and consolidate power," Arthur said.

"This is treason to the Ascendancy," Anabel said.

"You two killed your father to get a seat at the table. Treason is merely a complication." Arthur looked at them. "Aren't you two really all about the power and not the ultimate goals of the Ascendancy?"

The twins looked at each other, then at Arthur, and shrugged.

Anabel grinned and handed the drink back to Arthur. "Elise is mine."

"Fine with me." Arthur smiled at them both. "And as for you, Maks, I know all about your savage extracurricular games."

"What games?" Maksim asked.

Arthur rolled his eyes. "Don't play innocent with me. We all know you've been killing Mods."

Maksim flashed a worried look at his sister. For her part, Anabel seemed surprised about Arthur's knowledge but unfazed by the accusation. Reassured, Maksim looked back at Arthur. "How did you know?"

"I have the perfect Mod for you to take out."

"Even if I do that, you realize it will always be two against one. This will always be an unequal partnership once Elise is gone," Maksim said. "Then again, what's to stop us from taking you out right now, in addition to Elise, and claiming it all for ourselves?"

Arthur shrugged. "I accept that. For now, our interests are aligned. Isn't that enough?"

The twins glanced at each other and then back at their new partner.

"Then to us," Anabel said.

They all lifted their tumblers of scotch to toast their union.

CHAPTER
54

18 December

Moonlight dusted the grounds of Base 47, giving it an almost magical effect. Tonight was the night. Bayanai was finally going to make his move. He could no longer be content with stolen glances and wishes. It was all or nothing. He would ask Kirra out. All he had to do was find her. He walked along the glass passageways connecting the complex and saw something that made his heart sink. This was not how he wanted to find her.

In a clearing on a bench, Kirra and Etienne sat, arms wrapped around each other. The moment was perfect. But his timing was off. It should have been him, but he'd never made his move. The longer he stared, the more frustrated he became. He turned around and walked back into the main structure like a man walking to his last meal.

Inside, Bayanai paused at the door to the Base 47 head of security's office. He heard Laura's raised voice. It was out of character for her to yell, and he frowned. He turned to leave, but as he did so, he overheard Pierce's name. Intrigued, he nudged open the door and peered through the crack. She was too engrossed in the conversation to hear the door open. Laura faced the window and yelled into the phone.

"I'm doing what I can, Pierce. There's only so much I can do to cover for your team. If they were even half as competent as they are powerful, you wouldn't need to me to constantly undermine the SENTINELS." She put her left hand on her waist.

Bayanai sucked in his breath in shock. His heart sank. All this time, the mole he sought was his head of security? The woman he'd vouched for? How many times had he given her sensitive information and private details about the SENTINELS?

"I don't care. I've done everything I can. The rest is up to you." Laura turned, saw Bayanai peeking through the crack, and seemed to shrink in size. "Pierce, I have to go." Her voice sounded strained. She nodded. "I'm going to take care of it. Just let them be." She ended her call. They glared at each other for a moment.

"You weren't supposed to hear that," Laura said.

"Clearly." Bayanai entered the room and shut the door behind him. He stood tall to steady himself.

"I wish it didn't have to be like this." She picked up a table lamp and swung it at Bayanai.

Bayanai swerved and barely avoided being cracked in the head. "How could you?"

Laura dropped the lamp and lunged at the leader of the SENTINELS.

"How could I? How could I?" She practically shrieked at him. "You stand in your ivory tower and judge us when we have to make a choice." Laura toppled Bayanai and straddled him, applying all her strength to keep him down.

"What are you saying?" He struggled to get out from under her.

"You wouldn't understand." She leaned over, keeping

him pinned down.

He wasn't going to let her get away with this betrayal. He launched his hips up, twisted his body, and flipped Laura to the right. As he rolled into a sitting position, she caught his jaw with a right hook, sending him back against the wall. She stood and clenched her fists at him.

Blood dripped from his lips. She had decades of training over him.

"There's more where that came from." Her breath quickened.

"We don't have to do this. Just tell me what happened." He was no match for her skill, but perhaps he could use her desperation to his advantage.

She took two quick steps and jabbed at his stomach, but he danced out of the way. As he did, he grabbed her extended arm and shifted on his back heel. The move sent her crashing her into the wall behind him. Because he didn't have an offensive power, he had trained intensely in hand-to-hand combat. This was a perfect opportunity to use those skills.

With a speed that surprised him, she turned and grabbed Bayanai, wrapping her arms around his neck. They struggled for a moment before she leaned back. Together, they dropped to the floor.

Laura squeezed harder and Bayanai fought to escape her grasp.

"I've known you for two years. Why?" Bayanai's words came out choked and breathless.

"Nothing is ever so simple, so easy. Life isn't like that."

"Of course not, but you didn't have to betray us like this. Not to Pierce!" Bayanai, sensing her heart wasn't really in this fight, knew he had the advantage. He tucked his chin toward his chest and violently raised his head, knocking into Laura's head. Surprised and with a groan, she let go of him.

Bayanai pushed himself off the ground and slid toward the other side of the room.

They sat across from each other, chests heaving from emotion and exertion. For several long minutes, no one spoke. Bayanai scrutinized Laura.

"I'm sorry, Bayanai. I am so sorry. Pierce got to me. He blackmailed me. Threatened to expose my past and—" Her voice faltered, trying to hide years of shame.

"Why didn't you say anything? We could have helped you. It didn't have to come to this." He opened his hands wide. He could see in her face the struggle she was facing. He made his voice gentle. "Just talk to me."

She shook her head.

"I can wait all day," he said. "I used to tend sheep. Patience is woven into my DNA." He got comfortable and watched her.

Anger flashed in her eyes, then resignation. She sighed.

"I gave an order," she said. "An order that cost thousands of lives."

Bayanai looked at her pained face and wanted to reach out to her, but restrained himself. He needed to hear her out.

"Years ago I was in Afghanistan. We had found insurgents hiding in a village but the intel we had was incomplete. I sent a team in to wipe out the insurgents and to protect thousands of villagers. That team was led by Pierce."

The last bit hit Bayanai square in the chest. He'd known of her Marines background, of course, but it had never occurred to him to ask if she knew Pierce.

"He didn't succeed, and it was brutal. The villagers and his team were all slaughtered. He was one of only a few survivors. Now he's leveraged that against me. The thousands of innocent lives, his own life being thrown into the pit. He blames me for it all. And he's right." She drooped back against the wall, deflated like a three-day-old balloon.

"Laura, whatever happened, you can't hold on to it forever," Bayanai said.

She scoffed. "You can when you've seen the slaughter on video. I saw so many die. They didn't have to. It was my fault, and they visit me every night in my dreams." She closed her eyes. When she opened them again, she seemed more in control of herself. "I gave a bad order. Or I made a bad judgment call. Call it what you want. The long and short of it is that ever since he found out I was here at Base 47, he's been threatening to reveal the entire operation on the world stage." Laura rested her chin on her hand.

"What would happen if the world found out about the mission?"

"If they tug at the strings, governments could fall."

"What would happen to you if the world found out you authorized the mission?"

Now Laura looked like she might truly cry. Her eyes reddened and her breathing went shallow.

"He's threatened to do to my entire family tree what I saw on the slaughter footage. No one should die like that."

"That's a pretty powerful motivator." Bayanai studied her for a long moment, thinking about the burden she'd carried. "How do we find Pierce?"

"We can't. He's on his damn warship most of the time. I can't find it, and trust me I've tried. It's cloaked and never stops moving. It's impossible."

"Laura, impossible is my stock in trade. It may take us a while, but we'll get there." Bayanai wiped blood from his lip and slid his body up the wall. "We'll figure out how to stop Pierce and keep your family safe." He extended his hand to her.

Laura took a deep breath and, pushing with both hands,

stood up. "I'm sorry I made you send part of your team to Sydney. Pierce needed to distract you, and he thought it might focus the SENTINELS on the Swarm instead."

Bayanai squinted at her and squared his jaw. It was several long moments before he spoke. "Anything else you've done on Pierce's behalf I should know about?"

She shook her head.

He studied her a moment longer. "Okay, then."

"Sorry I attacked you. I panicked."

Bayanai laughed a little. "You really do have a great right hook."

Laura smiled ruefully before lowering her chin. "Bayanai, there's another thing. I'm not the only one here on New Atlantis spying on you." She walked him to the door.

"What do you mean? How far does this go?"

"I'm not exactly sure, Pierce skimped on the details. But whoever it is has powers. And is good at hiding."

"Well, then we have to keep this ruse going so we can find them," Bayanai said. "For now, you proceed as normal. Let Pierce keep thinking that he has you in his pocket. And you're going to tell me everything you know about his operation. We may finally be able to turn the tables on him."

CHAPTER

55

19 December

"Okay, just one more time, Mr. Florentino," Susan said. The physical therapist was a portly Japanese-American dressed in obnoxiously boldly patterned scrubs. She held his left leg on the bed. "Bend your toes."

The private hospital room was dotted with vases filled with gladiolas, star-gazer lilies, and sunflowers. The newspaper on the bed was opened to the opinion page. The top piece featured a GRIM spokesperson railing against Mods. Though the day was sunny, the blinds were closed and the room lights were dim.

Sweat dripped from Luca's forehead onto his white V-neck shirt. With his eyes tightly closed he white-knuckled the bars on the side of the bed and tried. His teeth gnashed against each other under the pressure. But nothing.

"Just breathe." She patted his leg.

He only grunted.

"Your family's been to visit?" she asked.

"When is Hector back? He doesn't ask as many questions as you."

"Not sure. Our schedules fluctuate." She began the

massage portion of the therapy session, pressing firmly on his right thigh.

"And no, they haven't visited." Luca frowned. "Not close."

"Oh, that's too bad. What about your friends? You seem to have a lot of love in your life." She tilted her head toward the display of flowers.

"I asked them to stay away. Haven't seen them in a long time. Better that way." Luca scratched the beard he'd allow to grow since the accident.

"I hardly think that's true."

Luca said nothing.

"Don't you have someone special in your life?"

"I did. But he hasn't been here in a long time."

"Maybe he tried to visit, but didn't know what to say to you," she suggested as she moved from massaging the thigh to his calf. "Sometimes people don't know what to say when other people go through traumatic experiences."

"I doubt it. Never had any trouble speaking his mind to me before."

"You know, I can cut that for you. If you'd like." She touched her face, intimating his beard.

"It's okay, just itchy. I kind of like it now." Luca turned to look at himself in the mirror. He hadn't shaved in weeks and if it were not for the nurses he probably wouldn't have bathed either. His once perfectly coiffed hair was disheveled and greasy.

"What would you say if this loved one were here?" She flexed his right foot back and forth.

Luca looked at her and sighed. He wished Hector were here. Or that he could more easily ignore her. "He'll never come back," he said, his voice dull as he looked up at the ceiling. He hoped that if he didn't look her in the eye he could be more direct. "We had some tough words. But no matter how many flowers he sends or cards I won't change my mind."

"You were the victim of a Mod attack?"

He looked at her with raised eyebrows.

She shrugged. "People talk."

"You just don't stop, do you?"

She simply smiled.

"Fine. Yes, I'm lying in this bed because a Mod hurt me. And I've accepted what's happened to me. The doctors have tried to give me some hope that I could have a full life, but I know the truth." Luca looked through the window to the LA skyline. What was once a welcoming sight now just felt cold and lonely.

"And what's that?" She began massaging his left thigh.

"That I'll never walk again. I'll never feel the grass under my feet. Never feel the sand creep between my toes on the beach."

Susan listened without comment and eventually moved to his left calf and began to massage it.

"And it's okay. God will take care of me." Luca folded his hands across his chest.

"What if there was a way for you to walk again? Some sort of miracle? Stem cell treatment? Cutting-edge technology? That kind of thing."

"There are no miracles, Susan. There are no quick fixes. A Mod did this to me, I'll be damned if I let another one touch me."

"So you'd rather sit here and wallow in self-pity instead of taking advantage of the opportunity to be whole again?" She flexed his left foot.

"Watch it, Susan."

"Sorry. It's just that if something like this happened to me I would want any advantage I could get." Susan removed a cloth from her bag and wiped her hands.

"That's you. I've made my peace with it." Luca turned his head away from her. "I'm tired. I need to rest."

"Of course, Mr. Florentino. Rest all you need." Susan threw the towel into her bag as she left his room, closing the door behind her. She walked to the elevator and waited. The doors opened and she was grateful that it was empty. She pressed the lobby button and once the doors closed, she transformed back into Josh. A tear slipped down his cheek.

"Oh Luca, why are you so stubborn?" The man he knew was no longer there and it cut him deeply.

CHAPTER
56

19 December

"What's wrong with you?" Timothy asked, his voice quiet.

"Don't you know that's the worst thing to ask someone?" CoCo countered.

"Fine. What's your problem?"

"Also bad."

Timothy Ellery

With exaggerated patience, he said, "My dear sweetheart, what do I need to do to make you happy?"

She threw her pillow at him, and he caught it neatly.

"What, no improvement?"

"No. You didn't mean it."

He put up both hands in the universal "I give up" gesture. He paced around her cabin for half a minute as she folded her laundry in silence. "I'm sorry. But I know you're upset about something. You won't talk to me. You won't tell me anything. It's been nearly a week since you've been in this bad mood. So I have to think I'm the problem. I can't do anything right. You snip at this, snipe at that. It's no fun,

CoCo, to be around you when you're like this."

She wrinkled her nose. "Have I really been that awful?"

Seemingly prepared to catch whatever she might launch at him next, he nodded.

She didn't say anything. She didn't throw anything. She created an illusion so Timothy would think she was still standing across the cabin, and she flopped on the bed. The months of working undercover with the Tribe wore on her. She sensed goodness from Timothy, despite his affiliation with the Tribe. She knew that if things had been different he'd be on the side of the angels, but his guilt from what happened in Miami weighed heavily on him. As much as she wanted to end Pierce, she wanted Timothy to fight for the right to determine his own freedom.

"I'm sorry," she said at last. "I'm not mad at you. But I'm not happy." Seeing the hurt look on his face, her illusion hurried on. "Not you, but here. Pierce is up to something really bad, and I don't want to be a part of it. I don't think you want too, either."

"CoCo, hon, we've had this discussion before. We don't have any choice. We don't have anywhere else to go."

"Doesn't mean I wouldn't rather leave than be here, helping him do awful things. You know, go on a mission and just not come back."

Timothy stared at the illusory CoCo, his mouth hanging open. When he finally responded, his voice was hard. "Don't even think of that. You know what happened the one time I tried to get away."

CoCo nodded. Like a savage gang, several of the Tribe had beaten Timothy up when they found him. He still bore several scars from that.

"I'm here for the duration. He'd find you, the twisted scum that he is. He'd make me help him."

"I know, I know," she said, miserable. The awfulness of

the last few weeks crushed in on her. The knowledge that her friend Carlos was alive. The fact that she had helped take George from Base 47 for God only knew what purpose, right out from under Emilio's nose, and the SENTINELS hadn't yet managed to come after them to rescue Carlos. Did that mean that they couldn't find the boat because of whatever shielding Pierce had used? Just recently, she knew, Pierce had found Ericka and her team sniffing around an old hideout in Poland. He'd bragged about defeating them soundly, but she had seen how haggard he looked when he came back. She fervently wished for the day she could rejoin their ranks. She worried for her friends.

"What do you want to do?" Timothy asked gently.

"I don't know. I just hate this feeling, knowing that I'm involved in bad things. I'm not really proud of myself right now," she said. Tears rolled down her tanned cheeks as well as those of her illusion, and Timothy held the illusion CoCo. "Timothy, sweetie, could you just let me be by myself for a little while? I don't think I'll be very good company, and as you already pointed out, I haven't been very good company for the last week. Just give me the day, and I'll have myself back together."

"You sure?"

She nodded.

"Okay," he said reluctantly. "I'll go work out and then go to lunch. Why don't you clean yourself up? Some fresh air might do you good."

"You're right," she said. "I just might go for a stroll on the deck later."

Timothy kissed her cheek and left CoCo to her tears.

The moment the door shut behind him, she dropped the illusion, walked to the basin and wet a washcloth. She held the cool cloth over her red and achy eyes while she replayed the scene with Timothy. Had she given away too much? She wasn't sure how she was going to get off this boat, but she couldn't stand one more day of it. For the last week, she had skulked around, looking for a means to communicate with New Atlantis, and had been stymied at every turn. She didn't want to use her normal way of reaching Emilio—email—because she was worried about Pierce and his goons snooping on her. She was certain the answer must lay behind one of the two doors in the forbidden zone of the boat. Project X or Hazardous Materials. She just needed an illusion strong enough to be able to get in and nose around until she found what she needed. And, of course, a means to get off the boat.

She was certain Pierce's plans were about to come to a head. The time for answers was now or never.

When CoCo had composed herself and formed enough of a plan to get past Pierce's guards, she headed down toward the brig. She was more careful than last time and maintained her illusion from the moment she stepped out of her cabin. While her illusion would never fool the surveillance system, there was something she could do. Builder had created a device that could short-circuit surveillance systems from a distance, and she had managed to secure one of those since she had discovered the Hazardous Materials room and its gruesome secrets a week before. Flattery and some batted eyelashes, and Builder had given her the device, which she thought of as a camera defeater. She had tested it out by using it on a camera in the cafeteria the very next day. The little red light had winked out and not turned back on until she pressed the device's button again. She wondered if the surveillance technicians even noticed the blip, and if they did, what they made of it.

Taking advantage of her ability to cast illusions, along with her handy camera defeater, she made it to the Project X room. She stood in front of it, trying to feel any psychic energy that someone on the other side might be emitting. It was early for lunch, just after eleven, but a cafeteria boy she didn't know was heading in her direction, carrying food. She maintained her illusion of the empty corridor. The cafeteria boy balanced a tray against his right hip while he held a badge up to the security sensor at the Project X door. It opened, and he walked in, setting the tray immediately on a rolling table. CoCo, still maintaining her illusion, walked in right behind him.

Quickly, CoCo took in the whole room. It was small and only had one other door, which she assumed went to the bathroom. There was a bed, which was in use, but she couldn't see the occupant through the cafeteria boy. To the side of the room were a rolling table tray, a chair and a small dresser. No television. No books. It was more like a cell than a room, and it had the feel and smell of long-term use.

"Wake up, time for lunch," the cafeteria boy said.

CoCo moved out from behind the cafeteria boy and saw a little body move under the blankets, although she could make out nothing but long blond hair. And then the room's occupant sat up and asked what was for lunch.

It was Emma.

CHAPTER 57

19 December

Dr. Patel walked into her office with coffee and a late-night samosa. She was exhausted and was waiting on her computer to finish running calculations that might determine the origin of the new element that had so far baffled them. She sat in her chair

Dr. Nicola Patel

and looked at the family photo on her desk.

Nicola had been thrilled when she and her family had been approved as colonists for New Atlantis, despite her former career with The Hastings Foundation. She viewed it as an opportunity to make amends for her part in The Hastings Foundation's nefarious activities by working for good guys. Plus, she got the added benefit of being able to spend more time with her family. Since Base 47 had relocated to New Atlantis, she had helped develop several new technologies that the SENTINELS used out in the field.

A knock at her office door brought her out of her daze.

"Come in." Nicola put her snack on the desk and glanced at her watch. "Oh, Bayanai. What are you doing here so late?"

He walked in and closed the door.

"Would you care for a samosa? I have an extra. The lady down the street from here makes the best ones in Crystal City." She held the bag out to him.

"Thanks, but it's okay. I need to talk to you." Bayanai gestured at the chair in front of her desk. "May I?"

She nodded and nervously sat back in her own chair.

"We've had two serious security breaches on the island in the past week and I need to know how they were able to get in without us knowing." Bayanai passed a flash drive to Nicola. "This contains all the surveillance—infrared, video, thermal—we have over the time period in question."

"Isn't this a matter for your head of security?" Nicola thought of the piles of work ahead of her this evening. It was already a late night as it was, and Bayanai's request could turn it into an all-nighter.

Bayanai took a breath.

Nicola frowned. "What aren't you telling me?"

"This is between us."

Nicola cocked her head at him and raised an eyebrow. She nodded.

Bayanai sighed. "Laura has been compromised. She's been working with the Tribe."

"Are you kidding?" Nicola rose in anger.

"I wish. Pierce had been extorting her for the last year."

"So is it her fault that Emma's gone? Shining and Jaako?"

"I'm afraid so." He slumped in his chair.

"Where did you get this?"

"From her. I want a second pair of eyes to scrutinize everything."

Nicola fought for self-control. It was a long moment

before she spoke again. "And why come to me instead of Ericka? Investigations seem much more her thing, and I'm up to my eyebrows on those explosions."

"Ericka has her hands full with some other assignments."

"Okay, then. What exactly am I looking for?" She took the flash drive, holding back a sigh. It was going to take more than tea to keep her going tonight. She was glad she'd just made an entire pot of coffee.

"Anything that stands out. Maybe energy signatures that are unknown or uncatalogued. I need to know how deep this goes. You can use this to cross reference." Bayanai handed her another flash drive. "This contains dossiers on every documented Mod that Base 47 knows about."

"I... I thought that you opposed registration."

"I am. Officially. I don't trust the whims of politicians to be judicious with that sensitive information. There are some people who would misuse this information and cause untold destruction."

She nodded.

"I don't need to tell you that this is of utmost importance. I believe Pierce has infiltrated the island several times," Bayanai said. "We know he's had Carlos since we thought he died, and he also has George."

"I'll get right on it. Can I bring Yukio in on this?"

Bayanai considered. "Okay, but no one else. She was quite a help during the Foxhound Project." Bayanai rose. "I also wanted to ask you about some new intelligence we have concerning the London office of The Hastings Foundation."

Nicola swallowed. She had tried to avoid any talk about the Foundation. She loathed the black mark it left on her life.

"Dr. Martin is still there," Bayanai said.

Nicola nodded. She took a few shallow breaths, pumped hand sanitizer into her palm and rubbed them together vigorously, as though purifying those years out of her life. "Anything in particular?"

"There seem to be massive energy spikes at their office on the Thames," Bayanai said. "I'm afraid that all of this leads right to their doorstep. Somehow, I think both The Hastings Foundation and the Swarm are involved."

CHAPTER
58

19 December

Dr. Frazier turned the corner of the Antarctic Research Center and ran smack into Captain W.G. Pierce. It was a sight she neither expected nor relished. He was in dark-green fatigues, set off by the glowing blue of the cryospore on his belt. He hadn't shaved in days and his buzz cut was overdue for a trim.

"Pierce! Bloody hell! What are you doing here?" She looked around for one of the many technicians employed at the station. To her horror she saw five of them passed out on the floor. "What did you do?"

"Don't worry, pretty doc. They're alive. I just need to talk to you for a moment." Pierce grabbed her hand. "In private." He manifested a burgundy door. Before she could protest, he pushed her through it and followed. The door clapped shut.

Julianne was immediately freezing despite the fur-lined winter coat she typically wore inside the center. Pierce had teleported them outside the station. Her coat was no match for the wind. It might be summer in the southern hemisphere, that time of year when the sun never slept, but that didn't make it warm.

"If you wanted to talk to me all you needed to do is just ask. No need for the theatrics!" Julianne shivered, trying to zip her jacket with trembling fingers.

"Oh, Julianne, I've missed your spark." Pierce laughed as he lit the air on fire to warm them up. He maintained a ring of fire close enough to warm them, but far enough that the flames wouldn't jump onto their clothes. "The cold doesn't bother me much anymore. But we could find another way to warm you up." He raised a suggestive eyebrow at her and grinned.

Julianne winced at the lewd implication. The thought of Pierce's Frankensteinesque body atop hers turned her stomach. "What do you want, Pierce?"

"How is the cryospore retrieval going?" Pierce asked.

Julianne didn't want to tell him the truth, not about the fact that Shining and Jaako weren't living up to expectations, and certainly not her suspicions that the retrieval had caused the Falkland Islands earthquake. Instead, she watched the flames, captivated by the way they refused to blow toward them despite the wind.

"I'm waiting." Pierce lowered the protective flames.

The wind cut at her body and shivering resumed. "We've been working on how best to get the child to create his force fields around the cryospores."

"And?" Pierce growled.

His gaze unnerved her. "He... It seems like he can only work for about twenty minutes at a go. We were able to retrieve about half a barrel, which we have safely stored for you."

"Why did you stop?"

"The child collapsed, bleeding from his nose."

"Doesn't sound too bad. Have you resumed operations yet?"

317

"We tried again this morning, after treating him and administering a regenerative serum designed to increase his stamina."

"And then what?"

"He didn't last five minutes before he started bleeding again this morning." Julianne frowned.

"Seems like he lacks the proper motivation." Pierce smiled.

"No, Pierce, he's just five."

"That didn't stop you using him to get the cryospores."

She frowned again. The point hit home. She wanted to contend that she was at least looking out for the child's safety, but she knew it wasn't true. She was merely being pragmatic. They had to baby the boy or they'd break him and he wouldn't be any use to them then. She had long ago dropped all pretense of nobility and any idea that she was in science for the sake of knowledge. She danced firmly on the dark side, although she had periodic moments of weakness. Or clarity, as her better angel sometimes referred to those moments. But even the dark side of her knew that using a child in this manner was tantamount to abuse. At night, she struggled to reconcile the fact that she had to force the boy to serve Pierce's mission with the fact that she knew it was wrong to treat a child like this. She shivered, as much from the subzero temperature as from her fear.

"Dr. Frazier, sort out this mess. Quickly. We both know that our employers do not take failure lightly," Pierce said. "And I need my supply." He raised the flames, encircling them higher.

Julianne slumped in her helplessness, grateful for the added warmth but worried about what he might do. He seemed to be losing his tenuous grasp on both civility and sanity. She sighed. "What do you want me to do?"

"What you were hired to do. Get the cryospores. Or the

next time you see me will be your last." Pierce opened and entered another burgundy door and gave a mad cackle as he teleported away, leaving Julianne alone in the frozen wasteland. The flames died down and she dashed to the nearest door.

CHAPTER
59

19 December

CoCo maintained her illusion all through Emma's meal. Emma slowly ate her way through a peanut butter and jelly sandwich, carrot sticks, and a small apple. Finally, Emma chewed her last, and the impatient cafeteria boy stood to take the tray and leave.

Alone, CoCo dropped the illusion, prepared for Emma's anger. She was not disappointed.

Emma jumped, started at CoCo's sudden appearance. "What are you doing here?"

"I thought we'd try to escape together."

"Why would I do anything with you?" Emma scooted away, putting some distance between herself and her former teammate.

"Do you want to get off this boat or not?"

The girl looked at her thoughtfully but said nothing.

From Emilio, CoCo had learned Emma had been kidnapped; she'd simply not known Pierce was behind it. CoCo wondered how being captive had affected the girl. "You reached out to me. Brought me into your head. Your dance studio."

Emma looked surprised. "That was you?"

"I know you have no reason to trust me, and if I'm right you can't use your powers," CoCo said as Emma reluctantly nodded. "But we're getting out of here. Both of us."

Emma's eyes welled up. She was on the verge of losing it or lashing out, but CoCo wasn't sure which.

"We need to figure out how to get off this boat. Pierce is about to do some really bad things."

"You chose to come here. He had to kidnap me to get me here," Emma said, her voice dripping with disgust.

"Emma, you're going to have to trust me. I've been undercover working against Pierce for almost a year. This would be a lot easier if you would get in my mind. You'd see what happened between me and Emilio. You'd see what I was doing, why I was doing it. What I was trying to accomplish by being here," CoCo said.

Emma narrowed her eyes at CoCo for a long moment. "My powers don't work unless Pierce turns something off that blocks them most of the time."

"Yeah, that. It's tied specifically to your power. When I first got here, they kept me in a room like this, and my illusions didn't work. It took a while before they let me out of there," CoCo said. "It prevents you from sending your power beyond the bounds of this room, which explains why you could reach out only when the door was open."

"Why should I trust you?"

"Well, hon, do you really think Pierce would let me know about you? I may have managed to convince him that I'd left the SENTINELS, but I could never convince him that I'd be willing to participate in your kidnapping."

Emma leveled her gaze at CoCo, considering this.

"And, when I get you out of here, you can read my mind to your heart's content. You'll see."

Emma considered it. Her gut and heart told her the

CoCo in front of her was telling the truth while her mind cried out for caution. But in the end her twelve-year-old's need to believe in her former friend and potential rescue won out.

"So you're not really one of them," Emma said. For the first time in months, she had a friend nearby. Someone she could trust. "But how did the two of you keep it from me?"

"Well, you did give me the tools I needed to guard my mind against telepathy. I think I got better at it than the others because of my power of illusions. And Emilio just counted on his luck to keep you from knowing what you shouldn't."

Emma gazed at her and nodded.

"I wish I knew that you were here a long time ago, but Pierce keeps so many secrets," CoCo said as she reached out her hand. Emma hesitantly reached hers out. Their hands met and Emma collapsed into CoCo's arms. Months of anger slipped out of her preteen body.

"You're right," Emma said, looking up at CoCo. "But there's a problem. We're locked in. We can't get out. And I'm not able to reach anyone on Base 47."

"I know. I have an idea for that," CoCo said. "When does the cafeteria boy bring you dinner?"

"Early, usually. Maybe six. But before that, someone will come and give me a shot to make me sleep again. I've slept nearly the whole time I've been here."

"How long until the shot?"

"Could be now, could be an hour. It's not so much about me as what he's doing elsewhere."

"Right, okay then. I'll be prepared with an illusion of you in bed, and we'll leave behind him after he gives the illusion the shot. Once we get out, can you call for Waleed?"

"I don't know. I haven't been able to call for anyone since I've been in this room, until the dance studio that one night. Sometimes I send messages when the door is open, trying to reach Waleed and Bayanai. But I never knew if anyone was listening."

"Well, when the dance studio came into my mind I thought that you might be behind it," CoCo said. "It was more like premonitions than your standard telepathy."

Emma shrugged. "Whatever they were doing messed my powers up."

CoCo had never seen Emma so despondent. It was a far cry from her bubbly self back on New Atlantis. "It's going to be okay."

"Do you have a way off this boat?"

CoCo grinned a sick grin. "As long as they don't shut down my powers, we can use my emergency escape."

"Emergency escape?" Emma asked.

"Plan B. You know, in case things ever got really bad and I had to get out of here in a hurry. But it would be better, safer if we can get Waleed to come get us."

Emma nodded and joined CoCo by the door.

"Once we get out of your room, we have one more stop before we leave the boat."

"You don't want to get straight off the boat?"

"Not without Tio Carlos," CoCo said.

"What?" Emma looked at CoCo, who grinned and shook her head. "He's not dead? He's here?" The girl's voice rose nearly an octave in her excitement.

"I saw him last week when I got down into this area of the boat. He's right next door. I couldn't rescue him then, and I've spent the last week trying to figure out how to get us rescued. That was before I found out about you. Now, I think maybe we have a real chance." Her eyes sparkled.

"He's really okay?" Emma persisted.

"Sweetie, he's hurt, but I think if we can get him to Jiya, he'll be mostly okay. But I have to tell you, Pierce did something really wrong to him, and to a bunch of others. Tio Carlos isn't alone in the labs next door. There are some other people there. Pierce has been stealing their powers."

Slowly, Emma nodded.

"It's his arm, isn't it?"

"Yes, sweetie, Tio Carlos is missing an arm. He's in some sort of trance or stasis or something. There's a guy there whose eye was gouged out, and—"

"Oh, no. Please, no," Emma said, and tears slipped from her eyes. She wailed and thrust her fists against her thighs.

"What, honey?" CoCo brought Emma to her chest and stroked her tangled hair straight.

"Pierce made me find that man. He had night vision."

"You've been helping him?" Shock frosted her question, and it came out sounding harsher than she intended.

"I had to," she said simply.

CoCo softened, seeing misery and shame in the girl's face. "Who else did he make you find?"

Before Emma could answer, CoCo heard the door's locking mechanism activate, and she held Emma close. "Get ready," she whispered.

The door opened, and Surgeon stood in the hallway, speaking with someone passing by. While he was preoccupied, CoCo snagged his entry key card and created the illusion of Emma lying face down in bed. She and Emma stood flat against the wall waiting for the grotesque man to step inside. Once he administered the shot to the Emma illusion and walked out, they slipped out behind him. When he disappeared down the corridor, oblivious to CoCo and Emma because of her empty hallway illusion and her camera defeater, CoCo asked the little girl if she could reach Waleed.

For a moment, Emma said nothing, and then tears welled up.

"What is it?"

"Nothing. I'm too scared to try. I got those people killed. I helped Pierce." Emma plunged her head into her hands.

"Emma, pull yourself together. We are losing our window to get out of here. I can only maintain our illusion for so long before they realize that you're gone." CoCo knelt next to the preteen, who slightly nodded.

They stood in front of the door marked Hazardous Materials, next door to the room where Emma had been held captive for so long. CoCo flicked the pilfered badge in front of the entry plate and the lock released. They entered, and the door closed behind them. CoCo looked at Emma, who was scrunching her eyes tight.

"Anything?"

Emma shook her head.

"Keep trying. We have to get out of here." CoCo looked around the room.

Three clear tubes were empty, but against the other wall were three clear covered tubes where the victims of Pierce's perversion lay in stasis. CoCo uncovered the tubes.

Emma walked toward the tube with Carlos. She reached her hands out, as though wanting to touch the body to make sure it was really him, but she couldn't touch him through the stasis tube. Emma sobbed.

"Shh!" CoCo said harshly. "We've got to keep ourselves together. Keep trying to break through. If you don't reach Base 47 and Waleed, they are going to do this to us." The words stopped Emma from crying. She wiped her face and sat down. CoCo opened Carlos's stasis tube so he'd be ready for immediate transport to Base 47 and then did the same for the other two occupied tubes.

At that moment, the door opened and a tech came in. CoCo pulled him into an illusion that bought them a little more time. She looked at Emma and whispered for her to try harder.

"I got him!" Emma shouted and jumped up. CoCo looked back in fear. She hadn't accounted for the noise and the tech got spooked. He looked around the room, trying to determine where the triumphant shout had come from. He felt under the monitor desk and switched the alarm on.

CoCo swore.

Emma began to cry again. She kept muttering "I'm sorry" over and over.

At that moment, Waleed's portal opened and Katrina came through. The portal flickered and disappeared behind her.

"Emma!" Katrina rushed to the girl's side. She then noticed CoCo.

"Hell," Katrina muttered.

Despite the gone teleportal, CoCo grinned in happy surprise at seeing an old friend. Katrina hissed at her and psychokinetically shoved CoCo, who crashed into the shelving behind her.

"Back off, CoCo. I'm not here for you." Katrina pointed at CoCo, minimally applying psychokinetic pressure on her. But upon seeing Emma, she relented. "Emma, I'm so glad to see you. You all right?" Katrina leaned down and hugged the girl.

Emma nodded and hugged back enthusiastically. She wiped away her tears. Finally, she was getting out of here.

"This is all well and good, but in about twenty seconds the Tribe is going to be here and we'll be doomed," CoCo said, the strain of the illusions getting to her.

"I'm here to bring Emma home. You're on your own, traitor," Katrina said.

"Katrina, CoCo's okay. She's still on our side," Emma said with certainty. "She's been undercover."

Katrina squinted her eyes in disbelief at Emma and CoCo and sighed. "Have it your way. For now." She pointed at CoCo, who was still against the wall. "You and I are going to have a long, uncomfortable talk when we get back to the base."

The strain of casting illusions while fighting off Katrina's psychokinetic pressure was too much for CoCo. Her illusion of the empty lab failed, revealing not just CoCo to the tech but also Katrina and Emma.

"Who are you?" The tech screamed as he stumbled in surprise.

"Damn it," CoCo said, the fear in her voice rising by the moment. "Katrina, some help here?"

Katrina looked from CoCo to the lab tech and shrugged. She levitated one of the monitors over to the unnerved tech and knocked his head with it. He squawked in surprise and dropped to the floor.

"Thanks," CoCo said. "What happened to Waleed's portal?"

"Whatever was blocking our ability to find this vessel must still be up," Katrina said as she put up a psychokinetic shield around them.

"Of course," CoCo said. "The ship's cloaking devices. Emma, I need you to focus all your might on Waleed." The room's door began to open.

Katrina used her power to keep the door from opening.

"Emma! Call for Waleed," Katrina said. "He must need us as an anchor for finding a spot to 'port in."

"Take my hand." Emma reached out to both CoCo and Katrina. The took her hands and together, the three of them mentally called for Waleed. For a few heart-stopping seconds, nothing happened. Then the black glittering globules that heralded Waleed's teleportal appeared.

Brute's fingers appeared between the door and its metal frame, and she began forcing the door open. Emma jumped back, but CoCo caught her. They focused harder.

"Keep trying. I'll hold her off as long as I can." Katrina psychokinetically pushed the door shut while Brute used all her strength to open it.

"Thank heavens," CoCo said, hearing a voice coming from the other side of the portal.

"Whatever you're doing, it's working," an obviously strained Waleed said. "It will help me keep the focus I need to keep the portal open."

Emma and CoCo closed their eyes tight and concentrated hard.

Once the portal solidified Emma pointed to Tio Carlos. "Send him through first."

Katrina glanced at Carlos but remained focused on keeping Brute from getting into the room. "Hey, what happened to his arm?"

"Pierce has it," CoCo said.

Katrina shook her head, looked at Carlos, and mentally lifted the strong man through the portal. The effort cost her, though, and Brute heaved the door open. The Korean came through the doorway followed by Surgeon.

Katrina erected a shield to protect the group from them. "I wonder why they bothered keeping them alive."

"Keep sending them," CoCo said, hoping Katrina's shield would hold against Jimin's enhanced strength.

"Drop her," Surgeon commanded.

Katrina ignored him, and the paralyzed Portuguese girl vanished through the portal, immediately followed by the man with gouged out eyes.

"I need those specimens, give them back to me," he yelled.

Jimin charged the shield. The impact caused Katrina to wince.

"Nope, sorry, Doc, no can do," Katrina said. "And it's going to take more to stop me." She maintained the force field and looked around the room for inspiration. She grinned and floated the white sheets over to Brute. Before Brute could react, she tied the woman up with one of the sheets and covered her with another, leaving her angry and hopping around like a deranged, unfriendly ghost.

Seeing his moment, Surgeon lunged for Emma. Realizing what he was doing, CoCo grabbed for Emma as well.

Emma did what all young girls do so well and naturally under such circumstances. She screamed bloody murder.

But Surgeon wouldn't let go. He kept pulling and pulling on the girl's left arm.

CoCo pulled Emma's right arm as the dangerous game of tug-of-war continued.

Emma was in pain. Both her arms felt like they would pop out of their sockets.

In desperation, she jumped into Surgeon's head. She screamed and screamed in his brain. Her screams increased and increased in shrillness and volume in his head until Surgeon finally let go of her arm to hold his hands over his ears.

"We have to leave now," Waleed shouted from Base 47 on the other side of the portal. "I can't keep the portal open much longer."

Emma yanked her right arm out of CoCo's grasp and ran through Waleed's portal. Just as she disappeared from sight, the first of Surgeon's reinforcements arrived.

"Just go!" CoCo ordered Katrina to hop through the portal. Katrina ran. CoCo's heart sank when she spotted Timothy. Looking around at all the electronic equipment in the lab, she knew the scene was about to get even uglier.

Instinctively, she jumped toward the portal, but just as she was about to make it off the boat, Timothy grabbed her, pulling her out of safety's reach.

"What are you doing?" Timothy yelled. "Have you completely lost your mind?"

He had his hands around her arms and was shaking her.

"Stop, you're hurting me."

"That's nothing compared to what happens when Pierce finds out you betrayed him."

CoCo looked at Timothy. "I'm so sorry," she whispered. She stood poised on the threshold of the portal.

Pierce stormed into the Hazardous Materials room. The containment tubes were empty. Three white sheets were strewn over the floor. Surgeon was knocked out on the floor in the corner.

"What in the hell happened here?" he bellowed.

Timothy sucked in some electricity from the room and sent a bolt at his CoCo. It struck her and sent her sprawling into the portal. The portal closed, leaving Timothy to face a furious Pierce.

CHAPTER
60

19 December

Arthur whistled a dark and twisty take on his favorite tune as he marched into the gothic-inspired dining room of the hidden headquarters of the Swarm. Outside, a brutal snowstorm raged on, but inside the secluded fortress they were warm. The firelight of the torches made dancing shadows on the walls.

Arthur sat at the head of a large intricately carved table. A tablecloth with a hexagonal design ran down the center of the table. The design had long been associated with the Swarm, and now the group used the pattern as a brand. The redheaded man joined him.

"How are the preparations coming along?" Arthur asked.

"All the supplies are being carried down as we speak. Everything will be in place by the solstice. We've been working on George to expand his control."

"Good. The plan hinges on him restoring the fragmented pieces of the mind." Arthur looked around the large room. Next to the recently returned Eye of Horus were several strange artifacts arranged on a shelf. He assumed those dated back to the inception of the Ascendancy, which the Swarm broke away from about three centuries ago.

"I know what is at stake."

"If the Scion can't host the Sentinel—"

"I know, I know, the New Reckoning can't happen," the redheaded man said and glanced at his watch.

"I see you have his prized Excalibur Quatuor." Arthur grinned. Maybe he should be upset that watch wasn't on his own wrist, but he wasn't. It wasn't to his taste.

"Partial payment for the kidnappings."

"Good choice."

"Is it true that the connection to the Sentinel is through a kid?" the redheaded man asked.

"Where did you hear this?" Arthur asked.

"As secretive as the Swarm are, there are quite a few who joyfully speak about the plans."

"The only way to make sure that our plan is fulfilled is to allow the blood connection to rise." Arthur leaned closer. "So, yes, the child is our conduit."

The redheaded man rubbed his chest.

"Can I see it?" Arthur asked.

The redheaded man shrugged and pulled down his shirt, revealing a hideous blue-tinged rash. Emilio had done this to him during the showdown battle on New Atlantis.

"That must hurt." Arthur studied the crusted-over rash in the glow of the torchlight.

"Every day. But I've ways of dealing with it. And I will have my revenge."

"You know why you can't," Arthur said. "Not yet."

Before the redheaded man could respond, their leader entered, followed by two guards cloaked in scarlet. They stood immediately and lowered their heads as he passed.

"Welcome back," the hooded old man said as his guards led him to his throne-like chair at the opposite end of the table.

"Thank you for seeing us, my sovereign," Arthur said as they both bowed.

"Now tell me about the twins and if the Ascendancy is usurped," the sovereign said.

"I have set Anabel and Elise on each other, and I will eliminate Maks once I return. Through your gift the Ascendancy is laid bare and the Swarm can now rise." Arthur looked at the hooded man. For a moment, he thought he glimpsed a smile.

"That pleases me. For so long the Ascendancy has consigned the Swarm to the shadows, but they never understood that the darkness is where we thrive. And now we will succeed where they failed. We have the Sentinel and the Scion. Soon the world will tremble before us." The sovereign ran his hands up and down the arms of the chair, seemingly considering his next words. "What of the so-called heroes? Are they following as we planned?"

"Of course. They got the eye, which led them to our operative in Egypt, who of course returned the relic." Arthur pointed at it. "Predictably, they searched out the abandoned bunker in Australia. They are as clumsy as they are honorable. They have no idea that they are just unwitting accomplices in our plans."

"See to it that they do their part and put a stop to Pierce once and for all. He's getting out of hand."

"We will fulfill your commands," Arthur said. "Thank you for seeing us."

The sovereign pushed himself up and out of the chair and walked away.

"The Sentinel will save us all," the redheaded man said as the sovereign passed.

"Yes, he will."

Once they were left alone, the redheaded man turned to

Arthur. "I meant to ask you, what is that tune you keep whistling? It seems familiar."

Arthur paused for a moment before replying. "Just a tune my father taught me." A smile crept across his face.

CHAPTER
61

19 December

When her phone rang, Maggie jumped in her chair at the kitchen table, knocking over an empty Chinese takeout container. It had been that way ever since the bomb went off in her office. The phone jangled. Sure a new threat was imminent, she jumped. Anger followed in its footsteps. Anger at her instinctive reaction mingled with fury at the unknown people behind the bombing.

As a reporter, her personal rule was to always answer the phone. Who knew what story might land in her lap?

But in the days since the explosion, the calls had ranged from uplifting to merely unsettling to deeply troubling. Most calls came from the general public, but some were Mods, politicians or celebrities. Everyone, it seemed, had an opinion. Judging by the unknown incoming numbers, she rarely knew what to expect. A handful had voiced their relief that she was not injured and wished her well. A couple had asked her not to give up on TheModsBlog because of the attack. But for each of those, there were several darker messages.

From her kitchen table, she had a view to the tip of

Manhattan. The Freedom Tower's lights shone bright on this cold evening. She had bought this apartment when she moved into her new offices, a prize, she told herself, for working so hard for so long. For the years spent toiling on travel pieces and nothing stories. She had finally made it. To the twenty-sixth floor, to be exact. But was she ever going to be safe enough?

Four different people had anonymously claimed responsibility for the explosion. Maggie knew many groups could be behind it, including the Tribe, the Swarm, GRIM, and Man First. Of those, Maggie had begun to think that one of the shadowier arms of GRIM might be behind the bombing, although no call from that organization had come through, as far as she knew. Publically, they had denied responsibility. At least a dozen calls had voiced disappointment the bomb hadn't gotten her, along with hopes that there would be more attempts on her life. Maggie had shared all the information on these calls with the officers investigating the explosion.

The second ring sounded on her phone, and she braced herself. She thought about the explosion and anger coursed through her veins. She took a deep and steadying breath before looking at the incoming number. It led with the country code for New Atlantis. She breathed a sigh of relief and answered on the third ring.

"Maggie Adams," she said.

"Bayanai here."

"Hey. What's going on?" She didn't want to talk, but it was better to get it out of the way.

"I'm glad you're okay."

"Thanks. Me too."

"Do they know who did it?"

Maggie scoffed. "They have a few ideas."

"And?"

"And so do I."

"Do you know who did it?"

"Four people have contacted me, claiming responsibility."

"But?"

"But I don't think any of them did it."

"Why?"

Maggie paused. She was the reporter here, and there were things one just didn't tell sources, even friendly ones. She shifted gears. "What's on your mind? Did you have a story idea for the blog?"

He cleared his throat. "Listen, Maggie, I want to make an offer, but I don't want to put you on the spot."

"Shoot." She got up from the table and walked a well-worn path from the table around the couch and back again.

"Do you feel safe, or are you worried about another attack?"

"Worried. We still haven't figured out how they got the bomb in the office to begin with. Plus, I've been worried for quite some time because of all the threats. You may remember that I hired security guards not so long ago." She stared out the window and frowned, wishing the investigation had already produced results.

"Yes, I remember." There was another long pause before Bayanai spoke again. "As I said, I wanted to make an offer."

"Yes?" It came out as a question, but with a grin hidden in it.

"Yes. I wanted to see if you would like to work from New Atlantis for a little while, until you sort out new offices for your staff."

Maggie expelled a breath she didn't realize she'd been holding as thoughts rushed through her mind. In the hours right after the explosion, after she had learned that the bomb had killed three of her own and injured a handful more, Maggie had come very near to shutting down the blog altogether. Fear and anger had ruled her life in the aftermath. Every time fear threatened her and she considered shuttering TheModsBlog, anger reared its vengeant head and talked her into keeping it running, at least until she figured out another course of action.

Finally, she spoke. "Wow, Bayanai, that's a generous offer. But—"

"I know, you need to think about it. You certainly don't need to answer me immediately. Think about it. You can bring a few of your staff members here, if you like. Waleed can handle the teleportals to get everyone here. We can get you set up in an office here at Base 47, or in an office building elsewhere in Crystal City. Just promise to think about it."

Maggie closed her eyes. "Thank you, Bayanai. I will think about it. I'll try to get back to you in the next couple of hours." She clicked off the line, her mind racing with possibilities. Could she do this? Should she do this? But in that moment she thought about the people she'd lost. Doing nothing would be a disservice to their memories. If she stopped now, how could she live with herself? With a newfound sense of purpose she made another call.

CHAPTER
6 2

19 December

Josh made his way to the dressing table and looked at the clothes laid out. The office, full of modern furniture, looked tidy despite Josh's normally messy habits. In half an hour he was to give Jaako's holiday closing speech to parliament, which would be televised.

As he donned the crisp, white button-down shirt, his phone rang. It was probably his agent. He had been ducking the agent's calls for days, ever since he had taken on his newest role of Jaako Aalto, prime minister of New Atlantis.

It could have been Luca. He wasn't ready to speak to Luca either. But he doubted Luca would be reaching out, not after their last argument.

Here he was, back in the thick of the world of superheroes, and he wasn't sure which was the life for him. Acting and the world of celebrity? Or saving the world and helping people, feeling more alive than he had in a long time? He had not come back to New Atlantis to get swept up in SENTINELS missions, but the longer he stayed the more at home he felt. It should be an easy choice, Josh thought wryly.

But it wasn't.

Josh relaxed fractionally when the ringing ceased and the phone shunted the caller to voice mail.

Posing as Jaako in public was an easy enough assignment. Even though he was a good actor, Josh hated the lying that he had to do in real life to sell the impersonation. Especially with family. He had almost slipped up the other night by kissing Birgitta and she had pushed him away, closing the bedroom door on his face. It gave him unsettling insight into the nature of that marriage.

The phone rang again, and he pondered what his agent might want now. Probably to find out when he could book his share of his press commitments for the film.

"Aren't you going to answer that?" Arian asked as she walked into the room.

"It's just my agent. He'll call back," Josh said.

"And how is Luca?"

Josh grimaced. "Which tie?" He buttoned up the shirt.

Arian raised an eyebrow but said nothing about his dodging the question. She picked up a deep red tie and folded up his collar as she slipped it around his neck to tie it.

"Do you do this for Jaako?"

"Only when he's going to be on TV. Between you and me, he never really does a good job on his own." She grinned.

Josh put on Jaako's jacket and shifted himself into Jaako's image. "How do I look?"

"Almost," Arian muttered. She picked up a pin and stuck it to the jacket. "He'd never be filmed without this on his jacket."

Josh looked down. It was the crest of New Atlantis.

Luli entered the room. She looked like she hadn't slept in a week. She handed a small photo of her son to the faux

Jaako. "Please put this in your pocket. Keep it as a reminder of why we are doing this."

Josh could hear the heartbreak in her voice. "Luli, no one wants to get your son back more than me. You have to trust Bayanai. He's smart. And with all the resources we have here at Base 47 it's only a matter of time before we rescue your son and bring him back safely," he said in soft, assured tones.

"It's already been a week," Luli said hoarsely. "I know that you are doing what you can and I know that Bayanai is doing everything he can. If I still had my powers now, Pierce would regret this." Luli clenched her fists and tears dropped from her eyes. Arian handed her a tissue, then put her arm around her.

"Yi and I chose to become New Atlanteans on the promise that we could provide better lives for our children and now—"

"Luli, we'll get your son back. Have a little faith." Josh hugged her and tucked the photo of Shining into his front jacket pocket. His phone rang again and Luli pulled away.

"You need to answer that?"

"No. They can wait," he said, sending the call to voice mail.

"I hate to break the moment, but they're ready for you, Josh. I mean, Mr. Prime Minister," Arian said.

CHAPTER
63

19 December

"Help! Someone help me!" A middle-aged man screamed as he ran toward a beautiful seaside villa in an exclusive Cape Town community.

Maks Wong

Moonlight bathed the grounds as a dark-haired predator followed the terrified man.

"Markos Vossen! You're on my list of Mods. You will not survive the night." A young Asian man pursued the South African. While his movements were methodical and measured, his prey was frantic, hysterical, and haphazard. Markos looked behind him to see how far away his pursuer was and tripped over a chair, skinning his knee through his trousers as he spilled onto the patio. In a fit of terror, he screamed and jumped back up. He ran to the doors, trying to get inside the villa.

"How do you know who I am? What I am?" Markos threw open the French doors on the patio and tore into the villa.

"I have deep pockets and even deeper resources that give me access to the most covered-up secrets. Like your ability to know the truth about any object. Must make working at a museum a breeze." Maks walked into the main room and looked around. It was quiet. Maks walked past the mahogany bar and heard the sound of metal on wood.

"How do you know that? I've never told anyone," Markos said. He hurled a silver-plated candlestick at the intruder, who dodged it easily.

"Is that the best you've got? This will be easier than the others."

"Others? What do you mean?"

"You aren't the first Mod I've hunted." Maks stalked Markos. "The first was a kid in Guangzhou. He could control any animal. But he just didn't know how to fight back. I target Mods who aren't worthy." He advanced on Markos.

"Please. Leave me alone and I'll give you whatever you want," the man with graying temples pleaded.

"Begging? So soon? And I haven't even begun to terrorize you." Maks pulled a suit of armor to the ground.

Markos' mouth and eyes widened at the crash.

"Sorry, that must have had some significance to you." Maks pulled a ceremonial blade from the wall and used it to slash a painting.

"Stop it! These are priceless artifacts!"

"You know, there are some who want Mods like you to be registered and treated like property." Maks jumped over a leather couch toward Markos. "Then there are those who treat you like gods. But not me. I think that if you're so ashamed of your solstice-empowered gifts, you should be treated like vermin."

"I never asked for powers."

"Of course not. But you've squandered them

nonetheless for the last five years," Maks said.

Markos inched farther back until he reached the wall in his living room.

"Go ahead. The first strike can be yours." Maks snagged a blade from the wall and tossed it to his target.

Markos looked down at the blade. "This is a ceremonial Zulu blade. It's priceless."

"I don't care. You have one chance. After that—" Maks said.

Markos swung wildly, connecting the tip of the blade with Maks' right cheek.

"So there is some fight in this dog after all... I like it." Maks smiled as he flicked blood off his lip. "Makes the hunt fun."

Markos saw his opportunity and broke for the stairs.

Maks leapt over the coffee table and pulled Markos off the stairs. He wrapped his arm around Markos' chest and yanked the blade from Markos' loose grip.

"Why are you doing this?" Markos struggled to break free.

Maks stood behind him and pressed the Zulu blade against his throat. "I told you. You don't deserve the gifts you've been given." Maks slit the man's neck and watched as the blood splattered against the white wall. He dropped the body onto the floor.

Tears leaked from Markos' eyes as he died.

Maks stood over the lifeless body of Markos Vossen and grinned. He wiped the ceremonial Zulu blade against the white drapes.

Maks grabbed his phone and dialed his sister, anxious to hear how she had dispatched Elise. Her voice mail picked up. He shrugged and walked out the villa.

"All right, sister. I'm on my way."

CHAPTER
64

19 December

Waleed's teleportal sent Pierce's three victims, along with Emma, Katrina, and CoCo, into the War Room at Base 47. The second CoCo entered the room, Katrina psychokinetically floated a pair of power-dampening handcuffs to her.

"Put those on," Katrina ordered.

CoCo, still shaky from Timothy's electrical push through the teleportal, hesitated.

"I can do it for you," Katrina said.

"She doesn't need to. I trust her," Emma said.

"Humor me."

"But—" Emma said. The look Katrina shot her instantly quieted the girl.

"Put them on. Now." Katrina stood with her hands on her hips and glared at CoCo.

CoCo put the cuffs on and slid into a chair, and Katrina nodded in satisfaction.

Waleed studied Carlos and Pierce's other two victims.

"Waleed, can you open a portal to Jiya so they can get treated?" Katrina said.

Waleed opened a teleportal to Jiya's ashram on the west coast of the island and Katrina floated the three victims through and gently placed them on the ground in one of her rooms.

"You should collect Bayanai and Arian and bring them here. There's no time to waste."

"Please bring Emilio, too," CoCo said. The pain of separation from Emilio ached. She longed to lay eyes on him. To drink him in. To finally hold him and let the last year wash away from her body.

Katrina sneered. "What? No. You're the last person he wants or needs to see."

"Please, just get him."

Katrina shook her head at Waleed. "Just Bayanai and Arian," she said firmly and Waleed vanished through one of his glittering black teleportals. Katrina turned to CoCo. "Why are you here?"

"Look, I know it looks bad, but this will be a lot easier if Emilio is here. Please, just call him."

Katrina shrugged. "Fine." She spoke into her cell phone. "Emilio? Yeah, get your butt to the War Room. There's something you've got to see." She clicked off. "He's on the way."

Glittering black globules heralded Waleed's arriving teleportal. Bayanai and Arian, Emma's guardian, stepped through. The portal vanished, though Waleed remained in the office.

"Emma!" Arian shrieked with delight and rushed to the girl. She picked Emma up and hugged her. When she did so, Emma returned the hug with equal measures of relief and happiness. "Oh, honey, I thought I'd lost you forever." Arian put Emma down and kissed the girl's cheeks and forehead. "I've missed you so."

Through her tears, Emma hugged her back. "I missed

you, too."

"What happened? You're too thin, too pale."

Emma shook her head and clasped her arms around Arian in another hug.

Arian spotted CoCo for the first time and frowned. "What's she doing here?"

Each time that question came up, CoCo felt the depth of her former friends' hatred for her. She wondered if she'd ever erase their doubt and anger.

"That's what I'm trying to find out," Katrina said. "Oh, and she insisted we call Emilio, so he's on his way."

Bayanai's eyes widened as he considered this news. "Then we'll wait to speak any more with CoCo." He turned to Emma. "Is there anything we can get you?"

"Ice cream," she said quickly. Then she looked down at herself and blushed. "And some clean clothes."

"We can certainly arrange that. I'll have some ice cream brought here. Chocolate or mango?"

"Mango."

"Mango it is. I'll send for it now." Bayanai made the order on his tablet and knelt next to Emma.

"Soon, you can go back home with Arian and get a shower and clean clothes. We just have a few questions first."

Emma slumped in her chair. "Okay."

Katrina butted in. "First, Bayanai, you need to know that Waleed teleported more than just Emma and CoCo back here. We got Carlos, and two more of Pierce's victims."

"Really?" A smile lit Bayanai's face. "Where's Carlos, and the others? Are they okay?"

"Waleed took them to Jiya at the ashram straight away, but I haven't heard anything since."

Bayanai nodded and turned to Emma.

Emilio burst into the War Room and quickly took in the

scene. CoCo sat up straight in her chair and beamed. She longed to rush over to him, but remained in the chair.

"What's she doing here?" he demanded.

"Babe, I'm back, and damn glad to be here," she said, smiling. "My cover's totally and completely blown."

Happiness washed over Emilio's face. "Really? You're back?"

"Really."

He rushed to her and she stood up. She placed her cuffed hands around his neck and they kissed deeply. In her happiness, it made CoCo think of the final kiss in *The Princess Bride*, which was to say it was perfect.

When CoCo finally opened her eyes, she saw confusion and doubt on all faces but Emma's, who simply looked happy to see CoCo and Emilio back where they belonged.

"Would someone please tell me what's going on?" Katrina demanded. "Last I heard, you two were splitsville. It was pretty public."

"It was all for show, Kat," CoCo said.

Katrina glared at her.

"Katrina," CoCo said, recalling how much Katrina hated that nickname. "We had to make it look real."

Katrina nodded, moderately appeased.

"Make what look real?" Bayanai asked.

"Take these cuffs off CoCo," Emilio said.

Bayanai studied them a moment then shook his head. "No, not yet. I need to hear more."

"She's one of us, Bayanai." Emilio stood shoulder to shoulder with CoCo.

"I won't risk her using her powers on us," Bayanai said.

"She won't. Trust me," Emilio said.

"Let her make her case then," Bayanai said.

CoCo took a breath. "It's pretty simple. Emilio and I had been talking about the fact that we knew Pierce was up to no good. That something was going on. After that mission when we lost Carlos, and we both felt to blame, we wanted to find a way to stop Pierce once and for all. We thought he must be getting information from inside the Base because of how that mission failed. We weren't certain, and didn't have anything solid to hang that on, so we couldn't really bring it up to you. So we cooked up the breakup."

"And?"

"We went back and forth about it for a long time." Emilio chimed in. "We knew only one of us could go. I didn't want to risk her life for this, so we decided I was going to go, but she jumped the gun and went instead. She managed to fall in with the Tribe." He looked at her and waggled a finger at her in a "naughty-naughty" gesture.

"So the breakup was part of her cover?" Katrina folded her arms across her body.

"Yes. It was so hard, but we had to make it believable. Otherwise, we wouldn't be able to get in with Pierce's people."

"But why didn't you tell me?"

"We believed Pierce had a mole here, and we didn't want that person to compromise whoever of us went under with Pierce," Emilio said.

"Who do you think it is?" Bayanai asked.

"Laura," CoCo said promptly.

"How did you know?" Bayanai asked.

"Are you kidding me? Our head of security?" Katrina blurted out. "Oh, this day just gets better and better."

The other SENTINELS exchanged looks that were equal parts shock and confusion.

"I was with Pierce when he was talking with her. I just found out yesterday, but I hadn't had a chance to let Emilio know. I also think he sent Plain Jane here, too."

"What?" Bayanai and Emilio said in unison.

"Yeah, I know. How are we ever going to find her?"

"I'll get Ericka on it."

"The Tribe has a way to track her using their tablets," CoCo said.

"What else do you know of Pierce's plans?" Bayanai asked.

"Not much. I wasn't fully trusted, and Pierce keeps things close. But he's trying to get something he calls a cryospore from the ice in Antarctica."

Bayanai and Emilio exchanged looks.

"You know about the cryospore?" she asked.

They both nodded.

"Well, he's got his scientists working on the means to extract it, including Dr. Roger Martin. He was updating Pierce, so of course I paid special attention. They don't know I heard them."

"What did you learn?"

"The way I understand it—and I'm no scientist—was that they were using Jaako and Shining to help with the extraction. How did they get them?"

Bayanai shook his head. "I'm still asking the questions here."

She nodded, stung. "Shining was supposed to be using his powers to safely encase the cryospores in force fields so they won't explode. But I've overheard the process is way behind schedule and not going well."

"Do you know where they are?" Emilio asked.

CoCo shook her head. "I'm guessing they're in Antarctica, where the cryospores are."

"So they're operating out of Antarctica?" Bayanai asked. "Big continent. Any ideas to help narrow it down?"

CoCo shook her head.

"I'm pretty sure the London office of The Hastings Foundation is involved because of Dr. Martin."

"What else did you manage to accomplish while you were under cover for almost a year?" Bayanai asked. "You showed up at some pretty key times and caused us a lot of trouble."

"Oh, like at the Cottonwood Pavilion, when Emilio and Kirra got George instead of Pierce? How do you think Emilio knew Pierce's people wanted him and where to show up?"

"Okay, I might buy that. But you came after him again."

CoCo nodded slowly. "I didn't have a choice, if I wanted to maintain my cover, but I did make it possible for the SENTINELS to find out that Pierce had Carlos by leaving a note for Emilio."

Bayanai thought about this for a moment. "What did they want George for?"

"I'm not sure."

Just then, a worker from the cafeteria arrived with the ice cream. Emma snagged the mango ice cream and sat next to Arian to enjoy it.

"Can we please take the cuffs off of her now?" Emilio asked.

Bayanai looked at Emma. "Have you been in her mind?"

Emma nodded, licking at her ice cream. She had hardly looked away from her ice cream since it arrived.

"And?"

"I trust her. I told Katrina that when we first got her, but she insisted on keeping the handcuffs on CoCo."

"She was right to do so, given the circumstances." Bayanai sighed. "Okay."

Katrina psychokinetically removed the cuffs, and CoCo rubbed her wrists. Emilio leaned over and kissed her.

"Emma, I'd like to go over a few more things with you," Bayanai said.

Arian stood. "Can we do that tomorrow? Emma needs

351

to rest. She's been through a lot."

Bayanai studied Emma for a moment and blushed. "Of course. It's been a long day for you. I'm just so glad you're back." He hugged the girl. "But I'm afraid you can't just go back to Arian's."

"Why not?" Arian demanded, crossing her arms over her chest and stepping protectively in front of Emma.

Bayanai put his hands up in a calm-down gesture. "We have to assume Pierce will want Emma back, and according to CoCo, his minion Plain Jane is on the island. We just got Emma back, and we don't want to lose her again. As such, I think the best course of action is for the two of you to stay here in Base 47, where it's safe, until we can sort out better security for you."

"Okay." Arian nodded reluctantly and grabbed Emma's hand, but the girl pulled away from her and walked over to CoCo.

"Thank you for rescuing me. I'm sorry I didn't trust you at first." Emma hugged CoCo, who returned the embrace.

"Hon, I'm so glad I found you and that you're back here safe and sound. That alone was worth all the awfulness I went through while I was with Pierce. We'll talk again soon, yes?"

Emma stretched a ghastly smile across her face and nodded. She hugged Bayanai, then Katrina and Emilio, before stopping in front of Waleed, who had silently observed the whole meeting. "Thanks for coming to get us."

He leaned down and hugged her fiercely. "Anytime, kiddo. Welcome back."

Emma turned to Arian and held out her hand. Arian took it, and they walked out of the War Room.

Bayanai debriefed CoCo for the next hour.

When he seemed to think they'd covered the most vital information, he turned to Waleed. "Can you 'port them back to Emilio's—I mean their—house? I don't want CoCo running around on the streets of New Atlantis until I've had a chance to announce to the rest of the SENTINELS that she's back. Otherwise, things could get nasty."

Waleed nodded. "My pleasure." Sparkling black globules appeared, and Emilio and CoCo stepped through.

Alone, in the privacy of their own house, CoCo leaned against Emilio and whispered, "I missed you."

"I missed you, too."

"Don't ever let us do anything like that again."

"Agreed."

Emilio nuzzled her ear. "How much did you miss me?"

Her kiss showed him, and he started to remove her shirt. She stopped him, and he looked hurt.

"It's not you. I just want to wash the Tribe off me. A good hot shower?" She grinned at him and raised an eyebrow in invitation. "And maybe you'll join me?"

CHAPTER 65

19 December

"I knew one of you would be coming for me the moment that ungrateful little twerp killed his father. You bitch, I never trusted you." Elise threw a large eighteenth century vase at Anabel.

Margaux Vu

"And now I have you alone." Anabel dodged the vase, which shattered against the wall behind her.

Anabel had surprised Elise as she walked into the private elevator in her high-rise condo in Zurich. Elise was straight from a board meeting, wearing an expensively tailored pant suit. Anabel was dressed for fighting, in a stylishly sleek but flexible pair of black pants and a sweater. Inside her condo, Elise managed to put a table between the two of them. She grinned.

"What are you smiling about?" Anabel asked, frowning minutely.

"I may be cornered, but I'm not exactly alone here."

Elise let loose an ear-piercing whistle.

Two women ran into the room. One, an Asian woman, was a petite thing, her hair pulled back into a tight bun. One of her eyebrows quirked up at such an angle that it always looked like she was contemplating something almost amusing. The other woman's face was framed by curly, shoulder-length hair. She had the healthy glow of someone who gets just the right amount of sun. The most striking thing about her was her arms. There were four of them.

"So these are the hired powers, huh?"

"Oh yes. After that assassination attempt a few years ago, I got some muscle for protection." Elise nodded at the four-armed woman and then smiled warmly at the other woman.

Anabel reached into her jacket and threw Chinese stars at the two women.

"I don't think so." The Asian Mod, a former member of the Tribe, magnetically caught the stars and launched them back at Anabel.

Anabel let out a gasp of surprise as they sliced her jacket and nicked the skin on both sides of her rib cage. She jumped behind the couch.

Elise took advantage of the distraction to make a run for the panic room hidden in her bedroom.

The four-armed girl charged at Anabel, using the super strength of her four arms to grab Anabel and squeeze her tightly.

"Easy, Joyce. I'm sure Ms. Springchild will want her alive," Margaux, the Asian Mod, said.

"Alive is more than you'll be." Anabel wiggled a hand into her pocket and clamped a plastic depowering bracelet on one of Joyce's arms. Joyce dropped Anabel and writhed in pain as the bracelet cut off circulation to her extra limbs.

Anabel smiled and slammed her right foot into Joyce's cheek.

Horrified, Margaux magnetically grabbed Anabel by controlling the iron in her blood and threw her against the wall. "What did you do to her?" she demanded.

"No less than she deserves, the freak." Anabel tried to grab for her gun.

"Oh, hell no." Margaux ripped the gun from her hands and magnetically deconstructed it. "I like your earrings." She held out her hand, and the earrings ripped out of Anabel's ears, surprising a scream out of Anabel. "You have more than just those earrings don't you?" Margaux smiled.

Anabel howled as a piercing flew from her belly button. Blood spurted from the new openings in her body. She clasped a hand to her belly and looked up at Margaux in angry surprise.

"Oh and you should really get your teeth checked." She laughed as she pulled several metal fillings out of Anabel's mouth without the benefit of a shot of Novocain to numb her first.

Anabel shrieked and held her hands to her mouth. Blood was everywhere. She breathed heavily and dropped to her knees from the pain.

"Now you aren't so fresh, are you?" Margaux lifted Anabel's head up. Margaux dropped her to the floor and stood over her.

Anabel was on her back and glared at Margaux with eyes full of murderous rage.

"I don't know who you are, but you can't attack Ms. Springchild and get away with it." Margaux grabbed the Chinese stars and magnetically held them over her, spinning, inches from Anabel's body. She turned to check on Joyce.

While Margaux was momentarily distracted, Anabel maneuvered her hand into her pocket and found what she was looking for. "You made a grave mistake."

Margaux didn't turn around, but called over her

shoulder, "Oh really? What's that?"

"You stopped watching me." Anabel slapped a power-negating bracelet on Margaux's ankle. Immediately, the stars dropped to the floor and Margaux's face soured.

A bloody Anabel stood, slowly but triumphantly, and edged toward Margaux. "This is for my rings." She slapped Margaux across the face. "This is for my fillings." She kicked Margaux in the leg. "And this is for trying to dominate me." Anabel slammed a defenseless Margaux's head on the floor.

Margaux whimpered but made no other sound.

"I came prepared, Elise. You hear that?" Anabel took a gun from the four-armed Mod and shot her in the head. From within the panic room she swore she heard a scream. She walked over to Margaux and aimed the gun at her. "And now for you," Anabel said.

"Not Margaux!" Elise yelled from the panic room.

"I may not have my powers, but I'm far from weak." Margaux kicked Anabel's legs out from under her. She landed with a thud and lost her grip on the gun, which clattered onto the floor and slid under a side table. Margaux rolled on top of her and squeezed her hands around Anabel's neck. Margaux's eyes tightened as she squeezed harder.

Anabel reached wildly around her, seeking anything she could use as a weapon. She found a lamp and whacked Margaux in the head. It was two too many blows, and Margaux dropped. Anabel smirked, then struggled to get up. She considered feeling for a pulse, but shrugged, figuring Margaux was out of the picture. She glanced around, seeking the gun. Not immediately spotting it, she walked down the hallway toward the bedroom.

"I've killed your honey, Elise," Anabel taunted. "You should know that I have all the intel on your security systems. You can't hide away any longer." Anabel made her way to the entrance of the panic room and pulled out the control pad. She started entering a code with her bloody fingers.

"I know you can see and hear me, Elise. I just want you to know that this is personal." Anabel wiped the blood from her mouth. "I am going to enjoy killing you, and I will take control of your portion of the Ascendancy. Your empire will be mine."

She pressed enter and the wall slid open to reveal a fully stocked and loaded panic room. Elise, face full of grief and fear, cowered in the back corner, aiming a gun at Anabel.

"Now you're just embarrassing yourself." Anabel picked up her Chinese star and aimed it at Elise.

"I'd think again, if I were you," Elise said. "Don't you see that Arthur is playing you?"

"You actually think Maks and I aren't prepared for his betrayal?"

"Then let me help you."

"I think not." Anabel cocked her arm, ready to let loose the star. But before she could, Elise shot her in the shoulder. The sound was huge in the small panic room.

Anabel screamed. Her arm fell to her hip, and she bitterly regretted her failure to retrieve her gun.

"Don't underestimate me. Go back to the playground." Elise walked over to Anabel.

"We can work something out."

"I don't think so. You killed my bodyguards, my love. Doesn't give you a leg to stand on." Elise walked out of the panic room. She stood against the floor-to-ceiling windows and tapped the barrel of the gun against her head and tried to gather her thoughts.

A guttural scream broke Elise's concentration. Anabel charged Elise, knocking her against the window.

Anabel fought her own pain as she maneuvered herself

behind Elise, holding her uninjured right arm around her foe's neck. With her non-dominant hand, she turned the gun toward Elise's side. The pain from the bullet in her shoulder was huge, and it took every ounce of will Anabel had to force her injured arm to obey. She squeezed the trigger.

"No!" The bullet zipped through the woman's body with devastating effect.

Anabel smiled as she let Elise's body slip to the ground, but pain shortened her victory. She'd aimed poorly. The bullet's trajectory took it through Elise before it entered Anabel's own side. Shocked, she fell to the ground. She watched the light in Elise's eyes go out shortly before her own did.

CHAPTER
66

19 December

A black teleportal opened on the third-floor stairwell of Wilshire General Hospital in Los Angeles. Three figures emerged.

"We have to get to the fifth floor." Josh started bounding up the stairs, his brown hair flopping from side to side.

"Wait up. Jiya isn't as fast as you!" Waleed helped the elderly Indian healer up the stairs.

"Can't. Don't know when the nurse is due," he said. "Meet me in room 526." When he reached the fifth floor, he flung open the door and darted down the hall.

"It's okay, Waleed. He's just scared. This infection came out of nowhere." Jiya had one hand on the banister and the other on Waleed's arm as they climbed up the flight of stairs.

Waleed and Jiya made their way to Luca's room and entered it. Waleed closed the door behind them. He stood with his back against the door to ensure their privacy.

Josh sat on the bed next to Luca, who was hooked up to multiple monitors and medicinal drips. Despair and worry filled his eyes.

"When the doctor called me to tell me he had contracted a potentially fatal infection, I was petrified that I might lose him." Josh put his hand on Luca's forehead.

"But the medication is working, right?" Waleed asked.

Josh studied Luca. "The doctors aren't sure if this is new or a complication related to his spinal injury."

Jiya walked to the opposite side of the bed and looked at Luca and then Josh.

"Jiya, can you please help him?"

"*Beta*, this pains me, but you told me Luca's feelings about powers. It would be against my better judgment to do this without his consent."

"What consent? He can't even speak." Josh put a hand on his forehead then swept it back through his hair in frustration. He took a fortifying breath. "He could die!"

Jiya grabbed hold of the rails on the bed, steadying herself.

"I'm sorry, Jiya. You are right, but ... this is the man I love." Josh looked back at Waleed, hoping for support. "You'd do the same for your wife, right?"

"That's different, Josh. She doesn't have the same beliefs as you say Luca does."

"If I do heal him, Josh, it could make the gulf between the two of you even worse." Jiya caressed Luca's hand.

"I don't care. I can't let him die." Josh leaned over and kissed Luca's cheek. "Doing nothing is like homicide."

Jiya sighed and closed her eyes in consideration. "You may be right that not acting would be like killing him."

Josh's breath exploded out of him. She might help after all.

"You accept it might create a karmic imbalance? There will be consequences."

"I accept anything." Josh said. "I just want him to be whole."

"You sure about that?" Waleed asked from his post by the door. "This will change everything between the two of you."

"It's already as bad as it can get. He hates me. But at least he'll be alive and able to walk." Tears welled in his eyes. "Please, I'm begging you."

Again, Jiya closed her eyes. "I will help, but I have deep reservations about this."

"Thankyouthankyouthankyou." Josh sagged in his relief.

Jiya placed her hands on Luca's chest. She closed her eyes and a warm, orange aura grew from her hands and enveloped Luca.

Josh and Waleed watched as the aged Indian woman worked her healing magic.

"It is done." Jiya opened her eyes. Her legs wobbled and she stumbled.

Waleed caught her and helped Jiya to a chair. She pulled out her glasses and put them on.

"Jiya, are you okay?" Josh asked.

"Just been a struggle. With the Falklands and this, I'm... tired."

"Thank you, Jiya." Josh studied Luca. "He looks better, doesn't he?" Josh kissed Luca's cheek. As he pulled back, he drew his eyebrows together in surprise. "That's new." Josh pointed at a white streak in Luca's black hair that had appeared in the middle of his bangs.

Jiya frowned. "I was afraid something like this might happen. I had such reservations about this healing."

"No, Jiya, I am so grateful. He's alive and he'll be able to walk. That's all thanks to you." He grinned. "It'll just take some getting used to." If this was the worst of the consequences, he had really dodged a big one. He leaned down to make a promise to Luca. "I'll be here when you wake up."

"Not sure if you can do that," Waleed said. He stood behind Jiya with his hands on her shoulders. "You need to be in New Atlantis. You have a job to do there."

Josh dropped his head onto Luca's chest. "I know. But I can't let him wake up without me being the first thing he sees. No matter what he feels."

"Josh needs to be here first. Then he'll come back." Jiya tapped Waleed's right hand.

An alarm from one of the machines sounded.

"I think it's time for us to go," Waleed said as he opened a teleportal. "Good luck, Josh. Let me know when you're ready to 'port back to the base." The portal closed as two nurses rushed through the door.

CHAPTER
67

20 December

A burgundy door materialized next to Roger as he poured hot water from an electric kettle into a large travel mug. The sudden appearance of the door in his office so startled him he spilled hot water everywhere. He cursed. Nothing good ever came through that door.

The door opened and a manic Captain Pierce strode out.

"It seems you lack the proper motivation to get the cryospores," Pierce shouted.

Dr. Roger Martin tried to quiet the angry man, but there was no calming him.

"What are you doing here?" Roger ushered him into his office, hoping that no one noticed the hulking man. Pierce looked even scarier than the last time Roger had seen him, and it took a moment to realize the reason. He had mismatched eyes now, and Roger couldn't begin to fathom why.

"I don't give a rat's ass right now. I want those cryospores immediately!" Pierce swayed and caught himself against the wall.

"We're doing everything that we can to safely extract the

cryospores. It's just taking longer than we expected. The child can't work for long periods of time." Roger tried not to look directly at Pierce, who was shaking and jittering in a way that reminded Roger of a documentary he'd seen about meth addicts. Tweaking, he thought it was called.

"Julianne told me that." Pierce stared hard at the Australian scientist. "I don't really care what the problem is. I want a solution. Now. Yesterday."

"We're working on the problem, and I think we have hit upon a solution."

"Thinking is not good enough. I have already lost the little telepath and I won't lose anymore. I... We need the cryospore immediately." Pierce telekinetically levitated Roger off the ground, then looked around the office. He spotted a photo of Roger and a woman.

"Who is this?"

"No one."

"Don't lie. I can feel your heart racing. Who is she?" Pierce leaned toward Roger.

Roger swallowed hard. He didn't want to involve Ursula in any of his work. Although he had told her the truth about what he did, he strove to keep his professional life separate from her. She was his respite from the madness of The Hastings Foundation and his work on the cryospore.

"She's—" Roger stammered as Pierce pinched his finger and thumb together, telekinetically squeezing Roger's throat. "My girlfriend."

"I see. Where is she?" Pierce pulled Roger closer.

Roger shook his head in mute denial.

"Where is she?" He tightened the telekinetic squeeze around Roger's throat.

He choked out an "okay, okay," and the hold released fractionally.

"Where is she?"

Roger slumped. "She teaches piano from her flat."

"I see." Pierce concentrated on the photograph of Ursula and used his stolen remote viewing powers to discern where in London she was. He latched onto her brainwaves. She was teaching a piano lesson, and her student wasn't bad.

"Such life in her." Pierce laughed as he telekinetically dropped Roger to the floor and summoned a burgundy door that opened to her flat. "I'll be right back." Pierce walked through the door.

***

"Keep going, Priscilla. That sounds wonderful. I can tell you've been practicing. Remember to feel the music." Ursula frowned when she heard a noise in the kitchen that sounded like a door opening. "Continue. I'll be right back." She walked to the kitchen. As she turned the corner, she saw the imposing green beret and tried to scream, but it was too late. Pierce grabbed her telekinetically and threw her through his door back to The Hastings Foundation.

***

Disoriented, Ursula ran to Roger. "What's going on? How'd I get here? What just happened?" She looked frightened and more than a little confused. Roger reflexively wrapped his arms around her.

"Love, keep calm. Everything will be okay," Roger said, though he couldn't fathom how.

Pierce returned to Roger's office.

"Pierce, what do you want?"

"What do I want?" Pierce looked furious and exasperated. "How many times do we have to go over this? I want the cryospores. Immediately."

"We're doing everything we can to do just that. Leave Ursula alone. She has nothing to do with this." Roger held his frightened love.

"Wrong. You have been distracted. By her. It's kept you from focusing totally on the problem. I can fix that." Pierce raised his hand to them.

Roger moved to place himself between the madman and Ursula.

"Hmm. How sweet." Pierce smiled. A burgundy door opened up beside him. "Go."

"Where are we going?"

"No questions. Go."

Roger grabbed Ursula's hand and they reluctantly walked through the door. Pierce followed.

***

Dr. Frazier was checking Shining's latest test results when the burgundy door appeared beside her. She stepped back and tried to compose herself for what she knew would come out. She was surprised and relieved to see her colleague Roger and a woman with dark curly hair emerge. Must be the girlfriend. Her relief vanished when Pierce followed them out. She looked at Roger and could tell he was scared.

"Just the person I was looking for." Pierce grabbed Julianne by the arm. "Take us to the kid. And bring Jaako too."

Julianne led them through the station to the holding cells. As she passed the technicians, she silently urged them to remain calm. It seemed like Pierce was holding onto his sanity by a thread and she didn't want to set him off. The last thing she wanted was for Pierce to flip out and cause any destruction. She opened the door to Jaako's cell and told him to step out, then removed Shining from his cell.

"Look at this. What a collection we have here." Pierce summoned another door and pointed them toward it. "Go."

Jaako looked at Pierce, the two scientists, and the unfamiliar woman. He opened his mouth, probably to ask what the dickens was going on, Julianne thought, then closed it. Instead, he took Shining's hand, smiled at him, and together they walked through the door.

The group emerged from the teleportal in the mining annex. Pierce telekinetically grabbed each of them and lifted them off the ground. He pushed them toward the piece of equipment that the technicians called the Cryospore Extraction Unit.

"You've been working on this for over a week. What's the holdup?" Pierce bellowed.

"Captain, we have tried, but the boy tires out too easily. We have reconfigured things several times, but the results are always the same." Julianne tried to hide her fear.

"Unacceptable," Pierce said. He turned to the child. "You are a powerful little kid. But this is getting a little old." He brought Shining closer to him. "Either you get back to shielding those cryospores or I will skin you."

Shining looked at Pierce with disgust and fear. He looked up at Jaako with eyes full of fright. His force field automatically surrounded himself and Jaako.

"Pierce! Leave him alone. You can't expect a child to do what you need out of fear," Jaako said.

"Don't tell me how to get what I want, you slimy son of a bitch." Pierce railed at the prime minister as foam filled the curls of his lips. "I will get what I want." He turned his attention to Roger. "What is it going to take to get this kid to work?"

"We've tried everything we can think of. But it comes down to one big problem. He's just a kid and you're asking too much of him."

Ursula looked at Roger in horror. "What have you done?"

"It's not what you think," he said, seeming to shrink. "Just let me explain."

"Explain? You are torturing a child. A child!"

"Enough out of you." Pierce telekinetically shut Roger's girlfriend up.

Roger puffed up. "Leave her out of this. Deal with me, not her."

"I see. Yes, you are the one who needs to fix this." Pierce dropped Ursula to the ground. She looked horrified and terrified as Pierce raised his hand over her.

"You don't have to do this. I can fix it. Let her go!" Roger tried to run to her but Pierce used his telekinesis powers to keep him away from Ursula.

Pierce then began to exert a gravitational force over her, increasing the density of the air around her and crushing her.

"No!" Roger flailed, trying to reach Ursula. "Stop it!" All he could do was watch Pierce crush the life out of the woman he loved.

She cried out at the intensity of the pain.

Shining moaned and clung to Jaako. The boy's force field still enclosed them both. Jaako covered Shining's eyes even as he himself swallowed hard and watched the spectacle. Julianne's mouth made a perfect O of surprise and shock.

Ursula never looked away from Roger as her bones broke and organs crushed under the pressure Pierce placed on her. At the end, the pressure was so great that she only gurgled as her jawbone broke in half. Blood spurted and oozed. All of them cried out for Pierce to stop, pleading with him as life left Ursula. As her body flattened and she bled, Roger wept.

Pierce smiled as he looked at the horrified prisoners.

"I'll be back in two days." Pierce pointed to the boy. "That should be enough time for you to fix this." He spotted the cryospore containment barrel near the Cryospore Extraction Unit and telekinetically lifted the barrel.

"And if he needs more motivation use this." Pierce pulled a cattle prod from his belt and threw it at Julianne.

"Pierce, I can't do this."

Pierce just looked over at the broken body and back at Julianne, sending the message.

"And just in case that's not sufficient, I'm stationing Alrick and Butcher here to keep an eye on things. Now get back to work." He opened a teleportal door and walked through with the barrel of cryospores following him in midair, leaving behind his prisoners with the dead woman.

CHAPTER
68

20 December

"How did Pierce get you?" Bayanai was perched on a light gray couch in his office, which was compulsively tidy and minimalist. The light streaming into his office seemed too bright for the topic at hand, so he stood and lowered the blinds. He wondered how badly Emma had been affected by her time with Pierce. He hoped that she was unharmed, but reality would likely tell a different story. Arian had said Emma hadn't slept much the night before. She shook until she fell asleep and woke screaming, which was a prelude to uncontrollable sobbing. Arian could do nothing but hold the girl and love her.

Emma focused her attention on her juice glass while she gathered her thoughts. "When's the last time you remember seeing me?" she finally asked.

"Heading back to Arian's the day you disappeared."

Emma furrowed her brows. "I just don't remember. I have a vague image of running back from the beach, but whatever drugs that monster Pierce and his goon gave me has jumbled up all my memories." She sobbed.

"We panicked when we couldn't find you."

Emma nodded and leaned into her guardian for moral support. Arian laid an arm over the girl's shoulders.

"I do remember something. I was almost home and saw a man on the sidewalk. I didn't recognize him then, because I just saw him from behind and he was wearing a hat. He dropped something and stopped to pick it up. I caught up to him just as he stood up. That's when I recognized him. It was the redheaded man. But before I could do anything, he grabbed my arm. He was so strong." She shuddered at the recollection, and the motion almost knocked some of the juice out of her glass. "I couldn't get into his mind. He was wearing a telepathy blocker. Then he pulled me off the sidewalk and nearly into the bushes. Except there was an open door, and Captain Pierce was on the other side."

"So the redheaded man kidnapped you for Pierce?"

"Yes."

"And Pierce was there, with his teleportal door?"

She nodded.

"Why didn't the MDA go off when he came in?" Arian asked.

Bayanai took a moment before responding. "For the past few months, the Mod Detection Alarm has been on the fritz."

Arian raised an eyebrow at him but nodded.

"What happened next? Where did he take you?" Bayanai asked.

"It's kind of hazy. Pierce looked scary and mean. Repulsive. The next thing I remember is my room on the ship."

"So you didn't know why he took you?"

"Not then." She frowned, then burst into tears. "Why did it take you so long to rescue me? I was terrified."

"We tried, Emma. We used all our resources, but we could never confirm that it was Pierce who had you. Or where you were."

For a long while, she said nothing, only cried. Arian held her tight and tried to soothe the girl.

"It's my fault." It came out in a hoarse voice, quiet and ashamed.

"What? What do you mean, Emma?" This time, the question came from Arian.

"He made me search. So it's all my fault." Fresh tears accompanied this latest admission of guilt. She set the juice down and hugged her knees to her chest. Arian held her.

Awkwardly, Bayanai leaned over and hugged the girl. After a few minutes, she continued narrating the details of her captivity.

"He made me search for other people with powers. And I found them. Sometimes he just had me tag them. That is, provide their names and powers and nationality but also to remember them for future reference. But sometimes he would get excited about a power and insist I tell him where to find that Mod immediately. He was searching for someone who could read minds or hypnotize people. I didn't understand then. Until CoCo came and told me about Tio Carlos and the others. And I found them. I found them all."

"The others? You helped Pierce find them?" Bayanai realized that George St. John had been one of the Mods she had found for Pierce.

Miserably, she nodded. She looked like she wanted the floor to open up and swallow her.

"And he hurt them. Took what made them special. All because I found them, and told him about them. He's an evil man, and I helped him. But I thought they were dead, not alive and in the room next door."

Finally, Bayanai understood. "Emma, we're going to stop Pierce and undo the many bad things he's done. But we're going to need your help."

For the first time, a hint of hope flickered across the girl's face.

"What do you know about Pierce's plans?"

"Nothing."

"I just wondered if you had picked up any stray chatter while you were on the boat. Can you make a list for me with all the Mods you tagged for Pierce?" Bayanai knew he should take it easy on Emma, but time was working against them. "I'm trying to get a complete list of the powers we believe he has access to. I know it's a lot, but can you do that for me? We'll need that info to put together a plan of attack."

"Bayanai, that's asking a lot." Arian rose and crossed her arms over her chest.

"I wouldn't be asking if it wasn't important. Or if there was another way. I know how much this hurts. But we need this information, or it will be that much harder to get Shining and Jaako back."

Arian closed her eyes and breathed deeply. Then she looked at Emma, who nodded. "Fine," Arian said.

"Anything that I can do. Just please, help me make it right." Emma stood.

"There's another matter," he said gently.

"Bayanai, she needs a break." Arian wrapped her arm protectively around Emma's shoulders.

"This will just take a moment."

Sighing, Emma sat back down and raised her eyebrows at him.

"You know Pierce also had Shining and Jaako kidnapped."

She nodded glumly.

"I want you to try to reach out to them. Figure out where they are so we can mount a rescue. Get information from them that will help us be successful in the rescue. Can you do that for me?"

"Emma, honey, are you up to this?" Arian asked.

Emma scooted back on the couch and shook her head.

"Bayanai. I don't think this is a good idea. Whatever Pierce did to her, it's affecting her powers," Arian said as she put her hand on Emma's knee.

Bayanai tried to remember the carefree child from before the kidnapping, but she had been replaced by a girl with what seemed like a lifetime of guilt and remorse. If she didn't snap out of her self-imposed torture, they might not be able to defeat Pierce. Perhaps Jiya could help.

CHAPTER
69

20 December

Swiss Magnate Killed in Home Invasion Gone Wrong

Maks read the updated alert on his phone. His stomach clenched and he fought to hold onto his composure. He had just returned to his penthouse apartment in Hong Kong. He had not heard from his twin sister since she had gone to take care of Elise Springchild. Now news outlets were reporting Elise's murder, as well as the deaths of two other unidentified women.

Like many twins, Maks and his sister shared a special, nearly psychic, connection. The feeling that something wasn't right with Anabel had permeated him since the night in South Africa. No. He would not allow the idea of her being gone to take a toehold in his mind. He called her number. Again there was no ring, just a service interrupted message.

"Damn it!" Maks threw his phone across the room. It hit the far wall and clattered to the floor. He was so distraught over the thought of losing his sister he didn't notice that he wasn't alone in the darkened apartment. He collapsed onto his sleek leather couch, consumed with fear. The primal need to hear his sister's voice overwhelmed him. He curled up on the couch and tried not to imagine a life without her.

"Why so glum, sugarplum?" a voice called out. Maks whirled and looked in the direction of the voice, which seemed to come from everywhere and nowhere at the same time.

"Who's there?" Maks leapt to his feet and strode toward the light switch.

"Forgotten me already, partner?" Arthur, seated in a side chair, grinned as light filled the room.

"What are you doing here? How'd you get in?" Maks glowered at his uninvited guest.

"I wanted to congratulate you on a job well done."

"How'd you know?"

"Of course I would watch to make sure you carried out your part."

"And what of my sister?" Maks asked.

"Alas, Anabel was outwitted by Elise." Arthur rose from the side chair.

"What do you mean? How do you know?"

"Well, of course Elise knew Anabel was coming for her."

"And how would she know that?" Maks demanded.

"I told her." Arthur smirked. "Three bodies were found at the scene. Anabel shot herself with her own gun." He shook his head in mock sympathy. "Ooof, that stings."

"No." Maks sagged back on the couch. The pit in his stomach grew.

"Elise was more prepared than Anabel expected." Arthur slowly walked to Maks.

"Leave. Get out of here," Maks said.

"I'm afraid I can't do that. You see, our original deal had the three of us seizing control, but now it's just you and I. And, to be honest, I don't think you'd make a very good partner." Arthur rounded the couch Maks had collapsed on.

Maks tried to focus, but the reality of his sister dying shook him deep. "What are you talking about?"

Arthur now stood behind Maks. He yanked the lamp cord from the outlet and brought the cord down around Maks' neck.

"What the—" Maks struggled to free himself as the cord tightened around his neck.

"I will have complete control over the Ascendancy and you will die." Arthur laughed as he pulled the cord harder.

Maks grabbed Arthur's hands and pulled them down fast, forcing Arthur closer as Maks thrust his head back into Arthur's chin.

"My tongue!" Arthur squawked in pain and let go of the cord.

Maks jumped over the coffee table, rubbing his throat.

"You made me bite my tongue." Arthur's words came out thick, full of anger and surprise.

Maks held his neck, ran to the front wall, and pressed the emergency button. The front door burst open and two bodyguards ran into the main living area from a back room. Maks signaled for them to attack the American.

They charged Arthur, grabbed him by the shoulders, and thrust him against the wall. Maks walked up.

"You thought it was going to be so easy to come here and dispatch me?" Maks laughed. "Seriously?"

"Actually, yes."

"That's it. Give me more reason to hurt you, punk." Maks punched Arthur in the stomach twice, then crossed to his desk and pulled out a Glock 43.

Arthur raised an eyebrow. "Come on, Maks. Nothing's happened that can't be smoothed over." His tone was cajoling. He didn't squirm in the bodyguard's grip.

"My sister's dead because of you, you asshole." Maks caressed the barrel of the gun against his cheek.

"You're just gonna shoot me? Then what?" Arthur grew belligerent as Maks walked over to him. "You think you can run the Ascendancy on your own? You're a fool!" He spat at Maks.

Maks wiped the spit from his cheek.

"You made a huge mistake," Maks said.

"Is that so?" Arthur smiled. "We both know that only one of us will walk out of here."

"You're right. And it will be me."

"Don't be stupid, Maks. You just want the power."

"There's no way for you to win. You walked into the hornet's nest and made them angry," Maks said. "You came to a gunfight without even a knife." He tapped the barrel of his gun against Arthur's forehead.

"Oh, but did I?" His eyes danced and he smiled slyly. He took a deep breath and let out a scream so high in frequency that the two bodyguards holding him let go of him to clasp their hands over their ears. They crumpled to the floor. Maks stumbled toward his dining table, dropping the gun to put his hands over his ears as well.

When the shriek finally ended and Maks recovered, he stooped to retrieve the gun and aimed it at Arthur. "What was that?"

Arthur took a deep breath and let out another piercing scream toward Maks. As the gun began to jiggle in his hands, Maks dropped the Glock again and covered his ears in a bid to block out some of the hellish noise. The scream seemed to go on and on, and the gun vibrated madly on the floor. The room went quiet, but it took Maks a moment to realize that. A moment later he also realized that while he'd been incapacitated, Arthur had collected the Glock. "What the hell?"

"See, Maks, I have an ace in my pocket too. I don't need hired help to get the job done." Arthur grinned.

"How? Are you a Mod?"

"In a manner. You see, while there are those who are gifted from the White Light Wave event, the Swarm discovered a way to transfer those gifts to others. A difficult and arduous process, but one they have mostly perfected. I was given the vocal cords from a man who had sonic powers. The poor bastard didn't even realize the potential he was wasting. I have worked and practiced and trained my voice. My power is impressive."

"Why are you telling me all this?" Maks said.

"I want you to know. I want you to know why you are no threat to me. That I could have taken you out at any point, but I enjoyed the game we played. Even if you aren't the most competent player."

"Please—" Maks said as he lowered his head.

"That's right. Beg. Beg me for your life." Arthur laughed.

"I can help you. Let me be your right hand."

"I think not." Arthur let out a high-pitched screech that shattered the floor-to-ceiling windows. The wind whipped around the living room, making the curtains billow out.

"And now to finish this." Arthur screamed at the bodyguards, leaving Maks for last.

They cried in agony as their ears bled. The sonic screech continued until it liquefied their brains and they fell lifeless onto Maks' polished marble floor.

When Arthur aimed his sonic power at Maks, he bent over in pain, bleeding from his ears and nose.

"See now, Maks? You are nowhere near my league. You never were." Arthur grabbed the bloody Asian man and dragged him over the broken glass to the edge of the apartment. "I wish that I could say that I liked you or that you had any redeeming qualities, but I make it a point not to lie to a dying man." Arthur smiled as he held Maks up outside the window. "Lovely view, isn't it?"

Maks was afraid to look around, especially down, but he opened his eyes briefly to see the streaks of lights coming from the busy road below him. He tried to speak.

"Shh. Shh. Don't. It's too late." Arthur cackled. "You don't need to say a word."

Arthur let go. Maks screamed as he plummeted fifty-six stories to his death. Arthur wiped his hands on his pants and watched the night skyline. He couldn't see or hear what was going on where Maks had landed, but he closed his eyes and imagined the scene for a few moments. He smiled, then took out his phone and dialed a familiar number.

"It's done. The Ascendancy is no more."

CHAPTER

70

20 December

Jiya urged the lucky Spaniard to enter her ashram first, and he opened the door. In the center of the room was Carlos, flat on his back on a single bed. A sheet draped over his body showed only the strong man's face.

"He's a sight for sore eyes," Emilio said as they walked to the Argentine.

"Gentle. He's still recuperating."

"And what about his arm?"

"Dr. Watanabe has created a cybernetic arm for him." She pulled the sheet down, revealing the prosthetic left arm. "It won't be a perfect match, at least not yet, but I do believe he should be better soon." She took Carlos' right hand and squeezed, sending an orange aura around his body.

"How long until he's back to normal?"

"I can only do so much. After that, it's up to him." Jiya began to sway.

Emilio looked around the sparsely decorated room for a chair. He found one, grabbed it, and brought it to Jiya.

"Thank you," she said as she sat. "What troubles you?"

"I'm that transparent?"

"This is only the second time you've been here. The first was right after CoCo left." She smiled at him.

Emilio cast his head down. She saw right through him. He looked back up into her eyes and forced a smile of his own.

"I thought that once she came back it would be just like it was. Like nothing ever happened," Emilio said. He sat on the floor at her feet.

"But?"

"I love CoCo and I owe her my life, several times over." Emilio struggled to find the words he wanted. "Her return should be the best thing to happen in such a long time."

"But you feel like there is something that you've lost since her time away?"

"Yes," he said.

"My dear *beta*, you are only human. And she has only just come home. Much has gone on between the two of you. No wonder you are so conflicted. You've had to hide your feelings to protect her and she's had to lie every day to stay alive."

He considered Jiya's words. She was right. Maybe it would just take some time to get back to where they were. He would do anything to make it happen.

"Sorry to interrupt."

They turned to see Ericka standing at the door.

"Ericka, what are you doing here?" Emilio stood up.

"Tracking down a lead."

"And it brought you here?"

"I go where the clues take me." She closed the door behind her and locked it. "How's Carlos?"

"He'll be fine. Just needs to rest a bit. Dr. Watanabe is coming soon to help him with his arm." Jiya leaned back in the chair.

"Good," Ericka said, looking at Carlos' new arm. "So,

what are you doing here, Emilio? I heard your girl came back?"

"I needed some advice. And Jiya's the wisest I know."

"Be careful what you seek. Sometimes there are unintended consequences." Jiya folded her hands in her lap.

Ericka scrutinized Emilio. He shifted. Something was wrong.

"I know that this was a ruse—CoCo's defection and all, but you have to be prepared. She was gone a long time," Ericka said. "It's going to be difficult."

"That's rich, what about you and Josh? You can't tell me that that's all just water under the bridge," Emilio said.

"What happened between Josh and me is totally different than you and CoCo," she said. "Some things cut deeper. You two were great together and will be again. You'll work this out."

Emilio eyed her and rose. "You said you were following up on a lead here?"

Jiya sensed the tension in the room and closed her eyes.

"I believe that one of the people responsible for the disappearance of Jaako and Shining has hidden herself in here." Ericka closed the blinds on the window and glanced at the door. She frowned, crossed back to the door, and locked it again.

Emilio looked around the room. To him the room was empty, save himself, Ericka, Jiya, and some furniture.

"What do you mean, *beta*?" Jiya asked.

"A Mod. One who has the ability to get in and out of places without detection," Ericka said.

Emilio perked up. "Invisibility?"

Ericka shook her head.

"Illusion-related powers?"

Ericka again shook her head and relocked the door.

"Wrong again, wouldn't you say, Plain Jane?" Ericka

grabbed an older woman by the sweater.

"Where did she come from?" Emilio asked, stunned to see the short woman, who seemed to appear out of nowhere. The woman was so nondescript Emilio couldn't find a single unusual feature about her.

"She's been here for a while," Ericka said.

"What? How did you know?" She tried to break free. "No one ever remembers me!"

"You came to my ashram to hide out?" Jiya pushed herself up and out of the chair and crossed to Ericka. She wobbled and put a hand on Ericka's shoulder and another on the police chief's satchel to steady herself.

"Careful, Jiya," Ericka said.

Jiya continued as though she didn't even hear Ericka. "This is a spiritual place."

"Don't take your eyes off of her," Ericka warned. "That's how she slipped by us the last time."

Jane closed her eyes tight and opened them, but Jiya stared straight at her.

"What do you mean last time?" Emilio asked. "I don't remember that."

"Of course not. She made you forget." Jiya stepped forward.

Jiya stepped toward Jane, who backed away from the old healer. Jiya smiled, then stumbled again. She kept herself from falling by grabbing the plain woman's arm.

"Let go of me," Jane said.

"I do apologize," Jiya said. She stabilized herself and stepped back from Jane.

"You're not going anywhere." Ericka took a set of handcuffs off her belt.

"Think again, dearie!" Jane crossed her arms and an almost imperceptible wave emanated from inside her, confusing and disorienting the SENTINELS. Jane used the moment to slip out of Ericka's hold and scamper toward the door.

"You may have gotten away right now, Jane. But karma will find you," Jiya said, staring at the escaping Mod.

A moment later Ericka and Emilio snapped back to reality.

"What are you doing here?" Emilio asked.

"I... I'm not sure. I thought I was following up on a lead." Ericka furrowed her brow.

"You were. She got away, but it's okay," Jiya said. "Ericka, you have to get to Bayanai quickly. We can track the Tribe."

"How would you know that?" Emilio asked.

"Because they were here," Jiya said.

"How?"

"The second time she used her powers on us I caught on to what was happening and third time she did, I slipped a tracking device into her pocket."

"You have a tracking device?" Emilio asked.

"No, I got one from the bag." Jiya pointed at Ericka's satchel.

"So you didn't really stumble. Nice moves." Ericka smiled at Jiya's slyness.

Jiya shrugged modestly.

"Then we'll get Waleed ready." Ericka neared the door.

"Yes, get the team together." Jiya reached out to Emilio. Ericka walked out of the room.

"Thanks for listening to me," Emilio said.

Jiya smiled at him as she shuffled toward him. "Try to remember that she's had a tough time too."

"You're coming?" Emilio said as he held the door open.

"Once a SENTINEL, right?" Jiya smiled.

CHAPTER
7 1

20 December

Jaako paced his puny holding cell, ruminating. It might be small, but it had the basics. A bed, a toilet, a sink, and a television. At first he'd been excited about the presence of the sink and toilet, which signaled access to water and therefore his ability to use his icy powers to perhaps escape. But he'd been stymied. He'd quickly understood that his room was equipped with some sort of power dampener, and he only had the merest of seconds to tap into his powers each time the door opened.

His room also had the requisite table and chair, along with a television that only seemed to receive one channel. This last was on for background noise because normally he couldn't stand to watch what was on the boob tube. Yesterday it was a terrible reality show featuring insufferable women, and today didn't look any better. Several days before, however, he'd gotten a newscast. He'd heard himself speaking about the Falkland Islands disaster and the rescue mission mounted by the SENTINELS.

That could only have been Josh's shape-shifting handiwork. The SENTINELS were letting him down. He thought they'd have rescued him by now. The longer he was here, the more he feared the unhinged Pierce would return. He closed his eyes and all he could see was Roger's girlfriend being crushed by Pierce. He shook his head, hoping to wipe it from his memory.

Daily, he and Shining had been trundled off to the mining annex, where they were forced to support the cryospore extraction process. The kid was supposed to use his force field powers to contain any energy released by the cryospore extraction and keep the cryospores stable until they were safely contained in reinforced barrels. Jaako had watched him work during the retrieval process. The boy sat utterly still, inside his force field, with his eyes closed and his forehead wrinkled in concentration. Somehow, he pulled off pieces of his own force field and encased the cryospores in individual force fields, which Jaako had seen through the clear suction hose. It was something else, he thought, those blue orbs flying through the hose, all wrapped up in clear bubbles like little gifts. It was a big task for a little kid.

Jaako himself was supposed to keep things cold enough so that any heat generated through the extraction process didn't cause any damage to the glacier. The last thing they wanted was a meltdown.

But so far, the kid hadn't been able to work his force field magic for long stretches of time. He just didn't have enough juice or stamina yet. Jaako didn't have any trouble keeping things cool. But he couldn't help the kid out. That was Shining's part of the deal.

And when Shining stopped cooperating Julianne would hoist the cattle prod. Most times the threat of the shock was enough for the child's force field to automatically power up, but the times when Shining was too drained it took actual contact to jump-start his power. The cries and screams from the five-year-old shook Jaako to his core.

Hope was in short supply inside Jaako. He thought his being prime minister might give him something to bargain with, but no one here cared for his title—only his ability to create and manipulate ice.

Jaako looked at the clock and saw his minder would arrive shortly to bring him breakfast.

How much longer would he be here before the SENTINELS rescued them? Or would he have to rescue himself?

It might be time to take matters into his own hands. Helping extract more cryospores wouldn't get him out of this predicament. If anything, that would encourage his captors to keep him longer. He needed a way out.

He turned the television to mute so he could think and resumed pacing. He roughed out an escape plan that required him to try something entirely new with his powers. He wasn't sure if they would work this way since he'd never tried to use his powers offensively. He thought of them more as simple parlor tricks. Perhaps he should have taken Bayanai up on that training offer when he'd had the chance. He might fail miserably, in which case nothing ventured, nothing gained. On the other hand, he might be free by day's end. But maybe not the kid.

He could live with that. They could always come back for the kid, once the SENTINELS knew where he was.

The clicking door lock told him his minder had arrived with the breakfast tray, and he tensed, standing right next to the door. The door slid open, and there was a pause before the tray and its bearer moved into his cell. The minder—Jaako didn't know his name—was midtwenties and wore thick glasses over small brown eyes. He had a smallish, squinched-up face that made Jaako think of a chipmunk.

"Good morning, Mr. Aalto. Omelet today."

Jaako offered a frosty grin and the minder crossed the

room to his table. Behind him, Jaako propped the door open with the small wooden chair. He knew his powers didn't work in his cell unless the door was open. He thought it had something to do with completing the circuit of the power-dampening system. That was the one flaw he'd detected with the power dampener.

The minder seemed to notice the door hadn't clicked shut, and he turned around, still holding the tray. "Close that door, Mr. Aalto."

"Sorry, that I can't do," Jaako said. Concentration furrowed his brow and ice crystals crackled in the air.

The minder shivered and looked at Jaako with confusion in his tiny eyes. He clattered the tray down on the table and clasped his arms over his chest as his teeth started chattering. "What are you doing to me?" The question took a while to come out, interrupted and strung out by stuttering bouts of chattering teeth.

"You're going to help me get out of here."

"Why would I do that?" Again, the question stretched out, punctuated by chatters and stutters.

"A bit cold, are you?" Jaako waited for the minder to nod. "I can make you colder. I can freeze the very blood in your veins."

The minder, apparently deciding speech was too much of an effort, nodded and looked at Jaako with an unblinking mixture of hatred and fear.

"Where is your access card?"

The minder could barely move he was so cold, so he looked down at his belt.

A high-pitched alarm screeched, jolting Jaako. The minder shivered and smiled at him.

"What did you do?" Jaako demanded.

"C-c-cold," was all the minder could say.

Suddenly, two guards burst into Jaako's cell, sending

flying the wooden chair propping the door open and crowding the small room. One pointed a tranquilizer gun at Jaako. The other carried a blanket, which he wrapped around the minder.

Jaako shrank back from the guard. He'd squandered his chance at escape.

"Don't do that again," the guard said. "When you tried to freeze Jimmy here, you triggered an alarm. We monitor the body temperatures of everyone here to make sure no one freezes to death. You'll pay for that." The guard shot the tranquilizer dart into Jaako, who sagged and collapsed to the floor of his cell.

Jaako's last coherent thoughts were of despair.

CHAPTER
7 2

20 December

The SENTINELS gathered in the large Base 47 War Room. Emilio and CoCo stood in a corner speaking quietly to each other. Everyone else avoided them as pariahs. Katrina, Etienne, and Kirra settled in a trio of chairs in the room's back row. Waleed sat in front with Luli, Jiya, Emma, and Arian. Next to Nicola, Ericka studied a display on her tablet, and when James rushed in at the last moment, he snagged a spot by her. Present at Bayanai's invitation, Maggie sat as far away from CoCo as possible, watching everything. She glared at CoCo and crossed her arms over her chest. Anyone sitting close enough to her would have heard her muttering the mantra, "There are no snakes, there are no snakes."

"Look at this." Etienne held up his phone to show a video to Katrina and Kirra. It was the commercial GRIM had put together after the Sydney incident. "That whole sand fight in Sydney was totally edited to make us look bad. They don't even show that we saved the people there and that no one got hurt. It's so messed up!"

Kirra stroked his arm and grinned at Katrina, who let out a small laugh.

Bayanai walked into the room and did his best to ignore how close Kirra and Etienne were.

"Everyone get seated. We need to start as soon as possible. As you know, three of our own have come back home," Bayanai said from the front of the room. "Emma and Carlos have been rescued—"

His announcement was interrupted by jubilant cheers and shouts of "Welcome back" and "Where's Carlos?" Emma lowered her head, momentarily embarrassed.

Nicola spoke up. "Yukio is with Carlos, helping him learn how to use his new cybernetic arm. I hear he's a quick study." More cheers followed her update.

Bayanai let the celebration continue for a few moments before signaling for silence. "Also, CoCo is back. Treat her as though she never left, because she always remained one of us—"

"Yeah, right," Etienne muttered.

"That's enough," Bayanai snapped. "We'll cover that territory in a little while. First, Emma can tell us what happened while she was held by Pierce."

Emma looked at Arian for assurance and slowly walked to the front of the room. Instead of saying a word, she looked at the faces of her teammates, the ones she'd missed for so long. She closed her eyes and tried to link her mind with the team, but she found herself alone in the little dance room in her mind where she'd held so many astral meetings with the SENTINELS over the last five years. She frowned. Where was everyone? She opened her eyes, and her teammates were all staring at her expectantly. How come she couldn't link them up?

She took a deep breath and looked at Arian, who nodded reassuringly at her. Emma bowed her head in thought. Instinctively, she knew she didn't want to have to relate the tale she was about to tell them, understood this might be the core of her problem in making her power work. But she couldn't dredge up the desire necessary to even fight to get her powers to work properly. Not if it meant reliving those awful months, those awful actions, Alrick's control over her, Pierce's increasing madness. No, she didn't want to think about any of it, let alone share it. A single large tear slipped down her cheek, and she ran back to Arian.

Arian comforted the girl for a long while. Jiya turned to Emma and beckoned. Emma stood and walked over to the healer. Jiya patted her lap and Emma half-sat on her, partly nervous to put her full weight on her but grateful to be in her loving arms. Jiya pulled her into a deep embrace and Emma broke down in tears as pure orange light engulfed them. Arian fought the urge to go to Emma. Eventually, Jiya released her grip and Emma rocked back, tears mostly dry. A tiny smile curled her lips.

Emma turned back to her teammates and this time, when she gathered everyone in the astral dance room in her mind, it worked. Reluctantly, she told about how she had been kidnapped and the atrocities that Pierce had committed on the Mods he'd forced her to locate while Alrick the puppet master guided her searches. She described the powers he now had at his command as well as those Mods she had found and simply tagged, who he might be able to find later. She shared her shame about her forced role in his activities, and in the astral dance room, they comforted her. When she broke the mental link, she sent everyone back into the War Room. She shook with tears as she returned to her seat between Luli and Arian, who both hugged her protectively.

"The ability for Pierce to steal powers from Mods has some serious ramifications for all of us," Emilio said.

"He's a dangerous man, and he seems to become more unstable every day," CoCo added.

Maggie cringed when CoCo spoke. Etienne, who clearly still mistrusted CoCo, shot CoCo a nasty look on Maggie's behalf, and Emilio glared back at him.

"I mean beyond Pierce," Emilio said. "Think about it. If there's a way to steal powers, and the Mods registration act goes through, then no Mod is safe from someone determined to steal their gifts."

Understanding dawned on each of the Mods in the room. If it was possible for Pierce to steal powers from unsuspecting Mods, then how safe were they really? What if others figured out how to do this as well?

"We should make attempts to identify who all these stolen powers originally belonged to, maybe even see if there's a way we can return them," Ericka said.

"This goes way beyond what I've been researching," Nicola said. "But I have to say you can't always return what's been taken."

"No matter, we won't be able to do that until we defeat Pierce once and for all. Emilio? CoCo?" Bayanai waved at them and the front of the War Room.

Emilio and a nervous CoCo headed to the front of the meeting room.

"I can't believe they let her back in here," Etienne muttered.

"Can we really trust her?" James asked.

Maggie shrank back in her chair, wrapped her arms protectively around herself, and narrowed her eyes at her once dear friend.

"Enough!" Bayanai yelled. "Hear them out."

"I know it's hard to swallow, but I never betrayed any of you. This was my idea," CoCo said.

Emilio put his hand on her shoulder and said, "Our idea."

She briefly looked back at him. "We needed to find a way

to stop Pierce. He was always a step ahead of us. But to get on his side, I had to make it look believable. And for that, I'm sorry."

Bayanai interrupted. "As you know, they were right, and there was a mole, someone who had been compromised by Pierce. We are using this person to send disinformation to him. So that leak has been plugged. Additionally, we have learned that Plain Jane has been on the island for quite some time, and we believe she participated in Shining's kidnapping. Just a little while ago, Jiya and Ericka managed to place a tracking beacon on Plain Jane, and Ericka is monitoring her location. Our hope is that when she leaves the island, she'll return to Pierce's ship and we can finally locate it and stop him."

"I wish I had better news," Ericka said. "Just before this meeting, the signal shorted out. I hate to say it, but I think that happened when she returned to the Tribe's boat."

Etienne swore under his breath.

Emilio looked at CoCo. "Is George on Pierce's boat?"

She shook her head. "I don't think so. I never saw him and I never heard he was there. Maybe he's in Antarctica." For a long moment, no one else spoke, so CoCo carried on. "Pierce amassed all the powers Emma told you about, but he's after the cryospore."

"That's probably the blue thing that was in his belt," Katrina said.

CoCo raised her eyebrows and nodded. "You're right. Anyhow, there are apparently tons of these tiny little things trapped in the ice shelves of Antarctica. The cryospore is a source of a new form of clean energy that The Hastings Foundation wants to monopolize. He's using Shining to extract them. Word is it's not going well. This is a good news, bad news situation. Good news for us because it means delays in their plans. But bad news because this increases the strains and risks for Shining."

"What I want to know is when we're going to get my son back," Luli demanded.

"The first step in that, Luli, is figuring out where he is. Thanks to CoCo, we have a general location. Antarctica. But now we need specifics. How are we going to get those details? Thoughts, anyone?" Bayanai opened the meeting to discussion.

The team kicked ideas around for a while before Nicola spoke up.

"Something unusual is going on at The Hastings Foundation's London office," she said.

"What do you mean?"

"They're using way too much energy, for starters. It spikes periodically. And it looks like it's coming from the building's sub-basement." She frowned in consideration. "I've been looking into it since yesterday at Bayanai's request but haven't been able to figure out just what they're doing."

"Whatever it is, we at least know that Henry Hastings isn't behind it anymore," Emilio joked.

"Why are we thinking about London? My boy is in Antarctica."

"I know, Luli, I know. But we may be able to kill two birds with one stone. If someone can infiltrate their office, we can get into their servers and search for information on the cryospore project. Their system is impenetrable from anywhere but on site. Trust me, we've tried hacking it. With any luck, we'll find documentation about the work—and location—in Antarctica. Second, we can figure out what the hell is causing those energy spikes."

"I like it," Emilio said.

"Me too," Bayanai said.

"It might not even be that hard to get into their offices.

I bet things are still messed up since Henry's death," Emilio said.

"Etienne, this sounds like a job for you," Ericka said.

"Sure, I can go snoop, but wouldn't it be better for me to explore what's going on with the energy spikes?" Etienne popped his gum as he spoke.

"As much as I hate to admit it, he's right," Katrina said.

"All right, the two of you will go in and discover exactly what this energy spike is all about. But only recon. Don't do anything," Bayanai said.

"Then who's going in to access the system from the inside?" Kirra asked, looking at the others.

For a long moment, nobody spoke.

"Arian," Emilio suggested.

The SENTINELS looked at Emma's guardian.

"Oh no. I couldn't. They'd recognize me in an instant. I'm the prime minister's chief of staff."

"There are ways to take care of that," CoCo said.

"But I'm not a SENTINEL," Arian said. "I don't have training in this kind of thing."

"We need your help on this one," Bayanai said. "We'll coach you through it."

"This will be a recon mission only. Arian, we'll get you into The Hastings Foundation so you can get us access to their network," Ericka added.

"Please, anything that will help me get back my son." Luli leaned across Emma and grabbed Arian's hand.

Arian studied Luli for a moment, took a deep breath, then nodded.

"Good," Bayanai said. "Etienne, you and Katrina will sneak in with Arian and discover the source of the energy spikes. Remember, we just need the intel at this point. Thanks, everyone. We'll gather here later when we have some answers from this recon mission."

The team walked out, but Bayanai nodded to Maggie, who remained seated.

"So is this the part where you tell me what's really going on?"

A thin smile curled his lips.

"Maggie, I think we can speak freely—off the record, of course."

Her eyes fluttered before she eventually nodded.

"I want to be as honest with you as possible," he said. "It wasn't just Shining who was kidnapped."

Maggie leaned closer.

"Pierce also has Jaako Aalto." Bayanai searched her face for any change. Her face didn't show any reactions to this news.

"And that's what Josh is doing here, isn't it?"

"How did you know?"

"I'm a reporter, Bayanai. There's a story here."

"Maggie, I asked you to come here to help us, not destroy us."

A long moment stretched out between the two of them.

"You know you're playing with fire here. If it ever got out—"

"It won't," Bayanai said with a confidence she soon felt.

"I hope for your sake it never does." Maggie got up and looped her handbag across her shoulder.

"I hope you can still report on the rescue. You'll be instrumental in showing the world how the SENTINELS are a force for good. Maybe we can even shut GRIM down."

Maggie arched her eyebrow at Bayanai and walked toward the door.

CHAPTER

7 3

21 December

The wind whipped around Arian, clad in a black overcoat and chestnut brown headscarf, as she walked the Canary Wharf section of London near the Thames. A pair of thick-framed glasses rounded out her disguise. She sipped the last bit of her coffee before walking into the high-rise building.

Her heels click-clacked across the tiled floor of the entrance hall. As she approached the front counter, a wave of uncertainty washed over her. What if there was trouble with her ID? Arian flashed credentials to the man at the security desk and he waved her through. With great relief that she tried not to show, she pushed through the turnstile. She punched the elevator button and stood alongside the others waiting for the lift. Two doors opened and most rushed into one car. Arian moved deftly to the empty one and walked inside. She pressed the door close button and then the button for the twelfth floor.

"All right, guys. Everything is going smoothly so far," Arian said into her comms piece, trying to squelch her fears a bit.

She wanted to help out the SENTINELS in any way

possible, but infiltrating the London office of The Hastings Foundation was not exactly within her comfort zone. She was simultaneously thrilled and anxious.

Arian held her breath, praying her cover would work. She gently touched the badge hanging from her neck that read "Shadi Ahmadi."

The elevator doors opened and she walked out into the lobby of The Hastings Foundation London offices. A young blond woman greeted her and escorted her past the desk.

"Good Morning, Ms. Ahmadi, it's a pleasure to have you here at the London office of The Hastings Foundation. We have you all set up in an office at the far end of the floor. I'll take you there. Have you been consulting for long?" the bubbly Brit asked.

"Hmm? Yes. Why yes," Arian said, remembering her cover.

"You'll have to forgive the offices, we've been in a state of shock following our founder's death," the woman said.

"Of course." Arian bowed her head slightly. "My condolences." She followed the girl through the office and past several large conference rooms full of people in white coats fervently discussing something. "They seem quite engaged," Arian said.

"What? Them? Yes. They are nearing the final stages of a project they've been working on for years," the receptionist said.

Arian looked at the whiteboards in the room and saw various notes about "cryospore" and "extraction" and sensed the receptionist was correct in that whatever they were planning, they were on the verge of completing.

"This is your space. We've set you up so you should have everything you need. Wi-Fi code is on the desk." The blonde opened the door to the office.

"Thank you so much. You're a dear. If I need anything

I'll let you know." Arian smiled and walked inside the plush office space.

"The bathroom is down this hall to the left and the break room is on the right just past it." The girl smiled and left.

Arian surveyed the room. She took a lipstick from her purse and twisted it. It wasn't really a tube of lipstick but rather a sophisticated anti-surveillance jammer designed by Dr. Patel. She touched the device in her right ear for reassurance. She spoke softly, hoping her friends at Base 47 were hearing her.

"We're in. I'll set the uplink in two minutes." She opened her briefcase and removed her laptop. She set up the computer on the desk and placed the lipstick next to her.

"Good. I'll keep you in touch with the others," Bayanai replied as Arian began the uplink from The Hastings Foundation to Base 47. "If everything goes smoothly we'll get the files simultaneously."

Arian inserted into her laptop a flash drive that would run a program to give her full access to The Hastings Foundation's protected files.

***

Etienne watched Arian walk off with the assistant. He and Katrina had a short amount of time to uncover the source of the energy spikes. Holding hands with Katrina, he kept them invisible and undetectable to anyone.

As Etienne and Katrina passed through the offices, they looked into the conference rooms where the scientists heatedly discussed calculations that Etienne could barely understand.

"What are they talking about?" Katrina asked.

"It looks like they're focused on the cryospore." Etienne frowned. "Looks like CoCo was telling the truth." They continued toward the lab facilities.

"What are we waiting for?" Katrina asked as they waited at the heavily secured doors.

"We can't phase through here. I'll short out the entire electrical system and we'll never get to the sub-basement," Etienne said. "We've got to be sneakier."

An overweight, nerdy lab tech waddled past them and placed his ID badge on the door sensor until it clicked. The door slowly opened and Etienne and Katrina walked through behind the lab tech. As he walked away, Katrina psychokinetically lifted his ID badge and made him stumble to disguise the movement. The tech looked around, shook his head, and opened a candy bar to take a bite. Etienne quickly increased his invisibility to shield the badge from view. He breathed and waited for the man to walk away. Etienne and Katrina walked toward the elevator at the end of the all-white corridor.

Etienne pressed the badge to the sensor on the wall and the elevator opened.

***

Arian looked up from her laptop to check out the office. It seemed quiet, and she hoped that her teammates were making their way down to the sub-basement. The status bar of the file transfer was at forty-two percent.

She ran her fingers through her hair and tried to calm herself down. She hated pretending. Lying. Being someone else, but this was no time to think about that. Anxiety about messing up filled her, but Bayanai believed in her, and she did not want to let them down. And poor Emma had just returned to them. She couldn't let her down. She had to be brave, for Emma, for Rami, for Shining and Jaako, and for herself. She concentrated on doing her part so they had a shot at winning.

Forty-nine percent.

Arian spotted the receptionist walking toward her. She reached into her briefcase and removed a file folder and pen so she would seem busy.

"Everything okay in here?" she cheerfully asked as she popped her head into the office.

"I'm good right now. Thanks so much." Arian hoped she sounded normal.

The woman closed the door and retreated.

"Bayanai, how are they doing?" she asked into her comms piece.

"They've made it to the elevator right now," he replied.

"All right. It's at fifty-two percent. I hope it goes faster. I don't like this."

"Relax. Everything will be fine."

"I wish you could have had someone else do this instead of me."

"Would that we could. The SENTINELS are too recognizable, but with your disguise, even someone who knows about New Atlantis won't recognize you. It's perfect. Besides, I needed Etienne and Katrina scouring the lower levels," Bayanai said.

Arian thought about the prime minister and Luli's son and wondered if they were okay, wherever they were. She shook out her hands as if banishing bad thoughts.

"You're doing great, Arian, just a little bit more. The uplink is working perfectly," Bayanai said.

"So what are you finding about Antarctica?"

"From the little I see here, this entire project depends on harnessing a great power. A resource, really. I believe that to harvest the energy source they needed Shining and Jaako. But until we get the all the files, we won't fully know the Ascendancy's endgame."

Arian nodded and decided to take a look through some of the files herself.

Sixty-six percent.

***

Even though they were invisible and intangible, they tried to be as silent as they could be in the elevator. The doors opened and they carefully stepped out and walked toward the end of the hall. It was marked Engine Room.

"This must be where the energy spikes are originating," Etienne whispered. They followed a lab tech as he placed the badge to the sensor and the large, thick metal door opened. They stepped into a narrow tube-like corridor.

"Uh, Etienne?" Katrina whispered as they lagged behind the tech.

"Just stick close."

The lab tech flipped his badge on the sensor and the red light blinked, but the door remained shut. They looked at each other. He again tapped the badge to the sensor. Much to their relief the door opened and they all walked through. A large circular machine was at the center of the room, and wires ran from it on all sides to monitoring stations. Etienne looked at one of the monitors, trying to figure out what the machine did.

"What's with all the heavy coats?" Katrina asked.

Suddenly the machine began spinning and the readings on the monitors spiked.

"Be careful, and stay out of the way," Etienne whispered to his teammate. He tried to mind-speak with Emma but she didn't respond.

***

Arian's eyes widened as comprehension dawned.

"Bayanai, I found the coordinates and schematics for the Antarctic base. I think that's where Jaako and Shining are." Arian told him where to find the information in question.

"Yes!" he said. "Great work, Arian. As soon as we get the full upload you are good. Just stay where you are."

Pride in her contribution replaced some of her anxiety. Now she just had to wait just a little longer.

Eighty-four percent.

***

Katrina looked on in awe as in the center of the dark circle a figure began to appear.

"This could be some sort of teleportation device," Etienne whispered on seeing a middle-aged man come through. The man looked defeated and weathered. As if life really had beat him up. "It's that Aussie scientist."

The scientist stopped, looked around, and addressed the engineer in the booth. "Leave the portal running. I just need to grab a few items and get right back to Antarctica," Roger said.

The heroes looked at each other. They were just supposed to find out what the energy spikes were while Arian downloaded the files. Etienne nodded at Katrina. Together, they charged into action.

They ran toward the bubbling teleport machine but before they reached it a klaxon sounded its alarm.

"What the?" Etienne said as he covered his ears. The sudden noise distracted him from keeping them invisible.

"Bloody hell!" Roger screamed as Katrina and Etienne materialized in front of him.

Katrina psychokinetically lifted Roger up and pushed him toward the wall.

"Step back, old man," Katrina snapped. She looked at the engineer and froze him in his tracks, but it was too late. He had already pulled a lever that had begun shutting down the teleportation device.

"Etienne! Now or never!" Katrina used her power to reverse the lever and keep the machine whirring.

"Stop them!" Roger shouted, even though he couldn't move.

"But what about the machine?" Etienne asked.

"Just do it!" Katrina shouted.

He had not wanted to short the systems, but they had no choice now. Etienne made his arm intangible. He stuck his arm into the first monitor and began running alongside them, disrupting each and causing them to spark and burn. The lights flickered and the portal dimmed.

"Katrina! If we're going, we better do it now!" Etienne said as he neared the large machine in the center.

"Come on! Let's go," Katrina said.

"I hope this works!" Etienne grabbed her hand.

They ran toward the teleportation portal, prepared to continue the fight on the other side.

***

Arian saw the progress was at ninety-seven percent. She jumped when strobe lights flickered and an alarm beeped madly. She hoped nothing had happened to Katrina or Etienne.

"Bayanai, something's wrong. What's going on?" Arian said but could not hear anything in return.

The receptionist burst into her office.

"What's going on?" Arian asked with a calm she did not feel.

"You have to come with me. There's been a security

breach."

Arian looked down at the screen and was relieved to see it reach ninety-nine percent. She grabbed her briefcase and coat and headed toward the door.

"Don't you want your laptop?" she asked.

"We're coming back in, right?"

"It may be a while. Security is a real stickler for procedures." She pointed back at the laptop.

Arian looked at it. One-hundred percent. "You're right. I should take it." Arian grabbed the laptop, closed it and put it into her briefcase, and ran out with the young woman. She said a silent prayer, hoping her friends were okay.

CHAPTER
7 4

21 December

"I thought being outdoors would brighten your mood, Mr. Florentino." Susan pushed her patient along the garden sidewalk of the hospital. Palm trees swayed in the breeze and the flowerbeds were in winter bloom.

"I'd rather be back inside." Luca stared off into the distance, seeing nothing. His arms were crossed in front of his chest and a frown threatened permanence on his face.

"You're alive. That infection could have killed you. The doctor said your spinal injury has healed and you'll walk. You just have to regain the muscle you lost while recuperating from the accident." She stopped the wheelchair and put on the breaks. "You're a miracle."

"Suppose so," Luca said, stroking his beard.

"Let's get you up. The doctor has cleared you." She held her hands out.

"I don't want to."

"Oh come on," Susan said with a cheer that struck a chord in Luca. "Stand up."

"Cut the act," Luca said darkly. "I know it's you, Josh."

The short Asian-American woman looked back at her

physical therapy patient and sighed. She stood, crossed her arms, and abruptly shifted into Josh Grant.

"That's what I thought." Luca sat back in his wheelchair.

"Fine. You got me. But I just couldn't let you suffer like that. And that infection could have killed you!" Josh dropped to his knees next to Luca.

"It would have been better."

"How can you say that? You're alive. You're here. You can walk. You just have to stand up." Josh implored him to get up. His cell rang and he silenced it.

"You should get it."

"They can wait."

"Can't you just leave me alone? Don't you get it? I don't want to see you. You violated my wishes. I asked you to not do 'this.'" Luca motioned to his legs. "And you deliberately did. You involved your Mod friends in my life and now I'm tainted."

Josh bit his lip. No matter what he said or did, Luca would find a way to crush him. "All I ever wanted is for us to be happy. We still can be. You just have to—"

"No, Josh. The accident was a wake-up call. I knew our relationship couldn't last. We're too different. I need someone..."

"Human?"

"You said it, not me. But, yes."

The answer stung. He wasn't sure what hurt more. Seeing Luca paralyzed and dying in that bed or seeing him here, whole, in the sunlight but separated by a chasm of belief.

"Luca, I'll give you all the space you want. When you're ready, we can go back to how—"

"Just stop!" Luca threw his hands up in the air.

It stunned Josh for a moment. "You know what I think?" Josh balled his fists at his side in frustration. "I think

410

you are relieved to be alive and whole, but your guilt is making you lash out at me—the man who loves you." It was a standoff.

"Here it is, Josh. I'm standing. Standing up. To you." Luca pushed his body out of the chair and wavered on legs he hadn't stood on in a month. Thrilled to see Luca on his own two feet, Josh reached out to steady him. Luca pushed his hands away. "You should leave. Before I do something I might regret."

"You don't mean that."

"I do." Luca gestured at his legs and then the white streak in his bangs. "I hate you for doing this. All of this is your fault. And you still think you can just slide off any culpability. Flash your million-dollar smile and I'll just forget that I was hurt because of you. Forget that being in your orbit means I'm in danger for my life. You Mods think you can act however you want and that there are no consequences. Your healer might have saved the day, but she might not be there next time."

The words slammed into Josh with the force of bullets. He wanted to hug Luca and never let go, but maybe this was one time in his life when going was the only option. He had run away from the SENTINELS. From the Mods. From Ericka. And now he would have to do the same with the man of his heart. He was in an impossible situation. He wanted to say the right thing. To fix it somehow. But this was something he couldn't fix.

"I don't care if you hate me. I love you and I did what I did because I love you. I couldn't live thinking I didn't do all I could to help you."

They stared at each other, the silence shouting their heartache.

"Go back to your friends. I don't want you."

Josh looked him in the eye. His shoulders drooped, and

411

he turned.

As Josh walked away, Luca crumpled back into his wheelchair and squeezed the armrests hard. He looked up to the sky for endless moments. Finally, he slipped his hand in his pocket and pulled out his cell. He dialed a number and waited. A cheerful girl answered.

"This is GRIM, where you can anonymously report Mod activity. How can I help you?"

CHAPTER
7 5

21 December

"This time with a little enthusiasm," Dr. Julianne Frazier said.

Beside her, Shining frowned and shook his head.

She knew the five-year-old was not in the mood to mount any sort of effort that didn't involve a family reunion. He sat cross-armed and cross-legged in the cabin of the Cryospore Extraction Unit. From her seat, she was able to operate the various functions of the machine and monitor the quantity gathered, while Shining was there to provide permanent stability for the cryospores as they came out of the ice and flowed into the collection barrels.

The Cryospore Extraction Unit was construction-worker orange. It was about fifteen feet tall and had an enclosed and thermally protected cabin for the operators. It used a drill to penetrate the ice. Sensors on the drilling tool could detect the presence of cryospores. A suction tool, also complete with sensors, extracted the cryospores from the ice and sent them to a cryogenic collection barrel via a reinforced hose.

They were in the mining annex on Antarctica, and the

only heat Julianne was feeling was Pierce's rage at their continued inability to extract the cryospores more quickly. The man's unpredictability grew every day. She feared he was as unstable as the cryospores themselves.

Rubbing her temples, she considered whether she had anything to offer Shining, anything that might tempt him to try harder. But nothing new rose to the surface. She'd tried all her treat offerings over the first few days, then had resorted to minor punishments for failure to comply or try harder. When she could get him to work, he worked halfheartedly for brief spurts of time and then needed enormous recovery periods before being able to resume. While she understood this was beyond his control, nothing could convince Pierce of this. He was unreasonable in his increasingly volatile state. In the aftermath of Pierce's visit, she was making use of more extreme measures. That was what the cattle prod beside her was for.

She felt completely out of options. The murder of Roger's girlfriend meant her own neck was on the line. She cut her glance to the site of Ursula's killing and away again. Some lowly and likely scared technician had cleaned up after. But Julianne couldn't clean the image from her mind. She shivered. And of course the murder had the opposite effect on Roger than Pierce intended. Instead of doubling down focus on the cryospore project, Roger had completely fallen apart in his grief. Julianne was pretty much on her own.

She had to get Shining to perform, and she hoped she wouldn't have to use the cattle prod again. Effective, but distasteful.

"Listen, Shining, I know you miss your mom and dad and sister. That you want to go home. But if you can just help me today make everything work right, I will get you home, back with your family."

Hopeful eyes studied her face, as though searching for the truth of her promise. Shining sighed, shook his head, and closed his eyes. He leaned back in his seat in a way that suggested he was willing to wait forever if that's what it took.

Then his eyes rolled back in his head, a red aura engulfed him, and an unfamiliar voice spoke through his mouth.

"THE WAY IS PREPARED

"THE TIME IS COME

"THE DEAD WILL WALK AGAIN."

She shivered, stared at the child, and drew as far away from him as she could in the cabin of the Cryospore Extraction Unit. She tried to brush the weird words away. What was that? Was he playing a prank on her? But the phrasing and cadence jarred her. That wasn't kid-talk. And what about that red light that enveloped him? Almost as quickly as the moment came, it was gone and Shining stared at her, dull-eyed. She studied him, trying to reconcile the Shining of the spooky red aura and strange words with the child looking at her now. She couldn't.

"Shining, here's the thing. If you help, you'll get to go home. But if you don't help, you'll never get to leave. Don't you understand how that works?" She patted the cattle prod.

He raised his eyelids a fraction and looked at her.

"Let's just try for a little while. And then we can take a break and you can have some fruit."

Resigned, he nodded. She started the Cryospore Extraction Unit's motor and let it warm up. Jaako stood about ten feet away from the Cryospore Extraction Unit, hunched over and waiting grimly to work, looking despondent, weak, and shaken up over his failed escape attempt. She was sure the only reason he didn't try to run from the mining annex was that one of Pierce's Mods, a guy named Dafydd who could clone himself, was watching him. There had been nothing in his manner that suggested he was

415

sticking around to help Shining. From far away, or up close, he seemed just like every other politician she'd heard of. Charismatic, selfish, and only semitrustworthy.

Julianne pulled up the machine's control monitor, which showed her the location of the drill in the ice. After about fifteen minutes, the monitor flashed, indicating the drill had sensed a pocket of cryospores. She retracted the drill from the hole and sent the suction unit down.

"Ready to collect," she shouted into a communication unit that connected the Cryospore Extraction Unit with the lab.

"Proceed," came the tinny response from the lab.

She signaled to Jaako, and he nodded back unenthusiastically. He held his hands out in front him. Ice crystals arced away from his hands and glistened in the air.

"Get ready," she said to Shining.

The child sucked in his breath, and his brow furrowed in concentration.

She punched a button and suction began. It sounded like the world's largest vacuum cleaner coming to life.

She watched the monitor and smiled as the level of cryospores in the collection barrel rose.

"Collecting," she said into the communication unit.

Within just a few minutes, however, she detected a change in pitch of the suction and powered off the unit.

"Collection halted. We're at twenty percent," she said into the communication unit. One-fifth of the way there in mere minutes. If they could keep up this pace, they could fill both barrels by lunch and get Pierce off her back.

In excitement and gratitude, she smiled at Shining and thanked him. He regarded her silently.

She retracted the suction tool and sent the drill back down. It whirred away for about ten minutes before its sensors alerted her to the presence of another cryospore accumulation. She swapped out the drill for the suction tool and waved at Jaako, who again nodded unenthusiastically back at her. She wondered what he was thinking.

"Ready to collect," she shouted into the communication unit.

"Proceed," the lab technician responded.

She activated the suction mechanism and saw Jaako hold out his hands and form ice crystals in the air to cool the temperature.

"Collecting," she said.

She monitored the screen. The collection barrel level rose steadily.

After a time, she said, "You're doing great. We're nearly there. Seventy-five percent." She glanced at him and saw he was trembling in his bucket seat.

"Stop," he finally rasped.

"We're at ninety percent," she said. "Just a few more minutes and you can rest."

"Please."

His voice sounded weak, and she could feel him shaking in the cabin next to her. She looked at him and saw blood trickling from his nose. She sighed and turned off the suction.

"Collection halted. We're at ninety-three percent," she said into the comms unit.

Shining collapsed back into his seat, giving in to the strain of actively placing permanent force fields around each cryospore. The difficulty of having to create multiple force fields that were permanent but away from his body drained him quickly.

"You did great," Julianne told him.

The fact that the suction hadn't tapered off meant there was plenty more to harvest at this zone. Once Shining recovered, she hoped they could fill the second barrel from that zone and call it a day.

The air crackled around them in the mining annex.

Alarmed, she looked to Shining, who had passed out. He lay limp across his seat. Blood still dripped from his right nostril. The glacier shuddered, and Jaako, who had been near the Cryospore Extraction Unit, stumbled and sprawled to the ground.

"What's going on over there?" a technician from the lab asked over the communication unit.

"Not sure," she said, panting. "Shining's down. I think it was too much for him. We hit the mother lode. But the air in here feels weird, and it felt like the glacier just moved."

The technician's voice changed. It sounded urgent when he answered her. "Julianne, get out of there now. All of you. Now."

The near-panic in his voice drove her. She lifted Shining onto her hip, called out to Jaako, and fled toward the mining annex exit, wondering what the technician had grasped that she hadn't yet figured out.

The ground beneath her shook. Believing it to be the beginning of all hell breaking loose at the mining annex, she doubled her speed.

CHAPTER
7 6

21 December

Katrina and Etienne skidded to a
halt in a metal enclosure the size
of a large elevator. There were no
buttons, only a touch screen
control panel. On it were The
Hastings Foundation's logo and a
few words in large red letters:
Arrived, Antarctic Research Station.

**Friedrich Metzger
"Butcher"**

Fighting nausea, Katrina patted down her own body,
making sure they had arrived through the teleportal in one
piece. It wasn't one of Waleed's smooth rides. The transition
from London to Antarctica had been choppy and reminded
her of the time she'd gone deep sea fishing with a friend's
family and spent most of that miserable day vomiting over
the side of the boat. "Ugh. We made it, but I don't want to
teleport that way again."

"Yeah, I wasn't sure the machine would function once
I—"

"Who are you? How did you get here?" The voice
squawked from a box in the top corner of the teleportation

chamber that Katrina hadn't noticed, and she jumped.

Something jangled from deep within the device. The humming whir of electronics switched to a clanging and banging. Once Katrina had driven her car for so long with no oil and at such high speeds that she'd shot an engine rod. This sounded like that, and Katrina instinctively grabbed Etienne's hand. "Phase us now!"

Etienne did, and they became intangible nanoseconds before the device exploded. Metal pieces flew throughout the teleportal chamber. They didn't feel the merest whisper as even the clunkiest parts shot through the space they had occupied moments before.

When he was sure the last bit of debris had sped through the air and they were uninjured, he released her arm and they both became solid again.

"Guess we're not getting back that way." Katrina stared at the smoldering and sparking pieces of the device. The smells of burnt plastic and heated metal hung in the air. The heat triggered the dry pipe fire sprinkler system, which released compressed nitrogen in the pipeline and allowed water into the pipes. Water spurted out the sprinklers, and Katrina psychokinetically buffered them from the shower with umbrella-shaped shields.

Etienne pointed at the reinforced door that separated the ruined teleportation device from the rest of the complex. "Let's go."

As they ran out, phasing through the reinforced door, Katrina dropped the psychokinetic umbrella shields. It looked like an observation or monitoring room.

"Check the mining annex," one of the frantic workers said.

Spurred into action by his colleague, one of the lab techs turned to run out of the room.

Katrina came to a stop and Etienne ran into her. In one

swift motion, she psychokinetically ripped all the electrical cords out of the computers and other machines in the room.

"Stop it," a shocked lab tech demanded. When Katrina looked at him with blazing eyes, he shrank back.

Etienne got the idea. He went intangible and phased himself through anything he could damage to prevent the techs from external communications. He didn't find any cell phones, but he damaged more than a few walkie-talkies and all the computers.

"Let's go," Katrina said.

They ran past the outraged lab techs and into a stark white hallway.

Katrina mentally shouted to Emma, but there was no response. She tapped her comms device, but there was only static. She swore under her breath.

"What's wrong?" Etienne asked.

"We need to let Emma know what happened and where we are. And I can't get through to her." Katrina patted her comms device. "This thing is giving me nothing but static."

"Could be interference from the—" he nodded in the direction of the busted teleportals "—explosion."

"We need to get away from here," Katrina said. Despite the physical exertion, she shivered. "Man, it's cold. I heard them mention a mining annex."

"Yeah, I heard that, too."

"I bet that's where they have Jaako and Shining."

"Makes sense," Etienne answered.

The pair had only expected to do a bit of snooping. But if they were here, they were going to make the most of it. Their recon mission had just morphed into the beginnings of a rescue mission.

"This place is huge." Katrina couldn't believe that The Hastings Foundation had managed to create this massive research and mining campus right under the noses of the world. If Pierce was here, the two of them couldn't take him on alone. They needed their team. The fiasco in the abandoned train depot was still fresh in her memory. Once they got farther away from the damaged teleportal machine, she called out again to Emma.

This time the girl responded immediately. "What happened to you guys?"

"We're in Antarctica." Katrina filled Emma in on what they'd learned so far.

"Be careful and I'll let you know Bayanai's plan soon."

"Okay," Katrina said. Although Emma had only been back a little while, it comforted her to no end. It reminded her of the good old days.

Etienne phased them into to a janitor's closet in the hallway.

"Why are we hiding in here?" Katrina asked.

"It's easy enough for me to keep us phased and invisible, but being in here will give us a break. Let us come up with a plan. Communicate with Emma without all the distractions," Etienne said.

After a few minutes Emma linked to Etienne and Katrina. None of what Emma told her was unexpected, but she was relieved nonetheless to hear the others were on their way. "Bayanai says priority one is finding Shining and Jaako, but to wait for backup. Do not engage. Waleed needs to focus on you to open the portal. Once you find Shining and the prime minister, let me know. We're gathering everyone to help back you up, but I'll stay here in New Atlantis to coordinate. It's going to be a few minutes before Waleed is able to teleport everyone there."

Suddenly, she was out of their minds.

Etienne phased his invisible head through the door to see if anyone was in the hallway. There wasn't. As he pulled himself back into the closet, the ground shook and cleaning supplies crashed from the shelves onto them and clattered onto the ground. Katrina squawked her surprise and rubbed her shoulder.

"What was that?" His voice was low and urgent.

"I don't know, but we need to tell Emma so they can factor it into their plans," Katrina said. "It might be nothing or might be something huge. Could be problems with the cryospore extraction, or maybe the glacier moved."

"I'll let Emma know," Etienne said but quickly grimaced. "I can't reach out. Something is blocking us. Maybe they got their defenses restored?" He cleared his throat. "I think we're on our own."

Katrina looked at her teammate in despair. She wanted to follow orders, but if they couldn't contact Base 47, perhaps Waleed wouldn't be able to teleport to their location and the team might not be coming after all.

"Great, so what do we do?" Katrina asked.

"You know, I've always been a by-the-skin-of-my-teeth kind of guy—"

"You reading my mind?" She grinned and cocked an eyebrow at him. "Let's save them."

"Yeah, but where? They could be anywhere," Etienne said.

"They were talking about the mining annex, remember? I say we start there," Katrina said.

Etienne nodded. They charged out of the closet and saw the emergency lights were on. Whatever caused the shaking had triggered the station's emergency protocols. They exchanged worried looks and moments later found a door marked "To Mining Annex." Heavy coats hung on pegs next to the door.

"Let's go." Etienne phased his head through the door. He was immediately blinded by the brilliant sun shining in a cloudless sky. The whipping sound of the wind shook him.

He pulled his body back inside. He was no stranger to long, cold winters, but this Antarctic summer was a bone-chilling difference from the London winter he'd just left. He hunched his shoulders against the shock of the bracing air.

"Here," Katrina said, pulling down two coats. "We're going to need these."

They donned the coats and opened the door. They both struggled against the wind to move forward. The icy air chilled them even through their coats and SENTINELS suits, which provided basic insulation from the elements. After adapting to the bright sunlight, they spotted a red snowmobile and piled on for a brief ride to the mining annex, visible from the main research building.

From behind them, Katrina heard the door open and bang shut and then a snarl. Etienne was focused on getting them to the mining annex, so Katrina turned to see who it was. Groaning, she turned back and hit Etienne on the shoulder.

"Go faster, it's Butcher."

"Can't." He glanced back and saw the foe charging toward them.

"We don't want him on our trail. You know what he does."

"I know. But I can't go any faster. You do something."

She turned around and mentally lifted Butcher into the air. Then she felt playful and spun him until she was sure he was dizzy enough that he couldn't stand. Then she spun him some more. Suddenly, out came Butcher's last meal in a hot steaming, streaming shot. Because she was still spinning him, the vomit spread far and wide until she let go of him and he dropped onto the ice.

She giggled and turned back around.

"What?"

"I just made Butcher puke. I don't think he'll be very

forgiving."

"Probably not the maniac you want mad at you," he observed dryly.

"Just get us there."

"If Butcher's here, his creepy handler can't be too far away," Etienne said.

"Just keep your mind closed, like Emma taught us. We'll be fine." Katrina tried not to imagine what Alrick, the German mind-controller, might do if he sank his mental hooks into any of the SENTINELS.

Moments later he stopped their red snowmobile next to a blue one already parked by the door to the mining annex. They climbed off.

Etienne made them invisible before he phased them through the door. Immediately, they felt warmer. Running straight toward the door were Jaako Aalto, followed at a distance by Shining in the arms of a woman Katrina didn't know. She smiled to see him and wondered briefly why Jaako wasn't carrying the boy. Katrina immediately tried reaching out to Emma. This time, it worked, and she let Emma know they'd found Shining and the prime minister. The running trio looked scared. She added that info.

Jaako ran right past Etienne and Katrina without acknowledging them, and Katrina realized they were still invisible. Etienne reverted them to visible, and the woman screamed when they materialized right in front of her. The scream alarmed Shining, who'd been passed out in Juliane's arms. He rousted himself long enough to deploy a weak force field to protect himself. It was strong enough to push him away from the woman, and he plopped to the ground. He looked around, dazed, and spotted Etienne. He squealed and jumped into Etienne's arms.

"You okay?" he asked the child. Shining just held tight onto him, saying not a word. Etienne went invisible, bringing Shining with him.

The woman yelped when he faded in front of her eyes.

Katrina cocked her head at the woman. "Who are you?"

"Where did they go? We need to get Shining back! And who was he?" In the scientist's panic, the questions came out with machine-gun rapidity. In the distance, Jaako stopped and turned toward the SENTINELS.

"Who are you?" Katrina asked again, calmly.

"Where did you come from?" the woman asked instead of answering the question.

"London. Who. Are. You?"

"Katrina!" Jaako said with obvious pleasure. He jogged toward the SENTINEL. "That's Dr. Frazier. It's about time you came to rescue me—er—us."

Katrina gave him a withering look.

His politician's smile didn't even flicker. "We need to get out of here. Where are the rest of the SENTINELS?"

"It's just us right now," Katrina replied, noting his strained demeanor.

"There's a snowmobile outside. Let's go." He turned and ran.

Katrina and Dr. Frazier followed him. Outside, Jaako turned away and threw his leg over a blue snowmobile and turned the key.

"Where do you think you're going?" Katrina put her arm out against the scientist, preventing her from boarding the snowmobile.

"We need to get out of here, now," Dr. Frazier said. "The teleportal will get us out of here—"

"Yeah, about that. It's no longer working," Katrina said.

"What? Then we're as good as dead here." Dr. Frazier threw her hands up in the air in despair.

"Why?" Etienne asked.

"Something went wrong with the Cryospore Extraction

Unit. I don't know what it's doing. We couldn't get Shining to contain all the cryospores into their own force fields and I think the stray cryospores are reacting to not being stuck and trapped in the ice, and the destructive force could destabilize the tectonic plates or even cause the entire ice shelf to calve," Dr. Frazier said. She hastened toward the snowmobile. "Think of the Falklands Island earthquake as a firecracker and all of the cryospores as ten times worse than the atom bomb."

All of them stared at the scientist.

"How much time do we have?" Katrina asked.

"I don't know," Julianne said, blinking rapidly. "Any minute. An hour. Never."

"You've got to be kidding me," an invisible Etienne scoffed. "What is it with you Hastings folks? Always got a world-destroying plan in place?"

Julianne looked down. "The farther away we get, the better. At least to the research station, but I doubt that will be far enough."

"Is there a protective bunker? Some place that we can hole up in until our team arrives?" Katrina asked.

The scientist flitted her eyes about, searching for options, then pointed toward the research station. "The basement in the research complex is fortified. It might save us. We can go there."

"Let's go." Katrina hopped onto the red snowmobile and felt Etienne slide on behind her with Shining in his arms. Jaako sat alone astride the blue snowmobile.

"Jaako, let's go," she said.

"Wait!" Panic filled Dr. Frazier's voice. She fought Jaako to get onto the blue snowmobile. "Let me on. You'll need me to bypass the security systems."

"That won't be a problem," Etienne said.

"Actually, it will. There are defense parameters in place

that prevent Mods from accessing the facilities without an override. I've got that code," Julianne said.

"Really? We were in the other part of the station with no problem," Katrina said.

"Just the bunker," Julianne said.

Katrina felt the ground shaking under the snowmobile. No matter what she may have done, she wouldn't just leave the scientist out here to die. And if she was telling the truth about the bunker override code, they'd need her. Katrina psychokinetically pushed Dr. Frazier onto Jaako's snowmobile.

CHAPTER
7 7

21 December

Luli's eyes lit up as Yi and Sying walked through the door of the War Room at Base 47.

Carlos Martin

"Mommy!" Sying hugged her fiercely.

"Thanks for the great big hug, sweetie." Luli looked to her husband, suddenly fearing he'd changed his mind. "What are you doing here?"

Luli and Yi had long debated her participation in the Shining rescue mission since she had no Mod powers and hadn't trained with the team since Shining was born. But just because she hadn't trained with the team didn't mean she wasn't fit and capable in jiu-jitsu. She was. She had been given a SENTINELS uniform on loan, and Yukio had devised an experimental exo-suit of next-generation materials and strong but lightweight metal alloys that would enhance her strength and give her an extra layer of protection. She'd still be going up against Mods, but the playing field would be somewhat leveled by the combination of the uniform, martial arts, and tech.

"We didn't want to be away when you bring Shining back." Yi reached out his hand and helped Luli to her feet.

"Yi, I know you don't approve of me doing this," Luli started, but he pulled her in close.

"Just get our boy back."

She kissed him and rubbed Sying's shoulder.

"I will." She held them both in her arms. "And we'll all be in San Francisco riding that trolley before you know it."

"And see the sea lions?" Sying asked.

"Of course." Luli grinned. "Maybe this time you won't run away from them."

"Mom." Sying rolled her eyes.

"Luli?"

Luli looked up and smiled sheepishly at Bayanai at the front of the War Room at Base 47, but she kept her hold on both husband and daughter.

"As you go through the teleportal, fan out," Bayanai told the collected SENTINELS. They stood by in their protective uniforms in the War Room, waiting to join Katrina and Etienne in Antarctica through one of Waleed's teleportals. Bayanai studied the group: Carlos, Luli, Ericka, Emilio, CoCo, James, Kirra, and Waleed. Each held a heavy parka from the team's supply closet.

Bayanai looked closely at Carlos, wondering if he would be a help or liability on this mission. Jiya had declared him healed, and he looked healthy. He was not a tall man, maybe as tall as his own five-foot-eight inches. He had a deceptively slight frame. No one looking at him would have an inkling that he was a Mod with super strength. Dr. Watanabe had fitted him with a cybernetic replacement arm that the Argentinean was familiarizing himself with. He hadn't trained with the team in the year since they thought he'd died, so he wouldn't be up on the team's latest strategies and lingo. Then again, Carlos had always been intuitive and able to anticipate the needs of his teammates and the possible courses of actions others might make. It was part of what made him such a good SENTINEL. Plus, he had a definite bone to pick with Pierce. A help, Bayanai decided.

Emma stood off to the side, watching; she wasn't going. Maggie, there for documentation purposes only, also wasn't going on the rescue mission, although she'd be publicizing it later. Bayanai had arranged through Ericka additional police security to protect Emma in the absence of the SENTINELS. Those officers stood at attention in the back of the War Room. Jiya sat quietly in a corner. If there were injuries in the battle, Waleed would have to 'port them back to the War Room for healing. It was an arrangement Bayanai didn't like, but since Jiya had opened the ashram, the healer had refused to set foot in any fight zone.

"If Pierce's goons are there, pick a target and be smart. Remember, we have three tasks. Save Shining and Jaako. Stop the cryospore device. And finish Pierce. Ready?"

"Let's go," Emilio shouted.

James and CoCo both whooped in agreement.

"Without me?" Josh asked as he walked through the door.

"Hey, what're you doing here?" James asked.

"I don't want you do this without me." Josh strolled toward his old teammates.

Ericka stared at him for a moment before turning away.

"Sorry, Josh, can't let you come with us." Bayanai crossed his arms over his chest.

"What? Threatened by me?"

"Of course not," Bayanai said. "You just have a different role to play this time. Besides, I want you here to make sure that Emma and the rest are protected while we're in Antarctica."

Josh sighed but nodded acceptance of the logic and decision.

"Parkas on." Bayanai surveyed the team. They looked eager, ready to win. "Waleed?" He gestured where he'd like to see the teleportal appear.

Waleed grinned, and the black globules that heralded his teleportal sparkled in the War Room.

As Ericka passed by, Josh stopped her. "Be careful down there." She nodded silently and turned back toward the team.

James was the first to vanish through the teleportal, and Bayanai knew he would conduct a quick recon while the rest of the team walked through. Ericka and Kirra crossed through the teleportal, followed by CoCo and Emilio, who were holding hands. Bayanai accompanied Carlos and Luli. The cold buffeted him when he walked through the teleportal from the tropical island to the frozen underside of the earth. What he saw was vast whiteness, and a shockingly clear and crisp blue sky. White buildings on opposite sides blended in with the landscape. He shivered in his heavy coat.

James zoomed to a stop right next to Bayanai and Luli and panted. "Katrina and Etienne have Shining and Jaako. No sign of George, though."

"Where?" Luli demanded. "Is Shining OK? Let's go get him."

"He's fine. They're not too far from here." James pointed to the direction he'd come from. "Also, there was some kind of explosion in the main research area. I saw a few of Pierce's goons, but not Pierce."

"Let's go get my son," Luli said.

Bayanai nodded his assent, and James started to lead them off. The other SENTINELS, following the orders from the briefing, spread out. Ericka and Kirra set out in one direction seeking the cryospore device while CoCo,

Emilio, and Waleed headed toward a different part of the research area.

***

CoCo, Emilio, and Waleed reached the doors to the research facility, and CoCo stopped. The other two bumped into her.

"What? Security?" Emilio asked.

"Yup." CoCo frowned and looked around. "Waleed?"

He nodded and teleported them just inside the doorway, where warmer air welcomed them. A researcher was coming down the hallway and CoCo hastily cast an illusion that would show him an empty hallway. She needn't have bothered. The researcher was so focused on his clipboard he wouldn't have noticed a pink elephant blocking the hallway. She maintained the illusion of the empty hallway once he passed by.

Everything she saw was white, and just looking at it made CoCo wish for a thicker coat. As they worked their way through the building, CoCo remained chilled to the bone from her brief exposure to the Antarctic summer. Hrmph. Some summer. She preferred a beach to the slopes.

"This way, I think," Emilio whispered. He pointed to a sign that read "Labs" and had an arrow leading off to the left.

CoCo and Waleed looked at each other and nodded. They followed Emilio's lead and rounded the corner. Emilio swore under his breath when a shot of electricity crackled down the hallway. Emilio dodged it, as did CoCo, but Waleed grunted in surprise mingled with pain when it connected with him.

CoCo looked past Emilio and clenched her jaw. It was Timothy, the Mod she'd faked a relationship with to help establish her cover with the Tribe. He looked pissed.

"I thought I'd find you around here," Timothy said. "Let go of your illusion, CoCo." For emphasis, he sent another bolt of electricity toward the area where he believed the three SENTINELS stood.

Again, it bypassed CoCo and Emilio and struck Waleed. He cried out in pain as electricity spasmed in his body. Emilio caught Waleed, but Timothy wasn't done. He shot another bolt of electricity at them. Again, it struck Waleed, who cried out and sagged, needing Emilio to support his entire weight. He was hurt, but conscious.

"Stop it," CoCo's illusion yelled. "What's wrong with you?"

"Don't you even start with me." He sneered at her and let loose a large electric blast at the illusory CoCo. "We're not on the same team anymore."

CoCo grimaced as her illusion dissipated. She hoped Timothy had known it was an illusion and not her real self. While he was distracted, the real CoCo had snuck around behind him and deftly attached a pair of power-dampening handcuffs to one wrist, then the other. When he realized what she'd done, he cursed her.

"I know you're confused and upset. You have every right to be." She looked at him with great sadness. She turned to Emilio. "We can't just leave him here."

Emilio looked from Waleed to Timothy. "Up to you. One patient, one prisoner. That's a lot for us to deal with in case we find the cryospores or Pierce."

CoCo frowned. "You're right, but it's safer to take him. I just wish we had something to keep him from yelling and warning anyone here."

Emilio grinned and pulled off his scarf. "This should help."

Waleed, suffering badly from Timothy's electrical attack,

opened a teleportal to New Atlantis. "I need Jiya," he said. Black globules glimmered, but his portal was as shaky as he was. It wavered and winked out of existence. "He scrambled me more than I thought." A frown creased Waleed's weary face, and he collapsed.

Emilio lifted Waleed over his shoulder in a fireman's carry.

CoCo pointed at Timothy. "Did you have anything to do with the explosion in here a little while ago?"

Timothy looked confused.

"You. Electricity. Explosions. Things like that happen around you," she said dryly.

"Wasn't me." His voice came out muffled by the scarf. "It was your guys. They ruined the teleporting machine connecting London to here. I was trying to find them when I found you."

CoCo sighed. "Walk." She pointed straight ahead, and Timothy complied.

***

James led Bayanai, Carlos, and Luli into the research complex but in a different direction than Emilio and CoCo had headed. Luli was so close behind Bayanai that she stepped on his heel a few times. Carlos rotated his cybernetic arm around, still getting used to its movements.

Suddenly, Shining shrieked, but none of the SENTINELS could see the boy.

"Mommy!" Shining launched himself out of an invisible Etienne's arms. As he did so, he left Etienne's influence of invisibility. He blurred into view as he landed in Luli's arms. She staggered under the surprise weight and hugged him with relief. Etienne dropped his invisibility and Katrina, Jaako, and Dr. Frazier materialized.

435

"Oh, my dear sweet boy." Luli held him tight and smothered his face with kisses, careful not to hurt him with her exo-suit. "Are you okay?"

He wept into her shoulder. "I missed you so much."

"It's okay, baby. I have you. We're going to get you back home." She clenched him to her. "Oh my god, I love you. I was afraid I'd never see you again."

"I want to go home. It's so cold here." He shivered in her arms.

"We'll go back to New Atlantis soon," Bayanai said. He looked at the scientist. "Who are you?"

"I'm Dr. Julianne Frazier." She stood tall.

"She oversees the cryospore extraction, and we may need her help with shutting down the operation safely," Jaako said.

Before Bayanai could say anything, the ground shook fiercely. Each of the SENTINELS struggled to stay upright.

"What was that?" Luli asked.

"This whole place is unstable. We have to get out of here," Dr. Frazier said. "We just came from the mining annex. It's bad. But the underground complex might shield us." She pointed toward the elevator down the hall.

Bayanai nodded. "Okay." This was too delicate a mission to dismiss any potential help, but he didn't trust anyone currently associated with The Hastings Foundation. He'd keep a close eye on her.

Someone called out to Bayanai. He turned toward the shout and spotted CoCo and Emilio making their way toward them. They were prodding someone wearing a makeshift muzzle and power-dampening handcuffs. Emilio carried Waleed. When they got closer, Bayanai realized the prisoner was Timothy. While Timothy was walking and doing as he was told, his face promised nothing but fury once the handcuffs were removed.

"What's wrong with Waleed?" Luli asked Bayanai as they walked toward where they first entered the complex.

Bayanai shrugged. When the group arrived, he studied the teleporter. He'd regained enough of his strength so that he could stand on his own two feet, but he was still shaking from his ordeal with Timothy. "Are you hurt?"

Waleed hooked his thumb at Timothy. "He electrocuted me. Messed up my powers. I can't 'port."

Bayanai glared at Timothy, then closed his eyes in thought. "Do you think you'll recover enough without Jiya's help to make a safe teleportal?"

For a long moment, Waleed considered this. At last, he nodded. "I'm feeling a little better, so maybe, in a little while. But not just yet."

"Okay, then. Rest and recover." Bayanai shivered as a door swung open and Ericka and Kirra ran in.

"It wasn't me!" Kirra shouted. "Something's wrong here. The ground is giving up."

"We know." Emilio gestured to the scientist opposite him.

"Oh. Okay. What's the play?" Kirra put her hands on her knees and caught her breath.

"Waleed can't teleport yet. Will the bunker protect all of us?" Bayanai asked the scientist.

"It should. It was built strong enough to withstand a nuclear blast." Julianne ushered them toward the elevator.

"Why'd you build something that substantial here?" Bayanai asked.

"There were some ... concerns about the cryospores," she said.

Bayanai's eyes flashed at this, but he did not respond to her. Instead, he looked at Carlos and pointed at Luli and Shining. "Keep them safe."

"With my life," Carlos promised.

***

"Looks like the gang's all here." Behind the heroes, Pierce stepped out of one of his signature burgundy door teleportals, followed by Dafydd. "Who do we have here?" He telekinetically grabbed Shining before the emotionally and physically exhausted child understood the threat and could generate his force field. The boy fought and kicked, but Pierce ignored him. "Here's the prize. And I think I really have to go now."

"Leave my boy alone!"

Surprised, Pierce turned his attention to Luli. "You shouldn't be here, Mommy." Pierce flicked his fingers and increased her personal density, crushing her to the ground, despite the protection of her exo-suit. Dafydd smirked.

"Mommy, no!" Shining pleaded. He extended his force field, tripping Pierce.

"Ack! You little sh—" The overpowered monster opened another burgundy door portal and flung the five-year-old through. He hollered through the door, "Take care of the boy." Pierce cast a furious look at the SENTINELS and raised his fist at them. One by one, he telekinetically pinned each of the remaining SENTINELS up against the wall of the research complex. Only Etienne's instinctive invisibility, invoked the second he heard Pierce's voice, had kept Jaako, Dr. Frazier, and Katrina from joining their team members against the wall.

"I don't think you'll make it to the bunker," Pierce said as he telekinetically ripped the elevator out of its shaft. Bayanai was in disbelief. Pierce was ridiculously overpowered. How could they defeat him?

Carlos, enraged by the sight of Pierce, struggled the hardest against the telekinetic hold.

When Pierce noticed Timothy had been captured by the SENTINELS, he slitted his eyes and growled. Pierce telekinetically pushed Timothy up against the wall and then squeezed his fist fractionally, increasing Timothy's personal density. Timothy moaned.

Katrina could still use her psychokinesis while invisible, and did so. She knocked Pierce off balance. He looked around wildly for this source of trouble, but saw no one. With his concentration broken, the SENTINELS all tumbled back onto the ground. He swung wildly with his super strong arm and busted a hole into the wall. A gust of frigid air whipped in.

"Come with me," Pierce said to Dafydd as he stalked through a burgundy door. "I'll send the rest of the Tribe to take care of them."

"Waleed, you feeling any better?" Bayanai asked as the team stood and took stock of their circumstances.

"A bit. Need a teleportal?"

"Yes. We need to get Shining back." They made their way outside through the broken wall into the area between the complex and the annex.

Before Waleed could create a teleportal, another one of Pierce's appeared, and the door swung open. Out poured the Tribe.

CHAPTER
78

21 December

George descended into Ghar Parau, his anxiety and fear growing with every step. His head pounded. Coupled with a headache that had started days ago, he found it doubly hard to think clearly. It had been hours since he'd followed the redheaded man into a cave he'd only recently learned the name of. He wasn't even sure what country the cave was in, although he thought it might be in the Middle East.

The treacherous decline sapped whatever remained of his strength. Along the way, he'd seen strange images carved into the cave walls. He traced some of them with his fingers. Some were hastily fashioned, while others seemed the products of time and craftsmanship. Nothing about what was going on made sense to him. The redheaded man led him deeper into the cave and George had no idea what he was supposed to do in here. All discussions about him had been out of earshot, and he couldn't read their lips. He wasn't sure how much farther they had to go.

"I've been coming to this cave for a few years now. It's not too tricky, but you have to be careful," the redheaded man said as he clamped his belay together, motioning to

George to do the same.

George hesitantly followed suit. After the redheaded man double-checked it and descended, George slowly lowered himself down the embankment. As he did, he thought he heard a low murmur from deeper inside the cave. When he asked about it, the redheaded man told him it was just generators at the sump, which was their destination.

When they reached the floor, they unhooked themselves and continued.

George had tried several times to use his powers to hypnotize his captors, but the power-dampening bracelet locked around his wrist prevented him from doing so. He felt hopeless. He wished Emilio were here to save him again. He had grown increasingly despondent as the days progressed. He hoped he would be released once he completed whatever task they wanted him for, then wondered at the potential consequences of his forced actions and worried how he'd face the man in the mirror. Would he even survive whatever these people planned for him to do? He thought about all the things he might not ever get to do. Never go on safari. Never skydive. Never fall in love. Never have a child. Regrets, mistakes, and sorrows joined forces with fear to consume him.

"Be careful here. It's dangerous," the redheaded man said, slinking across a narrow ledge. George clung to the wall and tried not to look down. His headlamp could pierce the darkness, but the overwhelming black devoured the light quickly. He shuffled along and knocked some rocks off the ledge. He grabbed the wall and listened as pebbles cascaded off the walls and disappeared completely. No sound came back to reveal how far that hole went. A few steps later, he slipped, and the redheaded man grabbed him.

"I said be careful. We've not much more to go." The redheaded man made it across the ledge and extended his arm to George to help him over.

As they rounded the corner, George saw a lessening of the darkness. Before long, they reached a point where light streamed out from a nearby room of the cave. It wasn't enough light that he could turn off his headlamp, but it helped him relax marginally. In the past few days he'd thought a lot about his life. He had wanted to be a SENTINEL for so long and now he wasn't so sure about it. It sounded amazing. They made it look glorious. But the truth was it was hard. Did he have what it took?

"Not too much farther." The redheaded man waved George along. They eventually came upon a well-lit area of the cave, and George turned off his headlamp.

It looked like an excavation site: lights and tables with monitors. The rock walls amplified the sound of the running generators. George could see fifteen people in the chamber running around occupied by various tasks. If he'd had trouble getting down here unencumbered, he couldn't begin to imagine what it had been like to haul the generators and other equipment down here. He could not discern what was going on. Each time he tried to ask a question, he was immediately silenced. He heard references to the winter solstice and something about a swarm, but he had no context into which to place these nuggets.

"Sit over there, George." The redheaded man pointed at a table and went to converse with two men in robes.

As George did so he realized his headache had stopped when he entered this chamber. He heard a familiar beeping sound. But it was so far out of place, so far out of context, that it took him an embarrassingly long moment to place it. A heart monitor? Here? Was someone down here? On life support? He looked toward the beeps, so unnatural in this cave, and saw a gurney surrounded in plastic. He could barely make out that there was a body on the gurney. The protective plastic atop the body must be to keep all the dust out and shelter whoever it was from the elements.

"On your feet, George," the redheaded man shouted as he walked over to him. "You're up."

CHAPTER 79

21 December

"Get 'em!" It was Brute. Behind her were Maru, Flame, and Washington. She rushed at Bayanai, Kirra, James, Carlos and Ericka, who formed a protective knot around Luli and Waleed. To the side, CoCo and Emilio held Timothy captive. Etienne, Jaako, Katrina, and Dr. Frazier became visible again next to them.

Maru Tamatoa

The ground shook and the Tribe struggled to stay on their feet.

Kirra focused her attention on the bits of earth inside the ice and used that connection to open a hole, which Brute tripped into, and closed it again. "Old tricks are the best."

"Good work, Kirra!" Etienne winked at her.

"You can control the earth?" The question came from Dr. Frazier.

Kirra nodded. "Among other things. Why?"

"The earth here is too unstable. From the cryospores. Don't do that again."

Kirra wrinkled her brow in concentration. After a moment, she said, "I feel it." She looked at James and pointed inland. "I need you to take me over there."

Without a word, he whisked her away.

Bayanai looked around. They were between the mining annex and the research complex, out in the frozen open. He and the nonfighters needed to find shelter, some place to function as Fight HQ.

"All nonfighters come with me. Waleed, Luli, and Timothy too. Everyone else, take them!" Bayanai guided a disgruntled Luli, Timothy, Jaako, and Dr. Frazier toward a corner away from the fight. He turned around, clasped his hands together, and pulsed his power out to the SENTINELS, boosting their own native powers.

"Why are you bringing me with you?" Timothy asked through the muzzle, his voice muffled.

"Not going to leave you twisting out in the wind." Bayanai sat Timothy across from the others. "Besides, I'd rather keep a close eye on you."

"Bayanai, let me fight. I can help," Luli said.

"I know that, Luli, but we need you as our secret weapon. In case things go south. Please," Bayanai said.

She reluctantly agreed.

The SENTINELS sized up the Tribe and chose opponents, but Carlos peeled off from the group.

"Where are you going?" Ericka asked.

"To save Shining." He ran off toward the mining annex, dead set on confronting Pierce.

Maru flew high up in the sky and sent a mini icy tornado at his opponents.

"Watch out, Ericka!" Etienne shouted as he pushed her out of the icy tornado's path. "Take him out!"

Ericka spotted Maru hovering cross-legged in the sky and aimed a fury of green blasts at him.

In dodging the blasts, he lost his control over the tornado. It dissipated into a puff of icy wind.

***

"I hurt everywhere," Luli said, taking stock of her exo-suit and making sure it was still functional.

"Lucky you have the suit. It could have been much worse," Bayanai said.

"We have to get Shining back."

"We will. I promise."

"Could you let me out of these?" Timothy asked through the makeshift muzzle as he held up his wrists in the power-dampening cuffs.

Bayanai shook his head.

"You think Pierce cares a lick about me? As far as he's concerned, I betrayed him along with CoCo." Timothy leaned his head back against the wall.

Bayanai removed the muzzle but left the cuffs on.

Waleed began moaning and then convulsing. Black globules popped up around the group.

"Uh oh," Jaako said as one opened near him. "Are you seeing this?"

"I am," Bayanai said, realizing that when he sent a power boost out, he had boosted Waleed as well. But due to his injuries he was unable to control the portals he was now unintentionally making. "Jaako, help Waleed."

"What is this?" Dr. Frazier asked, eyes amazed.

"Waleed can create teleportals, but I think his injuries have made them unstable," Bayanai told the scientist. The globules formed into a pair of glittering teleportals, both of which opened up into the War Room at Base 47. Bayanai watched with worry as Emma peered into one of the teleportals and Josh into the other.

Bayanai could see what was going on in the teleportal better than he could hear, although it was evident Emma was talking with someone else in the room. Then he saw Maggie looking through the opening as well, standing next to Emma.

Bayanai saw they were suddenly closer to the teleportal, as though they wanted to see more clearly what was going on the other side. When the teleportal leapt toward the pair, Bayanai realized with dawning horror that wasn't what was happening at all. The teleportal was growing. It was getting closer to Emma and Maggie, not the other way around.

"Step back," he shouted, hoping they'd be able to understand what he'd said, even though he'd been unable to understand what they were talking about on their side.

Maggie and Emma both leaned into the teleportal, perhaps to hear better what Bayanai was saying.

The next moment, they stumbled to the icy ground in front of Bayanai. Waleed, who under Jaako's care had stopped convulsing and begun watching the events unfold, looked stunned, but nowhere near as stunned as Maggie and Emma. Both had arrived on Antarctica without the benefit of coats. They began shivering immediately.

The second teleportal, into which Josh had looked, didn't deliver Josh next to Maggie and Emma. Instead, the part of the teleportal in Antarctica wobbled off toward the research station, as though seeking warmth. Waleed worked furiously to bring his teleportal back under control but could not. He watched with mounting disbelief as the teleportal snaked through the wall of the research station and vanished.

Bayanai closed his eyes for a moment to collect his thoughts. "Luli, we need to get Emma and Maggie some place warm and see about getting them jackets. Emma, can you call out to Josh? See if he's still at Base 47 or if he's here too?"

She strained for a moment, then she said, "I don't feel him."

"You don't think he could have been teleported into a wall or something?" Luli asked.

"We'll find him," Bayanai said.

Emma squeezed Waleed's hand, hoping that Josh had somehow made it safe.

"We need to get you two warmed up. But I want you here and safe, with me." Bayanai looked around. When he spotted Jaako, he smiled at the idea that occurred to him. "Jaako, can you make an igloo for these two?"

Jaako's icy blue eyes glittered as he nodded. He held out his hands and an igloo big enough for three or four built itself in front of them. Without delay, Maggie and Emma crawled in and huddled together to warm up.

**

James rushed Kirra around the perimeter of the complex and set her down.

"What do you think? Is it stable enough?" he asked.

She touched the snow-packed ground. "It's not good," she said. "Weak, very weak. Barely holding on. The bonds are breaking. Could get real bad. Real quick." She looked at her teammate. "Leave me here. I'll do what I can to make sure it doesn't crack in two."

James regarded her a moment, nodded, and darted off as Kirra closed her eyes and willed the earth to stay together.

**

CoCo ran at Flame, bolstered by finally being able to confront her after being forced to ally herself with the villainous Mod for a year to protect her cover.

Fire crackled around Flame's body. Fiery animals sizzled the ground around her, with a flaming pack of wolves running circles around them and turning the snow into slush. Flame herself wasn't on fire, so CoCo leapt and tackled her. They rolled around on the ground, each trying to gain the upper hand. Fueled by a year's worth of pent-up feelings, CoCo delivered a solid punch that knocked Flame out. CoCo stood, dusted the snow and slush off her uniform, and staggered away, looking to see where she was needed.

***

Washington, Pierce's right-hand man, grunted when out of nowhere a fist clocked his jaw.

Etienne dropped his invisibility and smirked as Washington worked out his jaw.

"You're going to regret that." He jumped at Etienne, only to pass right through him and stumble into the snow.

"You never could touch me," Etienne said as the mercenary picked himself up. Snowflakes clung to his uniform.

"We'll see about that." He pulled two knives from his belt. The blades shimmered in the frosty air.

Etienne stepped back and pulled out his escrima sticks.

The knives began to shake as Katrina dropped down into the fight. Washington struggled to keep the blades in his hands, but her power was too strong. The blades flew out of his hands and shot right into the wall of the research complex.

"Go help the others. I'll take care of him." Katrina flung Washington a few yards away and mentally grabbed all the negative energy in the area to supercharge her abilities.

Still holding his escrima sticks, Etienne faded into invisibility. Katrina's eyes followed him.

Washington, sensing her distraction, charged through the snow at Katrina and tackled her to the ground. Her protective psychokinetic shield sprang into place.

"Your powers can't protect you forever." He pressed his body against her shield. "But there's something you should know." He leaned over eye to eye with her. She was grateful for the shield between them. He pulled a gun from his holster and shot once. It ricocheted off her shield. Katrina's body shook with the bruising impact. He lifted himself off of her and aimed the gun at Bayanai. He smiled and squeezed the trigger. Katrina looked over in horror as Bayanai screamed and slumped over.

"No!" Katrina balled her fists tight and slammed the ground, an action that sent Washington flying hard against the wall, stunning him. The gun disappeared into the snow.

***

"Bayanai!" Jaako shouted.

For several long seconds, Bayanai didn't move or respond. When he did finally did, he patted his chest gently and then smiled weakly. At last, he said, "It's okay. I'm okay."

"Yeah, right. Washington's a good aim. Let me help you." Timothy got to his knees.

"No way. We need to get Jiya here," Maggie said.

"I'm fine. The suit is bulletproof, remember? It just hurts like a mother. I'm going to be black and blue there tomorrow." Bayanai closed his eyes. He was a Mod, but his gift wasn't flashy like Ericka's or impressive like Katrina's. His ability was tied to his confidence. The more confident he was, the better he was able to enhance the abilities of others. In times like this, he reminded himself of how far he'd come and how important this team, this family, was to him. That focus and renewed confidence in his team allowed him to fully access his powers.

***

"CoCo, watch out!" Emilio pushed her out of the way of the knife that Butcher threw at her. He rolled on the ground and watched CoCo take the snarling Butcher on.

CoCo created an illusion of her attacking him. He fell for it. While he was distracted, she punched him in his side. He grunted in surprise.

CoCo faced Emilio and smiled. Her face contorted and she fell toward her lover. Emilio grabbed her as she dropped. Behind her stood Butcher, grinning widely, his right hand holding a blade covered in blood. Emilio looked down at CoCo's back and found Butcher had stabbed her through a weak spot in her protective suit.

Butcher cackled as CoCo's illusion dropped. Blood dripped onto the snowy ground from her back as she hung limply in Emilio's arms.

CHAPTER

80

21 December

"ARGH!" The scream came from deep within the teleportation room. The debris was scattered all over the place and the tech workers sifted through to find the source of the screaming. They honed in on the sound and lifted a section of wall. What they saw underneath shocked them. It was Dr. Roger Martin, impaled through his shoulder on a metal rod.

"Dr. Martin! How did you get here?"

"Help me get out of this." He struggled to stay conscious. Blood flowed freely from the wound.

"I was following them from London, got caught up in all of this. Help me!"

"But if we pull you off you might not stop bleeding. Maybe it's better to stay here," the balding tech suggested.

"Just do as I say," he yelled through gritted teeth. He reached out his right arm and they took it. He breathed deep and nodded. They pulled. Roger yelped. They stopped.

"Don't stop."

The two techs kicked some debris away and dug in. They each grabbed a hold of the scientist and pulled with all their might. Flesh slithered around the rod as Roger came clear.

"Wow, are you okay?" the other tech asked.

Roger leaned against the wall. "All right, boys. What's going on here?" Roger held his left shoulder, taking slow, deep breaths in and out.

"We're under attack. Pierce and the Tribe are fighting the damn SENTINELS who came here. One of them destroyed our teleportal." He gestured angrily at the rod. "I hope that Pierce is demolishing them."

"Is that right? And where are they now?" Roger rotated his shoulder backward.

"Out near the mining annex. But we should get to the bunker for safety."

"Of course, safety first." Roger tipped his head toward them. "Let's go."

He followed them to the hallway. The elevator was also destroyed. A hole in the wall exposed them to the outside.

"What do we do now, Dr. Martin?" The bald tech looked on the edge of panic.

"We?" Roger started shaking fiercely.

"Are you okay?" The other tech reached out to keep Roger from falling.

Before their eyes, Roger disappeared and was replaced by a youthful brown-haired man. The tech snatched back his hand and repulsion flickered across his face.

"Never better, thanks for asking," the man replied as he pulled his left shoulder up and down. "As for the two of you, I would get to cover as quick as possible."

The two techs fumbled over themselves as they ran toward the bunker. Josh checked the wound on his shoulder. Though it had mostly mended when he shifted from Roger Martin to himself, it was still tender.

"Now, on to the fight." Josh stepped out of the hallway into the frozen wasteland.

453

CHAPTER
81

21 December

Ericka and Maru came at each other with a vengeance. She sent her green energy blasts at him repeatedly, but he used his control over the wind to divert the blasts away from him.

**Taneesha Jackson
"Flame"**

"Give me a chance," he teased as he flipped over her. "It would be fun. Cops and robbers. Stuff of legends, you know."

"You didn't have a chance then, you certainly don't have one now."

He called up the wind burst that splayed the snow all around Ericka, momentarily blinding her. She sent more short blasts at him and finally landed a direct blast to his chest.

He yelled and held his hands to his heart. Panting, he doubled over and fell to the ground.

She pressed the advantage, pulling his arms back with the efficiency of a longtime police officer. She whipped out power-dampening cuffs and tied him up.

"Seriously?" Maru snarled.

"Cops and robbers, right?" Ericka wrapped a zip tie around his feet. "Can't have you getting out and causing more bad weather." She left him on the ground and ran back to the group.

Nearby, the ground heaved, and Brute reemerged from her icy prison.

***

"You son of a bitch!" Emilio lunged at the savage German. He grabbed Butcher by the collar and flipped him. Butcher landed flat on the ground with a loud thud, the breath knocked out of him. Emilio put his fist to flesh over and over until Butcher was covered in more blood than skin.

Emilio was in such a blind rage that he didn't hear Timothy come up behind him. Timothy reached out his cuffed hands and stopped Emilio's fist.

"You've done enough," he said, looking Emilio right in his eyes.

Emilio raised his hand a fraction toward Timothy, then seemed to realize that Timothy was not the enemy.

"Go. Take care of her. I'll handle him," Timothy said.

"Wha? Huh? Okay." Emilio slowly stood, dazed. After a moment, he unshackled Timothy.

"Much better," Timothy said as electricity jumped off his body. Emilio tensed, recalling the last time he'd been subjected to his powers. But Timothy turned to Butcher. "This is for CoCo." He delivered one swift kick to the man's side.

Emilio nodded in satisfaction, walked back to his bleeding girlfriend, and lifted her.

"Turning on your team? I don't think so." Brute, holding a knife, ran past Emilio toward Timothy.

Emilio, who was carrying CoCo toward the Fight HQ, shouted. "Timothy, watch out!"

Timothy began to turn, but he wasn't fast enough. Brute's blade impaled him. He screamed at the pain. She twisted as she pulled the blade out, and he screamed again and fell to the icy ground. Satisfied, she turned her attention elsewhere.

**

Alrick, the possessing Mod, ran across the frozen battlefield and bent over his unconscious friend. He rolled Butcher over and felt for a pulse. Alrick preferred to stay on the sidelines, using his power of possession to have others do the fighting for him. He had stayed inside the warmth of the research complex, but when he felt Butcher cut down, he came out into the fray. He looked around, trying to see where he could do the most damage. See who would be the weakest link to exploit. He looked at CoCo and Emilio, but decided against it since CoCo was already down. He wanted to disable more SENTINELS. The more chaos he caused, the more easily he could manipulate them.

**

"Emilio, you have to check on him," CoCo whispered.

"No. I'm not leaving you," Emilio said.

"I'll be fine. He needs our help. Please." CoCo closed her eyes. Emilio could tell that she was in more pain than she would let on.

"CoCo—"

"Please," she said. Her breathing was shallow.

"After you're safe in the igloo." He carried her there, gently kissed her forehead and left to check on Timothy.

"How's it going, buddy?" Emilio asked when Timothy opened his eyes.

"Oh man. Not you." Timothy groaned and closed his eyes.

Emilio put pressure on Timothy's wound. "You're going to be okay. Just breathe."

"Is—is she okay?" Timothy managed to ask.

"Shh. She'll be okay. I've got you." Emilio willed his luck powers to work on Timothy's injury. "You're going to be all right. Just focus on your breathing." Emilio mentally yelled for Emma.

"Sorry, Emilio, but Waleed is still injured and can't 'port yet. You're on your own," she said from inside the protective igloo.

Emilio swore and dragged Timothy over to the igloo at Bayanai's makeshift HQ.

Timothy looked over at CoCo. "Was any of it real?"

She looked at him but said nothing. At the moment it seemed kinder than the truth.

***

Jaako stood stiff. His eyes glazed over.

"Jaako? What's wrong?" Julianne asked. He turned toward her, grabbed the collar of her jacket, and lifted her off the ground. She swung her feet and arms, trying to get loose. The air around her grew colder. Her feet dangled inches from the ground. "Freeze," Jaako said, his voice void of inflection.

Julianne started to do just that, her core body temperature dropping and her teeth beginning to chatter.

Bayanai looked up, concerned, and Maggie, her journalist's instincts roused, shimmied out of the igloo to see what was going on. She took in the scene and acted.

"Stop it!" Maggie beat her fists against Jaako's sturdy frame, trying to get him to let go of the scientist, but he wouldn't.

He looked expressionlessly at Maggie. "Away." Jaako held out his hand, and a growing beam of ice flowed from it. The ice beam hit Maggie square in the chest and pushed her away from the Fight HQ and toward the mining annex. With his other hand, he threw Julianne down, then created an ice beam that pushed her off after the reporter.

Jaako's behavior confounded Bayanai. The politician would never do something like this on his own, so something must have happened. And then Bayanai spotted Alrick, his face frowning in full concentration.

"Oh no. Alrick's got him," Bayanai said. "Jaako, stop. This isn't you."

In the igloo, Emma whimpered at the mention of Alrick's name.

Jaako looked down at the leader of the SENTINELS and lowered the ambient temperature around them dramatically. Bayanai's teeth chattered as he tried to focus, but it was too cold. He looked toward the incoming Emilio in despair. Suddenly, Jaako dropped to the ground in a heap and the air returned to the level of merely cold.

"What happened?" Luli asked.

"I happened," Etienne said as he turned visible. "As soon as I saw Alrick here, I knew he'd try to pick us off. But he can't possess what he can't see." Etienne shimmered into nothingness and stood guard over those at the Fight HQ.

***

"This is all going south, Bayanai. We've got to get the advantage here," Emilio said.

"Go turn the tables on the Tribe," Bayanai said.

Emilio nodded and turned to search the battlefield for Brute. There was hell to pay now. "You and me, Brute!" Emilio locked eyes with the Korean.

"Bring it! I've been waiting for this." Brute raised her fists.

Emilio charged, and Brute let swing a powerful roundhouse blow, which Emilio easily dodged. He kicked her in the chest.

"Go ahead. Hit me. All you do is make me stronger." She laughed.

"That's not exactly the plan." He rushed toward her. Emilio slid between her legs, jumped up behind her and injected her with a liquid blue tranquilizer that he'd pulled out of a pocket of his SENTINELS uniform. She seemed to wind down. She wobbled on her feet and passed out. "You're finished." Emilio pushed Brute onto the ground and stood. She wouldn't be out for long, but that wouldn't matter. Next, he pulled out the pair of power-dampening handcuffs he'd removed from Timothy and fitted them over her meaty wrists. He looked across the battlefield and tried to figure out where to use his powers to help most.

***

Gathering every last shred of her courage, Emma crawled to the edge of the igloo and peered out. All the fighting upset her, but nowhere near as much as the presence of Alrick. She'd felt him closing in on Bayanai's Fight HQ and had prepared herself to fight him to keep him out of her mind if necessary. But he hadn't chosen her. He'd chosen Jaako, and Jaako had hurt Maggie because of it, she was pretty sure. Although she couldn't see Maggie, so there was hope for her. But Emma felt like she needed to do something. Partly because she was one of the few who had any real practice fighting Alrick. Partly because she knew that if she didn't stand now for herself, nightmares of him might still haunt her when she was an old lady like Jiya.

She spotted him and retreated back into igloo. She concentrated on the odious man and pictured a gong and the mallet used to bang it. The second she felt the connection between the two of them, she mentally banged that gong.

Alrick shrieked physically and mentally.

It felt ... satisfying. So she whacked the gong again. Harder. While she normally didn't condone hurting people, she thought she might begin to enjoy this. He'd caused her such trauma during her captivity that she had a lot of pent-up anger and helplessness to expend. She'd prefer to target Pierce, but Alrick would do.

Just then, she felt the tickling in the back of her head that indicated Alrick was trying to become her puppet master. She glared and buckled down to fight his advances. She banged the gong again, but she could tell that was losing its effectiveness. What else could she do? Shuddering, she made another split-second decision. She violated her long-standing no-snooping policy. Shamelessly, she rifled through the contents of his brain, looking for the most humiliating moments of his life. There he was being bullied by the popular kids. She sought the times of helplessness. There he was, victim of an uncle doing wrong things. She sought the sourest of sour experiences. There were the beatings from a drunken father. There was the girl dumping him for someone richer. There was his mother favoring Alrick's younger brother. There was his own self-loathing of all his base bodily functions. Those were just the surface ones. She thought worse memories might exist, but she didn't have the time to dig around. She flashed those memories and feelings through his head like a life's worst of highlights reel.

The scratching at the base of her head stopped and she could feel Alrick shrinking back as he was forced to confront all the unpleasantness of his life to date.

She almost took pity on him. But she couldn't. This was war, and the SENTINELS needed Alrick out of commission. What could she do? She thought while the horrible replay of his worst moments filled the video screen in his head. And then she gave the biggest mental scream she'd ever screamed. It was a primal thing, full of fury and agony and desperation. The scream went on and on and on and on. She paused to take a quick mental breath and resumed the scream, notching it up the equivalent of thirty mental decibels. Alrick could do nothing. If he had screamed in response, it was a pitiful whisper by comparison and she'd neither heard nor felt it. If he had clapped his hands over his ears, they weren't blocking the internal sound from the Irish girl screaming in his head.

She screamed some more in this fashion until she felt it, and she smiled a little when it happened.

He stopped resisting. He stopped fighting. Somehow, she knew, he was curled up in a tight fetal ball on the icy ground outside. He would have the migraine to end all migraines, she thought. He was certainly out of this fight.

And, Emma thought, grinning, she hadn't felt this good in quite some time.

***

Jaako groaned.

"Back among the living, are you?" Etienne asked.

"What happened?" Jaako asked. His voice came at low and thick.

"Sorry about earlier, you got hijacked by the creepy

461

German puppet master, so I had to help you out," Etienne said.

Jaako frowned and rubbed his head. "What did you do?"

"Oh, I knocked you out. He can't control you if you're down," Etienne said.

"Ow."

"But someone else took care of Alrick," Etienne said.

Emma crawled partway out of the igloo. "That was me."

Etienne looked at her with respect. "Good work, kiddo." He turned back to Jaako and summed up the latest bit of the battle at the bottom of the earth. "I think they could use your help. This is your element, after all."

"My pleasure," Jaako said, his teeth showing.

Nearby, Flame rousted herself. She pushed herself off the ground. Her body was engulfed in fire.

"Good. Take on Flame." Etienne pushed the prime minister toward the pyrokinetic.

Washington had also risen and looked likely to cause problems. "Gotta go." Etienne grabbed his escrima sticks and took off.

Jaako approached Flame.

"I've always wanted to lay the smack down on a slimy politician!" Flame grinned and rubbed her hands together.

Jaako iced up his hands and threw balls of ice at her.

The ice balls melted against her burning body. "Fire beats ice, every time." She smiled deviously and threw her hands up in the sky. Fiery birds circled all around him. "See, that's what I thought. You politicians are all the same. All talk until the pressure is on." She laughed and turned the heat up even more.

"He may be all talk, but he's got friends who aren't!" James zoomed by her, using his speed to knock her down.

"You!" Her flames lessened.

"Yep. Me." James used his speed to suck the oxygen

away from the fire birds that trapped Jaako.

"Thanks for that, James. I'll take it from here." Jaako willed snow to fall from the sky and pile onto Flame, trapping her in a mound of snow. He touched the mound and flash froze it. He turned to walk away, then heard a sizzling sound coming from the ground. He turned and saw steam billowing into the sky, the heat and icy air mixing in an impressive display. Out of the steam emerged an angry figure.

"You thought that was going to hold me?" Flame charged and Jaako shuffled backward. He lost his footing, and he grabbed Flame to keep him upright. Instead, he pulled her down on top of him. They tumbled to the ground and tussled. Desperate, he created an icicle and pierced her side with it.

She screamed in pain as the ice melted and blood poured out of her wound. She closed her eyes and reached down to feel the injury. Taking a deep breath, she cauterized the wound, groaned, and passed out from the pain. Jaako squirmed out from under her and pushed her to the side. He stood, carefully avoiding her blood as he did so. He looked at the red pool distastefully and turned away. Jaako spotted the SENTINELS and walked over to them. He nodded to Bayanai, who slowly rose to meet him.

Bayanai surveyed the snowy battlefield. Katrina had just delivered a knockout blow to Washington. Emilio had beaten Butcher senseless. Ericka had handcuffed Maru. Emilio had tranquilized Brute. Etienne had neutralized Jaako while he was under Alrick's command, then Emma had taken Alrick down. Jaako had stabbed Flame.

The SENTINELS had defeated most of the Tribe, but now they needed to stop Pierce.

"We still have work to do here," Bayanai said.

Luli was finally starting to feel like herself again. She

spotted Washington's gun on the snow a few yards away. She hesitated only a moment before scooping it up and stowing it in her coat pocket without anyone noticing.

"Yeah, but how are we going to do this? Half of us are injured," CoCo said. "And Pierce is just too overpowered. We can't—"

"No!" Luli said. "Pierce does not get to win. I won't let him."

"Kirra said it's taking all she's got to keep the earth together and whatever we're going to do, we should do it fast," James said as he rushed back around.

Bayanai looked at Waleed and raised his eyebrows.

Waleed shook his head. "I can't make a teleportal yet. Still a bit scrambled."

Bayanai nodded. He looked at his teammates, knowing this could be their last stand. At the bottom of the world, this battle would determine if they, and the world, lived or died. "Katrina, would you lead the charge?" He pointed toward the mining annex.

CHAPTER
82

21 December

Shining stumbled out of Pierce's burgundy door teleportal, disoriented. He was back in the mining annex, and the whole area was thrumming. Tears streamed down Shining's face as he realized that his life was now in more danger than ever. He closed his eyes, and a familiar voice soothed him.

"Fear not, my friend, this is not the end."

"Amir?" Some relief crept into Shining's voice.

Pierce paid this weird utterance no attention. He directed one of the Dafydd clones around the machinery to monitor the shaky situation.

"Where have you been? I'm so scared." Shining sat.

"I'm always here, right with you." The words provided cold comfort to Shining. "Your mother and her friends will rescue you. You must not be afraid. Pierce cannot stop us."

"What do you mean?"

"We, you and I, can save the world. Together we—" But before Amir could finish, one of the Dafydd clones yelled.

"I got her." The Dafydd clone dragged a kicking and scratching Julianne with him while another clone held Maggie. "Almost frozen solid, though. Jaako got to her."

The clone shrugged. "Maybe it was payback."

"Let me go." Julianne struggled to twist out of his grasp.

"Pierce wants you." Dafydd shoved her toward him. She shuddered.

Pierce took a look at the two shaking woman and grinned. "Well, well, well. What do we have here?" He looked at Maggie for a long moment. "You're going to record my message to the world in a little while. Be good until I'm ready for you." He grunted at Julianne and grabbed Shining by the collar with his telekinesis, lifting him into the air like a scruffed cat. Shocked, Shining activated his force field, which disrupted Pierce's telekinetic hold on him. Shining dropped to the floor of the mining annex with an "oof" and rolled away from the green beret.

A scowl flashed across Pierce's face, but then a sunny chuckle followed it. Pierce pointed to the machine. "Playtime is over, kid. Get to work."

"Pierce, this place is about to go down. It's too dangerous." Dr. Frazier looked around in terror.

"Captain Pierce, she might be right. We have to be careful about the ice shelf. The shakes are more frequent. And there was that explosion earlier," one of the Dafydd clones said.

Pierce was opening his mouth to reply when he lost his balance, barely keeping to his feet. All the color drained from his face and his mouth opened wide in dismay and fear. Two clones continued to hold Julianne and Maggie while three Dafydds ran toward him. Two Dafydds propped him up while another opened Pierce's belt, threw out the spent cryospore and called for a fourth clone to snag a fresh cryospore from the collection barrel and pop it in place. That done, they closed the belt up and stepped back. For a moment Pierce's whole body glowed an exotic shade of blue, and then he was back in a flash of light.

Julianne stepped back a pace and pulled a hand up to cover her mouth. Her eyes widened with understanding and dread.

"Sir, are you all right?" The question came from Jane.

Pierce grinned at her. "I knew you were here somewhere."

"You did?" Her voice rose in obvious delight at his response. "You sure you're OK?"

"Better than ever. Now let's get to work."

Shining looked toward the exit.

"Don't even think about it, boy." Pierce growled, all good humor dropping from his voice. "Dafydd, Jane, watch Shining." Pierce shoved Shining, protected in his force field, in Dafydd's direction and strode to the orange Cryospore Extraction Unit. The first barrel was full, but he cursed Dr. Frazier's name for not filling the second barrel, despite the fact that just the day before he'd acquired a barrel of the precious cryospores.

"You have failed for the last time, Julianne." Pierce pointed at the scientist and flames flared around her. Maggie watched in horror as the ring of fire surrounded Julianne. There was no hope of escape. The crackling flames drowned out her screams, and he grinned as she flailed in panic. He opened his burgundy teleportal door, carried the full barrel through and returned empty-handed.

Two Dafydds and Jane circled the boy, whose force field prevented them from getting too close to him.

"And you," Pierce swung wildly around to face the reporter. "How fortunate for me that you tagged along. Again."

"What do you want?"

"I've always liked your spark, Maggie. It's the only thing that made you bearable these last years." Pierce stretched his torso and flexed his arms.

"Get to the point."

"You're going to record me. Show the world what Mod power can really do."

"You aren't a Mod."

"Aren't I?" He cycled through his powers, first pyrokinesis as he ignited a fire halo around his head, then telekinesis as he took out her cell phone and made her hold it to film, then density control as he put more weight on Maggie's shoulders than she had ever felt.

"I don't know what you've done to yourself or how, but it's clear that your body is not handling it very well," Maggie said, continuing the recording against her will.

"Do not presume to know anything about me!" The vein in Pierce's forehead pulsed. Then he spoke for the video. "I am a god among gods. I have granted myself power beyond power and I am the future. A new day has dawned and humanity has a new leader."

A deep banging at the door to the mining annex turned into pounding, disrupting Pierce's momentum. The Dafydds, Jane, Shining, and Pierce all turned toward the disruption. The door burst off its hinges and frosty air whipped through the mining annex.

Carlos stood in the doorframe. He looked around, spotted Pierce, and pointed at him. Pierce smiled with delight at this new development.

"You and I have unfinished business, Pierce." Carlos stood just inside the room. He pointed with his bionic arm to Pierce and then swung it back, hitting the wall. The impact rang through the annex and the steel buckled out.

"You don't look so good. Missing something?" A feral smile crossed Pierce's face as he pointed Carlos' own arm at him.

"I'll take that back now," he said evenly.

"It's hardly a fair fight, me having your strength." Pierce

advanced on Carlos. "And so many other powers."

The men circled each other in the time-honored pre-match way of boxers—evaluating the opponent, warily watching for a weakness, deciding when to make the first move.

Maggie, who'd been commanded to record video, continued to do just that, no longer mindful of the Dafydd clone behind her making sure she obeyed Pierce's orders.

Carlos feigned a punch. As Pierce began to dodge in anticipation, Carlos instead kicked at Pierce's right knee. The move surprised Pierce, and he failed to generate his personal protective force field in time. The kick connected. Pierce grunted and doubled over, and Carlos sent his knee up, intending to break Pierce's nose. Instead, Carlos struck something solid and groaned. Pierce had finally brought up his force field.

"How are you going to fight an opponent you can't hit?" Pierce, a superior smile affixed to his mouth, teased Carlos. Pierce stood, his self-healing ability removing the pain from his knee. "You got your one shot. Now it's my turn."

"No chance of a fair fight? Strength and skill against strength and skill? No force fields, no telekinesis. Just you and me."

"Now why would I want to do that?"

"Once upon a time, you were about honor and fighting honorably."

Pierce rammed Carlos' own powerful fist into his ribs, cracking several, and followed it up with a punch that broke Carlos' nose.

Carlos grunted in surprise, lost his balance, and fell to the ground. He tried to get back up, but Pierce pushed him, and he fell on his knees and arm. But Pierce wasn't done. Pierce wailed with all his strength against Carlos, battering him and knocking the breath out of him. The impact-resistant uniform could only buffer so much. Carlos began worrying about merely surviving this fight.

Maggie strained not to gasp with each blow Pierce landed on Carlos.

Mentally, Carlos called to Emma. "I'm in the mining annex and I need some help. Pierce is here, and he's got his goons watching Shining. I'm hurt." He paused for a moment, sighed, then continued. "This is a fight I can't win."

That admission, that he couldn't win the fight against Pierce, hurt almost as much as his screaming cracked ribs and broken nose did. Through his puffy, blackened eyes he watched Pierce with the wariness of a prize fighter who was only one solid punch from being knocked out.

"Stay down, Tio Carlos, and don't let him hurt you anymore. I'll get someone to come help," Emma said in his mind.

Grinning, Pierce watched Carlos slump in the haze of pain. Pierce stalked over to the two Dafydds and Jane. The boy sat in the middle of them, crying inside his force field.

"Dafydd, make some more clones. Have some take care of the strong man if he gets up. Have the rest protect the Cryospore Extraction Unit." Pierce began coughing. He held his hands over his mouth, and when he let go, blood stained his hands. Jane looked at him with a mix of concern and worry.

"Pierce, you need another?" a Dafydd asked.

Pierce waved him off and wiped his mouth. Out of the corner of his eye he saw Carlos stumble through the flames still burning around Dr. Frazier to rescue her and hobble to the other side of the Cryospore Extraction Unit. "Dafydd! I said to watch for Carlos." He noticed Dafydd's feet splayed out.

Battered though he was, Carlos still had some fight left

in him.

"Carlos, where are you?" he taunted.

Maggie moved in unison with Carlos in order to continue recording. The Dafydd clone followed her.

"You're insane, Pierce. You can't win." Blood dripped from Carlos' broken nose and his uniform bore scorch marks from his run through the fire.

"That's where you're wrong!" Pierce used his remote viewing powers to see around the Cryospore Extraction Unit.

Carlos rested against the wall. Suddenly, his bionic arm moved of its own accord. He realized Pierce was using his telekinesis powers to manipulate the prosthetic. He struggled against the unexpected movement, but he could not stop it. Pierce's telekinetic control over his bionic arm was too complete. The cybernetic hand slipped around Dr. Frazier's throat and squeezed. She cried out in horror and fresh tears streamed down her face while Carlos fought a lopsided battle to resist Pierce's power.

"Stop it!" Julianne cried out.

"You've forced me to do this, Argentine. It's by your hand that this woman will die." Pierce laughed.

The strong man let out a guttural yell as he steeled himself to fight Pierce's power. Carlos ripped his own cybernetic arm out of his shoulder in a bid to free Dr. Frazier. Shining and Carlos screamed in unison—Shining in horror and revulsion and Carlos in pain and fury. This time, Maggie couldn't keep her shocked gasp in. Her video recorded that sound along with Carlos' frantic removal of his prosthetic.

The separation hadn't seemed to help at all because Dr. Frazier still was not free. The bionic hand was still clasped around her throat. Focusing his will, Carlos snapped the bionic fingers off the hand. Julianne gulped a breath of relief as Carlos passed out into her arms, and she sagged under the surprise of his weight.

"That works for me. Now, back to the cryospores." Pierce spotted Shining and telekinetically lifted the boy in his force field into the machine. "Get me more cryospores."

Shining screamed as he was placed into the seat and the machine powered up. "I want my mommy!"

"Get me those cryospores, kid, or your mother won't live to see tomorrow."

Shining looked directly at Pierce but took no action. Tears slid down his wet cheeks.

"You don't have a choice here. You will do as I say or you can say goodbye to your precious family and your friends because I guarantee you that I will slowly kill them all in front of you if you don't get me those cryospores right now!" Pierce ignited the air and twisted a flame that encircled Shining in his force field.

Shining was delirious with fear and too scared to do anything. He tried to calm himself, but the flames grew hotter. He wanted to be brave and resist Pierce, but he was also a tired five-year-old boy who just wanted to curl up in a ball in the hopes it would all just go away on its own.

"Buckle up, kid." The flames danced on the invisible force field separating Shining from his tormentor.

"What about Jaako? Don't we need him, too?" Jane seemed to materialize from nowhere.

"Don't worry about it." Pierce pointed at Dr. Frazier. Immediately one of the Dafydds dragged her over to the engine and put her at the controls.

Shining took a breath. Dr. Frazier reluctantly set the machine to extract and activated the cattle prod. Shining screamed with fear and exhaustion as his force field appeared. The Cryospore Extraction Unit began extracting a new load of cryospores. Tears fell down the boy's cheeks, and a runnel of blood slipped out of his nose. He screamed each time he had to tear away a part of his force field for use on the cryospores.

Pierce smiled as he watched the monitor, which showed the rising level in the cryospore barrel. He turned his attention to the newly disarmed Carlos, who'd regained consciousness.

"Dafydd, take care of the Argentine," Pierce shouted.

Dafydd sent out four copies to counter Carlos.

"Take it easy, old man. You're lucky Pierce left you with one arm," Dafydd teased as his duplicates held Carlos down.

"What is that?" one of the Dafydds asked when metal squealed near the entrance.

Maggie's recording turned away from the drama unfolding with the Dafydd clones, Carlos, Pierce and Shining, and toward the entrance.

The wall separating the mining annex from the bitter Antarctic weather ripped apart. Standing there were the rest of the SENTINELS.

Katrina sent a psychokinetic blast that hit Pierce in the back, knocking him to the ground.

CHAPTER
8 3

21 December

George struggled to stand, mostly because he feared what he was going to be forced to do. He was led past the plastic sheets and told to sit beside the gurney. Doubt clouded his vision.

"Who is this?" he asked.

"None of your concern," the redheaded man replied. "Just follow our instructions."

One of the robed men, old and bald, walked in and stood on the other side of the gurney. He spoke in broken English. "You must heal the mind. Suffered much damage. Body is repaired, mind is not."

George looked at him in disbelief. "How do you expect me to do that?"

"Don't be an idiot, George. Your power will allow you to fix him," the redheaded man scolded.

"But I am not a healer. I can just hypnotize people."

"Yes. You heal mind. Make it think it's healthy. Then it will be healthy," the robed man said in an accent George thought was Russian.

"That's not really how it works." George tried to buy

himself some time. "Is this man in a coma?"

The redheaded man nodded.

George wasn't sure if he could use his power on someone in a coma to begin with, let alone instruct the comatose person's brain to repair itself.

The redheaded man unlocked the power-dampening bracelet on George's wrists and removed it. George tried to use his power to hypnotize his captors but he couldn't get a lock on their brains.

"The Sentinel must be healed," the old man said.

"Sentinel?" George asked. He had heard these men mentioning the Sentinel and New Reckoning but without further elaboration. Similarly, he had heard Bayanai and Emilio talk about a Sentinel and a Reckoning. He thought hard and tried to remember the context and the significance. He thought it was related to the guy who died when New Atlantis first formed. He'd even been to the memorial to him while he'd been on the island, but for the life of him he couldn't remember the name. Was it possible these were one and the same? He might be in more trouble than he feared.

"Enough. Come. Heal," the old man commanded. George hesitantly rose and stood next to the body. Reverently the old man placed George's hands on the comatose man's head and looked at the two men in the room. George was more scared than he let on. What could he do to heal this man? If this was the man who died on New Atlantis years ago, how could he be alive now? His mind spun with questions. His hands touched the man's curly hair. If he were somehow able to fix him, what would that mean? George began to tremble and sweat.

"Go on." The redheaded man encouraged as he gently tapped the gun he had holstered on his right hip.

"Right. Okay," George muttered. He wished he were strong enough to fight back. Strong enough to say no and run. But he was scared. And he wanted to live. He dropped his gaze to the man on the gurney. He opened his mind and dove into the brain of the man on the table. It was such a jumble in there that George felt like he was in a twisted cubist art painting. Nothing made sense. He usually was just able to walk into someone's mind and suggest to them what he wanted. This would not be the case here. He ventured forward and the horizon grew dark and cold. George looked up and saw an image that frightened him beyond measure.

George screamed and stumbled back.

"What is it?" The redheaded man picked George up.

"This man is damaged. He is not alone in his mind. There's someone else, something else in there with him." He struggled to articulate the wrongness he'd sensed in the man's head. "Something powerful. Dangerous." George fought the urge to drop to the ground. "Don't make me to do this."

"You must," the robed man demanded. "The Sentinel must rise again."

George shook his head and turned to away. The redheaded man pulled his gun out, cocked it, and held it to George's left temple.

"Do as he commands."

Heart pounding and with eyes wide, George returned to the comatose body and reluctantly put his hands back on the man's head. Immediately, he was sucked back into the man's world. He heard whispers.

My time is come
The vessel is ready
Open the mind
And the world will be saved.

Surely the world being saved was a good thing, but had

476

the dark and dangerous presence been responsible for the words? His heart raced as he tried to relax and reassure himself. The presence in the man's mind unnerved him mightily. Then a jumble of memories flashed before him. A man wrongfully imprisoned. A child crying alone in the dark. A collective ritual sacrifice. Through the haze of the man's memories, he heard encouragement from the outside world as a voice urged him to keep going.

George saw a crudely made toy of sticks and rope lying on the ground, and a child's eerie laugh came from the darkness.

The man's mind was too broken to be repaired. He felt haunted by that other presence in the man's mind. He heard the ticking of his watch and knew his time in this troubled and troubling mind must come to an end. He quickly said a few words and closed his eyes. Before he turned around he felt a tug in his heart and a deep ache.

There was barely time for George to craft a mental suggestion to leave behind inside the shattered mindscape. Maybe this artifact would enable healing him from afar. He whispered, "heal, heal" to form the artifact. As he did so, he felt his presence slipping from the man's mind.

George came out of the trance with a start. He looked around. The old man chanted in some language, Latin maybe, or some other archaic language, and the redheaded man stared directly at him. George felt certain he was doomed. He could not go back into the mindscape without rousing the beast inside the man's mind, and, based on the look in the redheaded man's eyes, he would not escape with his life no matter what he did. And if he helped them do what they wanted, what then? Trouble awaited mankind if this man awakened. He felt it deep inside.

He looked around, considering the potential consequences. Every single moment of a person's life offers an opportunity to change its course. Go left at the light and wind up in a car accident. Go right or straight and avoid it. But you couldn't know ahead of time the results. Decide to stop for a coffee and fall in love with the barista. Decide to skip that coffee and eventually die without having known the emotions that had inspired so many songs, so much poetry. All those little random moments that might make greatness or heartache the next inevitable step, and you never knew when they were going to happen, or what they were, or that they were the little decisions that defined your life.

He was at the crossroads of his life, but at least he had the benefit of realizing it. He could continue to help them, perhaps creating a monster and making possible whatever terrible thing this New Reckoning might be. Perhaps getting himself murdered in the process. Perhaps not, but wishing he had been once he understood the ramifications. Could he live with whatever atrocity resulted, knowing he'd been the crucial factor that made it possible?

Or he could refuse. His death would likely be swift. The redheaded man held a pistol and acted like he knew how to use it. But at least George would have the satisfaction of having chosen to do the right thing. Maybe, in his last act, he could find the courage he longed for all his life.

George would no longer be their puppet. He took off from the plastic enclosure and ran toward the empty void. Startled, the redheaded man pursued him and ordered him to stop.

George skidded to a stop right before the ledge and turned around with his hands held up.

"Come back. You don't want to do that," the redheaded man said as he pointed the gun at George.

The lights gleamed off the gun and George gulped. But courage and resolve filled him. "I don't know what that man did or who he is, but waking him up is a bad idea." George stepped back.

"George! No!" the redheaded man yelled.

"I won't help you." George closed his eyes and flung himself over the ledge. He plummeted silently to his death.

CHAPTER
84

21 December

"Stay down, Pierce," Katrina yelled. She focused her energy on neutralizing the man who had once trained her.

Pierce, sprawled out on the floor next to the Cryospore Extraction Unit, swore.

"Pierce is down. For now," Katrina hollered to her teammates. "I don't see Shining."

Even though Pierce's telekinetic hold on her waned, Maggie continued recording.

Luli rushed past Katrina. "Shining! Where are you?" She scanned the mining annex.

"Wait, Luli, don't," Katrina said.

Pierce, apparently waiting for a break in Katrina's concentration, took advantage of the distraction. With agility younger than his years, Pierce sprang up and faced his foes. Luli charged straight at him. Ericka stood on one side of Katrina, Bayanai the other. Next to him stood James and Etienne, who charged his escrima sticks. Behind them, Waleed stood protectively in front of Emma and next to Emilio, who held the injured CoCo. Next to them, the also-injured Timothy looked everywhere but at CoCo and

Emilio. Behind Waleed, Jaako stood erect. He exuded fearlessness and a willingness to battle if necessary. He scowled at Pierce, and his chin jutted out. In the far corner of the annex, Carlos remained in his lopsided battle with the Dafydd clones.

Pierce held up his hand to stop Luli. She hung suspended in midstep, as though she'd run into an invisible brick wall covered with fly paper. She was grateful that her exo-suit bore the brunt of the impact.

"Shining!" She frantically searched the annex for her son. "I'm here. I'm going to take you home."

"Not until I get what I want from him," Pierce said.

"Help me," Luli screamed to the SENTINELS, nearly out of her mind with worry. "We have to save my son."

Katrina and Ericka nodded to each other, a signal they had given one another many times. Ericka shot green energy blasts at Pierce while Katrina focused on reasserting psychokinetic control over Pierce. Katrina might be able to use her powers to keep him from moving forward, but she couldn't keep him from using his stolen powers. He clenched his fist, and Ericka and Katrina both grunted in pain as he increased the density of the air around them. The frigid air pressed in on them, and neither could maintain the assault on him. Ericka's last green energy blast fizzled in midair, while Katrina lost her mastery over her psychokinetic ability.

Emma scooted back against the wall, head buried between her knees. Given her recent victory over Alrick, she thought she might be strong enough to see Pierce again, but it was too soon. She sobbed.

Luli still hung suspended. She couldn't move, but she continued to cry out for her son and try to at least place her eyes on him. Bayanai went to comfort her.

"James, find Shining," Bayanai said.

Pierce anticipated this directive, and before James could zip away, Pierce increased the speedster's personal density. It happened in a nanomoment.

James swore. He was stuck in place, having become so heavy that he couldn't create enough momentum to move forward, let alone race off to find Shining. He was nearly as dense as granite. With microsized moves, he fought his increased density and worked to generate momentum.

***

Beside James, Etienne tried to turn invisible before Pierce could neutralize him. But he wasn't quick enough. When Pierce neutralized Etienne, his escrima sticks clattered to the ground. Pierce telekinetically hoisted Etienne and all the remaining SENTINELS in midair.

The Cryospore Extraction Unit roared to life, filling the air with the scent of diesel, and Jaako gulped.

"My son's in there! We have to get him." Luli struggled to fight Pierce's telekinetic hold over her, but even maternal love and desperation couldn't triumph here.

"Shut up, Luli," Pierce snapped.

"Pierce, man, what happened to you?" Bayanai asked.

"What happened to me? How dare you."

"No, seriously, look at yourself. You're a wreck. You were probably an okay guy, once upon a time. Now look what you stand for." As Bayanai said this last, he gestured at the mining annex and rumbling machine. "What are you trying to do here? What's this thing with the cryospores all about?"

Pierce's face reddened to an alarming shade, and his eyes bulged. For a moment, he didn't act, as though rage had paralyzed him. Telekinetically, he tossed Bayanai around the mining annex, flinging him against walls, the ceiling, the ground, all the while maintaining his control over the other SENTINELS, who watched in horror. All except Katrina, who saw an opportunity. Katrina closed her eyes and called into her body all the negative energy that Pierce was projecting. The risky move gave her a power-up. If she didn't voluntarily use that energy soon in a way she chose, that energy would come out on its own, as it had in the aftermath of Rami's death on New Atlantis back when this all began.

When his rage had almost played out, he deposited Bayanai's battered, bruised, and bleeding body on the ground in front of Emma.

She let out a little moan but couldn't lean down to help him. "Bayanai?"

He didn't answer, and she called his name again, more urgently. He still didn't answer.

"I'm a wreck? How dare you judge me." Pierce's voice didn't come out as rant. It came out in chilly, unsettling calm. "All I've ever done was serve one master after another. First the military, then the Ascendancy. Time and again, they let me down and broke promises. Well, I finally woke up. I realized the Ascendancy would never actually bring me into the inner circle, nor would they ever help me achieve a superpower. Why take orders from people when I can be a god?"

Pierce sneered at Katrina and her team as Maggie continued recording. "You take your powers for granted. You don't really deserve them the way I do. When the White Light Wave passed me by, I knew I had to act, to find another way. And I have. It took a while, but look at me now." He puffed out his chest. "I can—"

One of Ericka's green energy blasts knocked into Pierce's fist, and he looked at it with wide, surprised eyes before glaring at Ericka. She remained suspended in midair, but seemed to have fully recovered from his changing the air density around her. As he watched, Katrina also seemed to recover and aimed a torrent of pent-up and amped-up psychokinetic fury at Pierce. His utility belt started to unbuckle, and he panicked.

It was too much for Pierce. He lost control over some of his powers.

James was suddenly no longer burdened by all the extra density Pierce had saddled him with. One moment, he'd been nearly as heavy and immovable as granite, but the next his weight lightened, although he was still denser than normal. Buoyed by the momentum he'd been building up with micromovements and suddenly freed from the excess weight, he blazed through the mining annex at a rate none of the SENTINELS had witnessed before. Even the impact of crashing his dense body through the wall of the mining annex, Wile E. Coyote style, did little to slow his speed-fueled momentum. He had to burn off all the extra momentum before he would be able to control his actions.

Sunlight filtered into the mining annex through the hole James made in the wall, and chilly air entered as well. Jaako, seeing something he could do, created an ice wall to block the hole.

Pierce fought to rebuckle his utility belt. "Stop that! Stop that right now," he bellowed at Katrina.

"I should have thought of that long ago," she said as she continued to psychokinetically undo the utility belt, which held the cryospore that fueled his abilities.

One of the Dafydd clones broke away from the fight with Carlos to help Pierce.

"It's Katrina," Pierce said. "Stop her."

"I'm on it, Pierce!" Washington shuffled into the annex from the frozen outside. A look of relief flitted across Pierce's face. "The rest are still down out there, but payback's coming."

Ericka looked back and shot off three quick green blasts, which Pierce dodged.

A Dafydd clone ran toward Katrina, but before he could get there, she had psychokinetically pulled off the belt and was moving it through the air toward her. Blood fell to the floor from the cryospore port in Pierce's belly. Pierce fell to his knees and groaned, and as he did so, his telekinetic hold on the SENTINELS vanished. They dropped to the ground of the mining annex like so many rocks. The fall startled Katrina, and her control over Pierce's utility belt faltered. Washington was about to grab it when a Dafydd clone snagged it out of the air and ran it back to Pierce, who wrapped it around his hips with shaking hands. Washington saw Etienne's escrima sticks on the ground and picked them up instead.

The SENTINELS leapt to their feet.

"Now," shouted Ericka. Green energy poured out of her eyes and hit Pierce. He stumbled, still intent on the vital utility belt. But only Luli—who pulled a gun out—joined in Katrina and Ericka's assault. Emilio started to join them but realized that if he acted he would leave the others unprotected. So he, Jaako, and Waleed remained in place to tend to the wounded.

Washington ran up to Luli from behind and tried to knock the gun out of her hands. "You don't want to do this, I promise you."

"You know nothing of me." She used her exo-suit enhanced strength to overpower Pierce's right-hand man and flip him on his back.

"Luli," he said.

She paused and frowned. Never had Washington called her by her first name during all their time together at Base 47. But she disregarded the thought and punched him hard

485

in the stomach, her exo-suit delivering more intensity than she could on her own.

Luli aimed the pistol at Pierce, who'd finally managed to win out over Katrina's psychokinetic efforts. The belt was securely bound around his waist, although he kept one hand on the buckle for good measure.

"Pierce, make them stop that machine," Luli said. She sounded calm, and certain of success. "I want my boy back."

Shocked amusement washed across the man's face when he spotted her aiming the gun at him, leaving the barest hint of a grin behind.

"You're not going to shoot me."

"I want my boy back."

"Drop the gun, Luli," Pierce commanded, sounding like the drill sergeant he had been so many years before.

She didn't move.

"Where'd she get a gun?" CoCo asked Emilio, who shrugged.

Next to Luli, Waleed finally felt recovered enough from the dual attacks by Pierce and Timothy to create a teleportal back to Base 47 so Jiya could tend to the injuries of Bayanai, CoCo, and Timothy. Black globules formed near him, and his teleportal opened up. He urged Emilio to take Emma along with them.

"No one leaves," Pierce said. He threw a fireball at the wounded. It landed near the Fight HQ with a heat so intense it singed their hair, suffusing the air with an acrid odor.

The teleportal flickered. It no longer was a passageway from Antarctica to Base 47. But, it seemed, it was still a portal of some kind.

"Luli, what are you doing?" Jiya's voice came from far away and sounded distorted, but the shock was still evident. It was somehow coming through Waleed's damaged teleportal. Jiya, who'd been in the War Room waiting with

Yi and Sying for the team to return, could see what was going on, but could not enter the portal. "Luli, why do you have a gun?" Urgency laced her question.

The floor heaved again, more strongly this time, but Luli kept her eyes, and the gun, trained on Pierce. "He has my son, and I will get him back."

"Luli, don't—" Jiya said as Yi neared the portal.

After the floor and building moved again, none of the SENTINELS remained standing.

CHAPTER
8 5

21 December

"Uhm... guys..." Kirra shivered as much from the cold as from effort. It took all her strength to keep the ground under the ice sheet from splitting.

"Kirra," Emma thought to the Australian. "What's going on?"

"I don't know. And I don't know how much longer I can keep it together." Kirra steadied herself and used her connection to the earth to help her understand the effect that the volatile cryospores were having on the ground. "It's as if the earth is giving up. Whatever they're doing in there, they better do it quick. Otherwise, it's going to get ugly real quick." While she was holding the continent together she felt a deeper bond with the earth. She could sense the connective tissue holding the world together. Via that connection the cracks began to reveal themselves to her, radiating outward. One branched off toward the Falkland Islands. It seemed increasingly likely that The Hastings Foundation was behind that devastating earthquake. The rest splintered off and while she could have followed them there was a bigger task at hand. Kirra's hands shook, not from her powers, but from the tension in her muscles working to prevent, or at least stall, the splitting of the ground. Sweat beaded on her forehead as she worried for Etienne and the others.

***

The walls of the mining annex shook with a force that brought everyone to their knees.

"What the hell?" Emilio checked on CoCo and Timothy. "We've got to get out of here." He crawled to Waleed's distorted teleportal to Base 47. He placed his hand against the shimmering blackness, but his hand wouldn't pass through. The portal was only a window into a safe world. He locked eyes with Jiya on the other side.

She shook her head, worry in her eyes. "It's no use, *beta*, you're stuck there. We can't get to you."

Emma, still visibly shaking as much from the cold as from her terror of Pierce, mentally connected the team together and relayed what Kirra had told her. Through tears she said that if they weren't able to secure the cryospores, they'd be dead in minutes.

Realizing the perilous situation they were in, Emilio slowly nodded and turned back to his teammates, who were finding their footing.

The shaking had stopped.

***

"Keep Pierce's attention away from us," Emma mentally said to Ericka and Katrina.

Katrina nodded as Ericka made a beeline for Dafydd, or one of his clones, but was stopped by another clone. She looked over and saw Ericka send three quick blasts, knocking back one of the Dafydds attacking Carlos.

"Don't normally hit ladies, but you're—"

But she wasn't listening. She was remembering training. She took a deep, anxious breath and head butted him. His outraged cry of pain told her the contact had been as solid as she thought it was. She followed with a fierce kick to the clone's left knee and heard it break. He crumpled to ground, groaning and holding the knee.

Across the room, Washington picked himself off the ground and stumbled to Pierce, who steadied himself.

"What's the play, boss?" Washington eyed the blue glow of the cryospore powering Pierce from the belt buckle.

"I just need a moment." Pierce put his hand on his shoulder. "Make sure the kid gets as many cryospores as possible. I can't lose those." Pierce coughed and blood splattered onto the white floor. He shook his head at his loyal soldier and Washington set off toward the Cryospore Extraction Unit.

Ericka, feeling relieved and fueled by success, looked around for more action.

Someone tapped Ericka's right shoulder from behind. She looked over her right shoulder but saw no one. Then, remembering trickster's habits of tapping one shoulder but standing behind the other shoulder, she whipped her head around to the left. Still no one. A fierce knife jab to her kidney cut deep through her protective uniform. It doubled her over and left no doubt that someone was there. As she was bent over gasping with pain and surprise, she spotted women's shoes. Of course. Plain Jane.

Ericka sent energy blasts at the woman's feet as she held her own bleeding side, but none connected. She struggled to stand.

"It's hard to fight what you can't focus on, isn't it?" Jane asked. The plain woman slapped Ericka's face hard. "And nice try with the tracker."

Carlos spotted her trouble. He manhandled one of the Dafydd clones and launched him into the air toward Ericka and her opponent. The flung clone whizzed by Ericka and rolled into Jane, and Carlos panted from the strain and pain.

"Well, that's something," Ericka said as she nodded her thanks to Carlos. She whipped out a pair of power-dampening cuffs and slapped them on the middle-aged woman. She sat back on her legs, winced as she explored the stab wound and shook her head. "Now I see you."

Jane furrowed her brow at Ericka and sat silently.

"I'm not taking any chances with you." Ericka pushed Jane to a support beam in the wall and snapped a zip tie around her wrists, the power-dampening cuffs, and the beam. "Stay put." Ericka smiled at Carlos. "I know you want another go at Pierce, but let me take it."

Carlos smiled at her concern and pointed to her side. "You're up for that?"

"Feeds my rage." Ericka narrowed her eyes, full of glowing green energy.

"Give him hell." Carlos leaned back against the wall, trying to catch his breath, as green energy bubbled off of Ericka's body.

***

Katrina sent psychokinetic blast after blast at Pierce.

"Big mistake!" Pierce telekinetically lifted himself off the ground and turned to look at the Canadian. "You try that again, you have no idea what kind of pain I'll inflict on you." He shook his head and clicked on his force field.

The smile of victory slipped off Katrina's face. Hearing a change in the sound of the extraction, Pierce turned to the Cryospore Extraction Unit and saw Shining taking advantage of the distraction. He had climbed out of the machine and his force field pushed Washington against the wall. Julianne chased him.

"No." Pierce ran toward the boy and telekinetically lifted him back in the seat. "Get me those cryospores and don't stop until the tank reaches a hundred percent."

He gave a threatening look to Julianne, who averted her eyes. "Keep him in check, I'm not kidding. Washington, don't let them out."

Washington pointed and she climbed back into the Cryospore Extraction Unit and slumped in the seat. Again, she activated the cattle prod and set the machine to extract. Shining's force field flared, and he screamed. The unit started sucking up the valuable energy units out of the ice, and Shining was forced to share part of his force field with the cryospores as they emerged from the earth.

Another set of mini-quakes rocked through the mining annex.

The SENTINELS looked around, taking in the scene. Pierce was forcing Shining to work. The boy was crying inside his force field, but he was working, the torture providing sufficient motivation. Dafydd and his clones defended the huge orange machine from the SENTINELS.

Frantic to reunite with her son, Luli fired twice at Pierce. Both shots bounced off Pierce's shield. Pierce snapped his fingers. Fire jumped from his hands as though from a flame thrower. He directed it toward the injured group sitting off to the side.

The New Atlantis prime minister responded with a stream of ice. The wall of fire and the wall of ice sizzled loudly where they met. Those powers were too evenly matched.

"Stop it," Shining cried out.

The five-year-old's shriek startled everyone within

hearing distance.

"What is it, boy?" Pierce asked.

"The fires, the cryospores, it could—" And here words failed him. Shining closed his fists and then opened them while spreading his hands apart, mimicking the word "explosion" which had slipped his mind in his fear. "Make it stop."

"Pierce, he's right. This place could go at any moment! Don't you feel the ground?" Julianne added.

Pierce studied the boy and the scientist. The feel of the freed cryospores was thick in the air. The flames twinkled out, and Jaako panted as he braced himself with his hands on his knees.

"Jaako, get over here and help me finish up the extraction," Pierce shouted.

Jaako didn't move.

"Now, or that little matter you want private won't stay that way," Pierce said.

One by one, the SENTINELS turned and stared at the prime minister.

Pierce taunted the SENTINELS. "You really think your little island paradise could rise to such prominence in such a short time without some dirty dealings?"

Katrina looked over at Jaako. She seemed unsurprised at the implication. She'd long thought some of the rumors about Jaako being on the take were true.

Looking like a man whose world had just crashed and burned, Jaako shuffled toward the Cryospore Extraction Unit.

Luli watched this unfold, her jaw hanging wide open. "You're going to help Pierce?" She pointed the gun straight at Jaako.

"Luli, you don't understand. My life was in danger. New Atlantis was in danger." Jaako waved his hands in front of his body, hoping to calm her down.

"How could you?" Luli's hands shook with rage, but the gun remained aimed straight at Jaako, her finger on the trigger.

A series of minor tremblors shook the mining annex again. Luli lost her balance, and as she fell, she fired the gun twice more. One bullet went straight at the Cryospore Extraction Unit and one into the ceiling. The first bullet bounced off of Shining's force field and zoomed past Dafydd into the ground near the extractor hose.

Dafydd, out of clones and too zapped to create any more at the moment, dropped to the ground to avoid the line of fire. He didn't see Carlos moving toward the Cryospore Extraction Unit.

Carlos snuck up behind Washington and grabbed him in a one-armed choke hold. Washington flailed and slipped out of his grasp. He turned around and put his hands up as if to say time out. Carlos advanced.

"Carlos." Washington's face morphed into Josh.

Carlos' jaw dropped. "Josh? How did you get here?"

"Not now. Listen, I've got a plan."

Carlos nodded.

"Distract Julianne while I get Shining free," Josh-as-Washington said.

"You got it." Carlos called upon his reserve of strength to continue. His body wouldn't fail him now. He mentally reached out to Emma, hoping she would be able to help them stop the monster Pierce had become.

"I can't. I'm so scared." In his mind, Emma's voice sounded tired and hopeless.

Taking advantage of the chaos, Pierce telekinetically lifted Jaako over to the Cryospore Extraction Unit. "Time for you to earn your keep," Pierce growled at the Mod.

Under Pierce's watchful remote viewing eye, Jaako

concentrated his freezing powers on the actual area the cryospores were emerging from. Out of the corner of his eye, Jaako saw Carlos approach.

"Carlos, stay back. I need to keep the freeze on so this place doesn't explode," Jaako said. The very air around him chilled as he focused on keeping the hole in the ground sufficiently cold.

Carlos looked at the politician speculatively for a long moment, clearly thinking about Pierce's accusations. He shook his head and stalked over toward Julianne.

Josh-as-Washington climbed onto the Cryospore Extraction Unit and approached Shining. As Shining turned, Josh revealed he was masquerading as Washington. Shining's eyes lit up. Josh put his finger over his lips, urging Shining to stay quiet. Through tears Shining nodded understanding. He lowered his force field and let Josh touch him. The former SENTINEL leader picked Shining up and carefully moved out of the Cryospore Extraction Unit.

"Stay over there in the corner, but keep your field on. I'll be right back." Josh pointed to the corner and Shining nodded. He threw his little arms around Josh's neck and thanked him before running to where Josh indicated. Josh grinned, morphed his face back into Washington's, and turned his attention back to the device. He snapped the suction toggle to the off position and broke it so it couldn't spring into action again without serious bench time, then he picked up one of the escrima sticks that Etienne had dropped and gave it a full charge. He slammed it into the center of the Cryospore Extraction Unit, where he could do more damage. The stick vibrated as it released a charge that fried the equipment.

Carlos grabbed Julianne and held her close to him. He gave an intense look at Jaako, who avoided eye contact.

"Show me how to stop this," Carlos whispered to the

scientist.

"It's impossible to stop now. The cryospores have become unstable and that's why the quakes are happening. I wish I could stop it, stop Pierce. But the man is insane. Believe me," Julianne said.

"I do." Carlos let her go. "Get as far away from here as possible."

She edged toward the entrance.

Josh-as-Washington jumped out of the control area of the Cryospore Extraction Unit. He had just gotten out of the machine and moved several feet away when Shining began screaming.

***

"CoCo, can you hear me?" Emilio whispered.

"Is it over, did we win?"

"Not yet, mi amor." Emilio brushed her hair back and whispered an idea to her.

"Are you sure?"

"We don't have a choice. It's that bad." He leaned back and she took in the scene. Katrina struggled against Pierce while Ericka, wincing in pain from the stab wound, sent her energy blasts at Pierce. Though she couldn't see Etienne or Luli, CoCo knew they must be in the battle somehow. Just to her left were the other wounded—Timothy and Bayanai. Maggie was still very scared but filming the action with her cell phone.

CoCo looked over and saw the frozen window portal back to Base 47 with Yi pounding on the portal, to no avail. CoCo took a breath and reached her arm behind her to check out the stab wound on her back. Tenderly, she slid her fingers over it and flinched in anticipation, but it was not as bad as she feared. Emilio had packed the wound and it wasn't hurting as much. She reached out her hand and winced as Emilio helped her to her feet.

"You okay?" He studied her.

"I've a bad feeling about this," she said. They held hands and walked toward Pierce.

***

Outside, Kirra remained locked in concentration, focusing every ounce of her geokinetic power on stabilizing the land. She was burning so much energy in her effort that she no longer felt the cold. She shook from the exertion. Blood streamed from her nose. The red drops splattered on the dry snow like a Pollack painting.

***

"Maggie?" the voice came out of nowhere. She looked around. A shimmer showed her it was Etienne.

"Don't worry about me. I'm okay. Mostly." She paused when she realized he had made her intangible, which made it possible for him to phase her out of the telekinetic grasp that Pierce had her in.

"I'm going to get you over to the others," Etienne said as they moved unnoticed.

"This is insane. I don't understand how Pierce got so messed up. How all this came about."

"He's been stealing abilities from Mods and using this cryospore to power him. It's made him deranged." Etienne sat her next to Bayanai and made her visible to him.

"You were right." Blood dripped from Bayanai's lips.

"As much as I appreciate that, what are you talking about?" Maggie asked.

"You were right about not giving up." Bayanai gingerly

pushed himself off the ground.

Maggie frowned at him. "Be careful. You look worse than a ravaged chew toy."

"Feel that way. But this is my team, and I won't let them down." He looked out at the SENTINELS fighting with all their might against an enemy who was more powerful.

***

Josh-as-Washington quietly rushed over to Shining but couldn't get close enough because of the child's force field, and then saw what he was screaming about. On the other side of the annex, Luli charged at Pierce and knocked him to the ground. She climbed on top of Pierce and wailed her fists into him. Normally, this wouldn't have hurt him at all, but with the exo-suit's enhancements she connected again and again. His blood stained her suit with each hit as he tried and failed to use his force field.

The SENTINELS watched as Luli laid her rage bare against the man responsible for kidnapping her son, the man who had tormented them for years. Shining yelled for his mother and she looked over. She pushed herself up and off of Pierce and walked to Shining.

Smiling, she opened her arms and stepped closer. Josh-as-Washington tried to get closer to Shining but his force field prevented him. Shining's eyes watered as he neared his mother.

Pierce reached out his hand and flames shot out. They caught her from behind. The fire super-heated her exo-suit, which was partially constructed of metal, and she fell to her knees screaming in pain.

"No!" Shining shouted.

Luli tried to get out of the exo-suit but her flesh had already been scorched. She fell down on her side as the flames receded, and the smell of burned meat filled the air.

Shining's screams resumed and then crescendoed. Still encased in his protective force field, he rushed to his fallen mother and dropped to his knees next to her. "Mommy, Mommy, get up." He cried, shaking her gently and then with vigor as he tried to deny the loss all children most fear.

Josh-as-Washington leaned down to place his hand on the little boy only to stopped by the force field still protecting him.

Back at Base 47, Yi and Sying banged ineffectively against the portal, trying to break through.

"No Mommy, no, don't go," Shining sobbed as his force field enveloped her, and as it did a puff of smoke was all that remained of the fires that smothered her. "You're the only one who could help me."

"I love you, baby. Jiya's going to try to patch me up," Luli whispered raggedly to her son, her face charred and cracking. "Kiss me."

Crying, he did as asked. He was afraid to hug her, terrified his love would hurt the parts that Pierce had charred.

She turned to the portal and locked eyes with her husband and daughter. "I love you all. Be good and do good."

She closed her eyes and left the world.

Understanding bit deeply into the powerful little boy.

"No, you can't leave me, Mommy." He whimpered, hugging her with the intensity he'd not dared to show moments before.

Everything stopped. Moments seemed to stretch into eternity as each of the SENTINELS grappled with Luli's death. One by one, the team members externalized their anger and grief.

Pierce stood up with a perverse sense of pride and eyed

the fallen warrior.

"Pierce, you sonuvabitch!" Emilio ran toward him.

"You can't stop me alone." Pierce laughed as he telekinetically froze the Spaniard in midair.

"Who said he's alone?" A voice asked out of nowhere. Pierce grimaced and turned around. Behind him CoCo stood ready to fight.

"I just killed Luli, you think I'll do anything less to you, traitor?" He reached out and increased her density. She dropped to the floor and he smiled.

"Except, that's not really me," the real, battered CoCo said as she appeared next to Emilio. Pierce turned around a moment too late. They were holding hands. His luck power and her power of misdirection merged in a dazzling display of blinding light. The explosive blast hit Pierce, sending him flying. At the same time, the light blasts reflected off of Pierce and ignited a fire in one of the lighting fixtures. Pierce nervously checked his belt.

CoCo and Emilio both dropped to the ground, still holding hands, all their energy spent on their gamble. Josh-as-Washington ran to Pierce and helped him upright. But while Pierce was occupied with his belt, Josh pulled out a knife and drove it deep in Pierce's back.

"Washington?" Pierce wheeled around, but before he could do anything Josh shifted back into himself and thrust the other charged escrima stick into Pierce's buckle. "Josh, you son-of-a—" The resulting shockwave launched them across the room.

Jaako heard the thud of the man who had been impersonating him. But it was the crackling of the new fire that made him turn around. He sent an icy blast in the direction of the flames, extinguishing them. This time he had plenty of time to react, unlike when Pierce immolated Luli.

Pierce used his telekinesis to pick himself up and eyed his enemies.

Just then, a deafening boom shook the room as James finally returned from burning off all the excess momentum.

"Shouldn't have done that, Pierce!" James delivered an uppercut fueled by the increased momentum and power he had stored up. Pierce had tried to turn his force field on but James was far too quick. The punch rocketed Pierce into the annex's ceiling before he slammed into the ground.

"You did this," Shining shouted, in full command of his fury, and marched toward Pierce. "You killed Mommy." Shining's eyes rolled back in his head and his voice deepened. There was a distinct change in the boy's demeanor. "You've hurt for the last time." Shining's force field was perfect all around him, but it glowed with a reddish haze and crackled. It added to the thrum in the air from all the cryospores that had been released during the extraction process and weren't wrapped in some of Shining's protective force fields.

Red ribbons of pure energy extended from Shining's force field and danced around the annex, dipping here and there by unconscious SENTINELS, rousing them. Emilio and CoCo came to with a start, trying to figure out where the battle stood.

Pierce looked unnerved by the advancing Shining. He created a burgundy door, but couldn't open it because Katrina psychokinetically kept it closed. If it was just one injury he would have been fine, but he suffered from a pileup of injuries: the knife still stuck in his back, the concussive blast from Emilio and CoCo, the Mach 4 punch from James, the shock in his buckle from the escrima sticks, the beating he took at the hands of the dead Luli. His cryospore flickered and the blue glow faded. His hands shook and he dry-heaved to the side. His heart thumped in his chest, the strain almost too much for him. But he wouldn't give up. Not to them. Not ever.

As Shining approached, he exerted his control over the cryospores, that ability Pierce had so valued, and rushed them toward the old man. Perhaps sensing the boy's plan, Pierce erected his own force field, but the glowing blue cryospores passed right through it. Within moments, there were so many cryospores within Pierce's force field that he could barely see out.

James whispered to Ericka, "Did you know he could do this?"

Ericka shook her head, her eyes wide with disbelief and worry. "I don't think this is a Mod power."

"We have to stop him," James said.

"I don't think we can."

"This is your end." Each word Shining spoke was punctuated with deep red energy ribbons racing toward Pierce. Bayanai limped closer to the boy, but the energy surrounding Shining's force field kept him away.

"This isn't Shining," Emma said mentally to the group.

"What? How do you know?" Bayanai asked.

"I can't explain it, but something has overcome him. He's there but not." Emma moaned and put her hand to her head.

"We can't do this, Shining. We have to let the law take it from here," Josh said.

"He killed the boy's mother. There must be a Reckoning." The words came from Shining's mouth, but they weren't his voice. Shining lifted his hand toward Pierce. The red aura around him darkened in intensity, and red ribbons seemed to float around his hand.

"A Reckoning?" Emilio asked CoCo. "This is bad."

"Bayanai, we can't let him do this." Katrina shouted over the noise.

"Stop him!" Maggie's shout joined Katrina's.

"Shining," Ericka said. "Don't do this. This isn't self-defense. It's murder."

Shining looked over to Ericka and with a blink she hit the ground, immediately unconscious. Josh crawled over to Ericka and put his fingers to her neck. Grateful to find a pulse, he grinned weakly and looked back at the other SENTINELS.

"Shining, no." Fear filled Bayanai's heart. If Shining was this powerful, how could any of them stop him?

"There is more to this than you know," the otherworldly voice said. "The past will never die. He is always with us." Shining pointed at Pierce and opened a hole in the villain's force field. "Sacrifice is the only way to make whole again." Deep red energy ribbons shimmered in the air as they circled and wove their way inside Pierce's field.

"Make what whole?" Katrina asked.

"Not what, but who." Again, the words came from Shining's mouth.

A spark ignited the cryospores inside Pierce's force field. Even though the force field contained the heat, an intense wave of warmth radiated away from Pierce. In anticipation of Pierce's death, at which time Pierce's own force field would wink out of existence, Shining formed a secondary force field around the man to contain the damage that he expected any moment.

The SENTINELS watched in horrified fascination as their former leader was immolated within his own private force field. The crackles and explosive booms continued for several minutes after Pierce's force field failed. Jane wailed until she lost her voice.

Maggie wondered at the boy's potential. Was it just Mod power, or more than that? Either way, he was only five, able to destroy Pierce and contain the fallout. What would he be capable of at ten?

Shining next turned his wrath on Jaako. The red ribbons advanced from Shining's aura, pointed like arrows at Jaako.

"You are guilty. You could have saved this woman. He didn't have to lose his mother." The voice rumbled out of Shining and throughout the annex.

"Shining, I was trying to watch out for you. That's why I was here," the politician said.

"You lie." The boy pointed at Jaako, and then he looked to the teleportal back to Base 47. He pointed at it, and the portal fully opened. Out rushed Yi, Sying, and Jiya. The boy, surrounded by the red shimmering aura, beckoned to Sying. Wiping tears off her face, she walked to him. Yi ran to his wife's body and wept over her.

Jiya spotted CoCo, Bayanai, Carlos, and Waleed, who were all injured, and she made her way to heal them.

White light, so bright that it was nearly blinding, burst out of Jaako's head in a corkscrew beam. It went straight to Sying's head.

"Now you have his power, Sying," the boy said.

She let out a soft breath and ice sparkled and fell to the ground.

"What did he just do?" Katrina asked Yi.

"There is more to Shining than you ever knew. So much that his mother and I kept secret." Tears slid down Yi's cheeks as he held his wife in his arms.

"What do you mean, more?" Katrina advanced on Yi.

Yi looked down at his dead wife and seemed to shrink. No one understood the words he mumbled, and Bayanai, drawn by the conversation, stepped closer.

"What?" Bayanai asked.

Yi swallowed hard, and his breath hitched in his throat. It turned into coughing, until he was finally able to speak again. "We were afraid. We didn't understand."

"Afraid of something like that?" Etienne gestured at the aftermath of Pierce's combustion.

"It was never like that—"

"We'll discuss this later," Bayanai said. "Back at the base. We need to get moving."

The emergency exit door burst open. Kirra stood in the doorway. "I don't know what happened in here, but the earth's fine now," she said.

Etienne ran over to her and hugged her.

At last, the crackling and fire died down inside the second force field Shining had constructed around Pierce. The moment Shining released the force field, eight lines of white light beamed out of the remains and shot straight into the atmosphere.

"Why didn't it come back to you, Tio Carlos?" Emma asked.

"Don't know, and honestly I wouldn't want it back after it had been tainted by Pierce," he said, patting the shoulder socket where his left arm had been.

The boy watched this for a moment with a satisfied grin. Suddenly, the red shimmering ribbons vanished, and he dropped to the ground.

Bayanai caught him before he hit. "He's out," he said softly to the others.

"Good. Any ideas how the hell he just did that?" Etienne asked.

"That wasn't Shining. It was someone else," Emma said. "I can't explain it any better. But it scared me."

"Scared me, too," CoCo said.

"Like possession?" Etienne asked.

Emma shrugged.

Katrina frowned. "What are we going to do about the Tribe?"

"Everyone but Timothy," CoCo said. "Please?"

Bayanai drew a deep breath and thought.

"If I may?" Josh walked close to Bayanai. "I know a place where you can imprison them."

Bayanai raised an eyebrow, and Josh whispered. Bayanai closed his eyes and considered. At last, he nodded.

A haunting voice weaved its way inside the annex, repeating a phrase over and over.

The four forces will show the way
A loss restored
Must unite the children
For peril awaits.

EPILOGUE

I

21 December

Deep within Ghar Parau several robed men chanted an ancient phrase over and over. The words hung in the air, as thick as the subterranean dust.

The redheaded man shuffled back from the ledge where George St. John had just leapt to his death. Without him, there was no way to repair the damage to the man on the gurney. And with his death, any hope for retribution against Emilio was gone. The redheaded man's fingers traced the blue-tinged rash across his chest, and he tried to catch his breath as he fought anxiety.

A strange warm wind rushed through the cave. He looked toward the area blocked off by plastic sheeting. He ran toward the enclosure and pushed back the curtain.

In the center of the room, the man on the gurney shifted. A screeching sound echoed from the cave entrance toward the sump. The redheaded man looked in the direction the sound had come from. Eight separate white lights streamed toward him.

A loud whoosh followed and flattened the robed men, who continued to chant even as they fell. The lights hovered directly above the man on the table and dove into his chest.

The man heaved and levitated above the table, then

screamed.

The redheaded man looked on in awe. He was witnessing the rebirth he'd waited to see ever since locating the man five years ago on Santo Antao island off West Africa. He had allied himself with the Swarm so he could see the New Reckoning come to fruition. Now moments away from the transcendence, he could hardly breathe. Perhaps he would have his revenge still.

The figure rose and burned bright. The cavern lit up, and the redheaded man tried to shield his eyes, but it was just too much. He reached up to touch the figure, but the heat seared him.

The entire cave rattled as red energy blasted off the levitating man, striking and felling the redheaded man, whose last thoughts before losing consciousness came from the cave's depths.

His mouth formed the shape of the name, but did not say it. Rami.

The day of the Reckoning
Has come.
The Sentinel has risen.
Earth will renew.

EPILOGUE

2

21 December

Arian walked quickly past the crowds in central London, partly from nerves and partly to try to warm up. She had fled The Hastings Foundation's offices after the emergency with only her laptop. She was grateful she'd worn a headscarf for disguise because it provided some measure of warmth. She was sure her companions were the cause of the security alarm. In the excitement, she had lost her comms unit. She couldn't shake the sinking suspicion that something bad had happened. She tried her cell but she couldn't get through to any of the SENTINELS. Once she found an entrance to the London Underground, she took it, seeking primarily the warmth it promised. Halfway down the stairwell, a knot in the pit of her stomach twisted. She doubled over, panting. She at least had the wits to hold tightly to the handrail lest someone coming down the stairs knock her over. But the crowds heading downstairs swerved around her without comment.

When the pain eased, she went to the bottom of the stairwell and leaned against a cool tile wall, trying to regain her composure. Something was wrong. She could feel it.

Something in the very ether had changed, and in that instant the question about the true outcome of one vital event rushed into her mind and demanded an answer.

Eyes closed against the memories, she held her aching stomach. She slowly lifted her shirt. She slid her hand along her belly and felt a long horizontal scar, one which had healed over four years ago.

Pain, fear, and bitter remembrance took over. The doctor's visit in Tehran that had become an emergency delivery. The complications. The awful words that her infant was stillborn. She had never seen the body, despite wails and demands.

Certainty she had been deceived filled her. Her son might have lived. A tug at her heart begged for the truth. She whispered hope into the air.

"Amir?"

EPILOGUE
3

23 December

Mourners dressed in black filled the Sun family's small home. Yi stiffly greeted Maggie and Focus. To Maggie, it seemed that only pure willpower kept the man upright and moving through the motions of dealing with grief socially. She was grateful that Focus had made the flight to New Atlantis to be her rock.

The house was a contradiction. A Christmas tree stood in the corner, though its lights did not twinkle. Christmas-themed snow globes lined a mantle. But every other horizontal surface held pictures of Luli, or Luli with her family. Mourners paused to look at and occasionally comment on the photographs. Grief hung in the air.

"I'm so sorry for your loss," Maggie said, her voice catching. "Luli was a class act and a fierce family protector. I liked her."

Yi nodded and closed his eyes. "Thank you."

"How are Shining and Sying?" Focus asked.

"It will be very hard for them."

"May we share our sympathy with them?" Maggie asked.

Yi nodded, and Maggie and Focus walked off in search of Luli's children.

Maggie turned down a hallway lined with framed family

photos and bumped into CoCo, who offered Maggie a timid smile.

"We have nothing to say to each other." Maggie turned away and ran right into another CoCo, this time standing next to Emilio. "What is this? Which one of you is real?" she asked in exasperation.

"I am. The first was an illusion. I just want to apologize."

"If you truly want to apologize, you can start by leaving me out of your illusions. That was an awful thing you did to me. And this is no place to talk about that."

"I'm so sorry—" CoCo said, but Maggie turned and stalked away, leaving the apology nowhere to land.

As she'd turned away, Maggie had seen CoCo bury her head into Emilio's shoulder. Part of Maggie was pleased that CoCo was hurting, but deep inside she knew that what CoCo had done to her was only to create and maintain her cover with the Tribe. No matter. She was not yet ready to forgive. Maybe when the nightmares stopped.

Continuing their search for Luli's children, Maggie and Focus instead found Bayanai speaking quietly with Waleed at the dining room table.

"Are we interrupting?" Maggie asked.

Waleed smiled and shook his head at them.

"Come on over," Bayanai invited.

"How is everything? In the aftermath of Antarctica?" Maggie asked as she and Focus joined them at the table. "Did you ever locate George?"

Bayanai shook his head in answer to the final question. "Maggie, everything here needs to be off the record. This is a wake."

Maggie's eyes grew large and she blushed. "I'm so sorry. I wasn't asking as a reporter. I meant team and morale. I'm still struggling with everything I saw, and I'm so sad for Luli's family."

Bayanai studied her a moment and nodded. "It's rough all around. We're also worried about what might be coming."

"What do you—" she started. Then recognition dawned. "The prophecy."

He nodded.

Maggie closed her eyes and repeated the prophecy from the showdown. "The four will show the way. A loss restored must unite the children for peril awaits."

Bayanai cocked his head at her. "How'd you remember that?"

"Recorded it. Listened to it a few times." She shrugged. "Plus, as a reporter, I have a pretty good memory for quotes."

"Right."

She waited for them to respond further, but they seemed too grief-stricken or distressed to reply. She was about to set out when Bayanai stood and beckoned her to step away from the table to speak privately.

"This is more serious than we've let on," Bayanai said. "I need your complete trust and discretion. We can't reveal that Jaako lost his powers. Or that Josh is pretending to be him for the time being."

"What you're suggesting is unethical. Jaako's the prime minister. Josh is impersonating a duly elected official. You are walking a thin line here."

"It's far more complicated than that, Maggie."

"The truth will always out."

His face was pained.

She regretted accepting his invitation to New Atlantis. "We're looking for Luli's children so we can share our condolences."

Finally, Maggie and Focus found Luli's offspring in the kitchen with Emma and Jiya. They watched as Sying practiced her new ice power by creating a cube of ice in a glass of water.

"Good job," Shining said. "Now, make two."

"Hi, Maggie." Emma waved at them.

"Hi, Emma, Jiya," she said and then looked at the Sun children. "Shining and Sying, I am so sorry for your loss. I respected your mother a great deal."

Sying grunted and didn't look at her.

To Maggie, it felt like the temperature in the room dropped five degrees.

Emma must have felt it too, because she said, "Sying, did you do that?"

The girl grunted again.

"Hey," Emma said. "That's pretty good. You're getting better with your powers really fast!"

EPILOGUE
4

24 December

"My fellow New Atlanteans, it is with a heavy heart that I stand in front of you today." Prime Minister Jaako Aalto glanced around at the those who'd gathered at Dini Square for the unexpected appearance. Nearly five hundred people had been curious enough about the unexpected speech to take time out of their busy holidays and crowd into the square. Bayanai stood next to Crystal City's police chief near the front of the crowd but off to one side. They nodded and smiled at Jaako, and he dipped his head in their direction in acknowledgment of their unspoken support. When he looked back at the video camera, he resumed speaking into the microphone.

"Today I bear not a message of holiday tidings. Rather this occasion marks my final appearance as the first elected prime minister of New Atlantis." The politician closed his eyes. Even on stage, he heard the shocked gasps and whispers at this announcement. He took a deep breath before opening his eyes and continuing. "I am resigning the office, effective immediately, to spend more time with my family. Deputy Prime Minister Doug Harp will shortly be sworn in to succeed me."

Harp smiled and waved as the camera panned to him.

"Why don't you tell them why you're really resigning?" The question came from the edge of the stage, but it had been shouted and could be heard across the entire square. The venomous voice sounded familiar to the politician, and his blood chilled. The politician shot a look over at the police chief, and Ericka started making her way up to the stage. The prime minister's security detail stood sentry around the open-air stage. One shot a menacing look at the heckler, who was positioned right next to the stage's stairs.

"It has been a great honor to serve the citizens of New Atlantis, and—"

"Tell them what really happened down in Antarctica," the voice said. "Better yet, tell them who you really are."

The security officer stepped toward the heckler. "Sir, further interruptions—"

The heckler, a streak of white shot through his otherwise dark hair, ignored the officer and dashed past him onto the stage and straight at the politician. The security detail shouted, but he paid them no heed. He leapt at the politician, and in one fluid motion had wrapped his arms around him. They both landed on the wooden stage with a thunk in a tangle of legs and elbows.

Involuntarily, the politician began to shape-shift. He was no longer the prime minister of a tiny island nation but rather a millionaire actor. Panicked, he looked down at his wrists and saw exactly what he expected. Power-dampening handcuffs. He glared at the heckler, his once beloved, and wondered how Luca had pulled this off, where he had gotten the intel about Antarctica, about his masquerading as Jaako.

The crowd buzzed in anger and surprise. They sounded dangerously close to rioting. He didn't even need a quick glance at the crowd to tell him there was no forgiving this abuse of Mod powers. Then he realized the cameras were still trained on him, and this moment was being live broadcast. He groaned and looked at Luca. "Why?"

Luca stood, sneered at him, and addressed the crowd. "See this?" He pointed at Josh, who still lay on the stage. "He's exhibit A of why powers registration should be mandatory around the world. But that's only the half of it. Everyone knows that Josh Grant is a Mod. And look what he managed to pull off. It was a rather large acting job, wasn't it? Imagine the damage that Mods with unknown and untracked powers could do."

Three members of the security detail tackled Luca. One roughly pulled Luca's arms behind him and cuffed him. Luca, arrested, continued ranting about the urgency of powers registration and fearmongering about the Mod menace.

Red-faced and furious and apologetic, Ericka finally made it to the stage. She pulled Josh to his feet. "Let's go. They're going to eat you up if we don't get you out of here." She walked with Josh, leaving the stage to a crestfallen Harp, who had stepped up to the microphone to address the unruly crowd.

"Calm down," Harp said. "We will get to the bottom of this. It is clear the real prime minister is missing. I will initiate emergency search protocols immediately. In the meantime, I am still the deputy prime minister of New Atlantis."

Exiting the stage with Ericka, Josh looked back, trying to get an idea of the fallout. What he saw frightened him badly. "This changes everything. We can't walk back from this."

GRATITUDE

Writing a sequel was in some ways more challenging than writing the first book. We kept wanting to top the first book by adding more and more and more. Often, one or the other of us acted as the good angel, taming the other's wilder authorial instincts. Sometimes, like an incorrigible kid, we aided and abetted, amping up the adventures in the narrative. At every step, we fretted the story didn't have enough drama, intrigue, action. Or, alternately, that there was too much. We had to know when to give, when to press, and when to stretch. Working together has enriched our lives, and we are truly grateful for your support as we crafted the latest story set in the Children of the Solstice universe.

We are grateful to John Dylan DeLaTorre, who has given so much for *Collision*. He's been a sounding board, a beta reader and a constant source of support as we worked through creating this book. Thank you for your time and thoughts and perspective. We could not have done this without you.

We owe great thanks to our wonderfully supportive friends and family members who encouraged us to keep going and never stopped asking when the second book was coming out.

Some of those friends went a step beyond by serving as our beta readers. Thank you for helping us spot problems in the draft when we were too close to the story to see them. You have helped us refine our manuscript and we are truly grateful for your help.

This book would not be possible without the amazing efforts of our two editors. Matthew Arkin of My Two Cents Editing again provided an early critique that helped shape and focus our story by offering guidance on how to strengthen the plot and storyline. Lourdes Venard of Comma Sense Editing again served as our copyeditor and proofreader. She helped tighten the pacing and language and provided valuable feedback on the story. Thank you both.

The book looks as great as it does because of Alex Sanchez and John Kaiser. Alex drew and inked the cover art. He also provided the character sketches used for many of the chapter breaks, as well as images for promotional materials. John designed the cover and logo and inked the supplemental artwork. Thank you both.

It was a pleasure working with all of you.

With deepest gratitude,

Baltimore & Jennifer.

REVIEW

Many thanks for choosing our superhero book. Please consider writing an honest review about *Collision* and posting it on Amazon or Goodreads. There are few things more valuable for book sales than honest reviews from a variety of readers. Reviews are the best way readers discover great new books. We truly appreciate it.

ABOUT THE AUTHORS

Baltimore Russell is a writer, actor, and producer. He and his husband created the *People You Know* new media series, which aired on HereTV and Amazon Prime. He's an avid reader and collector of comics. Almost from the time he learned to work a pencil, he could often be found creating his own stories. He lives in New York City with his husband, John Dylan DeLaTorre. *Collision* is his second book.

Jennifer Pallanich is a communications consultant specializing in the oil and gas industry. She is a recovering trade journalist who bylined over half a million words about the oil and gas industry. She published the nonfiction book *Flacks & Hacks: Trade Secrets Journalists Want PR Pros to Know*. *Collision* is her third book. She loves to read good versus evil stories. An avid scuba diver, traveler, reader, and writer, she lives with a lab mix named Houdini in Houston.

www.ingramcontent.com/pod-product-compliance
Lightning Source LLC
Chambersburg PA
CBHW020822030726
47496CB00001B/50